OFF BALANCE

PAINTED BAY 1

JAY HOGAN

SOUTHERN LIGHTS PUBLISHING

Published by Southern Lights Publishing

To request permission and all other enquiries contact the author through the website

https://www.jayhoganauthor.com

Trade Paperback ISBN:978-0-9951325-4-2

Digital ISBN: 978-0-9951325-3-5

Digital Edition published September 2020

Trade Paperback Published September 2020

First Edition

Editing by Boho Edits

Cover Art Copyright © 2020 Reese Dante

Cover content is for illustrative purposes only and any person depicted on the cover is a model.

Proofread by Lissa Given Proofing

Printed in the United States of America and Australia

For my family who read everything I write and keep on saying they love it all, blushes included.

ACKNOWLEDGMENTS

Meniere's Disease is a disorder of the inner ear that presents with varying degrees of severity from mild to severe, and which can profoundly affect a person's life. Each person's experience, although having commonalities, may be vastly different. In this story, Judah is diagnosed with a reasonably moderate to severe form of the disorder. I want to especially thank my sensitivity readers, people living with Meniere's Disease, for helping me craft Judah's character and experiences. Any mistakes are my own.

As always, I thank my husband for his patience and for keeping the dog walked and out of my hair when I needed to work. And my daughter for all her support.

Getting a book finessed for release is a huge challenge that includes the help of beta readers, editing, proofing, cover artists and a tireless PA . It's a team effort, and includes all those author support networks and reader fans who rally around when you're ready to pull your hair out and throw away every first draft. Thanks to all of you.

PROLOGUE

Judah

Boston Opera House

Precise, flexed, perfect—a string of dancers pick their way across the stage.

Sinuous, staccato, smooth transition.

Water on glass.

They circle my back. Sharp feathered breaths.

I lock the spot. Explode, snap, spin, repeat. Centred, balanced.

Down, stretch, move.

Damn buzz in my ears.

Audience hush of approval.

A flash of crimson in the wings—heads nodding, counting, shaking, feet riding the rhythm on the floor, landing every jump, frowning —long notes for the next rehearsal. Maybe a patient reminder of how young I am, how lucky, how much work I've yet to do.

But I wasn't lucky.

Leap. Landed. Next mark. Ready.

I was prepared.

Seven years of discipline, sweat, control, loneliness, and crippling pain.

Grand jeté. Landed. Next mark.

Some days I flew, some I barely walked—anything for this. The roar of the audience, the thunder of the ovation, always dance, always ballet. A lifetime of dreaming and determination. Surviving the bullshit, the taunts, the bullying, the bewildered family. Getting out, getting on, getting noticed, getting chosen, getting a chance. Boston.

Temps levé. Move. Circle. Wait. Count.

Dancing till my knees gave way and my feet bled into the tape that barely held my skin together. Dancing through the calf tears and the shoulder pain, the stress fractures and tendonitis, the ankle strains, and the back spasms. Second soloist by twenty, first by twenty-two, talented, remarkable, gifted. All for tonight—a principal role if I proved myself, if I soared, if I was ready.

I was more than ready.

This was mine.

Pas de chat. Move. Mark.

And I was fucking flying.

The pregnant hush, the sharp gasps, the rise of the orchestra as the choreography found expression in the stretch and punch of my muscles. I knew it by the bright eyes of my fellow dancers. I knew it by the reassuring glance of my best friend and principal as she soared past me on stage. And I knew it from the critical eye of the crimson-shirted artistic director, my lover, counting every beat from the wings.

I knew that scowl, inside and outside the bedroom—hard, rigid, hungry, unforgiving. He'd rail at my mistakes and I'd deserve it, but he pushed the hardest, the closer I came to perfection. Disappointment earned disinterest. There's be no disappointment tonight.

Tonight, I had him at my feet, and my heart flew.

Penché. Diana's wrist in my hand for balance, her leg thrown high behind. Down. Circle. Move.

I hit my mark at the front of the stage, followed with a short run of double tours, checking my recently recovered right ankle on the final landing. Turn. Prepare. Check the wobble. *What the hell?*

The buzz in my ear roaring.

Modified Cheshire Cat lift—worked into the programme because Grant was evil like that. A difficult catch, then lift. Landed. Yes! A defining moment. Mine.

Vision blur. Ears full. Curious heat. Mental check. Solid? Have to be.

Questioning eye. Diana's.

I lift a chin. I'm fine. We've got this. Hit it.

Flying feet.

Brace. Knees lock.

Stage curtains swim. Audience heave. Floor rolls. Bile.

Blink hard. Steel jaw. Fight.

Diana in my arms, grip slipping, heart pounding.

The floor swells beneath my feet. The world turns upside down. My right elbow falters.

Diana's eyes flash fear and shocked disbelief.

My legs dissolve, my stomach in my throat. I crumble to the boards.

The roar in my ears.

The gasp of the audience.

The sickening crack of Diana's wrist as it shatters in the fall.

CHAPTER ONE

Judah

Painted Bay, New Zealand. 8 months later

"Jude, get your arse the hell out here! We need to leave now!" My front door shook on its hinges.

Judah.

"Fuck off." I weaselled my aching head further under the pillow and ignored the bile that bit at the back of my throat. My brother was an arsehole.

A spark of guilt flared in my chest, then was gone just as quickly. *Whatever.*

The hammering continued. "Jude!"

Judah.

"If you don't get your arse out of bed and on that damn boat in five minutes," Leroy shouted, "I'm gonna come in and drag you out myself. I need your help to seed the nursery ropes before we lose the spat. Maybe you could try not to be a total waste of space, yeah?"

Fucker.

"Okay, okay, I'm coming. Shut the hell up, will you? Jesus, Leroy, we own the fucking business. Who cares if we're ten minutes late?"

"*Mum* owns the business, arsehole," Leroy continued to batter at my aching head. "Not me, and certainly not *you*. We're doing this for her and you're gonna damn well earn your keep. Who works for seven years and has nothing to show for it?"

A fact I wasn't proud of, but it wasn't like professional ballet came with bonuses and a stock portfolio.

"Plus, you're not *ten* minutes late, it's a fucking hour after I told you we'd be leaving."

Shit.

"So if you don't like it, you can fuck off out of this boathouse you've been wallowing in rent-free, and get a damn job."

There was always that. Point taken. "All right, don't get your panties in a twist. I'll meet you in the boat."

"Ten minutes, Jude."

Judah.

"Ten minutes or you can pack your fucking bags."

"Yeah, yeah. Make sure to tell Mum that. I'm certain she'll be thrilled at you booting her other son off a property you don't even own." I didn't need to see him to know the exasperated fury on his face, and a piece of me cringed at the satisfaction the image gave me. He might be an arsehole but I wasn't exactly helping myself.

"For fuck's sake, Jude"—

Judah.

—"just . . ." He sighed and dropped his voice. "Just get yourself out here, will you? Jesus, what the hell's wrong with you?"

I rolled my legs to the side and somehow got myself to a sit. Go me. The fact it took a few moments for the room to stop waltzing in my brain was neither here nor there, but it was enough time for the sour stench of vomit to jam up my nostrils and turn my stomach, again.

Looking down, I found most of last night's cheese and crackers staring right back at me from the floor in front of my feet. A vague memory of leaning over the side of the bed in the midst of the spins sprang to mind. I squinted down at my chest and sideways at the bed. Clean. Thank Christ for that, and for wooden floors, and for the fact I hadn't just put my damn foot in the middle of the putrid puddle. Note to self: don't eat cheese in the middle of a vertigo attack.

The phone on my bedside table flashed with a message, and since it seemed the safer option than standing right then, I reached for it. A stream of texts from Terry sat front and centre on the screen. *Shit.* Somewhere in my foggy brain I recalled him giving up on my sorry arse the night before and leaving me to drown in my warm cloak of self-pity.

Are you okay?

Text if you're okay.

What the fuck, Judah?

Text me!

I'm gonna wring your bloody neck.

I guess he was pissed. But he was going to have to get in line with that last text.

I fired off a quick apology but hadn't even put the phone back on the table when it rang. I thought for a second about ignoring it, then—

"What the hell, Judah?" Terry was very definitely pissed.

"And good morning to you too. Look, I'm sorry—"

"I've been worried sick." He ignored my apology. "You promised you'd answer the text I sent when I got home, so I'd know you were all right."

"I was a bit—"

"Shit-faced are the words I think you're looking for, arsehole. Or maybe legless? How about pissed as a newt? I'm rather partial to munted, myself."

"Sorry." And I was.

The line went quiet for a minute and I pictured Terry figuring out how far he could push things. Though we'd known each other in school, our adult friendship was all new and shiny, and we were still getting the lay of the land between us.

"Shit. Well, as long as you're okay," he finally said. "For fuck's sake, you don't make things easy on yourself, do you?"

Singing to the choir, mate.

He continued, "I'd have stuck around, but Hannah's sitter was on the clock and I needed to drive her home."

"It's fine, Terry. I don't need babysitting. I shouldn't have drunk that much. It's my own fault."

More silence, then Terry cleared his throat. "Were things okay after I left? Did um . . . did you have a . . . you know?"

I said nothing.

"Fuck. I just knew it. I should've stayed."

"No. I said, it was my own fault. And it wasn't a bad one." *Liar.* "I need to get my shit together, I know."

"You so fucking do, man. People care about you. But . . . whatever. It's your life. Are you working today?"

"Yeah. Leroy's waiting on me now. I have to go."

"Damn. Be careful. And come by tomorrow so I can lay eyes on your sorry arse. You haven't been to the store in a week and Hannah's missing you."

Shit. Terry being angry with me, I could handle. Disappointing Hannah? It was too easy to love Terry's daughter. Nine going on fifteen. Cute as a button with a core of spiked steel. "I will. I promise. I gotta go. Talk later."

I threw the phone on the side table and pushed slowly to my feet. A half dozen empty beer bottles clanked out of the way as I teetered around the pool of vomit and stumbled against the wall to steady myself, every goddamn bone in my body weeping in exhaustion.

Stepping over my clothes, which I'd somehow managed to successfully worm out of before crawling into bed at some stupid hour past midnight, I worked my way over to the bathroom, then held onto the jamb, trying to keep my anger in check at Leroy's cutting comments.

"What the hell's wrong with you?"

Arsehole. Leroy knew exactly what was wrong with me. Exactly why I was stuck back in this fucking arsehole of a town, in this fucking boathouse, helping out with the shitty family business. He'd heard every sorry bit of it without a single fucking question, a single comment, nothing except an emailed plane ticket and a note to say the business would need reimbursement. Yeah, I bet Mum didn't know that part.

I needed to stop letting him rile me. It wasn't like we'd *ever* got on, even as kids, as different as it was possible to be. That damn streak of family responsibility he possessed lay a mile wide. I'd told him he was crazy when Dad died and he chucked in his veterinary study to come home to run the family mussel farm instead. But I think he half expected me to join him, and that's where we came undone.

My path had always lain elsewhere and my determination to get there, single-minded. So when I headed back to Boston the week after the funeral to continue my ballet career, the gulf between us only ripped further apart. My current demise was probably as close as he was gonna get to payback and he was making the most of it. I might not like it, but I could almost understand.

The toilet mocked me from the far side of the bathroom, but I got there in one piece and took a piss sitting down, earning myself a witches kiss while I was at it and wishing I was one of those people who had no symptoms between attacks. Yeah, good luck with that.

Unsteady on my feet—check. Fatigue—check. Nausea—check. And about as mentally sharp as a head full of jellyfish—check.

A quick once over in the mirror to check for bruising from where I'd hit the floor trying to get to bed came up clear, but the direct confrontation with my face was hardly flattering. Black circles ringed my eyes, a skittery expression on my face, and then there was that inviting stench of alcohol and vomit.

"Jude!" The bedroom windows rattled in their frames. "Now!"

Judah. "For fuck's sake, I'm coming."

I reached across the battery of makeup and lotions and potions which used to encompass my morning routine in the days when I gave a fuck, grabbed one of the pill bottles from the shelf alongside the mirror, and stared at it. The bastards helped with the vertigo but they knocked my fatigue into eye peeling exhaustion and ramped up the nausea. Food would help, but the very thought made me gag. Fucking rock and a hard place. Still, I had to work. I wasn't giving Leroy anything else to use against me.

But damn, I hated this, hated these pills, hated everything that my whole fucking life had been distilled down to.

The bottle hit the wall with a clatter, popped its lid, and scattered pills from one end of the bathroom to the other.

Fuck, fuck, fuck.

I scrambled around on my knees, my stomach heaving in my throat till I had all the pills in my hand. Then I deposited them, dust and all, back into the bottle, save one, which I threw down my throat with a palm full of water. I took another for the nausea and added my usual diuretic, then made sure to grab my emergency supply in case I had another attack on the boat. God, I hoped not. But I'd only forgotten it once, and the embarrassing crawl back to the boathouse on my hands and knees ensured I'd never forget it again.

If they had a pill for the fucking tinnitus, it might make my daily rattle actually worthwhile, but no chance of that. Still, it could be worse. The background buzz wasn't too bad, although the category-five cyclone in my ears during an attack left a lot to be desired.

The splash of cool water on my face was sheer fucking bliss and it was worth another just for the lift in mood. I even managed a face-cloth to my chest and pits and ran my fingers through the sticky knots in my unruly mess of dark hair—avoiding the question of exactly what the fuck that shit was—and wondered how much longer I could avoid the local hairdresser, or local *anything* for that matter.

A quick gargle of mouthwash, enough to send my gut clenching again, and I was good to go—that is if you considered a sallow-faced, raging-gay pretty boy with a bad haircut, patchy dark stubble, black-ringed eyes, and a current attitude that could do with some work even on a decent day was your idea of good.

But hey, it worked for me. The vastly edited hygiene ritual made for a much faster exit strategy, which would've been great if I actually had anywhere to go or anyone that I cared two shits about looking good for. That my ex-best friends, ex-lover, and high-flying dance mates would've walked past me on the street without an iota of recognition said it all.

I scraped up the worst of the mess from the bedroom floor and deposited it in the toilet, mopped at the rest with a damp towel, and then chucked that in the wash as well. No diarrhoea this time though, so hey, go me. Yet another shocking nuance to this shiny new life of mine.

Avoiding the full-length mirror with its damning opinion of my increasingly soft waistline and woeful loss of muscle definition, I pulled on some fresh clothes, tucked my jeans into my waterproof boots, grabbed my jacket from beside the front door, and stumbled outside to where my arsehole brother stood leaning against the wharf office. Converted from the original whaling storage and loading shed, it was a cavernous space complete with a loading door and chain block directly over the water, which we still used for moving heavy stuff on and off the mussel boat.

Leroy had a pile of black longline floats at his feet and a scowl the depth of the Marianna trench. People said we looked alike and I guess we did—dark hair, high cheekbones, and a certain grace as we moved that I put down to genetics. But there were also differences. At nearly six feet, I was slightly taller than Leroy, though he had more muscle. My hazel eyes to his blue. My bright-as-a-flower gay arse, to his straight-laced deeply ingrained hetero one.

But as pissed off as Leroy appeared, I ignored him and took the time to appreciate the fresh skin of morning light over Painted Bay and suck in a lungful of air, redolent with salt and new rain. I loved the sea, the one joy I'd never shaken from growing up in this godforsaken town.

Perched on bluffs overlooking a rocky coastline carved with a complex system of sheltered bays and surging seas, Painted Bay was one of a string of small towns that ran along this section of the East Coast—a fishing and marine mecca. As a teenager I couldn't wait to put it behind me. But as an adult? Yeah, I wasn't blind to the attraction, and residing in the boathouse meant living with its beauty only metres away.

Not even Leroy's arse fuckery was going to ruin that splash of daily mana. To that end, and in general just to fuck with him, I didn't rush locking my front door and made sure to check my mailbox as I passed. Leroy's sighs escalated with each passing second. so I smiled and slowed my pace even further.

As I got closer, he cast a disgusted eye over me. "You look like crap."

I snorted. "Gee, thanks."

He leaned close and sniffed. "And you smell like a fucking brewery bathroom. I thought booze screwed with your whole *thing*?"

I couldn't remember Leroy using the correct name even once. "Yes, it does."

"Then why fucking drink?"

Good question. Still holding his eye. "Cos it feels better."

"Better than what?"

"Better than *this*."

He stared at me for a minute before his gaze slid away. "Typical."

But when he turned to walk off, I grabbed his wrist. "And what the hell does that mean?"

He spun to face me. "That it's just like you, thinking of no one but yourself. Coming back here, expecting everyone to fall over backwards for you while you do nothing to help yourself. Oh, poor Jude," his voice mocked, while my fists clenched at my sides. "Did you hear what happened? Had to give up his big career. Jesus, you had Mum googling night and day to learn as much as she could so she could help you when you got back, and what do you do? Piss everything away in booze and self-pity. Well, grow up, little brother. Everyone loses shit in their lives, and they just have to get on with it. The problem is, you've never had to face anything you couldn't charm your way out of—"

The crack of my fist on his jaw and the jangling sting of pain was the first I knew I'd hit him. But the second punch? Yeah, that sucker was fucking deliberate and had been a long time coming.

He staggered against the weathered planks on the office wall, holding his jaw. "Why you little—"

I jumped to the side as he lunged, shoving him back into the wall and stabbing a finger at his chest. "You've been dying to have your little say, haven't you? But you know nothing about me or what I had to give up or how hard I had to work to get where I did. And you know even less about what it's like to grow up in a town where you never fitted in, in a school where you were the only gay boy for miles, where wanting to dance and being good at it came with a side order of derision and what-the-fuck-are-you? You're the one who should know all about charming your way, mister star fucking rugby player—you did it all through high school, after all."

"I worked damned hard for those grades." Leroy pushed off the wall. "Unlike you."

"I was working on *my* career too. I danced more hours after school than you ever put into your rugby. You wanna know how a lean fem guy like me can throw a punch that knocks you off your feet? Because I fucking *had* to learn so I could hit back. *And* because I worked my arse off in the gym and fight training to do my *job*. My *dancing* job. Twelve-hour days, seven days a week, sometimes five shows over a weekend. Have you ever danced a two-hour show on a broken foot? Don't you fucking dare talk to me about *charming* my way anywhere."

"Are you boys done swinging your dicks?" Martha pushed Leroy aside as she stormed out of the office. "Because if I'm disappointed in you, your mother would be heartbroken. What the hell is wrong with you two?"

I caught Leroy's eye and looked away. Martha was right. Martha was always right. At sixty-two, she'd run our small private wharf for fifteen years with an iron fist and an attitude equal parts mumma bear and rattlesnake. And I'd been on the wrong end of her acid tongue often enough as a kid to recognise the warning signs.

Her gaze narrowed. "Just as I thought. Well, if you're done ruining my morning, get your wilful butts into that boat and head out. Your mother doesn't pay you to act like idiots. Do I make myself clear?"

I was tempted to point out that Leroy ran the business and my mother didn't pay me at all, but I thought that might be pushing it.

Leroy scuffed his shoes. "Sorry."

Martha levelled me a look and I felt ten all over again.

"Yeah, sorry."

"Good. Now piss off, both of you. You're making the place look untidy. And make sure to take that rucksack with your lunch. She made you pot pie today." Martha stepped back into the office and slammed the door.

Leroy and I grimaced at the same time. Our mother's cooking was famous for all the wrong reasons.

Leroy stared at the closed door. "You'd think she ran the whole damn place, not just the wharf."

I snorted. "You wanna say that loud enough for her to actually hear?"

He looked at me like I'd grown a second head.

"Okay, so maybe I shouldn't have hit you." The admission nearly choked in my throat but was clear evidence of Martha's woo-woo power over me.

Leroy rubbed his jaw. "Yeah, well, I didn't really mean it about you charming your way out of everything, either."

I rolled my eyes. "Yeah, you did."

He laughed. "Maybe. Anyway, that's some punch you've got there. Not bad for a guy who wears a tutu."

I raised my hand and flexed it open and closed. "Fucking hurts."

He eyed me speculatively. "Did you really dance on a broken foot?"

I shrugged. "More than once."

He took a second to digest that. "That's pretty hardcore."

He had no fucking idea.

"But you really do need to stop with the booze."

And he was right. "I know, and I will. It's just . . . hard right now. And today's not just because of the booze. I had a night of it, to be honest."

His brows crunched. "You have one of those . . . things again, that you get with the um . . . whatsitsname?"

I huffed. "Can you not say the fucking words for once, Leroy? Meniere's disease. Vertigo attacks. Take your pick." To be fair, Leroy hadn't witnessed an attack yet, but even so.

He rolled his eyes. "Jesus Christ, all right. Did you have a bloody vertigo attack?"

I blew out a sigh and loaded a couple of floats into my aching arms. "Yeah. As you so eloquently said, I can't charm my way out of this one, can I?"

His expression turned serious. "I didn't mean that. But you can't keep using it as an excuse either. You have to find a way to deal with it—"

"An excuse? That's what you think? At the risk of punching you again, I'm gonna pretend you didn't just say that."

Leroy shrugged. "Whatever. Stop drinking and start looking after yourself, and maybe I won't say shit like that. But if you're gonna stay here, you have to help out, be on time maybe. Now, let's get this stuff loaded."

I bit back a million snarky replies dancing on the tip of my tongue and decided it wasn't worth it. Leroy had always needed to be hit between the eyes to change his mind about *anything*. Stubborn had nothing on him. And to be honest, I was too fucking tired to deal.

"So what do you think is in those pies?" Leroy aimed for small talk as we carried a huge coil of rope between us and threw it on the boat.

I wiped my hands down the front of my jeans and cast the knapsack a dubious look. "Ten bucks says it's leftover topside roast from yesterday."

Leroy winced. "Jesus, that shit was tough enough first time around. But I've got rugby practice later, so there's no avoiding it."

I threw him the knapsack and scooped up the last of the rope. "Serves you right. But fair warning, if I don't spew on the way out there, it'll be a fucking miracle."

Leroy climbed into the boat and I followed.

"Star rugby player, huh?" He shot me a smug look.

I shook my head. "That's what you took out of all that? How about homophobic arsehole instead?"

I left him frowning and went up front to secure the extra floats.

CHAPTER TWO

Morgan

"Thanks for the lift, Morgan." Leroy rapped his knuckles on the hood of my Toyota Hilux and headed up the path to his mother's 1880s settler homestead, nestled about half a kilometre up the hill from Painted Bay wharf. He usually walked home after training, the town was barely five minutes away, but with the rugby change rooms still under renovation, I'd offered him a ride to get him into a shower before he was arrested for singlehandedly breaking some air-pollution bylaw. My car stank like a loggers' smoko room minus the hairy eye candy, if you were into that sort of thing, which I could be, on occasion.

"See you next week." The headlights on my Hilux illuminated his path until his feet hit the front steps, and I took the time to appreciate the family's sprawling rabbit warren of a house for the millionth time. A century ago its homesteaders had run whaling ships in and out of the tiny cove and made themselves a nice little nest egg, but when the whaling boom eased, the whole town fell on hard times.

Leroy's parents bought the place in the nineties when tourism took off, with the grand idea of farming mussels about a kilometre up the coast. The wharf and pier that came with the property were exactly what they needed. The house had the best spot in the town, and with the tide lapping at the lower reaches of its boundary and the odd dolphin for a neighbour, there wasn't much not to like. It sure as hell beat the tiny little cottage that came as part of my fisheries officer job, with no view and a fishing charter operator as a neighbour. The free fish were great. The smell of his homemade chum, not so much.

I cranked Aerosmith to full volume and threw the Hilux into gear, praying my fridge had some beer. I got as far as the end of Leroy's drive when a flickering light on the pier at the wharf down the hill caught my eye. I checked my watch. Nine thirty. Aerosmith went to mute.

There were no vessels tied up as far as I could tell, other than Leroy's workboat. So what the hell was with the light? My gaze tacked left to the boathouse and the soft glow behind its windows. Leroy's brother, no doubt. Most of the town knew he was back, but not many had seen him, odd in a town of fifteen hundred people. A bit of a problem child, according to Leroy, but the guy was entitled to his privacy.

The flickering light niggled at me. Boats, harbours, lights, and illicit night-time activity were a fisheries officer's bread and butter. Curiosity and suspicion came with the job, and I wouldn't sleep if I didn't check it out.

I headed down the hill to the wharf's parking lot, cutting the engine and pulling over just before the gate so I didn't alert whoever it was. The front door of the boathouse was closed and all appeared quiet, so I made my way across the broad planks of the wharf to the start of the pier, keeping to the shadows.

At the end of the old wooden structure, about thirty metres away, a figure sat leaning through the safety rails, staring into the water. It looked innocent enough, but I'd been caught out before. My hand went to my chest and I mentally slapped myself. I still had my training gear on, my stab vest sitting useless in the Hilux. Rookie mistake.

I studied the figure again. They looked to be alone, hoodie pulled over their head, legs dangling, just gazing into the water where a light bounced around in the incoming swell creating an undulating circle of blue-green flecked with silver. I'd risk it.

Keeping to the thick wooden beams at the edge so as to minimise the sound of my approach, I made my way along the pier, stopping about five metres away. Whoever it was, they were fully engrossed in what was going on in the water, no voices, no sound other than the lap of the waves against the old piles. I relaxed a little. Whatever I was intruding on, I doubted it was anything illicit.

I straightened and gave a slight cough, which was greeted by a sharp intake of breath. The hooded head whipped around, and in the reflected glow of the submerged light, I caught the flash of some killer cheekbones and an unruly lock of dark hair dangling over a pair of startled eyes. Young eyes. Beautiful eyes. So beautiful, that for a second, I forgot what the hell I was doing and simply let myself fall into their green-and-amber stippling until—

"What the fuck are you doing sneaking up on me like that?" The young man wriggled his legs out from under the rail and shot to his feet. "Jesus Christ, you nearly gave me a heart attack." He dusted off his hands on his jeans as his gaze raked slowly over me from head to toe. Blatant and appreciative.

I felt the jolt of it down to my balls.

Then he stilled, eyes wary. "I've got nothing worth stealing if that's what you're after, unless you've a hankering for cold pizza and a shot of Jack. That said, you're welcome to one, or both, as long as you keep quiet and don't scare the fish."

I snorted, taking in the slight sway of his lean body. Shorter than my six foot two, he was nice, very, very nice. My gaze flicked to the half-empty bottle of whiskey at his feet alongside an open notebook packed with scribblings, but no sign of pizza.

His gaze followed mine. "Oh, crap." He turned and peered over the safety railing into the water and grinned. "I guess you're shit out of luck with the pizza. Must've knocked it over the edge when I stood. Serves you right for scaring me."

I joined him at the safety rail, elbows almost brushing, and peered down at the school of jack mackerel churning the water like a thousand silver knives as they feasted on the remains.

"Clearly meat lover fans." He watched the roiling water with a definite smirk tugging the corner of his mouth. I was watching him, not the fish, when he swung back around, bringing us eye to eye. "So, how about you? Got a preference?"

There was no misunderstanding his meaning, and every word in my brain fried to dust.

His brows peaked. "Cat got your tongue?"

Holy fuck. Who was this guy? I hadn't felt so damn flustered since my not-yet wife goosed me within the first minute of meeting her parents.

"Hawaiian," I choked out.

He laughed, hazel eyes sparkling. "Well, that seals it. We can't ever be friends. I'm not sure I should even be seen with you." He reached for the open notebook on the deck and wobbled on his feet. I grabbed his arm to stop him falling, but he jerked away. "I'm fine. And I'm not drunk, if that's what you're thinking?"

I was, but his eyes were clearer than I expected.

His jaw set. "I've only had one. I'm just . . . tired."

That looked to be an understatement. The more I saw of his face, the more I recognised the tell-tale signs of chronic sleep deprivation and a deep-seated exhaustion. I should know. "It's none of my business," I said softly. "But I apologise. And I didn't mean to sneak up on you like that."

He pressed a hand to his chest. "My god, he talks. So, why are you here, then? Because you did sneak up on me."

Back to those eyes. The brightest hazel. Not to mention that sexy-as-shit beauty spot sitting high on his right cheekbone. And now I'd seen it, I couldn't unsee it. Damn, he was beautiful. He was also older than I'd first thought, which was somewhat reassuring given my visceral and unexpected reaction to him.

I dropped my gaze to the safety of the feeding frenzy below. "I, ah . . . just saw the light and was curious. It's late. I wanted to check who it was and if you were okay. And now I know. So, you like watching fish, then?"

He glanced at me and shrugged, but a smile made its way through the nonchalance to light up his face. "They look pretty cool in the light, don't you think? They shimmer. All that silver striping, like dancers in some gaudy Vegas show. Fifteen minutes of fame and all that. I used to come down here as a kid and do this. It helped me relax. Guess it still does."

"So, you're local then?"

He didn't lift his eyes. "I wouldn't say that. It was a while ago now."

The water below still bubbled with action as the last of the pizza met its fate in the green depths of a full tide, and I wondered things I shouldn't about a young teenage boy who came down to find peace in a simple thing like this. Fat ribbons of kelp twirled between the giant timber piles that had stood there for nigh on a century.

"Mackerel love it around these old wharves," I told him. "Sprats and piper too. The piles break the swells and give them some shelter from the bigger predators."

He glanced at me with curious eyes and I was lost in their gold-stippled green. "You know your fish."

I lifted a shoulder. "I grew up fishing. Sounds like you do too."

He pulled a face. "Not like that. God knows, I don't have the patience, and I'm not all that sold on the whole hook-in-mouth thing, either. But this?" He turned back to the water. "I like this."

We stood in silence watching the school of jack still working on their unexpected bounty. It should've been uncomfortable but wasn't. "Do you have a favourite?"

He bit back a smile. "Fish, you mean?"

Never let it be said I didn't have game. Standing here with a

gorgeous guy, talking about fucking fish. "Yeah, why not? Thrill me."
It was too damn close to a flirt to pretend otherwise, even if he'd
started it. Most men didn't pick me as open to the idea quite so fast.
Or at all.

His eyes widened and he gave up trying to hide the smile. "Well,
in that case, I guess it depends if you're talking species specific to
New Zealand or open to international contenders?"

I snorted. "Now you're just taking the piss. But for the sake of
argument, I'll open the question up to allow global responses. I'm
very much against marine xenophobia. The ocean's a big place, after
all."

He laughed and all the bunched muscles in his back and shoulders relaxed like an outgoing tide. It smoothed out the wary lines and
warmed the cool edge to his demeanour, and I liked it, I liked it a lot.

His head tipped back and his gaze swept the night sky as if
searching for an answer. My eyes slipped to the smooth curve of his
neck and soft lobe of his ear and . . . For fuck's sake, what was I
doing? I guess it had been a long time between drinks.

"Mmm." He dropped his gaze and locked eyes. "In that case, I
would have to say, manta rays. Big, I know, but technically still fish.
And, as I always say—" He winked. "—size matters."

Jesus George. I was pretty sure my tongue disappeared down the
back of my throat to lick my arse, but I wasn't about to check. I
cleared my throat and hoped for the best. "Yes, well, an excellent
choice. A little short in the water around New Zealand though."

He nodded. "True, but I did get the chance to swim with them in
Indonesia a few years ago. They were so elegant and"—he pinned me
with that look again that damn near curled my toes in their socks—
"very, very sexy."

The words rolled off his tongue and straight into my rugby shorts
with barely a polite introduction. Not that any was needed, apparently, judging by the happy dance going on down there. The guy
was . . . fun, and we were very definitely flirting. I hadn't had fun like
that in a long time, but I also very definitely needed to stop. He might

not be as young as I'd first thought, but he was a lot younger and more fiery than was prudent for a mid-thirties, woefully unexciting guy like me.

"Your turn." He leaned back on the railing and studied me with laughing eyes.

I blew out a sigh. "Well, it's a tricky question. But like you, I have no hesitation. Octopus. Hands down. Sneaky, smart as shit, expert hunters, and . . . equally sexy." *Good God, what was I doing?*

He fought back a smile and nodded seriously. "Mmm. Tricky question—tricky answer. But a definite yes to the sexy bit. All those . . . tentacles." His eyes danced provocatively. "But"—and he waggled a finger at me—"they are *not* fish, mister smart guy."

Well, look at that.

"They are, in fact, molluscs, I believe."

I grinned widely and nodded. "Clever man."

"Yes!" He fist-pumped the air. "You didn't think I knew that, did you? So I believe that eliminates your answer from the competition leaving manta rays as the deserved winner. I'll collect my prize later." He raked his gaze over me once again, leaving scorch marks on my skin, and then focussed back on the water. "They're nearly done."

I watched him watching the fish, not caring a jot if he knew it. He'd made his interest clear. Taller than his litheness first implied, he was close to six feet if I had to guess. Lean, but with this sense of barely restrained strength bubbling just below the surface. An energy that revealed itself in a restless shifting of feet and fists shoved merci- lessly into the front pockets of torn jeans, forcing the material tight across a curved muscular arse that had *bite me* written all over it.

But there was also a dull anger and grief alongside that power. Like you'd find in a caged animal. The idea stole my breath, and all I could do was stare, which was guaranteed to get me—

He turned suddenly.

—busted.

A sly smile stole over his face. "Like what you see?"

Shit. I raised my hands. "No, sorry, I didn't mean to . . . I'm not . . ."

The smile dropped like a stone and all those harsh edges returned. He pushed away from the corner pile with a dismissive snort. "Like hell. But whatever. Maybe it's time for you to leave. But in the interest of full disclosure, you have no idea what you're missing."

Oh, I thought I had a fair idea, and just thinking about it almost got me hard—er. "I didn't mean that you weren't . . . that . . . I just . . ." I dropped my hands, remembering the word prudent. "You're right. I should go. I'm sorry if I disturbed you and for the . . . misunderstanding."

I wasn't in the closet regardless of what the guy thought, but I didn't owe him any explanations either. The last thing I needed was a rumour I'd been cruising down at the local wharf. God help me. When had my name and the word cruising ever been in the same sentence? Never, that's when. Sally would laugh her damn head off.

A flash of uncertainty crossed the young man's face but was gone just as quick. "Well, have a nice life. And for fuck's sake, have a shower. You smell like a damn locker room with none of the attraction."

Yeah, he was fun.

I bit back a smile and left him to it, feeling the heat of his gaze on the back of my head all the way back to my Hilux. Safely behind the steering wheel and away from the temptation to offer the man all my unborn children, I sat for a few seconds and stared at the shadows where he'd been standing, wondering if he was still watching me, wondering if I should've given a different answer.

I dragged a weary hand across my jaw, flipped down my visor, and stared at the photo taped there.

"I bet you didn't see that coming." I fingered the dog-eared image. "So, whaddya think?" I glanced back to the end of the pier. "I'm losing my mind, right?"

I grinned at the woman who'd stolen my heart all those years ago. She held a full glass of champagne in a toast to the camera, my camera. Our fourth wedding anniversary. We'd splurged on a ridiculously expensive bottle at some hotel on Waiheke Island. Cost me a week's wages. Then we'd fucked each other senseless in a room with a view over Half Moon Bay. One of the best weekends of my life.

"On second thought, you probably had something to do with it, you little minx. Pulled a few strings? Badgered the bearded old guy till he gave in? You were always trying to loosen me up. But you might've overshot the mark with this one, sweetheart. He's too young, too prickly, too . . . something." I squinted into the dark. "And too . . . not you. Come on, let's get home. And stop with the damn matchmaking."

I threw the Hilux into gear and tore back up the hill toward home.

Judah

I slowly sank to the pier and watched the stranger's headlights make their way up the hill, acutely aware we hadn't even exchanged names. For the better, undoubtedly. Way too tempting. The cool of the wood travelled straight through my threadbare jeans as I sank back against the upright pile with a sigh, because *damn*, the man made a fine exit. Compression skins under not-too-loose rugby shorts, cradling all that muscle, enough to make a red-blooded gay man's mouth water.

I didn't care how much he'd protested, there'd been enough heat in those gorgeous brown eyes to sear the fucking skin off my damn bones. Straight, my arse. Not that he'd really answered that question, to be honest. But he'd sure as hell hightailed it out of there as fast as he could when I'd pushed. *Fucker.*

Which brought me to the fact I *had* pushed. I'd hit on him. *Son of a bitch.* Where had that come from? I didn't even know the guy, not that it was a pre-requisite necessarily, but he could've been anyone. Even at the top of my game, I didn't take risks like that. I'd burned plenty of time in the clubs and gay bars of Boston—hot and popular like professional dancers were want to be. Shake my booty, throw in a few moves, take my shirt off to show all those hard-earned ballet abs, and I rarely left disappointed, let alone needing to fork out for a drink. Not what you'd call emotionally satisfying, but it did the trick, so to speak. God, I could barely remember it. But I'd always been careful.

Still, I'd had a shit few days, and if I was looking for a distraction, Mr Tall, Unwashed, and Beautifully Bearded was an epic distraction. Not my usual type, especially the beard bit, though this one was short and tight. But my usual picks ran to overly groomed, chiselled gym bunnies who didn't mind being shoved around a bit in bed, or up against a wall, or whichever surface was closest as long as nobody saw them. Bossy and me were a match made in heaven, which didn't always sit well with some, but fuck 'em.

So, no, definitely not my usual. This guy smelled of sweat and ocean and soil. And who knew that shit could be as sexy as Tom Ford on smooth skin? Had he belonged to me, I wouldn't have let him anywhere near a damn shower, regardless of what I'd said. Nope. Licking the man from top to toe, slowly—making damn sure to get in all those dangerous dips, curves and creases would be a lot more fun. And holy shit, who the hell had I just turned into? Lusting over David Attenborough in a jockstrap.

But Mr Whoever He Was, he was a genuine, no-nonsense, weather-toughened, earn-my-respect-if-you-dare man. Rugged and patently untouchable. The type I hadn't seen in a long, long time. Certainly not amongst the ballet fraternity or their groupies. Stereotypes be damned. They were there for a reason.

He was also the sort of man who'd take one look at me and see high-maintenance drama with a side order of rabbit-food brunches and label shopping, sauced by a demanding and well-followed Instagram account. And he wouldn't be wrong.

Not because I loved it—I didn't—but because it was what most of my friends expected and lived. And to be honest, the life of a ballet dancer left little time for a lot of other recreational pursuits. If I got out of a five-square block around my apartment and the rehearsal studio once a month, I'd have been doing well.

Guys like him were rare in my world. I hadn't seen many since—I chuckled as the memory hit—since I used to sit on the same bloody wharf as a testosterone-fuelled teenager who'd just discovered he liked his meat swinging not perky, and watched the brawny fishermen offload their catch. Which wasn't a euphemism, but oh how I'd wished it was. The fact that I might have jerked off in the boathouse afterward on more than one occasion was no one's business but my own, and damn, but I'd forgotten all about that as well. I perhaps needed to revisit the whole not-my-type thing, after all.

Then again, maybe I was just horny. I hadn't had a hook-up in . . . so long I could barely remember. After my diagnosis, I'd avoided the clubs. What if I had an attack in one? The whispering, the looks, the pity, the suffocating kindness of the few who stuck around, the friends who'd have to get me home.

I'd used Grindr a couple of times, but it had never been my style. Nothing wrong with the guys I hooked up with, they were hot and eager and right up my alley, but I'd felt disconnected in a way I'd never felt before. The whole thing was unsatisfying and laden with anxiety. My hand was at least safe. If something happened, I didn't have to deal with an audience. It had become less of a worry in the months since, but I hadn't quite got the balls up to try again.

Which was why my out-of-the-ballpark reaction to this older hottie eyeing me like a tub of his favourite ice cream had come as a bit of a shock. Ditto my less-than-subtle, completely ill-conceived invitation to him to tango. Understandable with a couple of shots under my belt, but I hadn't lied about that. I was stone-cold sober.

Still, I'd gotten so used to settling for inspection-without-erection, my fears overwhelming any want, that this sudden desire had caught me off guard. I glanced down to where I still sported a semi and blew out a sigh.

Well, shit.

CHAPTER THREE

Morgan

"Put the shovel down, Randy." I pocketed my phone, raised my hands, and planted my feet in front of my white Toyota Hilux with Fisheries Officer emblazoned down the side. "Don't do anything stupid. Mary will be expecting you home for dinner, right? Be a shame to spend it in the Whangarei lock-up instead. I expect she'd be pissed. She's a good cook, Mary."

Randy's eyes darted from the beach car park and his bright red Ford Focus to the sack at his feet, which I'd caught him hauling up from the sea, and then back to me. The shovel rested on his right shoulder, its shaft in a firm grip.

"You'll never make it," I warned him. "If you've run more than ten metres at a time in the last ten years, I'd be shocked. Besides, even if you did get home, we'd only come get you, in front of Mary."

Known to his mates as Scarecrow, Randy was fifty if he was a day, sucked on Camel filters as if they were oxygen, and had one of the scrawniest arses known to humanity. He was also one of the wiliest and recidivist shellfish poachers on the East Coast. His only saving grace lay in the fact he never sold a single one, just took them for himself and his family, his very large family.

"How many *tuatua* have you got in there?" I indicated the sack. "One fifty is the limit."

Randy rolled his eyes. "I'm not stupid."

I merely raised a brow. It wasn't the first time we'd done this dance. "I'm not gonna find any *toheroa*, am I? They've been off-limits for twenty years."

"As I said, I'm not stupid." Randy's knuckles pinched white around the shaft of the shovel.

"Hasn't stopped you before. What about *pāua*?" I kept my hands wide and neutral.

"A few, not over the limit." His gaze shifted sideways.

"Uh-huh. We'll soon see. Now, if you'll stand back and let me do a count, we can get you home to the missus before dinner."

Another eye flick to the car park and I tensed. Randy might be relatively harmless, but there was always a first time.

Ten years as a fisheries officer and nothing surprised me anymore. Baseball bats, tyre irons, gutting knives, attack dogs, floats, boiling soup, spare boat engines—I'd been attacked with all of them and had the scars to prove it. The protective vest gave me some comfort, but it wasn't a magic bullet. On the whole, the Randys of the world were the least of my worries. Organised poaching gangs with multi-million-dollar industries to protect were the serious threats, but you never could tell for sure. Abalone were found across the globe, but the blackfoot pāua variety, with their brilliant coloured shells, were only found in New Zealand waters and were extremely valuable on the international market.

"You realise that if you're gonna keep this up, you really should change your car," I joked. "Every fisheries officer north of Whangarei knows this one on sight."

Randy grunted. "I keep telling her that, but it's hers . . . Mary's, I mean. She likes red."

I stifled a smile. "Well, she's going to be mad as a hornet if it gets impounded, because you are a whisper away from that, my friend. Now put that shovel down before I have to stop pretending you aren't threatening me with it, and let's see what you've got in there."

He stood fast for a moment, and I wondered if this was going to be the time Randy crossed the line. Then his whole body deflated like a curled-up hedgehog and the shovel dropped to the sand along with my fear. Thank God for that.

He picked up the sack and upended his harvest on the beach. I had a good eye, and although the number of pāua looked to be within limits, there were significantly more than 150 tuatua.

I sighed. "Randy, Randy, why do you make things so hard on yourself? You know there's another fine here, don't you?" I waited till he moved back a bit, then began counting the shellfish into piles. Out of the corner of my eye, I caught sight of a police four-wheel drive pulling into the car park and some of the tension left me.

Randy saw it too and stabbed at the sand with the toes of one foot. "Mary's family are coming for the weekend. There's like a fucking million of them and she had it in mind to cook a whole lot of fritters."

"Then why not wait and bring one or two of them down with you when they got here? You could've taken all of these and more with a couple of extra people."

"She wanted them tonight."

"Well, it's gonna cost both of you." I finished the piles and added them up. "Two hundred and eighty-five. You're lucky they're up to size or I'd be handing you another infringement on top. But 135 over means a $250 instant fine."

Randy hissed.

"Yeah, a lot of money for a few shellfish that you could've had for free if you'd just waited a day and brought your family. Now I'm gonna let you take your 150 this time, but make sure to get that fine paid. Tell Mary hello and that she needs to make better decisions. Two hundred and fifty dollars would've brought you a hell of a lot of fish and chips to go with those fritters."

"Maybe you could tell her."

I backed away with my hands up. "No way. I like my balls exactly where they are, thank you."

Randy snorted and started packing his limit of shellfish back into his sack while I wrote his infringement notice.

"Now get out of here." I handed it to him. "But let me make something perfectly clear first." I eyeballed him so there'd be zero misunderstanding. "I'm gonna be passing along to my colleagues and the police what happened here today. You raise that shovel of yours one more time in my direction or the direction of any other fisheries officer or officer of the law, and you'll find yourself in deep shit, understand? And Mary will have your guts for garters. Do I make myself clear?"

Randy's gaze slid to the side and he gave a curt nod. "Yeah."

"Good. Now go."

He hauled his sack into his arms and trudged across the thick golden sand to his red beacon of a car in the parking lot. The police vehicle flashed its lights my way and I gave Jon a wave, pleased I'd followed my gut and called to see if he could play backup.

When Randy was gone, I returned the confiscated shellfish to the sea, finished my paperwork, and tried to keep my mind from skirting, yet again, to a man with bright hazel eyes, a quick wit, a fondness for watching silver jack in the dark, and an ability to tie my tongue in knots in a matter of seconds. Cursing myself for not even getting a name, I hadn't been able to get him out of my head. I was tempted to see if Jon recognised the guy, but that was only asking for a whole lot of teasing that I had no mind to endure. Best keep my mouth shut.

Done with the paperwork, I drove up off the beach to where Jon was parked in his 4WD, his feet up on the dash, snoozing. As the sole charge cop for the district, and me the lone fisheries officer, we provided a second pair of eyes or hands whenever the other needed it. The fact we got on as friends was an added bonus, bonding over a love of rugby, hair-raising eighties music, and a loathing of all things city, including, but not limited to, shopping malls, crowds, traffic, clubs, congested beaches, and the apparent self-entitlement virus contracted by all people under the age of thirty.

I dropped my driver's window and leaned out. "Thanks for having my back."

He waved it aside. "Pleasure. That guy's getting more unpredictable by the day. Paula at the tackle shop thinks it's early dementia. His dad was the same, apparently."

"Poor bugger."

"Yeah. You got time for a pie and a beer before footy practice?" he asked with a conspiratorial grin.

"I haven't gotten over that one time when our beloved coach made us run sprints on that belly of beer you poured down my throat. I spewed from one end of the field to the other. Then I had to clean it up before Alison McCree took her dawn yoga class the next day."

"Don't recall you resisting much at the time." Jon winked.

I shrugged. "It was a good brew. And you clearly didn't get the text. Training is off. Coach's brother is in town. But yeah, I'd enjoy a pie if you're still interested. Just a Sprite though. I've got an incoming fishing boat to check at six thirty. Don't know what the hell we're training for in February anyway? The social league doesn't start for another six weeks."

Jon flashed a knowing smile. "Coach has a mind to win this year. His brother is coaching Kaitaia."

I stared at him. "Has he lost his freaking mind? Half our team had to be bribed to play with the promise of a free handle of beer after each game, and the other half can barely recall how to throw a rugby ball from the dim dark years of their youth. And then there's people like you and me who fit nicely into both categories."

"Hah!" Jon dropped his feet to the floor. "I'll have you know, Connie says this body has never looked so good."

I snorted. "Connie's your wife. She has to say that shit. I'm five years younger than your embattled forty years, and I *know* this body has seen better days."

Jon laughed and threw his 4WD into gear. "Yeah, well come on,

Richie McCaw, let's see if you can keep that pie and Sprite down this time. I'll see you there in twenty."

Judah

"Throw me the last of those floats," Leroy shouted from the bow. I was busy trying to keep the boat steady while he made some adjustments to the long line anchors. "These cultivation ropes are way too heavy. They're dragging the long lines under."

I furnished him with three extra floats and watched as he added them to the backbone. When he was done, I headed for the wheelhouse and waited for him to get back on board. The sooner I was home and in bed, the better. It had been a long arse day and I stank of sweat, salt, and the ripe odour of mussel shells left in the sun. We didn't normally work these hours, but keeping with my current luck, Leroy's part-time help had abandoned us. Patrick was in Auckland at some family thing, and Sheena had disappeared, God knew where. That girl had a time clock running on Cora's patience.

Both had been part of "Mother Cora's social work programme" for local youth who deserved a break. It was a discreet but well-known local fact that if you needed a safe place to send a young person for a few months while they worked out their shit, Cora would provide it if she could. That included a job, though it might not pay well, and a bed in the homestead, if it was needed.

Most came and went quickly, but at twenty-two, Patrick had found a home in the town and been at the farm over a year. Sheena? Well, the eighteen-year-old was still a work in progress. I'd be all over Mum for letting her get away with simply not turning up, but I was hardly one to talk right now, so yeah, there was that.

But it meant we'd been out on the aquafarm for damn near ten hours, the constant swell doing shit for my queasy stomach, which was still adjusting to the change in meds my GP, Finn, had wanted to try. I was tired, irritated, and hungry. We'd managed half a surprisingly tasty sandwich each at noon, but that was it. But I wasn't hungover, so I suppose that counted for something.

Since my previous attack, the subsequent altercation with Leroy, and a routine doctor appointment two days later, I'd been making a concerted effort to keep to a single beer a night. It hadn't helped that Leroy had followed me into the crammed waiting room for my appointment and then asked my doctor if he would talk to me about my drinking.

Fratricide had never looked so fucking good, and it was all I could do not to deck Leroy there and then. He shrugged off my blistering glare like I'd deserved the calling out, and half the damn waiting room stared like they expected a gin bottle to fall from my pocket when I got up.

Finn Alder, my young, ridiculously handsome in a blond, Clarke-Kent kind of way, presumptively straight, and annoyingly no-bullshit doctor, then, of course, nailed me in an embarrassing conversation. I'd been honest, mostly. And to his credit, he didn't lecture. But the head shake, epic sigh, and the height his eyebrows rose into his hairline kind of said it all. I was suitably mortified.

He, of course, recommended abstinence, but the fact he was right didn't make it any more palatable. So he said if I had to drink, I needed to keep it to a minimum and note everything in my trigger journal. Oh joy. Way to put a downer on it.

Then he climbed all over me for failing to make an appointment with the Auckland specialist he'd recommended and fired a consult note to over a month before, and yeah, those crumbs of humble pie I was eating were starting to mount up.

But I wasn't about to admit how fucking terrified I was to go. Listening to an endless reiteration of exactly how much my life sucked and how much worse it might get before it got better, with no cure in sight, blah, blah, blah, hardly sat high on my list of life-affirming experiences. Not when I was barely making it out of bed each day.

So I'd chickened out. Ostriches and all that.

I promised to make the appointment as soon as I got home, but sensible man that he was, he called through to the specialist while I sat pouting in his office and made it for me, eyeballing me all the while. I felt about twelve years old. But to be fair, I was acting it, so there was that.

I didn't speak to Leroy for the next two days except to tell him it was the last time he was to step foot in that office. Bad enough he had to chaperone me there since I wasn't allowed to drive, but coming in with me was a definite no-go. If he wanted to know something, he could fucking ask like any other half-decent human being who was supposed to care.

It would be fair to say I was still pouting.

Leroy made his way into the wheelhouse with a towel wrapped around his waist and a jacket over the top. He nudged my hip to vacate the helm. "Let's head back. I'm done for the day."

"I can take us in—"

"I've got it." He elbowed me aside and I huffed my way to the stern to sulk like a fucking kid and pretend not to recognise the theme brewing in my life. If there was one thing my brother was good at, it was making me feel like a total waste of space. I might not be able to get in the water, but I could at least manage the boat, and he knew it.

"I won't steer us into the wharf, you know," I shouted from the back.

"Never said you would." He kept his back to me.

"I get enough warning to hand over." *Mostly.*

"I know."

"Then why—"

He spun, frustration written on his face. "It's our business, Jude, our only income."

I knew the "our" part of that statement didn't include me.

"It's nothing personal, but if we lose a boat, we're screwed. I can't take that risk."

Nothing personal? Like hell, it was nothing personal. I was good enough to haul rope and floats and all the other shit, but not good enough to helm the fucking boat that I'd spent years doing as a kid. He might not say it outright, but it was crystal clear Leroy didn't trust me anymore. Not that I could blame him. I barely trusted myself.

I hunkered down on the floor of the boat, sheltering from the gusty northerly that had eaten at us all day, and dropped my head to my knees. As was apt to happen when I had a few spare moments, my thoughts ran to the bearded, brown-eyed man I'd met on the pier all those nights ago. He had a local feel about him. I'd thought about asking Leroy, but we hadn't exactly been talking much after the whole doctor fiasco, and Mum was fussing around me like a mother hen. That shit needed no further encouragement.

My phone buzzed and I pulled it out to find yet another text from Terry to add to the bazillion others he'd sent since I hadn't shown at his hardware store as promised. Managing to avoid his thoughtful arse was kind of impressive in a town of fifteen hundred people, but less so if you considered the fact that if I wasn't out on the boat with Leroy, I barely left the boathouse. And up until then, Terry had been too polite to push things by just turning up on my doorstep. I had a feeling that was about to change.

Where the fuck are you? I'm done being nice. Be at the store tomorrow by 9 arsehole or I'll set Hannah on you.

Shit. Was I a bastard friend? Yes, yes, I was. Terry was the only one of my old school mates who'd even bothered to visit when word got out I was home with my tail between my legs. Not that I was welcoming any fond reunions at the time. But Terry persevered, and we'd met a few times for coffee or a beer at the boathouse, and I appreciated it far more than I let on. He knew about the Meniere's, not because he'd asked, but because he hadn't.

I texted back, **K.**

To which he replied, **A single letter? That's all you've got? Jesus, Judah. Just be there.**

I shoved my phone back in my pocket and contemplated what a shit friend I was. But as long as it wasn't pity Terry was doling out, I was good with it, so I needed to up my game. And God knew I could do with a friend, even if I didn't intend on being in this stain of a town forever. As soon as I figured out what I wanted, I was gone. I needed my life back again and some kind of independence.

The white tips of the choppy swell broke in lines against the side of the boat and set my head nodding.

Being so reliant on people was screwing with my sanity. I couldn't even drive to get away from the place, from Leroy, from my mother, God bless her. My world had shrunk to a tiny boathouse in a two-bit town, and I was backhauling mussels to earn my keep when only months before I'd been sailing over the boards in Boston—the ballet world at my talented feet.

I hated that people looked at me like they didn't know what to do with me anymore, even my family—like I was this uncomfortable problem in their lives they wished they didn't have to deal with. Well, join the fucking club.

Self-absorbed, narcissistic, SOB? Absolutely.

Because mostly I hated that I couldn't seem to stop hating and moaning and despairing. I hardly recognised this new cynical and ungrateful me—no longer the confident, easy-going guy who made people laugh. Before my head had exploded my life. Before my ballet friends smiled and walked the long way around me. Before my body fucked up on itself.

I pocketed my phone and stared daggers at Leroy's back till the harbour entrance came into view and my grumbling stomach drew me out of my funk. I reached for my knapsack of food and—

—fell back like a fucking stone, like a puppet whose strings had been cut. Even my eyelids drooped. My head flopped and cracked against the side of the boat, the jolt of pain ripping through my skull, but I couldn't move.

Thank Christ I'd been sitting and Leroy was focussed on berthing the boat, not me. With my head lolling useless against the interior of the hull, I watched his back, waiting for him to cotton on, but luck was on my side. They might scare the fucking bejeezus out of me, but drop attacks didn't last long, seconds mostly, and by the time we were pulling into the pier, I was pretty much over it, other than the residuals.

But it was the first I'd had in months, almost since the beginning. *Fuck, fuck, fuck.* It was all I needed.

When the boat came to a stop, I stumbled to my feet, grabbed the side for balance, and looked up to find Martha and my mother staring down, concern etched deep on their faces. *Shit.*

Mum opened her mouth to say something, but Martha—bless her cotton socks—tugged at Mum's wrist and shook her head. "Leave it," she said, and I could've kissed her.

I held Mum's gaze and pleaded with my own. The last thing I wanted was to hand Leroy any more ammunition to confirm how useless I was. She glanced from me to Leroy, to Martha, and then back to me, her jaw working in earnest.

Martha caught the rope to tie us up, but I kept my attention on Mum, unsure which way she was going to go. In the end, her shoulders slumped and she sent me a weak smile before heading back to the office. I let out the breath I'd been holding and glanced at Martha. She gave a curt nod, but there was no missing the worry in her eyes. If I didn't want a visit from her later, I'd have to make this right with my mother.

"You throw, I'll catch." Leroy climbed up onto the pier and stared down at me.

I took a moment to steady myself, my legs still a bit wobbly, and then started throwing up the leftover rope, ties, tools, and other equipment, all the while trying to keep my guts where they belonged. I could've begged off. It would've been the sensible thing to do. I could've been honest or at least told Leroy I wasn't feeling great, but fuck that.

Martha looked ready to jump in and rescue me, but I fired her a warning glare and got there in the end. I should've walked along the pontoon and taken the damn stairs up, but where's the fun in that? I deserved a fucking gold medal for not face planting at the top of the ladder, but I did it. Go me. Martha was less impressed, shaking her head in disgust and walking away.

We got the equipment stowed in the large metal shed behind the wharf office and Leroy waved me off with a reminder I was expected for Sunday lunch up at the homestead. *Dammit to hell.* On the positive side, he didn't need me for the Saturday morning shift as Patrick had a day to make up, and I had Sunday off. Two whole fucking days.

Relief brimmed in my eyes, and without thinking, I wiped at them, pretty sure I wouldn't have made it through another day without falling asleep on the boat or bringing on a major attack from sheer exhaustion. Alcohol, lack of sleep, and fatigue were high on my list of triggers, and now hunger, apparently.

"You okay?" Leroy came up on my shoulder.

I turned away. "Fine." God, they were going to etch that word on my damn headstone.

I gathered my coat and backpack and headed to the office to face the music with my mother. Martha was doing busy work outside, recoiling ropes and stacking floats that didn't need it. I nodded my thanks and she grunted what I could only assume was some form of approval as I passed by.

I didn't give Mum a chance to get going before I wrapped her in a hug. At five foot nothing and sixty kilos soaking wet, she barely stood to my chest, and I buried her face in my shirt to hide her tears.

"Hey, I'm okay. I promise." I pressed a kiss to her choppy brunette bob.

She pulled back and stared up at me, blue eyes wet and shining. "Don't lie to me Judah Benson Madden. I saw you go over, saw that look on your face when you pulled in. You were pale as a ghost. That was nothing like that one you had at home."

Or the others you don't know about.

"You just flopped sideways like a rag doll and didn't move. That was one of those drop attacks, wasn't it?" She pulled at the collar of my shirt and patted it flat, her cheeks wet.

I took her hands and held her gaze. "Yeah, it was. I've only ever had a couple, and none since I left Boston."

"They're scary, Judah. You could've hurt yourself. You could've fallen overboard. It must be . . . terrifying." She cupped my cheek and my eyes filled, because it was, terrifying, in every respect. "Do you feel them coming?"

I blew out a long sigh and took a step back from her hands to stop bursting into fucking tears. "No, not with those."

"Then how can you protect yourself? How can you . . . ?"

I took her by the shoulders and kissed her forehead. "As I said, they're rare. I get warning with the others; a full ear, a rush in my tinnitus, light-headedness, even just feeling a bit off."

She shook her head, unconvinced. "Does Leroy know about these?"

Shit. "No, but I'll tell him, I promise. I'd kind of hoped I wouldn't have to."

Her gaze steeled. "You have to tell him, Judah. They're dangerous on the boat. Are you sure you should even be—"

"Please, Mum, I'm fine. But yes, I'll tell him. And they only last seconds, not like the others. They just leave me feeling a bit weak and nauseated. And I'm never in the water. I wouldn't take that risk. But I have to live my life, Mum. I can't hide away."

She said nothing at first, clearly struggling with her instinct to protect me.

Join the club.

But eventually she nodded. "Okay. I hear what you're saying. I'm just finding this all so . . . hard. And I know that's selfish, because it's you who has to go through it, not me. But it's everything you had to give up, your career, Judah, your life. And then coming back here. I know it's not what you ever wanted, and I worry so much. You're so quiet, so . . . angry all the time. I want to make things better, but I know I can't. And you won't talk about it. You must miss dancing so much, baby." She put her arms around me. "I just want my bright boy back."

I sighed and pulled her close. "Me too, Mum, me too. I'm sorry for not talking, but it hurts, you know? And it's like I can't catch my breath before something else happens, some new way this disease finds to screw with my life. Plus, Finn is still messing with my meds and I'm so damned tired, all the time."

"You shouldn't be out on the boat so much. You need to rest. You have to let me help more—"

"No, please. I know you mean well, but I have to work this out on my own. And I can't sit around all day, it'll drive me crazy. But I will talk to Leroy, okay? Even though he thinks I'm ducking work as it is."

Her chin lifted. "I should talk to him."

"No." It was the last thing I needed. "I'll do it. This is my life now, and I'm getting the hang of it, kind of. I'll tell you if there's something you need to know, I promise."

She pressed her lips together and frowned. "You promise? If I leave you alone, you *promise* you'll talk to me?"

"I promise." And God help me, I would, even if it was only to keep the worry from her eyes. "But please, let *me* talk to Leroy."

A heavy sigh broke her lips. "All right. I worry for him too, you know? He was never as easy going as you. He takes life seriously. And when you didn't stay long after your dad died—"

"I would've lost my role—"

"I know that, son. You don't have to convince me. Your dad wouldn't have wanted you to lose that. But Leroy couldn't understand, and I'm not sure he ever will. I don't want you boys fighting."

I thought I was done with feeling guilty, but there it was. I cradled her face. "He's not exactly making it easy."

She frowned and chewed her lip for a moment. "I know. But are you sure you're safe to work out there?"

"Perfectly." *I hoped.*

She took a step back and eyed me. "He says you've been drinking."

Goddammit, Leroy. I closed my eyes for a second and fought for patience. "Mum, please."

She gave a heavy sigh and raised both hands. "I know, I know. I just worry."

"It's your job, I get it. But please, let me do this my way. I'm getting there."

She patted my chest. "Okay."

"Thanks." I kissed her cheek. "I love you."

"You too, son."

I headed out the door, nearly running into Martha who startled backwards.

"I wasn't listening." She flustered, running her hands down the front of her black slacks. "Well, not much," she added with a wry grin. "Good job."

I kissed her on the cheek as well and nodded to the closed door. "She might need a hug."

Martha nodded and ducked inside, and I stood for a second to let the turmoil in my head settle. This time last year I'd been dancing on tour in London. A lifetime, a broken heart, a career collapse, a life-shattering disorder later, and here I was. Diana's voice echoed in my head from a couple of months after my diagnosis. *Suck it up, buttercup. Life shits on you sometimes.* Not one to mince words, Diana.

My attention wandered to the other side of the wharf where Leroy was busy talking to some fisheries officer, the two of them watching a local fishing charter unload. My gaze lingered on the uniformed man's face and—*no fucking way*—I nearly dropped my knapsack off the side of the wharf.

If it wasn't Mr Bearded and Ruggedly Handsome from the pier—the man I'd whacked off to one or five times over the last week. But who was counting? *Well, fuck me.* Of all the men I could have propositioned, I'd of course chosen someone my brother was guaranteed to know. The mussel farm and fisheries department had a close working relationship.

Then the rugby gear sprang to mind and the rest of the horrifying picture came to life. The night at the pier had been training night, which meant my brother and the guy I'd hit on played freaking rugby together. Yeah, my luck just fucking ran like that.

I saw the minute he recognised me as well—the way his expression froze on his face and his whole body braced. *Yeah, guess who?* And since there was little point in hiding, I took another long look, and damn, the man still looked a treat.

He did a good job of gathering himself and refocussing on Leroy who was busy chatting away like they were friends. And just why that rankled me so much, I wasn't prepared to dwell on. But before I could make my escape, he looked my way for a second time, and Leroy's gaze followed.

Leroy frowned and waved me over, like he'd rather not. *Shit.*

I wandered across, taking my own good time, which earned me a suitable scowl from my brother. *Whatever.* I wasn't about to make this easy on fish guy.

"Morgan, this is my younger brother, Jude—"

"Judah," I corrected, which earned another scowl.

"*Judah*, this is Morgan Wipene, our local fisheries officer."

Morgan. Nice name. "Jordan?" *Yeah, never said I couldn't be a bitch.*

Leroy glared, whereas Morgan bit back a smile—the man wasn't fooled for a minute.

He threw out a hand. "*Morgan.* Perhaps I should spell it?"

Oh, he was good. I fired him my best withering look but took his hand anyway. His grip was firm and warm, and if I held on a little longer than was strictly necessary, who could blame me? "Maybe you could write it down so I don't forget. So many men, after all."

I smiled at Leroy's sharp intake of breath. Who said this wasn't going to be fun?

Morgan blushed brightly and a twinge of regret played havoc with my smug satisfaction. Yeah, I was being a total dick.

"Lucky them," Morgan said softly, surprising me.

Leroy's eyes flicked between us, the crease between his brows growing deeper by the second. "Do you two know each other?"

"*Know* is a relative word, wouldn't you say, Morgan?" I answered drily, thrown by Morgan's unexpectedly sweet comment. "We've met, briefly, no names exchanged."

I waggled my eyebrows at him, then stepped back before I gave in to the increasing urge to climb the man like a tree, my brother be damned. "Whereas you two are clearly *old* friends." My gaze travelled between them. "Let me guess. You met at the local Residents Against Drift Netting meeting? Ballet Not Bait Fishing—I'm an inaugural member of that one. Or, how about—and this is one for the fisheries officer—Size Matters."

Morgan looked about to swallow his tongue, while Leroy looked ready to pop a blood vessel, his cheeks blazing.

"What the fuck, Jude?" he choked out.

"Judah."

"I don't give a shit. Can you at least not insult the guy? He's a friend. We're in the same rugby team, for Chrissakes."

"Yeah, I'd worked that one out for myself." I remembered those yummy skins under the man's training gear. "Sweat and boots with studs or, alternatively and much more intriguing, studs with boots." I grinned and Morgan blushed, he fucking blushed.

Leroy looked ready to blow a gasket, but Morgan simply laughed. "He didn't insult me, Lee."

Lee?

"And I happen to agree with his comment about fisheries officers. Size does, indeed, matter." He opened his hands wide. "We are but a tool of the community." He nodded. "At your service."

He gave slight emphasis to the words tool and service, and my tongue got a little friendly with the roof of my mouth. Trying to keep a straight face, I pursed my lips and stared at him, letting him know I knew exactly what he was up to.

I wagged my finger in his face. "Very slippery, Mr Wipene. But don't think I haven't got your number. On the ladder of witty repartee, you still have a way to go to even spy me in the rankings well above your head."

He leaned in. "If I got that close, Mr Madden, I'm pretty sure that's not what I'd be looking at."

I opened my mouth, then closed it again. *Goddammit.* The man had game. An unfamiliar warmth hit my cheeks that hadn't seen them in years. So much for thinking the guy was on the down-low. I'd been a total dick, again. I saw an apology in my future, damn it all.

A sideways glance at Leroy revealed he'd likely need a crane to lift his jaw from the deck it was currently plastered to. I winked at Morgan. "I think you've shocked the sensibilities of my straight-as-a-die older brother."

Morgan followed my gaze. "I doubt it. Lee knows I'm bi."

Definitely not closeted. And also, what the fuck? Leroy was friendly with someone who had a bend either way right in the middle of the words sexual attraction? My world view rattled somewhat on its size-twelve assumptions.

"Yeah, I do." Leroy ratcheted that jaw of his back into place and managed to look smug as shit. "So, fuck you. And what the hell's up with you anyway? Morgan simply asked who you were and if I could introduce you. Then you all but flip him off."

He asked? I turned to Morgan. "You asked?"

He shrugged and flashed me a pair of unexpected dimples that came with an adorability factor of ten. "Seemed like a good idea at the time. But then I've been known to get it wrong, on occasion." A somewhat pointed reminder of our encounter on the pier.

Well, shit. There was nowhere to hide after that. I blew out a sigh. "Yeah, well, sometimes you catch people when they're not fit for human consumption. A state I have more than a passing familiarity with at the moment. Leroy's right. I owe you an apology."

Morgan snorted. "Wow, how did that feel?"

It was really hard not to like the guy. "Like swallowing horse shit. But now I think I'll leave you two to talk. Excuse me." I made to head off, but Leroy's constipated look gave me pause. "What? Something else I've done wrong?"

His lips turned up in what might've been the beginning of a

smile, but I hadn't seen it often enough lately to be sure. "Not a thing," he said smugly. "I was just recovering from the part where you said I was right."

I narrowed my eyes. "Don't push it. And did I say that? Cos you know how bad my memory is lately, what with the *thing* and all."

His smile dropped instantly.

Yeah, don't think this makes up for you not giving a fuck about me for most of my life. Dear God, could I sound more sorry for myself? And did my brother deserve it? Maybe. Didn't make me any less of an arsehole.

I chanced a last look at Morgan, who was watching me with a curious expression like he knew he'd missed something, and I realised Leroy obviously hadn't said anything about what had happened to me. The idea of him protecting my privacy jolted me hard, and I didn't know whether to be grateful or pissed about the fact that it was most likely because he was uncomfortable about the whole thing. My vote went to the latter. After all, it was pretty much how I felt.

"Nice to have met you *properly*, Morgan." We exchanged polite nods and I escaped toward the boathouse before I crashed on the deck of the wharf. I needed meds, food, a shower, an encounter with my right hand, and a year's worth of sleep, and good luck with the order of those. It was going to be first come first served.

I changed into loose yoga pants and a sweatshirt, gabbed my meds and a leftover sandwich, and got as far as the lounger on the deck when sleep won out.

CHAPTER FOUR

Morgan

I THUMPED MY KNUCKLES ON THE DOOR OF JUDAH'S BOATHOUSE for the second time, figuring I had about a minute left to appreciate the current geographical alignment of my balls before Judah handed them to me. If I'd been a betting man, I'd have put money on this being up there with one of my more idiotic decisions. But like all the other stupid ideas I'd had over the years, I didn't pay a lick of attention to that voice of reason and knocked again.

I'd watched Judah, *not Jude*—though it begged the question of why Leroy seemed hell-bent on ignoring his brother's preferred name —head into the boathouse a good hour ago, and as far as I knew, he hadn't left. Not that I was stalking the guy or anything. The fact I just happened to be doing an inspection of the fishing charter's catch, which just happened to be in spitting distance of the boathouse, wasn't my fault.

The fact that I'd spent the next twenty minutes writing it up in my vehicle—carefully hidden in a quiet corner of the car park behind the electricity transformer with an excellent and unobstructed view of the boathouse—instead of taking it home as I usually did was admittedly, less convincing.

The fact that I'd then sat another ten minutes, chewing on my pen, talking to my dead wife—who'd gone surprisingly silent on the matter—and staring at Judah's front door over my steering wheel with not a damned excuse in the world to still be there, I busily ignored with everything I had.

But when it came to the fact of me knocking at the guy's front door, I was all out of excuses. Five years in Painted Bay and this was the first time I'd been even remotely interested in anyone, let alone a guy, for fuck's sake. And as for knocking on their front door? I raised my eyes heavenward. "I'm holding you responsible," I whispered.

None of which got me a reply from inside the house.

I peered through the window to the side of the door and saw . . . nothing. The prudent response would be to take that as a sign and simply leave. Judah would be none the wiser and it would save me the embarrassment of facing his undoubtedly less-than-impressed reaction even if he did answer.

Pfft. Like that was even an option. Refer back to stupid decisions. Not to mention the dead woman who'd been whispering in my ear about taking chances for the last week. It wasn't a ghost thing, I hadn't lost my marbles or discovered some latent psychic ability, it had just always been that way between us.

Sally had been buried so deep in my heart and my head that not even death had shaken her free. Admittedly, her voice was softer these days, and at times I had to listen really hard, but that was okay. Life moved on, eventually. It had taken a while, but we were letting each other go, making room for the living or, in Sally's case, for flying, because she'd have been first in line for a pair of those wings or someone would've regretted it.

The moving-on thing was happening whether I liked it or not, and most days I was fine with it. But some days? Yeah, some of those still fucking sucked. And making room and letting go had never in my wildest dreams included a *guy*. And not just any guy. Oh no.

Judah Madden.

I could hear Sally laughing her sweet patootsie off from here.

The young man had been stuck in my head on replay like a bad jingle since that first night on the pier, and Lord knows I'd tried to switch him off. He'd been mouthy, defensive, vulnerable, cheeky, a little sad, and just this side of sweet. All in all, a pretty intriguing package if you were into that kind of thing, which apparently, I was. News to me.

When I lined Judah up alongside Sally, I could barely find any lines of intersection, and it was doing my head in. How could a prickly, artistically inclined, snarky, and far-too-young-for-me *man* with his life in upheaval—which was all Leroy would say on the matter—get under my skin almost as quickly as the driven, capable, fiery-but-reliable woman I'd loved with all my heart? It felt wrong on so many levels, just not the levels that were holding the reins on my common sense, evidently.

Talking with Judah was like playing verbal tennis, with me as the lower-seeded competitor. You never knew quite how the next set of words you lobbed were going to be returned. But I also hadn't felt as captivated, frustrated, or turned on in ages, since . . . Sally. Okay, so one line of intersection. And when Judah sent me packing with a flea in my ear? Well, let's just say I drove home with the biggest damn smile on my face.

But Judah Madden also screamed trouble with a capital T. And watching him with his brother hadn't in any way reassured me. Judah had complicated threads sitting just under that surface calm he worked so hard to maintain. Complicated, emotionally sticky, and downright hazardous to my *uncomplicated* life, and I wasn't at all sure about getting close enough to pull on a single one of them. And therein lay the problem.

I didn't do complicated, or trouble, or even intriguing. I enjoyed watching them dance from a distance, could even admire and dip my toes in every now and then from the safety of a hook-up. But actively invite them into my life? Not in a million years. I liked calm. I enjoyed quiet. I preferred predictable.

Sally might've been a spitfire and shaken up my world, but for all that, she was safe, solid, grounded in herself and what she wanted from life. Judah felt . . . none of those things. Which threw up all sorts of questions about what the fuck I was doing at his door.

I took a step back and weighed my options.

My dad had a life mantra: "You can't live life by hiding from it." It sounded good, though he was inclined to take it a little too much to heart, zig when he should have zagged and such. Like throwing our money away on half-baked ideas or ill-conceived generosity. It caused a fair bit of trouble in our household, and some prudence on his part wouldn't have gone amiss, but then he was all about risk.

Which was why I wasn't.

That aside, there was one thing I *was* sure about. I'd felt more alive in the fifteen minutes I'd spent with Judah Madden than I had in a long, long time.

Walk away.

Take a chance.

The ongoing civil war in my head.

And so before I could talk myself out of it, I took the steps down from the front door of the boatshed and walked across the old concrete launch ramp. A glass wall with ranch sliders had taken the place of the original wooden launch doors and my heart ticked up. Standing inside it would feel like you were on top of the water. At the far side, I turned the corner and found Judah curled up on one of two sun loungers on a small deck that sat above the sand, shaded from the last of the evening sun. He was fast asleep.

My breath caught in my chest as I stood transfixed by this elusive snapshot of a completely different side of the man I'd faced off with twice already. Judah's long, lean body wrapped in a loose yoga pants and a long baggy sweatshirt, lay curled on its side, legs bent, revealing the full curve of a muscular and mouthwatering arse. His face rested on his lower hand, the upper tucked between his knees, and a thin curtain of messy dark hair striped his forehead. My fingers itched to brush it aside.

He looked impossibly young, in that way only deep sleep could render someone—relaxed, peaceful, open. Everything the wide-awake and prickly young man wasn't. The contrast was startling, and I ached to know why.

"I didn't take you for a pervert, *Mr* Wipene." Judah lifted his head and attempted to scowl at me through sleepy eyes, the end result more comical than irritated.

I tried hard not to laugh. "I, ah, knocked on your front door, but there was no answer."

Judah arched a brow. "Perhaps because I was asleep . . . on my deck, after a long day minding my own business . . . unlike some." Then his gaze dipped to an ant covered sandwich and a few pills on a plate beside him and he swore, "Fuck." He shook the ants off the pills and swallowed them dry, then looked up. "Is there something I can do for you or can I get back to sleep?"

Right. So much for taking a risk. It didn't seem I could find a good side to get on with this man. If he'd ever been interested, he clearly wasn't now. "Forget it. My fault. I'll, ah, leave you to it."

I got as far as the ramp.

"Oh, for fuck's sake. Just . . . hold up." Judah pushed himself to a sit and waved me back. "It's not like I'm going to be able to sleep wondering what could possibly have possessed you to come visit. So, spill."

It was hardly a welcome. "It can wait."

His brows dipped. "Now you're just pissing me off."

I rolled my eyes and walked back to the deck. "Fine. I, ah . . . well, to be honest, I'm not exactly sure *why* I'm here, other than we seem to have got off on the wrong foot and I'd like to remedy that, if I can."

He raised an eyebrow and frowned. "Did my arsehole brother put you up to this? Is this his way of getting in my head? Sending you to work those cute little dimples you've got going on and charm your way into my confidence? If it is, then you can tell him it's gonna take a hell of a lot more than a sexy man in a uniform to shoehorn me out of this place."

I couldn't help but laugh. "Wow, whatever those pills were, they must've been something if you think this uniform is sexy. You need to raise your bar a little, Judah."

Judah's mouth curved up in a slow, sexy smile, and every hair on my body stood to attention. "Let's test that theory, shall we?" He twirled his finger in a circle. "Take a spin, Mr Fisheries Officer."

My mouth gaped. "What? No. Don't be ridiculous."

His smile grew. "Humour me."

I stared at him a few seconds longer, then spread my arms and turned in a fucking circle, wondering what the hell I was doing. I swear Judah choked back a laugh. Or maybe that was Sally; angels could be bitches too.

"Mmmm. Just as I thought," Judah said in all seriousness. "Tight in all the right places and an arse to bounce a quarter off. I'm sorry, but the verdict is indisputable. Too fucking sexy for your own good." He cocked his head and winked.

A flush ran to my cheeks and it occurred to me that was twice in one week he'd made me blush, which was twice as many times as I'd blushed in the previous however many years it had been since I'd last crushed on a guy—which was just this side of never. Fucked on the rare occasion, very rare. But crushed on, never.

I shook my head and ignored the rush of warmth in my belly at his flattery. How long since anyone had complimented me like that? I did all right with women, but I didn't fool myself. Cover model, I was not.

"You're an idiot," I brushed him off. "Not to mention, clearly in need of glasses."

He frowned, looking genuinely perplexed. "You don't think you're sexy? Come on. I bet you have all the boys licking at your heels, not to mention other more . . . interesting places." He drew his bottom lip between his teeth and my body instinctively responded. How did he do that?

But then, I'd been about one fuck shy of a monk's life for the last five years. Just enough nameless sex to keep the flag flying, but only at half-mast and wilted against the pole. Mostly my dick had given up on me, fully expecting the last post to ring out at any moment, whereupon it would be rolled up and packed away, only to be brought out on special occasions as a kind of memorial.

I didn't for a minute believe anything Judah Madden said about me. He was young, hot, and sexy as shit, and clearly knew how to play to an audience. Leroy hadn't told me much about his younger brother, but I knew Judah had been an up-and-coming ballet star until something happened. Enough to let me know the man could work a crowd.

I wasn't sure how we'd gotten onto this, but I wanted off it again, quickly, sensing it was all part of some well-scripted performance Judah used to keep his defences solidly in place and keep people like me off-balance. But it was a game that didn't interest me in the slightest. I was here to see if the *other* Judah Madden—the one fascinated by a simple school of mackerel swarming around a submerged light—actually existed.

"Behave." I narrowed my eyes at him. "Are you always this way?"

He dropped the sexy smirk and eyed me warily. "What way?"

"This whole act you've got going on. The 'reel them in with a bit of bait and charm, take what you need, and throw them back into the water before they find out anything about you' act?"

He chewed the inside of his cheek and studied me.

I fully expected the next words out of his mouth to send me packing. So be it. It would save us both a lot of time.

He got to his feet, opened the ranch slider, and my heart sank. Jesus, was he just going to leave me standing? It wouldn't surprise me.

"Leave your shoes outside." He stepped into the boathouse and glanced back to where I was standing with my mouth open. "Well, are you coming?"

I ran a hand over my beard and his eyes followed. "I'm not here for a hook-up, Judah." Just call me a fucking martyr and be done with it.

His mouth turned up at the corners. "Just as well, Morgan, cos I'm not offering one."

Oh. I walked up the dozen or so steps made of old wharf piles onto the deck, wistfully noting that in a full tide you'd be able to step right off the bottom one into the shallows. "In that case, yes. Should I have left my stab-proof vest on?"

He flashed me a wide smile and my eyes locked onto that sexy beauty spot high on his right cheek. "Very possibly." He laughed and disappeared inside.

And just like that I was back dangling at the end of whatever fish hook Judah had me on this time. I hesitated about two seconds before I followed. But since he'd stopped just inside the door, I had to quickly sidestep to miss running into the back of him and—

Holy moly.

I came to an abrupt halt as the room unfolded before me.

He was a young guy, so it wasn't like I was expecting meticulous, but I hadn't reckoned on a scene straight out of The Hoarder Files, either. Every flat surface exploded with clothes and boxes, papers and magazines, weight equipment and suitcases. Various large framed photos of ballet performances were stacked three deep along the walls, and a mound of what looked like woollen leggings, sweatshirts, and what I guessed were ballet shoes took up most of the single cream linen armchair shoved in the corner. A matching couch held another pile of jeans, jackets, and T-shirts as if they'd been upended from a suitcase and never moved.

Not to mention a slew of empty bottles, everywhere; beer, tequila, wine, rum, you name it. Judah either drank to live—which yes, worried me somewhat—or he'd been on a serious mission of drinking to forget *something*.

Huh.

A few puzzle pieces fell into place as I recognised signs of the latter, even his prickly manner. When Sally had died, I'd done a fair bit of my own drinking to forget, not to mention pushing people away. My gaze flicked sideways to Judah's mask-like expression. There was a story there.

"Love what you've done with the place," I deadpanned. "Must have been a great party."

He had the grace to look a little sheepish, like he was seeing the room for the first time. "Yes, well, I, ah, might have gotten a little ahead of myself inviting you in. I, um, haven't been entertaining."

I couldn't help the laugh. "No kidding. Nothing says *I'd rather not be here* than unpacked bags."

His spine stiffened. "For your information, I'm not usually this bad. I actually like a clean space . . . mostly."

"How long have you been back."

His cheeks tinged pink. "A couple of months."

I snorted. "Imagine what you could achieve with a bit longer."

His jaw set. "Yeah, well, I've been a bit preoccupied." He went to clear the clothes from the chair and stumbled. His face drained of all colour and he struck a hand out for the wall.

I was there in a second, my arm sliding around his tight waist, slipping under his sweatshirt to connect with skin, lots of warm, smooth skin. His gaze jerked to mine, then away, but he let me lead him to the couch before quickly disentangling himself.

I shoved a pile of clothes on the floor so he could sit and then knelt at his feet. "Are you okay?"

"I'm fine." He kept his eyes closed. "I just need a minute."

I stayed where I was, and while Judah took his time, I indulged my curiosity about the state of the room. Beneath the surface bedlam lay the lines of a nicely set up space. A set of whitewashed wooden coffee tables, a chunky jute rug, some beach-themed prints, pale-blue-and-cinnamon curtains with a soft patterned shell motif, and some hand-blown glass ornaments.

A half-wall separated the lounge from the bedroom area, its large bed buried under a mound of pastel duvets and cushions. While along the sidewall of the boathouse, a small but fresh-faced and surprisingly tidy galley kitchen sat all decked out in stainless steel and cream cabinetry. And at the sea-end of the boathouse sat that wall of glass to the ramp, with its no doubt stunning view of the sea, if only you could see it through the closed drapes.

Beneath the clutter, the boathouse was charming, or it would've been if you could appreciate more than ten percent of it, and if the overwhelming impression wasn't one of sour alcohol, stale air, and unwashed clothes. The kitchen was the only space that looked relatively clean and remotely inviting.

When I turned back to Judah, he was watching me.

"I haven't had a man on their knees for me in a long time." His eyes twinkled shamelessly. "A pity I'm not exactly up for it."

I patted his thigh and stood. "Just as well, because as someone quite recently said, I'm not offering. You look whacked."

His expression softened, betraying the lines of exhaustion around his eyes. "I'm just hungry."

I remembered the ant covered sandwich on the deck. "When did you last eat?"

"I'm fine—"

"So help me, Judah, if you say that one more time . . ."

"Half a sandwich at lunch," he muttered.

I folded my arms.

He shrugged. "We were busy."

Cook for him.

Shut. Up.

I checked my watch. "That was eight hours ago. I'll get you something."

"You don't need—"

"Stay where you are. And please tell me I can open the curtains, maybe even a window or two?"

He sunk back into the cushions and waved his hand. "Knock yourself out."

I hauled open the drapes and threw back the slider. A salt-laden breeze and a splash of mellow evening sun hit the room in a welcome rush.

Judah shielded his eyes for a minute, then slowly dropped his hand.

"You okay?" I checked.

"Fi— Yes, perfectly."

I headed to the kitchen so I wasn't tempted to do something stupid like throw a blanket over him or fluff up his pillow, for Chrissakes.

"Am I gonna find any food in that kitchen of yours?" I kept my voice level.

"There's some stuff in the fridge, I think. Or at least Mum put something in there a week or so ago."

"A week?" I warily opened the door and was almost knocked flat by the aroma of food well past its due date. "I take it you haven't looked in any of these containers since she put them here."

He winced. "That you sound so horrified only reinforces how little you know of my mother's cooking."

"That bad, huh?"

He nodded. "Let's just say, Martha Stewart she isn't, but not for the want of trying. She pores over recipes expectantly, as if at any minute one of them will turn her into Julia Child. It hasn't, in case you were wondering. But that hasn't stopped her trying, and none of us have the heart to tell her."

I began rearranging the fridge contents to see exactly what I was dealing with as he talked. The conversation was a glimpse under the prickly façade, and I didn't want to put him off.

"As kids, Dad had this big German Shepherd that I'm sure died from hardening of the arteries. We were forever sneaking him food under the table, even Dad. He and Mum had this big love-affair marriage. He'd never have hurt her feelings by telling her how much her cooking sucked."

"So she has no idea how bad she is?"

Judah laughed. "Hell yeah, she knows. But she doesn't let a small thing like that stop her. She hosts Sunday lunch at the old homestead most weekends, Martha and Leroy's workers included. It's always a crap-shoot what you'll get served, but everyone still goes. I'm half convinced she fails at recipes deliberately, just to keep the joke running. Most of what she cooks *is* edible, just not quite . . . right, if you catch my drift."

I grabbed a handful of containers from the shelves and held them out to show him. "Well, you should have got rid of this lot days ago. Most of it could walk itself to the bin if you pointed it in the right direction."

Judah shrugged. "Sorry. To be honest, I mostly just pick. Cheese, eggs, yoghurt, that sort of thing."

I grunted. "Is that a ballet-weight thing?"

He laughed with a lightness I hadn't really heard before and I wanted to bottle it so I could play it back later.

"Nah, I ate a *lot* better when I was dancing. This is more of a lazy, fuck-my-life sort of thing."

Jesus, he was cute when he wasn't being a total dickhead. "Does that mean you *can* cook?" I eyed him with suspicion. "Cos I have to tell you, judging by the state of this place, I have my doubts about your proficiency in the kitchen or the relative food safety rating attached to it."

Another laugh. "Yes, *Dad*, I can cook. Nothing flash—grilled meats, salad, pancakes, that kind of thing, but I do all right."

"Except for now, apparently." I grabbed a dozen eggs and a loaf of what looked like homemade bread, some mushrooms that had seen better days but would do, and a block of cheese. "And lay off the dad thing. What are you? Twenty-two?"

"Twenty-five."

And okay, I felt a little less of a pervert.

"You?"

I glanced up and rolled my eyes skyward. "Thirty-five."

He threw me a wicked smile. "So not *quite* dad material, but pretty fucking close—"

"Don't even." I pointed my knife at him, trying to ignore the way those dancing hazel eyes went straight to my dick. This was such a bad idea. "And it's gonna have to be an omelette, take it or leave it."

"Considering you're cooking for me and the fact you're holding an enormous chef's knife that I didn't even know I had, I'm not gonna argue."

"Wise man. You can sit at the breakfast bar and grate the cheese."

His brows crunched. "I thought I was supposed to be taking it easy?"

"You can take it easy grating the cheese." Not to mention, I wanted him up in my space more than was remotely healthy for me.

He sighed and got to his feet while I broke the eggs in a bowl and kept one eye on him as he made his way over, in case he wobbled. But he made it in one piece and it wasn't long till he was filling a plate with grated Emmantel while I got the rest of the ingredients sorted.

"So"—I swept the knife over the interior of the boathouse—"tell me more about this. Not enough closet space?" I put some bread in the toaster and the mushrooms into a small pan to wilt with some butter and seasoning.

He stopped grating and regarded me with a cool stare. "Is that what this is about? Some quid pro quo? You cook and I spill my guts?" He pushed back from the counter. "No, thank you."

I sighed. "It was a simple, and dare I say it, obvious question sparked from curiosity, not the fucking Spanish Inquisition. Have you always been this suspicious?"

He didn't answer for a few seconds, those bright hazel eyes searching my face for something, I wasn't quite sure what.

I put a second much larger skillet on to heat, threw in another wedge of butter, and ignored him. He'd talk or he wouldn't. I wasn't going anywhere until I fed him, but I wasn't going to play the "let's pretend none of this is happening" game, either. There was something about Judah that hooked under my skin and tugged.

It took a minute, but eventually he relaxed. "Suspicious? No. But yeah, I've always been cautious, with good reason." He reached for an open notebook on the counter and closed it with a slap. "As the only gay kid in the district and with a penchant for ballet, makeup, and a major obsession with the Spice Girls, I was a convenient target for the usual dipshits, most of whom were friends with my brother who did fuck-all to stop any of it."

Ah. It wasn't a side I'd ever seen of Leroy personally, but I knew he was fairly black and white about a lot of stuff. Not that it was any excuse if what Judah said was true.

He continued, "And the ballet world isn't exactly known for its generosity of spirit, either. It's cut-throat and competitive. It feeds on insecurity and gossip, both of which I've been the target of and participated in, much to my regret. Friends come and go, depending on the arc of their career or yours. Can being a friend be useful or work against you? Can it get you the attention of someone who matters? That type of shit."

He stared at some point over my shoulder and I caught the emotional sting in his eyes.

"Ouch."

His gaze met mine. "Pretty much. I'm not saying I didn't have good friends, because I did. But I've been burned a few times as well. So forgive me for holding back on putting out the welcome mat when someone two licks above a total stranger asks for my life history."

"I wasn't asking for your life history," I pointed out, shaking the pan as it came to the heat. "I simply asked a question about settling back in."

"You were." He sighed and pushed the plate of cheese my way. "You just didn't know it."

I poured all the eggs into the pan at once and turned to face him. "In that case, I'm sorry. It wasn't meant that way. Just ignore it."

He gave a weak smile. "Shit. I'm being a sensitive dick, aren't I?"

I worked the eggs without looking up. "You're entitled."

"But you weren't to know. I tell you what. Maybe let me eat first, and we start with you."

I glanced up from the pan. "Deal. Fire away."

"So, how'd you find your way to this tiny slice of New Zealand and into the ranks of our esteemed fishery officers."

I smiled. "Now you're just taking the piss."

He popped a handful of grated cheese into his mouth and licked his lips slowly, watching me watching him doing it. "Maybe, but I'm still interested."

Good God, the man was sexy. "All right. Have it your way." I topped the huge omelette with the goodies, folded it, gave it a few seconds to heat through, and then slid it onto a chopping board. "You get two thirds," I said. "I've had something already. You got some plates somewhere?"

Judah nodded and got to his feet, looking a little steadier as he delivered a couple of plates to the counter and buttered the toast.

I stood alongside him and divided the omelette, feeling the heat of his body on mine as our hips brushed for a nanosecond, a nanosecond that lit me up like a Christmas tree. You'd have thought he'd shoved his tongue down my throat judging by the zing that travelled up my spine.

"But if I'm gonna tell you the sad, short story of my life," I said, sounding a lot more put together than I felt, "I'll need a beer. Assuming there's some left." I nodded to the overflowing box of empties at the end of the kitchen.

His eyes flicked sideways and back, with just a hint of defiance. "In the vegetable drawer of the fridge."

I shook my head. "Of course they are. You?"

He hesitated. "Make mine a water. But please, have your beer."

I filled him a glass, grabbed a beer for myself, and we headed out to the deck where at least we had somewhere to sit.

We took a lounger each, facing each other, and he shovelled a forkful of eggs into his mouth, dropped his fork to his plate, and groaned in appreciation. "Holy shit, you really can cook. This is amazing."

"Good." I tried not to stare as another forkful made its way between those lush lips. Tried and failed. Mostly because the man enjoying my cooking—and wasn't that a fucking rush—was the Judah I'd first met on that pier a week ago. Gone was the attitude and the snark, and in its place, this open, sexy, intriguing young guy simply enjoying the moment. The difference was startling . . . and beguiling, and I really, really needed to stop staring.

"What?" Judah spoke through a mouthful of eggs, his fork poised halfway to his plate. Then he swallowed and a slow, sexy grin spread over his face. "Ohhh."

Busted.

He pointed to my untouched plate with his fork. "Eat, before it gets cold and before I'm tempted to come over there and blow you just for looking at me like that."

Shit. "I wasn't—"

"Sure you weren't." He smiled again and went back to his eggs, leaving me still staring at him.

Judah Madden was doing my head in. I hadn't felt so damn rattled by a guy or *anyone* in a long, long time, and I didn't like it. Okay, so that was a lie. I liked it more than I should, but I didn't understand it, and I sure as shit didn't need to be encouraging it.

"I refuse to engage with your delusions," I grumbled and focussed on my eggs.

He chuckled but said nothing and we finished our meal in silence.

"So . . ." He deposited his plate on the deck and sank back on the lounger with his hands folded over his flat as a pancake stomach. "What's this sad short story of your life then? And how the hell did you end up in bumfuck, back-of-nowhere Painted Bay?"

I scooped the last of my omelette into my mouth and added my plate to his before grabbing my beer. "Not much to tell really. And I'll have you know, I love this place, so don't dis it. When I was growing up in the epically mind-numbing suburbs of east Auckland, I would've killed to have all this on my doorstep."

He laughed and shoved his hair back away from his face. "When

I was growing up, I would've swapped you for less than a packet of crisps. So how'd you get to be a fisheries officer?"

"I had a high school friend whose dad was big on fishing. He took us out all the time. We both got our diving certifications before we were fifteen. I've always loved the ocean—on it, in it, beside it, any way I can get close."

Judah's eyes twinkled. "Sounds like me and dance."

Huh. "I suspect my talent might not stand up to the comparison, but maybe so. I studied marine biology at university, and as much as I loved the subject, I worked out pretty quick that I hated being in the lab and I wasn't too hot on working with lots of people, either."

Judah's brow creased in a puzzled frown. "I wouldn't have picked you for a loner. You did a good job talking your way into my house, if you are."

I groaned. "Now I'm embarrassed."

He grinned. "Don't be. It was a compliment. I don't get *handled* that often . . . unless I want to be."

Our gazes locked, and oh yeah, we were definitely flirting again. I wasn't sure how I felt about it, but the butterflies in my belly were probably a good indication, and I cleared my throat. "I'm gonna ignore that. And no, I'm not a loner, as such. I *was* married for five years."

That sent his eyebrows to the roof and I was tempted to lick my finger and score an air point.

"Married? I wouldn't have guessed that, although I don't know why. But you said, 'was.' What happened?"

"Now, who's being blunt?" I studied him for a second, then took the plunge. "She died five years ago. Pancreatic cancer."

"Oh shit, I'm sorry." He immediately reached over and squeezed my hand. "Trust me to be a dick."

"It was my choice to answer. But maybe we can leave the rest of that topic for another time."

He dropped my hand but held my gaze for a long moment. "Of course. But is it okay to ask if that's the reason you came to Painted

Bay?" He wriggled back on the lounger again, and I couldn't help but notice the way those damn leggings tightened around his thighs and cupped his package. He adjusted himself, pulled his sweatshirt down, and then laughed when I caught his eye.

Fucking tease. I had no idea what we were doing, but there was no denying I was having fun. Judah was so comfortable with his body, so sure of his sex appeal. I couldn't relate in the slightest, but I could admire him for it.

"It was part of the reason I came here," I finally answered his question. "I was ready for a change, but I also wanted to escape the well-meaning but suffocating concern of my family."

Judah rolled his eyes. "Another thing we have in common."

I cocked my head. "There's a story there too, by the sound of it."

He shrugged. "Like you said, a topic for another time."

My turn to hold his gaze. "I *am* actually good with people, or at least I'm comfortable meeting and chatting with them—you have to be in this job. But I don't like working shoulder to shoulder with the same people day in and day out. I like planning my own time and being largely my own boss. So when the opportunity came up for a fisheries officer position in South Auckland after I graduated, I grabbed it. Haven't looked back since."

Judah brushed an errant dark swipe of hair from his eyes for the millionth time and nodded as if that all made sense. "You and the fishing friend still see each other?"

A sharp blade twisted in my chest and I hesitated before answering. "No. Lonnie died in a diving accident before we graduated. I was supposed to be out with him that day, but I needed to study. He, ah, decided to dive alone."

Judah slapped his palm to his forehead. "Fuck me. That's two for two today. Jesus, Morgan, that's rough."

"Yeah. I blamed myself for a while. I'd kind of known he'd go off on his own even though it's the cardinal rule of diving."

Judah sighed. "I get that. Just like I get you have to know how fucked up and ridiculous it is to think like that."

The laugh that bubbled out of my mouth caught me unawares. I wasn't sure I'd ever had that said so bluntly to me. Judah had this uncanny ability to weave a magical lightness over me. "You're something else, you know that?"

He raised his glass of water in a toast. "Can't say I haven't heard those words before, although I don't remember them said with quite the same intent."

I rolled my eyes. "I can imagine. You're hardly one of life's wallflowers."

"God forbid." He visibly shuddered and we both laughed. "So, you've lost a couple of important people in your life, then."

I winced. "Three, actually. My dad too, as it turned out. A few years ago."

Judah's eyes popped and he took my hand again. I wasn't even sure he realised he'd done it, and my stomach wobbled just a little.

"What happened? Oh god, there I go again. Is it okay to ask?"

I nodded but stabbed a finger his way. "But don't think I don't know what you're doing. Keeping all the attention on me."

He batted those long fucking eyelashes my way and I had the sudden desire to feel them move against my inner thigh or even . . . Nope, not going there.

Judah smiled in that way he had as though he'd read my mind and filed it away as evidence. "I have no idea what you're talking about," he said innocently.

"Mmmm." I gave him the stink eye. "Like I believe that. But okay. Mum and Dad owned a pharmacy in Blockhouse Bay. Mum's family comes from Christchurch, pretty standard background, nice people. My Dad's family is Maori and closely involved with their iwi. As kids we grew up flitting between the two. Anyway, they sold up and retired in their late fifties to follow other interests. Mum was big into food-bank and charity stuff. And Dad did a lot of outreach work through the iwi. And then a few years later he ran a red light and got sideswiped by a van, totally his fault. We still don't know what really happened. He was a good driver, but I guess he just wasn't concentrating."

Judah's expression grew serious. "I'm sorry. I know what it's like to lose your father."

I held his eye, trying to see beyond his words. "I guess you do. He was a huge part of our lives, my life, a larger-than-life character. Not the most practical or forward-thinking, but he had a big heart and our house was always full of people and plans. He gave a lot, too much as it turned out, and not just of his time."

"You're talking about money, right?"

I nodded. "He left a financial mess. He and Mum had a good marriage and she was pretty tolerant of his impulsive, generous nature, but none of us really knew what was going on. Paying off his debt wiped out most of his insurance and savings and a fair chunk of Mum's as well."

"Shit. That sucks."

"Cody, Jenna, and I moved her into a small apartment in town, but she misses their old house and Dad. Jenna's a furniture designer in London, so Cody and I keep an eye on Mum. She's pretty independent and has a full life even if she has to be a bit careful with money. Cody's married with a three-year-old spitfire called Logan, and another on the way. They're financially tapped out, so I top Mum up money-wise if she needs it for extras."

"You're a better son than me," Judah said with a bitter edge. "When my dad died, I came home for his funeral, stayed a week, and then went back to my life and left Leroy to sort everything out. It's still a bone of contention between us."

Judah dropped my hand, but the warmth of his touch lingered. I took a long swallow of beer and then met his eyes. "I somehow doubt it's as simple as all that."

He shrugged. "Yeah, it pretty much is."

I didn't believe that for a second but let it go. "Did your dad support your dancing?"

A smile lit up Judah's face. "Yeah, he did. And looking back, I was an ungrateful little tyke about it. They both made sure I got the dance teachers I needed, plus they financed me into boarding school in Wellington when I was sixteen, so I could go to a good ballet school."

"I guess it worked?"

"I was lucky enough to get into the New Zealand Ballet's special programme for boys and then snagged a mentorship. And when I was eighteen, I got plucked out of a class to audition for a ballet scout from Boston, who'd observed me through the glass door. In Boston, I completed my degree in performing arts while dancing with the Boston Blue Ballet Collective, and the rest is history."

It was pretty damn clear Judah was a major talent, but I sensed his defences go up as he talked, and I didn't push it. "Impressive. They sound like great parents. And you were just a kid. I'm not sure any kid really understands what their parents give up for them."

Judah sighed and a crease bit between his eyebrows. "I doubt my brother would agree. Leroy could give you a sermon on all the ways I was ungrateful, but to summarise a boring tome, I'll give you the high-lights. I never came home, or at least not as often as I should have, even from boarding school. I'd spent so fucking long aching to get out of this place, to not stand out like a sore thumb for all the wrong reasons, and to have my ability considered something special and not a freak show, that I came up with any excuse not to return." He looked around and snorted. "So much for that. The more cynical among us might say I'm getting my comeuppance. I know Leroy would."

"I'm sure your parents understood."

Judah's brow wrinkled. "I'm not so sure. Maybe at first. But later? I think they were mostly . . . disappointed. Once I left New Zealand, I only returned once, for Dad's funeral. I was hitting the big time, or so I thought. I wasn't interested in looking back. And then Dad died and it almost made it easier, you know?"

Only too well.

"Then it all crumbled, and whaddya know? Here I am."

"I take it Leroy didn't understand?"

"You might say that. When Dad had the heart attack, Leroy immediately dropped out of vet school to come home and run the business. He was less than impressed that I only carved a week from my schedule for the funeral. But I think he mostly doesn't approve of the fact I've come back *now*, like it's because it suits me or something, which I guess it does. Even though it's handed him all he needed to hit me with every 'I told you so' he's ever thought about me."

Judah listed them off on his fingers. "That my training was a waste of time and money; that Mum and Dad spoiled me; that Leroy could've done with some of that money; that I was ungrateful for what they'd done; that dancing wasn't a real career anyway, so what did I expect; that it wasn't for real men, that *I* wasn't a real man; that it was unreliable, that *I* was unreliable; and so forth and so on." He circled his finger in the air.

"Wow." I put my empty bottle on the deck and sat up. "That's a lot of assumptions, maybe on both sides."

He side-eyed me. "How well do you know my brother?"

Fair question. "Outside of rugby and the times we've met up because of my job, probably not much. He's a friend but not a close one. I only meant—"

"I know what you meant."

Ouch.

"Leroy seems to think Dad's death didn't rip me apart the same way it did him." Judah's voice thickened and it was my turn to reach for his hand. He threaded our fingers together and I tried not to think about how good it felt.

"But it fucking did. I was in the middle of class when the call came. My flatmates practically had to carry me home. I couldn't even get my shit together to book my tickets back to New Zealand. I could barely think. Dad always had my back. Mum's great, but she's more the quiet presence in my life. Dad was the anchor when shit hit the fan, and with me, it did, more often than anyone liked." He gave a weak grin. "I miss the hell out of him."

He went quiet and my attention slipped to the soft lap of the incoming tide beneath the deck while I studied his face in the growing shadows. He looked . . . lost. "Can I ask why you came home? I gather something happened, and you don't have to answer, of course." The tension returned, but he didn't immediately shut me down, which was progress.

"To be honest, I'm having trouble keeping my eyes open, and that particular story needs at least a passable attempt at me having my shit together even if it's just so I can lose it again. So, for now, let's just say it was a medical thing, and it ended my career."

"Damn. I'm sorry. To be living your dream and then have it snatched away from you . . . I can't even imagine."

His expression softened. "Oh, I think you might understand more than most."

I breathed out a sigh. "Yeah, I think maybe you're right. And on that note, I'll leave you to it." I slipped my shoes on before getting to my feet. "Get some sleep. You look like you need it." I turned to leave but he grabbed my wrist.

"I'm not being a prick," he said with a serious note. "It's just . . . a lot. And I really am tired. I wasn't lying about that."

I covered his hand with my own. "I don't think you're being a prick, and I didn't think you were lying. And you're under no obligation to tell me anything at all. But I've enjoyed this, talking with you. Maybe we could, ah, do it again sometime, if you're interested?"

Judah's vibrant eyes studied me intently. "Yeah, okay. But let's keep it light. I can't deny I'm attracted to you; hell, my dick's had your name on speed dial for a fucking week."

Oh Lord. I felt my cheeks flushing to beetroot.

"But there's only two options here. We can fuck and then wave at a distance, or we can get to know each other with none of the other. I'm not up to blurring the lines between the two at the moment. My life is . . . complicated. Take it or leave it."

I let out a slow breath. "I'll take door number two, then. I'm not after a hook-up with you, Judah. And I'm not sure I'm ready for anything else either. Friends is . . . good. We're both grown-ups."

He nodded. "Long as we're clear."

"Crystal."

"Though some of us are more grown-up than others." His eyes flashed in amusement. "Just saying."

"And we were getting along so nicely," I said drily and offered him my phone. "Shall we exchange numbers?"

He typed in his number and sent himself a text.

I took my phone back and held out my hand. He stared at it for a moment, then reached up with a warm grasp and an eye lock that went on way, way too long for what we'd just agreed to. I pulled free and arched an "are you kidding me?" eyebrow his way.

He shoved his hands in his pockets with an unapologetic grin. "Never promised I'd actually be any good at keeping to the whole friendship thing."

I snorted. "Behave. Right. This is me leaving. Talk later."

I hadn't made it past the first stair when the rumble of a powerful outboard caught my attention. "You get many boats launching at this hour?"

Judah came up on my shoulder. "Not often, but then it is almost full tide."

I wasn't buying it. "Mmm. I'm gonna check it out."

"I'll come with you."

"No. You stay here." I jogged across the ramp and back up onto the wharf via Judah's front porch, then ducked behind the back wall of the storage shed. Seconds later the heat of Judah's body lined up against my back and his head popped over my shoulder.

"I thought I told you to stay back."

"You did." His warm breath stole along the side of my neck. "And yet here I am. What's happening?"

I turned my head enough to put our faces just centimetres apart and dug deep for my best fisheries officer scowl. At this distance, Judah's eyes took on the deeper shadows to reflect a dark emerald green. "You're going back to the boatshed, that's what's happening."

He smiled and tapped me on the nose with his finger. "It's cute you think you can tell me what to do."

I opened my mouth to do just that when—

"Look."

That same finger pressed against my jaw and turned my head in time to see a guy loping across the wharf toward a car with an empty boat trailer idling in the car park. With the trailer facing me, I couldn't make the plate on the vehicle.

"You think they're poachers?" Judah sounded excited.

His face was so fucking close to mine, if I'd reached out with my tongue I could've licked the sea salt from his cheek right over that damn beauty spot, and the place where his finger had touched my jaw still burned a bright note on my skin.

I could barely focus. "I . . . um—"

The throaty engine revved and the launch's nose poked out from the other side of the pier.

"Shit." My gaze flicked to the car park where the vehicle and trailer were looking to leave.

It could be nothing, but it just didn't feel right. On the other hand, between the launch and the car, I'd seen at least three men. Getting eyes on the boat was a priority for any future encounters . . . but also that vehicle . . .

Judah picked up on the problem straight away. "You take the boat, and I'll see if I can get a look at the plate on the car." He was off before I could stop him.

"No—fuck." I muttered a string of curses and took off for the pier, keeping one eye on Judah who was doing a surprisingly good job of keeping to the shadows and staying low and light on his feet. All that damn ballet. Which wasn't going to stop me killing the man when I got hold of him again.

Poaching was big business with lots of reasons to avoid being caught—massive fines and confiscation of boats and vehicles for a start. It wasn't uncommon to launch a boat at one point and pick it up at another, and this definitely carried the stench of something illicit.

I got to the pier in time to catch a brief glimpse of the departing boat. With only a couple of running lights on, it was only enough to get me the basic model and an idea of colour—blue or green with a fat white stripe—though not the name. I took a quick photo, though I doubted it would show anything in the burgeoning night. Still, it was something. Poachers changed out their vehicles pretty often, but boats were harder to turn over without raising interest. Someone would recognise it, and I made a mental note to run it by Jon.

I headed back toward the car park to see how Judah had done before I wrung his scrawny neck. He ran across to meet me, looking exhilarated.

"It was an old Holden Commodore," he puffed. "Silver or sandy gold, it was hard to tell. I still couldn't see the plate, and the trailer didn't have one attached. That's suspicious, right?"

It was hard not to smile at his enthusiasm, but I was too damn angry to find him cute.

"And there were at least two guys. Someone else was driving when our guy got in. I tried to catch them up the hill. I'm pretty quick on my feet but—"

"*Our guy?* What the hell did you think you were doing?" I stabbed a finger at his chest and immediately regretted it.

His eyes flared in surprise, then narrowed, and he shoved my hand aside. "What the fuck? I was trying to help." He stepped back and glared at me.

It should've been enough to warn me, but I'd worked up a full head of steam on the run over. "You could've gotten yourself hurt. If those guys were serious, they don't mess around. There's a lot of money tied up in what they do, and they wouldn't have thought twice about doing whatever it took to shut you up."

I was way overreacting, but I couldn't seem to shut my mouth. Just the thought of him hurt . . .

"But—"

"Why do you think I wear a stab-proof vest?" I talked right over him. *Stop it.* "It's not to keep me warm, dipshit. It's because I know the risks, and I know what I'm doing. I'm not playing detective, getting my jollies for a bit of excitement." *Fuck.* I jolted at the harshness of my own words.

"Hey!" Judah reared back, the sting clear in his eyes.

"Shit, I'm sorry—" I reached for him.

He slapped my hand aside. "Who the fuck do you think you are talking to me like that? This is *my* family's property, not public space, as it happens. If anyone has a right to check on any suspicious shit, it's me, not you. Technically"—and he made a point of stabbing *my* chest with *his* finger—"you need a warrant, *Mr* Fisheries Officer, or whatever it is you guys use, to even be on our land, right?"

A debatable point, as we did, in fact, have powers of search on private property related to wildlife, but it was a grey area and not one I had any intention of raising with the highly pissed-off man in front of me.

"Judah, I'm sorry. I didn't think—"

"Well, think on this." He took a deep breath and gathered himself. "It's time you left." He brushed past, knocking me with his shoulder as he went. "And maybe don't bother using that number. Good night, Morgan."

CHAPTER FIVE

Judah

I BRACED A HAND ON THE ICE-WHITE TILES AND JERKED MYSELF off to the image of a man who had no business occupying my boathouse shower on a Saturday morning, especially after I'd thrown his sorry arse off our property less than twelve hours before. And yet here he was—in my head. And where was my hand? On my fucking dick. Go figure.

The upside? I actually had the energy to expend on a little self-pleasure. I'd managed to sleep until eight and it had been five days without a full-blown vertigo attack—the drop attacks didn't drain me quite the same way. Go me. Maybe the meds were finally working. It was enough to have me looking at the world in a better light, at any rate.

So Morgan had been married, huh? And there he was again, front and centre in my pea-sized, lust-addled brain. Still, I hadn't seen that particular twist coming. But then, an attractive guy like that, it made sense that someone nailed his arse down at some point. I couldn't imagine losing someone so important after such a short time.

And judging by the tone in Morgan's voice, the loss was still painful, still fresh. What would it feel like to be loved by someone, by a man, by Morgan, so deeply? There was an intensity to him that promised you'd never have to question it. He'd show you every day.

I shook my head at the thought. Like Morgan would be remotely interested in someone as fucked up as me. For a quick fuck? Sure. For more than that? He'd have to be a raging masochist.

Nothing said doomed relationship like a guy with no job, no prospects, a bad attitude, and a chronic illness. Which is why I needed to keep this thing between us to friends. I liked Morgan, more than was good for me or explicable from the brief time we'd spent together. I liked him enough to know that if we started something, I'd miss him when it fell apart. But if we kept it to friends, then maybe he'd stick around for me to enjoy, and I liked the idea of that, liked it a whole lot.

I dried off, threw on some old dance leggings and a T-shirt, and froze once again at my reflection in the full-length mirror, briefly contemplating a life where I didn't have Meniere's and could give free rein to the attraction I felt for Morgan.

How the hell had this become my life?

I stared at my reflection and realised the answer didn't matter. It was time to stop wallowing. Enough.

I sucked in a deep breath all the way down to my diaphragm and my thighs flexed like they were hopeful or something, tentatively lifting me up on the balls of my feet.

Move. The imperative pushed at my brain.

I stretched a leg behind, teetering a little, testing the weight I hadn't carried in months—arms out, reaching for that point of balance, clocking into the 'office' I worked in, the place I called home, and hearing that silent but familiar addictive mental click when I reached it and tipped over into weightlessness.

There. Like a soft sigh in my head. The rush of connection, the sweet sing of my body surging to life, adrenaline ticking up my heart.

Try.

A fouetté spin. And then a second. The centrifugal pull to another, and another. I nailed them all. But a stutter on the sixth as the world tipped slightly with the roar of the sea in my ears. I fell out of the spin and hit the floor in a graceless lump.

Fucking fuck, fuck. I grabbed a nearby boot and threw it at the mirror, a spiderweb of cracks exploding across its face. Less than a year before I'd have done thirty-two spins without breaking a sweat. Five was a joke.

No. More. Wallowing.

I gave myself five minutes to fall apart, then scrubbed my hands down my face, ripped the sheets from my bed, and threw them in the wash. That done, I stood barefoot in my kitchen and studied the current state of my tiny house while I chewed on a slice of stale toast and jam.

The picture told a sorry tale. I could've started my own recycling plant with the number of empties from my determination to single-handedly underwrite the local liquor wholesaler.

It wasn't hard to imagine what Morgan must've thought—nothing good, for sure. I blamed my perpetual brain fog for even inviting him in. These days my grey matter functioned like a rusty, poorly tuned Lada, as opposed to the hot-pink sharply primed Audi convertible it used to be.

His opinion shouldn't matter. Morgan was an overbearing boor, if somewhat sexy, because that shit couldn't be denied—cue my recent shower scene for confirmation. Not that we'd be crossing paths again if he could take a hint. I didn't need yet another person treating me like a pretty but fragile ornament, thinking they knew what was best for me.

And if only he'd stop texting me an endless supply of more than decent apologies, I might even begin to believe it. The man had a good line in grovelling and my resolve was wavering.

I'm an arse.

Yep.

I have no excuse.

Nope.

I should never have said what I did and I'm sorry . . .

Too late.

I was worried for you . . .

Ah, shit.

I would never have forgiven myself . . .

Goddammit.

You were right to be angry.

Fuck.

I hope we can still be friends.

A pestilence upon all your houses.

When I woke and read them all, I'd texted one word. **STOP**.

He had, and I'd been checking my phone ever since.

I choked on the last bite of toast, washed it down with a guzzle of some ginkgo biloba herbal tea shit that tasted like cat's piss, which my mother had read somewhere was good for Meniere's. Who the hell knew? But I wasn't averse to trying anything that didn't actually hurt and which my doctor okayed. Though, what chance it had of balancing the copious volumes of alcohol I had, up until recently, been chugging back, I wasn't sure.

Having undoubtedly dealt my Meniere's a fatal herbal blow, I proceeded to crank up Uriah Heep's *Wonderworld* and set about making some sense of my living space. The drapes were still open from the previous night—the image of Morgan standing at the slider never crossing my mind for an instant, nope not at all. Nor his laughing brown eyes or the touch of his warm hand in mine.

I threw open the slider, sucked in a belly full of salt-laden air, and turned my attention to the teetering piles of clothes, unpacked bags, and boxes of miscellaneous crap strewn from one end of the boathouse to the other. My stomach clenched in protest and I briefly considered simply closing the curtains and going back to bed, but I didn't.

Unpacking meant staying, which was why I'd avoided it, clever Morgan. It meant giving up pretending things were going to change, that any of my stuff was going to get miraculously shipped back to Boston, along with me, to a life that had once promised everything I'd ever wanted.

And it was well past time I dealt with the fact.

Two hours later, I crashed out on my sofa, a miracle in itself considering I hadn't seen the bottom cushions in three weeks. Uriah Heep had moved on from *Wonderland*, through *Sweet Freedom*, and were finishing their *Sea of Light* album, crooning about how to turn around my useless life. From their mouths to my ears, allowing for a couple of hiccups along the way.

A third load of washing juddered away on the spin cycle; the skip beside the wharf office bulged with the sheer number of trash bags I'd carted out; and I could finally see the top of the dining room table. All up, not a bad job. The last notes of the song faded to black, and I was debating the relative merits of a ham-and-salad sandwich over my mother's dubiously named and even more dubious-looking beef hot pot she'd left the day before, when a knock sounded at my front door.

Perfect timing. I'd been expecting Terry all morning, coming to exact his revenge on me for not turning up to the hardware store the minute it had opened this morning, as per his instruction.

"Come in. It's open." I made my way to the kitchen to put the coffee on and reached above the stove for the dark brown sugar, which Terry preferred and used in quantities enough to make my teeth ache. "Coffee before emotional evisceration, I always say. And I'm not avoiding you, I promise."

"I, um, wouldn't blame you if you were, but I think it's maybe safer if I stay outside."

Morgan. *Shit.* I froze and turned slowly in place.

He stood at the door, shifting uncomfortably on his feet. He was decked out in his fisheries uniform with a flush on his cheeks, a freshly groomed beard, a pair of sexy aviators, and looking too fucking goddamned delectable for his own good.

"I, ah, just came to apologise in person and to leave you this." He lifted his glasses onto his cap and put a brown paper bag on the small table just inside the door. Then his eyes widened comically as they swept the spotless room. "Ah, wow—"

My hand shot up. "Not a word." I pointed at the package. "What's in that?" I made no move to approach, mostly because I was torn between slamming the door on his face and kissing him senseless with a side order of bending him over my pristine couch. Or not. Since he was an overbearing boor, after all.

He shrugged. "You can look for yourself when I'm gone. But it's not part of my apology, just so you know . . . although I could, of course, change that, if you indicated it might, you know, get me back in your good books, maybe?"

I sniffed and folded my arms across my chest to show just how far above all that nonsense I really was, and his disheartened eye roll was kind of epic.

He blew out a sigh. "Yeah, thought not. Anyway, I just saw it and thought of you. Simple as that. But"—he eyed the bag—"you know what? I'm just gonna take it with me. It was a stupid idea—"

"Leave it." The words were out before I knew it.

His hand froze above the bag. "Ah, okay?"

I doubted anything Morgan Wipene did would be considered stupid, so the bag had me intrigued and all kinds of nervous.

Then, as if he'd only just noticed, Morgan's gaze slid slowly south and he sucked in a sharp breath. And I suddenly remembered I was wearing pale ballet practice leggings that clung to me like a wet T-shirt, a crop top that barely fell to my waist, and not much else. The combination left zero doubt about my musculature or the fact my dick ran to hoodies rather than open necks.

Not that Morgan seemed to take issue with the statement based on the hungry look in his eyes. I switched weight from one hip to the other and watched as he damn near swallowed his tongue. Say what you like about men in tights, there's not a gay man alive who doesn't appreciate the way they frame a package in all its glorious detail.

"Eyes up, Mr Fisheries Officer."

His gaze shot up to meet mine, and a cute-as-shit flush danced on those cheeks. "Fuck, sorry." He bit back a grin.

And shit . . . dimples as well.

"But I, ah, do feel, in the true spirit of *friendship*, that it would be an injustice not to mention the fact that"—and his gaze dipped again —"damn, that's a good look on you, for a Saturday."

I snorted. "I'll have you know it's a good look on me *any* day, sunshine." Then I shooed him away with my hands. "But be gone before I set the dogs on you. I have somewhere to be and I can't have any distractions."

He pulled a face and rubbed at his neck. "Okay, but can I just repeat, at the risk of you ripping me yet another one, that I'm really sorry I acted like such a dick. I still think you should've stayed safe, but there's no excuse for what I said. And it's not me. Not really." He shuffled on his feet. "Anyway, that's all I came to say."

Damn, he was cute. "Well, I'll think about it, no promises. And I won't be swayed by a bribe, if that's what that is." I glanced at the bag. "Or any of that cute little act you've got going on. I'm made of sterner stuff."

He nodded. "Understood. Have a good day, Judah. And, ah, the place looks great, by the way."

Cheeky shit. "Thanks. It wasn't for your benefit, if that's what you're thinking, so you can wipe that smug look off your face."

"Furthest thought from my mind. Take care."

I made sure to close the door before he'd even turned his back, then flew to the window to watch that impressive arse in all its tight, uniformed glory bunch and stretch its way across the wharf to the car park on the far side. Good God, the guy was sexy. So yeah, I had that whole sterner stuff, non-forgiveness thing in the bag. It sat right next to my not-being-swayed season ticket to any view I could get of the man's epic butt.

And yes, my resolve needed some work.

I ate lunch while staring at the small but oddly menacing and still unopened brown paper bag on the breakfast bar. I don't know why

I'd avoided opening it or why it bothered me so much, but it did. I hardly knew Morgan, so why would he give me *anything,* especially after my snotty dismissal of him?

The thing wasn't heavy, but it wasn't light as a feather either. It came with me to the bedroom while I changed and then out onto the back deck while I hung out the last of the washing. I shook it a couple of times deciding it was a single object. I took a good smell through the paper, ruling out bath bombs or recognisable food items.

But eventually I couldn't put it off any longer.

I grabbed the thing and took a deep breath. Then I opened it slowly and peered in from a distance like it might contain anthrax.

Huh. Not anthrax. Not unless anthrax came in the form of a small, perfectly formed snow globe, with a black manta ray swimming through the middle of a million sparkling flakes.

Well, shit.

I fucking loved it.

Morgan Wipene was going to be the death of me.

I shoved it as far away as I could, glared at it, snatched it back, and gave it another shake.

And smiled.

It was cute as fuck and just the kind of ridiculous shit that spun my wheels. How could he possibly know?

I pulled out my phone and stared at his texts. My life was a car crash. The last thing I needed was some sexy guy in a fucking uniform clogging up my common sense. And yet there was the whole sense of inevitability between us that fucked with my head. Because, no matter what I told myself, or him, friends *without* benefits between us was about as viable as an ice cream on a hot summer's day, and likely to last as long.

But since when had a lack of common sense ever stopped me? It wasn't like my life could take any more of a nose dive, so what the hell?

I sighed and pulled up the keyboard.

Cute move. Coffee, your place, today at 4? Text me the address.
And there better not be a scrap of dust in sight.

Morgan

I read Judah's text and a smile of relief crossed my face. The snow globe had definitely been a risky move.

I'd seen it in Jam's Antiques and Collectables when I'd dropped off a pair of waders for him that morning and couldn't resist. Jam—full name Benjamin—had given me an odd look and then laughed when I'd told him the edited version of the story, that I'd offended Leroy's brother, knew he liked mantas, and could he please shut the fuck up about me ever having been in his shop.

"Jude, right?" He eyed me closely.

"Judah," I corrected, noting his eyebrow tick up. "And don't start with that nonsense." I pointed at it.

Jam studied me for a minute. Thirty-ish and with a hipster haircut, ear gauges, and cool tattoo sleeves, he needed to own an impossibly trendy coffee shop in downtown Auckland, not an eclectic curiosity shop in tiny, nowhere Northland. But he'd bought his deceased grandmother's house two years before, apparently tired of the corporate life in Dunedin. He hit on me the first day he arrived in town and I'd turned him down flat. Mostly because he screamed *complicated* in all the ways I generally avoided. We'd been friends ever since.

"Judah, huh?" He slid me a sly smile.

"Stop it. It's nothing like what's going on in your dirty mind."

"Shame."

"We've only met a couple of times, and both times I managed to piss him off. This is kind of an . . . apology."

"Aha." Jam peeled the bar code off the bottom of the snow globe, stuck it in a brown paper bag, and handed it over with a wicked gleam. "That'll be fifteen dollars."

My eyebrows hit the ceiling.

He shrugged. "They're a collector's piece."

My gaze narrowed. "A collector's piece? They have *Made in China* right next to that bar code you just pulled off."

"Do you see any others?" He swept a hand over the crowded space full of bric-a-brac, musty rugs, used surfboards, assorted china, two ancient stuffed penguins by the front door, and a million things you could barely imagine, let alone want. But somehow, he did a good business, so there had to be something of value hidden beneath the clutter.

I shook my head. "No."

He gave a shark's grin. "See, rare as hen's teeth."

I laughed and handed my credit card over. "Ring it up, Arkwright."

He did and then walked me to the door.

I had a sudden thought. "You know you really should come to rugby practice."

His eyes bugged out. "You can't be serious."

"Not to play." I snorted. "God knows there's enough lack of talent without adding you to the mix."

His face said it all. "I'll try not to take offence."

"Do that. But there's a couple of guys in the team you might like."

He laughed. "Yeah? Nah. Not that I don't appreciate twenty hot, sweaty men in tight shorts, particularly if they're anything like you, but I prefer to watch them in a club with a long dry martini in my hand, if it's all the same to you. Still, I'll keep it in mind if I run out of thumbscrews and hair shirts. I hope the gift works."

And it apparently had. The fact of which had me inordinately pleased. I grinned like an idiot at my phone. Today at four, huh. A summons in all but name. But if Judah wanted to hold the reins, I was quite happy to let him, for now—see where he went with it while I decided what the hell I was expecting out of this. Friendship, sure.

But I wasn't kidding myself. That *something* that sizzled between us wasn't going to be easy to keep under wraps, and I needed to decide exactly how far I was willing to go before it exploded in our faces.

I thought for a minute, then smiled and texted back. **Is this a date?**

I could almost see the scowl settle over those fierce eyes.

He texted back. **I'd be asking for a lot more than your house to be groomed if it was a date.**

I laughed out loud, catching the attention of a young family returning to their car. I gave the kids a wave. They gave me the stink eye, which likely meant I'd probably written up their dad for too many shellfish at some point.

My thumbs pecked out a reply. **Other than my beard, I don't groom and have no intention of starting. Take it or leave it.**

There was a few seconds delay before he answered. **Then you better prepare me. On a scale between wire-haired terrier and old English sheepdog.**

Sasquatch. I hoped the silence at the other end was because he was laughing not choking.

Noted. In that case, if we do ever have a date, which is now highly unlikely, I'll make sure to bring my clippers.

I grinned and texted him a thumbs up along with my address, then pocketed my phone and secured my stab vest in place. The gusty northerly had kept most shellfish seekers off the beaches, but I'd been keeping an eye on a boat anchored over a reef not too far offshore. Blue with a fat white stripe. Could I be that lucky?

I'd talked with Jon about the boat, and between us we'd done a bit of investigating, unearthing a few who met the same description, all within a thirty-kilometre radius. I'd been doing the rounds of the boat-launching sites when I saw this one purely by chance.

But even with binoculars, it was too far offshore to get a good look at the three men aboard or tell if they were hauling stuff up or weighting it down to retrieve later. But my Spidey senses were jangling, and just as I was debating whether I had time to hang around any longer, the boat suddenly came to life and headed south.

Shit. I threw my vehicle into gear, headed up over the soft sand, and onto a track that led to the coast road. The boat dipped in and out of view, and it wasn't long before I lost them. I planted my foot and headed two kilometres down the road to the next boat ramp where I pulled the fisheries vehicle behind a motorhome to keep it from view and found a spot to watch for the boat's arrival.

It took far longer than it should've for the white striped launch to come into view and I cursed. If they *were* poaching, they'd dumped their catch to pick up when it was safe. *Fuck.*

Eventually it pottered into sight, its occupants relaxed and joking. One of the men waded to shore jangling a set of car keys and tipped his cap at me. "Afternoon."

Fucker. "Afternoon." I kept my voice friendly. "How was the fishing?"

He turned to his mates still in the boat. "He wants to know how the fishing was?"

The helmsman held up a string of what looked to be perfectly legal-sized snapper. "Not bad. Lost a few along the way, but you know how that goes."

"You the skipper?" I asked the helmsman.

He nodded. "For today."

"You been diving?" I nodded to the tanks and gear in the back of the boat.

All three exchanged a quick look before the skipper answered. "Nah, too murky."

"Aha. Mind if I take a look?"

The skipper threw a line to the man onshore and waved me over. "Knock yourself out."

I wouldn't find anything. They were too fucking smug. But I waded my way across anyway so I could eyeball the set-up and the men more closely. The boat's name was almost impossible to read, but it was there. Salt Maiden. I took a photo.

The skipper answered quickly, "It's booked with a signwriter to get that redone next week."

Of course it was. "Make sure it is. I'll be making a note. Consider this a warning. Can I see all the documentation please, including your ID? You the owner?"

"It's actually my cousin's."

Of course it was.

"I can call him if you want. But I can show you what you need."

"Please. Nice motors." I pointed to the twin oversized outboard motors well beyond anything needed for recreational fishing in these waters.

"Yeah, my cousin's a bit of a petrol head," he explained.

I wasn't buying. He was too slick, too . . . wrong. I went through all the paperwork and their ID's—Paul and Shannon Laird. The third man had no ID with him but gave me a name—Nick Martin. It was all above board, including their catch.

And then I spotted it, next to a bait bucket and behind the diving gear in the stern. A single pāua, legal size. I picked it up and took a sniff. Fresh from the sea.

"Thought you were only interested in snapper today?"

He shrugged. "We were. Picked that up when we went ashore for lunch by the triple creek outflow. Part of someone else's catch I guess. Taking it home for my niece."

I stared at him, not believing a word that came out of his smarmy mouth. It was all too slick. "Right, well you boys have a nice day."

"You too, officer. Keep up the good work."

"You can be sure of that." *Motherfuckers.* I headed back to my vehicle, steam coming out my ears, positive they'd stashed their haul somewhere to come back for. I wrote it up and made some notes for myself, including a couple more sneaky photos of the men as they got the boat on the trailer, the car towing it a Subaru, not the Commodore we'd seen in Painted Bay. I'd run the names past Jon and see what he thought.

My thoughts ran to Judah and a smile broke over my face. My

day was about to take a turn for the better. I threw the Hilux into gear but had barely made it out of the car park when Cody called.

"You talk to her" was all he said before handing the phone to our mother. I braced myself. It didn't happen often, but when Mum got it in her head to go off about our father's thoughtless stripping of all their accounts, how she wished she'd never married him, and how she deserved to be living a much easier life, it was hard to turn her around.

It took twenty minutes before she'd run the usual gamut of complaints and the fact that none of their friends believed what an arsehole he'd been. Because yes, there'd been a lot to love about my father. He was fun, generous, the life of the party, and sarcastic as shit. But he'd also been thoughtless, single-minded, and completely ignorant of the effect of his *generosity* on us. If he wasn't already dead, I might have had to kill him. Something we could all joke about, minus the laughter.

"Thanks." Cody breathed his thanks into the phone once she'd exhausted herself and handed it back my brother. "I was two seconds away from matricide."

I laughed. "What set her off?"

"The usual. Looking through some old photos."

"Does she need an injection of funds?"

Cody hesitated. "Can you afford it? We're strapped with the new baby coming—"

"It's fine. Your turn will come."

Cody grumbled, "Sure it will. Have you been on a single date in the five years you've been up there?"

"None of your business."

Cody nearly choked. "That means you have. Holy shit. Why didn't I know this?"

Gleeful shouts echoed in the background. Tess, no doubt.

"Tess wants to know who she is?"

"Or he?" None of my family cared two hoots who I dated, but even before Sally, women tended to be my default.

"He, she, they, we don't care— Ow, don't hit me."

"Forgive your idiot brother," Tess shouted. "I haven't cleaned the red off his neck for a while."

I chuckled. "It was a woman, but just casual. Nothing came of it."

Cody huffed. "Damn. I want you noosed with some kids so I can lord it over you when ours get older, but whatever." He went quiet for a minute and I knew what was coming. "Still, it's been five years, man. You shouldn't waste your youth."

"Jesus, Cody, you make it sound like I'm past my use-by date or something."

"Well . . ."

"Shut the fuck up."

Cody laughed. "No, seriously, I mean it. You're a great guy. I don't like to think of you alone."

"I'm fine. You say five years like it's a long time. I say five years like it was yesterday. But I take your point, and yeah, maybe I am getting ready to try again." A pair of bright hazel eyes sprung to mind. "Just don't push, okay?"

He blew out a sigh. "All right. But maybe you could come for lunch or something. There's this new woman at Tess's work—"

"Bye, Cody."

"But—"

I disconnected the speakerphone and turned at the signpost for Painted Bay, chuckling at what Cody would think if he knew exactly how close I was to being ready to try again. He wouldn't be upset about me dating a guy, but he would be surprised. Well, join the club.

Not that Judah and I were dating, of course. Not that it even crossed my mind.

I headed into town to pick up some milk and tried not to be overly optimistic about the whole coffee meet up. But one thing was certain: it wouldn't be boring. I doubted anything involving Judah ever was.

CHAPTER SIX

Judah

TERRY LEANED ON THE POLE OUTSIDE HIS HARDWARE STORE, wearing a grin from ear to ear. "Oh. My. God." Then he called over his shoulder, "Hannah, call the gendarmes, the Pink Panther's on the loose."

I flipped him off and finished crossing the street. "Could you say that any louder? I'm not sure they heard you down at the wharf. Besides, this town could do with a bit of class."

He laughed. "And it still could. You look dressed for an 80's throwback night at a gay bar. Afternoon, Alice." Terry nodded to a middle-aged woman with wide eyes and a disapproving set to her lips. "Off to bridge, are we?"

She nodded at Terry, then skewered me with a look. "Keep your voice down, young Madden. We don't all need to know your business."

"I'm delighted you think I'm young, Alice." I gave her a wave. "You're looking a bit scrumptious yourself."

"Pffft." She smiled and straightened the row of gold buttons on her crimson dress. "Maybe fifty years ago. Those trousers are very pink, young man. I'm not entirely sure they're appropriate."

I jogged over to meet them. "Excellent. That's exactly the look I was going for." I pressed a quick kiss to her cheek.

She blushed brightly, then grunted something about impertinent young men and moved off.

Terry leaned in to whisper, "You'll be the talk of the bridge crowd in about five minutes flat."

"Another thing off my bucket list. Besides, I thought you'd be happy to see me out of scruffy jeans and a sad T-shirt."

He clapped me on the back. "I am. It's just very . . . gay, even for you."

"I know. Great, right?" I stared down at the violent pink jeans ripped in all the right places and my favourite black net shirt I'd spent fifteen minutes digging through my drawers trying to find, only to panic that I might have thrown it out. Another ten minutes found it in the skip by the wharf office and all had been right with the world.

"I take it you've turned the corner from composting your body in that rubbish tip of yours formerly known as the boathouse?" His gaze narrowed. "You're wearing makeup—" He fisted my shirt, pulled me close, and took a sniff. "—and cologne, you tart."

I waggled my eyebrows at him. "I am. Are you jealous?"

"This is Painted Bay, Judah." He unfisted my shirt. "Not even the women here wear makeup. Well, other than Joyce Wickliffe, but that's because she's currently got her heart set on Gary at the service station."

"Really? I thought he was married?"

Terry tsked. "Call yourself a local. You should be ashamed."

"I don't call myself one," I pointed out.

"Just as well. Gary's wife shot through a month or so back, taking all her belongings, meaning he's newly available, and the lovely Joyce was knocking at his front door within an hour to commiserate, muffins in hand."

I couldn't help but laugh. Being one of the few available straight young men in the district, and with a business to draw in customers, Terry always had the latest gossip. Most women, old and young, took one look at his baby blues and gave it all up on a platter.

Terry was, of course, mostly oblivious. Always had been. I'd had the biggest crush on him as a young teenager, even though I was a year behind, and what a great behind it was. That he was now my one and only friend in this godforsaken town I counted as supreme good fortune on my part.

"Getting back to the makeup..." He swiped a finger over my lower lip and licked it. "Watermelon splash, I do believe."

"How in the hell—"

"Hi, Judah." Terry's nine-year-old daughter, Hannah, hobbled her way slowly from the store onto the sidewalk. "Watermelon's the bomb. Though I like the cherry as well."

I held up my fingers in the form of a cross. "Get thee behind me Satan. Cherry flavoured *anything* is the work of the devil, and I'm not entirely sure I can be friends with anyone who disagrees. Lime crush is the only acceptable second."

"Ew." Hannah screwed up her nose. "That's gross. Lime makes your farts stink like toilet duck."

I snorted and pushed my sunglasses on top of my head. "I'm not sure there's any answer to that. In which case, you win, and there's only one thing to do—"

"Ice cream?" Hannah's eyes bugged with delight.

I grinned and ruffled her hair. "You got it, gorgeous." I handed her a twenty-dollar bill. "Get your dad hokey pokey and boysenberry for me. They'll give you a carry carton. And keep the change."

"Really? Thanks, Judah." She hobbled to the café next door and disappeared.

"You didn't have to do that," Terry said, taking a seat on the bench outside his shop.

"I'm buying my way into her affections, one ice cream at a time." I plonked my butt next to his.

He snorted. "Waste of money. You're already there."

My heart tripped. "Really?"

"Like you wouldn't believe. She's watched all your performances that she can google, although I drew the line at following your Instagram account. Those tights you guys wear are pornographic. You may as well just paint your dicks cream and be done with it. Did it ever bother you? Your dick preceding you onstage most of the fucking time."

I choked out a laugh. "You get used to it."

"I'm not so sure. What if you chubbed up at some hot guy in the front row of the opera house?"

I turned to stare. "Chubbed up? What are we, ten? And no. I can't say that's ever happened to me. Now, if you were asking about the dressing rooms? All I'm gonna say is what happens backstage, stays backstage. Most professional male ballet dancers have bodies you can only dream about, my friend. And in the male corps change room, you can barely turn around without being stabbed in the eye by someone's dick."

Terry rolled his eyes. "An image I may never be able to get out of my head. But if I ever find myself dreaming of *male* ballet dancers' bodies, I'll make sure to come and talk to you. Mind you, dreaming about sex, *any* sex, is as close as I get these days. Having a nine-year-old daughter puts a profound dent in your sex life, let me tell you. My dick's been ignored for so long, it gets excited at the reruns of *The Golden Girls*."

"Good God. And I thought I was bad."

"How long?"

I blew out a sigh. "Five months. You?"

"Eighteen."

I was pretty sure my jaw hit the lump of discarded chewing gum on the pavement between my feet. "Holy shit. I feel so much better now."

"Glad to be of service," he grumbled, and we bumped fists. "So, you're here, in town, at my store, and the earth hasn't swallowed any of us up. What happened? You run out of lube? Hand's all chaffed?"

Hannah reappeared with the ice creams in a carry holder, and we all took a minute to get in those first strategic tongue swipes which determined the success or not of everything that followed.

"No, arsehole, that arena is just fine, thank you very much, although yes, a bit solitary." I eyed Hannah. "Sorry for the language."

She shrugged. "I'll live."

"I think I reached my limit of slob."

"You stank." Hannah pinched her nose.

"Hannah!" Terry eyeballed his daughter. "Though she has a point." He glanced again at my clothes. "But you appear to be rebounding . . . spectacularly."

I shot him a killing look.

He laughed. "No, honestly, you look good. It suits you. If you like pink. I just haven't seen you in all your glory before."

I licked at my ice cream. "I like colour. What can I say? But back in the day, I was hardly going to make myself any more of a target, was I?"

"I guess not."

"Well, I like it." Hannah gave me the once over. "Although everyone can see your nipples."

I pulled out a corner of my net shirt and studied it. "Too much?"

She leaned back and gave me the once over. "Nah. You can pull it off."

"How about you go finish your homework, sweetheart?" Terry took Hannah's free hand and kissed it.

"Daaaaad."

"Go on. Let the adults talk. Well, one adult and one snarky flamingo with a killer pirouette."

I raised an eyebrow his way. "My arabesque would make you weep."

His expression grew serious. "You know, I'd like to see that one day."

I took a long lick of my ice cream and pretended not to hear. I hadn't danced or even put on a pair of practice shoes in eight months, a fact Terry knew only too well.

"Yes please, Judah." Hannah's eyes lit up. "I want to see you dance. Promise you will."

I shot daggers at Terry.

He grinned and gave his own ice cream an insolent lick.

Bastard. I smoothed my expression and turned to Hannah. "I'll do my best, munchkin, but I can't promise."

Thankfully she didn't press it and disappeared inside the store. I slid my sunglasses back on my nose and we sat in silence for a bit and finished our cones.

It was oddly comfortable, this new-found friendship between Terry and me, and I was still getting used to the fact. Almost like we'd skipped the preliminaries and moved straight to the old woman stage. And it wasn't as if we'd been best mates in school. He'd been a year ahead. A good-looking nerd with a thing for music. We'd met in my first school drama production, but we'd done little more than hang around a bit, me drooling over his arse in a teeny tiny crush, and him indulgently letting me without getting all hung up about it.

Straight as an arrow, he'd had his eyes set on a career in literature and dated all the right girls, until Amber. They were both sixteen and Hannah was the life-changing outcome of that brief relationship. They'd moved in with Terry's parents since Amber's wanted no part of the pregnancy. Amber stuck around for a few years while they both finished school, but then flew the coop when things got tough. She handed full custody to Terry and that was that. Terry managed to buy the town's hardware store with the help of his parents and built it into a successful business. But things hadn't been easy.

"How's Hannah been lately?" I tipped my head toward the inside of the store as I licked my fingers.

He followed my gaze. "She should be using her crutches, but she refuses to. Says it's bad enough feeling like an old woman without looking like one. God knows what's gonna happen when she lays eyes on the braces they've got underway for her. She barely talked to me throughout the entire measurement appointment. But she needs them. Her knees have been really bad. The size of fucking grapefruit. And now they're trying a new biologic to suppress her immune system, so guess who's the lucky guy who has to inject her?"

"Shit."

"Pretty much. She's good about it, but that doesn't make it any easier. I sometimes think we should just replace every arthritic joint she has now and be done with it. I hate seeing her in pain and I hate this fucking disease. Juvenile arthritis can go and get fucked."

I reached for his hand. "You wanna rail at the gods of health in chorus for a while, because I've got room for a good tenor? But keep your eyes off my soprano slot, bitch."

He laughed and slumped back on the bench. "Fuck you."

"You couldn't handle it."

"I've no doubt."

I slouched alongside him. "So she's digging her toes in about the elbow crutches?"

"I've never known a kid so determined." He glanced my way. "Well, maybe one other."

"In my case, stubborn is the word I think you're looking for. Also, pig-headed works," I answered.

"Well it didn't do you any harm, did it? Look what you achieved."

I snorted. "Yeah. Fucking poster boy for success, that's me."

Terry turned and smacked me up the back of the head. "Jesus, Judah. Stop with all the fucking self-pity. If Hannah even gets a glimpse of something like you had in her lifetime, I'll die happy, you ungrateful prick."

The brief and surprising tirade from my otherwise even-keeled friend brought me up short. And he was, of course, right. Hadn't I just spent my whole fucking morning trying to drill that exact idea into my brain?

I squeezed his hand. "I'm sorry. Seems like I didn't throw my arsehole attitude out with my gross sweatshirts, after all. Shocker."

He laughed despite himself. "Yeah, well, I may be a teeny bit oversensitive." He picked at a thread on one of the rips on my thigh. "Fucking pink jeans. In Painted Bay. Anyone would think you craved attention. Did you not have something more subtle for your debut with the locals."

"You think I'm making a statement, don't you?"

He sighed. "Yes. I think you're making a statement. But after all those years of trying *not* to draw attention to yourself, I also think it's pretty damn great. But most of all I'm thinking, thank fuck you're doing something other than just sitting in that depressing boathouse, wallowing in your bad luck, and drinking yourself into an even worse state. And if it takes a pair of pink jeans and a"—he pulled at my black net clubbing top—"whatever the fuck this is to get you out here, then I'm all for it. Just give me some warning next time so I can find my damn sunglasses."

He wasn't wrong, about any of it. After the clean-up and Morgan's gift, I'd stared at my wardrobe and thought, fuck it. I needed to touch that part of myself again—colour, life, energy, fucking in-your-face, deal-with-me attitude.

Was it a finger at the town that had tried to suck every creative and desperately gay part of me dry as a fucking bone as a teen? Damn right. Was it to see how Morgan responded to this side of me? Absolutely. No point in wasting my time if he couldn't handle it. But more than all of that, when I'd looked in the mirror, I felt more like me than I'd done in eight months.

"Yes, well, I may have gone a bit overboard." I finished my cone and rested my head back against the window. "Rebound is a thing, you know."

A red Honda Accord passed by on the other side of the street, it's driver staring my way. One look and I was thirteen all over again. My stomach curled up. "Jesus, don't tell me that fucker is still around after all these years."

Terry followed my gaze. "Kane? Yeah. He's got a farm not far from here. Organic, I think. But you can settle the fuck down. He's not like he used to be in school."

I huffed loudly. "I'm not buying. Of all the arseholes that gave me a hard time, he was the worst. I pissed blood for a week after that kicking he gave me."

Terry winced and raised his palms. "I know, I know. I'm just saying he's not that guy anymore. Went off to university an arsehole and came back pretty quiet. That's all I know."

"Yeah, well, if he comes anywhere near me, I'll have something to say about it." I rubbed at my ear.

Terry's brow creased. "Tinnitus playing up?"

I pulled a face and waved his concern aside. "A little. Probably all that cleaning."

He grunted. "I don't know how you live with it. And for the record, I *am* sorry about the whole Meniere's thing. I didn't mean to make it sound like it was anything less than fucking devastating for you. I just . . ."

"I know. And it's fine." I faced him with a smile. "I like that you don't pussyfoot around me. Makes me feel . . . normal. God, I hate that word."

He snorted hard enough to have to wipe his nose on his sleeve.

"Classy, O'Connor. See, this is why you need me in your life."

"Yeah, well, heaven forbid you ever fade into normal, Judah. The world would spin a little dimmer."

My heart caught in my throat. It was one of the nicest things anyone had ever said to me.

"Noooooo, don't look at me like that." He covered his eyes.

"Aw, you do love me." I pulled him in for a hug.

"Oh god, okay." He returned the hug and patted my back bro-style, then pulled away. "And I thought the lip gloss was a nice touch, by the way."

I bit back a smile and raised a brow. "You want some?"

"No. Don't make me smack you again. You want to meet for a

beer in about an hour if you're still feeling brave? Shock the rest of the locals."

"I can't." I shifted my butt on the bench and straightened a non-existent crease in my jeans.

His eyes narrowed. "If you're worried about what people might say—"

"I'm not." I could lie, but this was a small town and I didn't want to start that shit with the only friend I had in it. "I'm actually going for a coffee . . . with someone," I muttered under my breath.

He leaned in and circled a hand around his ear. "I'm sorry? I'll need you to repeat that, because I'm sure you just said you were having coffee with someone who wasn't me."

I shoved him away. "Arsehole."

"Mmm. So, who is this mythical creature who's managed to pry you out of your pity palace?"

I threw up my hands in despair. "Do I not deserve *some* sympathy, for fuck's sake."

"Of course you do." Terry patted my hand. "And that was it right there. Now spill. Who's got you so flustered? Oh. My. God. Is this an actual coffee *date?*"

I glared at him. "It's not a date, and I am *not* flustered."

"Sure you're not. You're wearing pink jeans for fuck's sake."

The man was impossible. "All right, all right. It's Morgan Wipene."

Terry gaped. "Morgan—"

I grabbed his arm. "Keep your voice down."

Terry blinked rapidly, then broke out in a wide grin. "You're going on a *date* with mouthwatering Morgan, our resident eligible widower?"

I peered at him over my sunglasses. "*Mouthwatering Morgan?* What the hell? And it's not a fucking date."

Terry shrugged. "That's what the women call him. And it is *so* a date. You dressed for him, Judah. You care what he thinks. Ergo, it's a date."

"Do they really call him that?" I ignored the sour taste at the back of my throat. "And it's *not* a date." I looked around to make sure no one was listening. "We've just talked a couple of times. I was a bit of an arsehole, to be honest—"

"Shocker."

"Shut up. Anyway, I figured I owed him an apology, so I suggested coffee."

"Huh. I had no idea he was gay, or bi, I guess, or whatever, but that explains *this* a whole lot better." He swept a hand over me. "You're on the pull."

"I am not. And we don't all need a bar code for alphabetic identification, you know?"

He eyed my outfit with a smile.

"Whatever. Don't stereotype. Besides, he's not my type at all."

Terry chuckled. "Aha. Sure he isn't. Tall, dark, and apparently, delicious. What a tosser."

"At the risk of repeating myself, fuck off."

"It's *my* bench, outside *my* shop. You're the one who has to fuck off."

"A minor point," I grumbled as the sound of Hannah singing to herself floated out the door of Terry's store.

Hannah.

"I might have an idea," I said, looking over my shoulder through the store window.

Terry turned in his seat to face me wearing a sly grin. "About Morgan? You want some tips?"

I flicked his forehead. "As if. And no, it's about Hannah and her crutches. Just let me think about it for a bit first." I wiped my clammy hands on my jeans, but fear aside, the idea could be exactly what I needed.

Terry frowned and tilted his head. "Okaaaay. Well, the problem isn't going away anytime soon, so there's no rush."

"Good. In the meantime, I need a bike," I told him.

He stared as if I'd lost my mind. "You? On a bike? Jesus Christ, get inside before you change your mind because, damn, I'd pay good money to see that." He started to get up, then froze and sat back down again. "Hang on. Would it be safe with the vertigo attacks? What if you had one while you were riding?"

"Then I'd fall off, wouldn't I? What do you think would happen? I usually get some warning, at least enough to pull over, but if not? Well, it's not a long way to fall, and our roads aren't exactly Auckland central. And I can do without the parental concern, Terry. I get enough of that. Do you want to sell me a bike or not?"

Terry didn't look convinced.

"Come on. I can't keep walking everywhere. It could be months or years before I can drive again, if ever." I said it fast so I didn't have to think about it. "And I'm tired of lugging my groceries down the hill. Just show me the bikes."

He stared a moment longer, then nodded. "You're right. It's not my place. And you're in luck. We've got a special on helmets." He got to his feet. "Come on. You have the overwhelming choice of four. But if it's groceries you have in mind, might I suggest the one with a basket."

He ducked just in time to miss my hand.

Fifteen minutes later, with my shiny new bike in hand and helmet hanging off the handlebar, I stood peering into the hair salon two doors up from the hardware store, wondering if my well of courage had perhaps bottomed out for the day. My Boston hairdresser had been my one big splurge. Stage lights hid nothing, and I had to endure a ton of stuff in hair and makeup that no self-respecting haircut would ever agree to, so I took care to keep it in good condition. The fact my hairdresser also happened to be the hottest thing to wield a pair of scissors and dressed in skin-tight, black leather pants had nothing, of course, to do with it.

But staring through the window at the line-up of blue rinses and perms in Painted Bay's local stylist had my hair shortening by a good two inches as my follicles gave a collective gasp of horror. That and the fact the sign said the salon doubled as the local dry cleaners. A spot removal free with every cut.

I was about to chicken out when the forty-something stylist stuck her head out the door. At nearly my height and dressed in a floor-length kaftan of outrageous orange, she had a million smile lines framing a pair of cheeky brown eyes and an easy, welcoming air. She studied me for a second, then planted a hand on her hip.

"If you're looking for a rinse to match the colour of those jeans, I wouldn't recommend it." Her teasing laugh carried the length of the street and I instantly liked her.

She crossed the two metres between us in a couple of strides and ran her fingers through my hair, tugging at the ends and sifting through the layers. "You've been staring at my door for five minutes," she said with a wry smile. "So I'm guessing by the talented cut that's hidden under this tangle of regrowth that you might have questions about my ability to meet your high standards. Am I getting close?"

I winced. "Is there a right answer to that question? As in one that won't get my balls chopped up and handed back to me as hamburger?"

Another laugh and another assault on my hair as she spun me around to get a look at the back. My head lurched from the sudden movement and my tinnitus growled, but I swallowed and willed it back down.

"Mmm, hmm. Huh. Okay, yeah."

I looked over my shoulder and raised a brow. "Meaning?"

"Meaning, I've got this. You can sit yourself down in my chair and hand me your trust. That and a ton less money than whatever you've been paying to have this done in the past." Her eyes twinkled.

I narrowed my gaze. "That might well be true, but you don't come with an arse to bounce a coin off, chocolate eyes, and the sexiest scruff in Boston. Although, hang on—" This time *I* turned *her* around and took a quick peek at her arse. "Nope. Nicely shaped but lacking the necessary testosterone accompaniment."

She grinned. "I feel oddly comforted by that. I'm May, by the way." She threw out her hand and we shook.

"Judah."

"I know who you are, Judah. Word gets around."

"Let me guess, it was my charming manner."

"That and the pink jeans. But seriously, don't be fooled by the small-town shop frontage. I ran a salon in downtown Auckland for ten years. I'll see you next Saturday at ten if that works."

"I don't think—"

"I always find that works better." And she was gone.

With my afternoon trip down the rabbit hole complete, I shook my head and wheeled my new bike, complete with basket —*goddammit*—along the sidewalk toward my coffee *meeting* with the apparently mouthwatering Morgan. I made a mental note to keep that little moniker to myself until I could wring the most embarrassment from it. My day was looking up.

Two shops down and that thought became a distant memory as the increasing tinnitus I'd been trying to ignore all day suddenly roared to life along with a rising stomach and that godawful rolling panic I'd come to dread.

Oh god. No. Not here.

My world tipped and swam at the edges as my feet tangled and the bike clattered to the ground. I lurched toward the storefront, desperate for some kind of anchor. I'd almost reached it when the sidewalk rolled up under my feet and I was gone in a fog of free-falling vertigo. No up, no down, nor any idea of where the fuck my body belonged in space as I flailed for the security of any solid surface to cling to.

In seconds I'd gone to my knees on the sidewalk, losing the contents of my stomach in the process. Seconds later, I was on my face, bile-soured ice cream filling my mouth.

I spat it clear and fumbled for the slide of pills I always carried. But I couldn't get my fucking fingers into the pocket of my too-skinny jeans to pull the damn thing out.

Fuck, fuck, fuck.

I shoved and shoved, tears streaming down my face as my stomach once again surged up the back of my throat, my eyes flicking to and fro like a fucking metronome—my head spinning into that black pit of sickening vertigo, where all I could do was hold on and hope I could get somewhere safe.

CHAPTER SEVEN

Morgan

"Judah!" I windmilled for balance in the middle of the
road while the driver of the car I'd nearly run into shouted obscenities
at me. I deserved it. I'd seen Judah go down on the opposite sidewalk
and simply taken off toward him. The car moved on and I scuttled to
where Judah still lay on the ground outside the pharmacy with Kane
kneeling alongside.

"Get . . . fucking . . . hands off . . . me." Judah shoved at the man
who was trying to roll him to his side.

I dropped to my knees. "Judah?"

He grunted and turned his head to face me. I almost wept with
relief. "Morgan." His hand fumbled for mine and I grabbed it. "Get
him . . . away . . . please."

I frowned at Kane on Judah's other side. His pale face stared back
in anguish. I didn't know what the hell was up between them, but
right now Kane's feelings weren't my concern. I flicked my head for
him to back off and he did.

Judah's hand shook in mine. "Thanks."

"What happened?"

His eyes were doing some odd dance back and forth, almost like a convulsion, but he was conscious and there were no other involuntary movements that I could see.

"Judah, can you hear me?"

He nodded. "It's my ears . . . dizzy." He turned and heaved up on the sidewalk again, not much more than bile.

Henry appeared from inside his pharmacy with his phone in his hand. He handed me a packet of wet wipes. "I saw him go down. Does he need an ambulance?"

"No." Judah's grip tightened. "No . . . ambulance. I'll be . . . okay."

Like hell. "Judah, you need help—"

"No, I don't. I have . . . Meniere's."

What the hell was Meniere's? I looked up at Henry.

He nodded. "It's a middle ear disorder. It causes bad vertigo attacks and a whole lot of other stuff. If that's what he has, then no, he doesn't need an ambulance, but he could be like this for a few minutes, or even hours."

"Hours?" I cradled Judah's cheek and turned him to face me. "How long do these last, sweetheart?" I sensed Henry's inquisitive eyes land on the back of my neck. Too bad.

Judah's lashes fluttered, his eyes still dancing beneath them. "A few hours . . . sometimes longer. Need my pills. Helps with the . . . vomiting."

"Do you have them with you?"

"Is he okay?" May arrived from her salon to join the gathering crowd. "I was just talking to him."

"I'm . . . fine," Judah answered.

I had to smile. That damn word.

"Yeah, you look just peachy, hon," May shot back, then looked at me. "Can I help?"

"He needs his pills."

"Pocket." Judah tried to reach down, but I got there first.

"These?" I held up a small oblong pill container.

He nodded. "The cream one."

Henry took a look and nodded. "Stemetil. Anti-emetic. Should help the nausea. I'll get some water." A minute later he reappeared with a glass, and between us, we managed to get Judah upright enough to swallow the pill."

"What about these others?" I held the container up.

Henry peered at them. "Valium, I think. That'll help with the spinning. I'm not sure about the others."

Judah blinked slowly, keeping his gaze locked on mine as though he was holding on. "Home . . . please."

The flicker in his eyes was disconcerting and I sent Henry another questioning look.

"Nystagmus," he said matter of fact. "It happens with vertigo. When your body's balance goes, the eyes move involuntarily. Nothing to worry about."

"Can he see me?"

"Yes, but maybe not as clearly."

"I can see you." Judah squeezed my hand. "Feel really bad . . . Morgan. Need . . . home. Sorry."

"No apologies." I brushed his cheek with my fingers. "I'll get you home."

"I'll take him if you like." Terry O'Connor got to his knees beside me, breathless from running. "When did he go down?"

"Is he okay?" Jam arrived in a flurry from his shop across the road to join the gathering circle of townspeople. "Should I call Jon?"

"No, he's okay." Henry answered.

Jam caught my eye. "Judah?"

I nodded and turned back to Terry. "It happened a couple of minutes ago. He said he has Meniere's?"

Terry sighed. "Yeah, that's right. Shit. He'll be hating this. Right in the middle of fucking town, and all these people."

"They care about him." I eyed Terry with interest. "You guys are friends? I didn't realise."

Terry nodded as he stroked Judah's hair. "We are, not that he makes it easy."

I snorted. "I can imagine."

"We knew each other a bit in high school."

"Terry." Judah grabbed his friend's hand. "Don't want . . . *him*."

Terry glanced up at Kane and shook his head. "Sorry, mate."

Kane rubbed the back of his neck and backed off. "It's fine. I understand. I'll, um, get going. Maybe you could let me know?"

Terry shrugged and glanced at Judah without answering. Kane took off. It was clear I was missing something between them, but it would have to keep.

"So you've seen these attacks before?" I asked Terry, who nodded.

"Only once. At his place. I got him his pills and helped him to bed. I wanted to stay but he sent me away—said he just needed water to drink and a bucket to vomit and piss in until the spinning stopped. Nothing to do but ride it out, apparently."

"Jesus." I stared into Judah's eyes that held no trace of the brightness that usually danced there and swallowed hard. "You okay," I whispered.

He gave a weak smile and nodded. My heart stuttered in my chest.

"How often do you get them?" I kept my eyes on Judah, stroking his forehead.

Judah answered, "Once a week, sometimes more. Need to be . . . better . . . looking after myself."

"Hell yeah, you do." Terry shook his head.

I flashed him a warning glance. *Not the time.*

Henry huffed in frustration and threw his hands wide. "You should have said something, son. You don't even fill your scripts here. It's better if people know what to do so we don't screw it up for you and call an ambulance. No one's going to think any less of you."

Terry raised a brow. "Really, Henry? This town doesn't exactly have a great track record in that regard with Judah, does it? Besides, he's still getting used to the idea himself. It's fucked over his life pretty badly."

"Still here, guys," Judah said weakly.

Henry hesitated. "Sorry, son. But the town thing was a long time ago."

"Doesn't mean he trusts it any more than he used to," May chimed in. "Lived through a bit of that myself. Not exactly the fitting-in type."

Henry grunted. "Shocker."

May booted him with her toe and they shared a smile.

"Still right here," Judah rasped, and I could've hugged him for his sass.

"Enough." I eyed the others pointedly, then focussed back on Judah. "How are you doing, sweetheart?"

Judah winced. "Crap. Home, please. And if you call mum, tell her I'm fine and I don't want coddling."

I nodded, then looked to Terry. "Thanks for the offer, but I'm fine to take him home. I might not know him as well as you, but I think I can manage."

Terry studied me for a second as if trying to read my thinking. "He said you two were having coffee."

The fact Judah had even mentioned it to his friend gave me a ridiculous rush of pleasure. "We were."

Terry's gaze shifted to Judah. "That okay with you?"

Judah closed his eyes and nodded, and I let out the breath I didn't know I'd been holding. Complicated had taken a sharp turn into thorny and I was apparently fine with it.

"Won't be a minute." I squeezed Judah's hand and got to my feet. "I'll get my vehicle. Is that his?" I indicated to the bike.

Terry glanced sideways. "It *was*. He'd just bought it. But now . . . I'm not so sure. I can refund it, no problem."

I didn't even need to look at Judah to know. If he'd bought the bike, there was a reason for it, an important one.

"How about we throw it in the back of the Hilux and let Judah decide when he's recovered," I countered.

Terry flashed me a knowing look. "You might know him better than you think. Go get your vehicle. He'll need to lie on the back seat."

I made shooing motions at the small crowd gathered on the sidewalk. "How about we give Judah some privacy?" Everyone quickly dispersed after wishing him their best, and Judah looked equal parts mortified and appreciative, with a fair dollop of surprised in there as well.

———

Pink fucking jeans. I smiled to myself as I gave the grey duvet a shake and let it settle over Judah's legs, covering a tiny, beautiful tattoo of a male dancer poised on an ECG heartbeat next to his ankle. Seeing it had helped mitigate the shock of getting up close and personal with the contorted and scarred reality of the rest of his feet.

Jesus, what a mess. The price of being a ballet dancer, I could only assume.

Knobbly joints, corns, crooked toes, and blister scars, not to mention the incision line that ran up the back of his Achilles. Pretty, they weren't. But all those years of training, the pain, the injuries, and every sacrifice Judah had made to live his dream were written in every twisted bump and scar.

He wiggled down a little in the bed to get comfortable while keeping his eyes on a large framed photo hung opposite the bed. His still point, he'd explained—a spot he used to keep a focus while the world spun in his head. An attempt to keep his stomach where it belonged, a fingernail grip on reality.

Getting Judah out of my vehicle and into the boathouse had been a steep learning curve in exactly how bad these vertigo attacks were. This wasn't just a bit of dizziness. Judah was completely at the fucker's mercy. He couldn't walk a step on his own or even get to his feet unaided. How he managed on his own completely baffled me. He clung around my waist like a kid as we stumbled our way inside, side-swiping the front door jamb and the dining room table in the process.

We had a bit better luck in the bathroom where I manhandled him to sit on the toilet so he could piss. He managed that well enough, holding onto the vanity so he didn't pitch sideways while he shooed me outside. He left his shoes off and his jeans undone. They were a bit twisted but there was no way on earth I was going there.

He took a couple more pills to help with the spinning, then we lurched our way to the bed. He tried to keep a little water down, but most of what he swallowed found its way back into the bucket I'd grabbed from his tiny laundry and put on the floor at his side. Ghostly pale, he trembled on occasion but remained tightly focussed on that damn photo.

A few locks of hair caught in his long dark lashes and I smoothed them to the side, my fingers brushing the cool of his forehead and coming away damp. His eyes flicked briefly my way, no smile, just a nod of thanks before his gaze returned to the dancers in the photo.

I tried to see what he saw, and it took a second to sink in. The male dancer was, in fact, Judah—centre stage with some ballerina. The photographer had caught him mid-leap, his female partner mirrored at his side. My breath caught in my throat. *Holy shit.* He looked fucking gorgeous.

It was everything I'd felt that first time I'd seen him caught in a single moment in time. That bridled energy he possessed, like a desperate itch under his skin, fists jammed in his pockets. The photo revealed that same energy unleashed and put where it belonged, centre stage, and it was captivating. His body sang, radiating strength and power, and he looked . . . joyous. Beautiful and controlled, and hot as hell.

A thrum lit up my body and sizzled just beneath my skin, raising every single hair. I shuddered and his gaze flicked to me in question.

"So beautiful," I answered, dropping my eyes to his and wishing I could paint some life back into them.

He gave a careful nod. "Diana."

He thought I'd been referring to the ballerina? I took his hand. "Yeah, she's lovely, but I meant you."

His eyes went wide.

"So very beautiful." I couldn't resist and pressed the briefest of kisses to his forehead.

He said nothing when I sat back, just stared. After an excruciating few moments when I thought for sure I'd screwed up, he stretched a shaky finger to my lips and rested it there. "Thank you." Then he turned back to the photo.

I didn't know why he'd allowed me into this desperately personal space, allowed me to see him like this, but I could only hope it meant he trusted me. How he dealt with these attacks on his own, I had no idea. It worried me, and I needed an answer even if I had no real right. Whether he'd give me one, who knew?

I remembered the night on the pier, how he'd swayed, and I'd thought he was drunk. Was it to do with this? And if so, what the hell had he been doing down there at night on his own? If he'd had an attack, he could've fallen in. Fuck, he could've drowned.

But they were all questions for another time. I took a seat on the floor by his head and reached for his hand. He resisted for a few seconds, then let me wrap it in mine. He'd told me it could take twenty minutes, an hour, two, ten, or even longer till the attack subsided. He never knew.

"You should go," he said, keeping his eyes on the photo.

"You should be quiet," I answered, keeping his hand and settling my back against the bedside table. "Tell me if you need the bucket."

A palm cradled my cheek and I startled awake. I had no idea how long I'd been out, but my neck felt and moved like a rusted hinge.

"Shhh. It's just me." Judah's face slowly came in to focus. "It's late."

My eyes blinked rapidly as I got my bearings and took in the lengthening shadows in the room. Evening. The green-gold of Judah's eyes filled my vision, so close I could swim in them. They danced a little more than earlier and came with a small, wondrous smile that loosed the worry around my heart.

"You look better," I said, leaning into his hand and that delicious press of skin on skin. "How long was it?"

He shrugged, his thumb tracing small circles on my cheek. He lay on his side with the buttons of those pink jeans tantalisingly undone. "A few hours. The worst has passed. I'm not spinning, but it never leaves without a solid parting kick. Like a massive hangover."

I covered his hand with mine. "Headache?" It was in the way he held his head, so damn carefully.

"That, a stiff neck, and a little unsteadiness. Sometimes the nausea hangs around, but it's pretty good tonight. You didn't have to stay, you know?"

I turned my face so I could kiss his palm. "Yeah, I did. I wasn't going to leave you."

He pushed the hair back from my face and smiled. "You're a good man, but I would've been okay. Not my first rodeo. I manage most of them on my own."

"Yeah, another time you need to tell me just how you do that."

He raised a pointed brow.

"I know, not my business. But I was there. I know how hard it would be. Anyway, we had a coffee date, remember? I wasn't letting you get away that easily."

He chuffed in amusement. "Not a date. Still, rain check?"

"I was banking on it."

Those bright eyes sparkled. "Good. But in the meantime, I was lying here thinking of you, and that got me thinking about . . . omelettes."

I couldn't help but smile. "Omelettes? That's what springs to mind when you think of me? I'll try not to be offended."

"But they were really, *really* good omelettes," he teased. "Besides, what else should I have been thinking of." He batted his lashes.

Little minx. "Yeah, I'm not touching that. Friends, remember?"

He screwed up his nose. "Friends."

"What time is it?"

"A little after seven."

"Do you need to stay in bed or—"

"God no. I'm gonna watch you cook. My balance isn't great the first couple of hours after an attack, but I can sit and wield a knife."

"I'd settle for some conversation." I brought his palm to my lips and pressed another kiss there while he watched me intently.

He slid his hand from mine and reached over my head for his glass of water. He took a guzzle, then fell back on the bed.

"I'm pretty sure the palm-kiss thing doesn't come under the whole friendship umbrella though. And that's three kisses now, Mr Wipene." He eyed me pointedly. "Just saying." There was an edge of wariness there I couldn't ignore.

I got myself up and sat on the side of the bed, careful not to bounce the mattress. "Is this okay?"

"Sure." But he didn't look.

My fingers found his jaw and nudged his gaze around to me. "I apologise if I overstepped."

His brow creased. "That's not what I meant. It was a stupid thing to say. I seem to do that a lot around you—say stupid shit. You . . . unsettle me. I haven't had a lot of good men in my life, so I'm not totally sure what to do with you. Chasing you away is an entirely viable option, and one I've invested a little time in, as you might've noticed."

I grinned. "Pink jeans?"

A blush stained his cheeks. "Maybe."

"Was that part of some test? See if I ran away?"

He picked at a thread on the duvet. "Yeah, well, as I said, good men have been thin on the ground in my life or, to be more accurate, in my bed."

"Well, *technically*, I'm *on* your bed, not in it."

"In my defence, it looked like you might be heading that direction sometime soon. Still does, if I'm honest."

I chuckled and brushed a lock of hair from his eyes. "So you thought you'd what? Head me off at the pass? I thought we'd already established we were doing the friend-zone thing?"

He gave that comment the eye roll it deserved, shuffled sideways, and patted the bed next to him. "I was giving that friendship thing a week till my nuts got me in trouble. You?"

I stretched out alongside his lean, warm body, every hair on my skin standing to attention. "To be completely honest, all bets would've been off if you'd turned up at my house in these jeans with that rip in the arse the size of two of my fingers, not to mention your nipples sticking through that ridiculous black netting."

He laughed. "Not exactly the reaction I'd been expecting."

"Or maybe, exactly it." I pinned him with a look.

He replied with a cheeky grin. "Maybe."

"Mmm. Well, in the spirit of full disclosure, I *was* trying to make it at least two weeks, just to prove a point, but only if I could forget the image of you in those fucking tights."

Judah snorted. "So how's that working out for you?"

I turned and propped myself up on my elbow. "Abysmally. And just for the record, I'll require another peek to confirm my suspicions."

"Your suspicions?" His eyes danced with mischief.

"About the state of your . . . Johnson, your danger noodle, your trouser snake—"

He threw his head back and laughed, and for a second, I was lost in the sheer unfiltered joy of it. Then he stopped as suddenly as he started and rolled to face me, a slow, sexy smile spreading over his lips. "Can I just point out that we are once again sliding way to the left of the friendship zone."

I kissed the end of his nose. "Mmm. I believe you might be right. So how about this? Fuck the damn friendship zone."

He laughed again. "I concur wholeheartedly. And on that note, there is *one* way to get some definitive empirical evidence on the state of my . . . Johnson, if you're interested?"

Was he kidding? "Definitely interested. But there's a small problem with that idea."

His brows peaked. "Do tell."

"I'm damned sure I won't be satisfied with just a peek, and I'd rather wait to attend the whole show, if I'm lucky enough to get an admission ticket sometime in the future."

He stared at me for a long moment and then slid both arms around my neck and wriggled close enough that I could feel that row of undone buttons on his jeans. My arm circled his waist to keep him there so I wouldn't be tempted to just rip the damn denim right off his flirtatious arse.

"Such a fucking gentleman." He breathed the words against my lips. "Whatever am I going to do with you?"

"You could kiss me." *Please.*

His nose twitched. "That quick drink of water aside, I'm pretty rank."

I held his eyes. "I don't give a flying fig."

He shook his head and pressed closer. "You're something else. But how about you let me take another swig of water first? Freshen things up a little?"

"If you must." I reached for the glass and watched, my dick keeping time with every movement of his throat.

He waited till I put the glass back, and then the solid length of his cock slid up against mine, burning through the denim to set my balls on fire. His gaze hovered right in front, languid and laughing, begging me to fall, and I scrambled for a fingerhold on the edge of the cliff.

"So, here's an idea." He rubbed our noses together and I lost a little more ground. "Why don't I kiss you?"

"Mmm." I licked a stripe up his face and revelled in the rough stubble that grazed my tongue, the strength in the arms that held me. It had been so long since I'd kissed a man, and my dick was banging at the door of my trousers to get free. "Now why didn't I think of that?" I said, sounding light-years more together than I felt.

He leaned in and gently pressed his mouth to mine, brushing his lips from corner to corner, before sliding a tongue over the crease and licking his way inside. And, oh god, it felt so good, so damn good. I opened at the first touch and he dipped right in, sweeping through my mouth, hot and demanding.

Any question I had as to where Judah might sit on the control spectrum was answered in that singular kiss. One of his hands wrapped around my throat, squeezing gently, angling my head exactly where he wanted it, and I was so fucking on board. I might've had three inches and twenty kilos on him, but there was no doubt who was in the driver's seat.

He pushed me flat and straddled my hips, grinding down on my aching cock as his hot tongue danced through my mouth like a flame. Then he lifted both my hands above my head and held them in place as he pulled me apart one kiss at a time.

First, a string of them peppered up the short beard of my jawline to the soft fleshy lobe of my ear, which he suckled and nipped. Then he kissed each eyelid and cheek. Then another string layered down my throat to the hollow at its base, drawing an embarrassing groan of appreciation from my lips.

"Fuck yeah," he murmured in approval. "Tell me when you like it, Morgan, just like that. I wanna know your buttons. I wanna see you fall apart."

He nuzzled into my neck while still grinding away, and I arched up and threw my head to the side, exposing more for him to take.

"So fucking hot." He ran his tongue up the long slope of my shoulder back to my jaw, then nibbled all the way around and down the other side. Then he released my hands with a warning to stay put and trailed both sets of fingers down the length of my arms and across my chest, lingering over my shirt-covered nipples, before sliding both back up and around my neck.

I lay there, held in his firm but gentle grasp as he drilled me with a look so heated, I was surprised my cock didn't go up in smoke.

A flicker of concern passed through his eyes. "Okay?"

I held his gaze. For whatever reason, I trusted him. "Perfect."

He pulled a plump lip between his teeth and turned my head from side to side. "You are so beautiful, Morgan." He released my neck and ran those fingers over me again. He didn't say anything but I knew to keep still.

He leaned over and suckled my nipples into his mouth through my shirt one by one. I didn't move a muscle, keeping my hands above my head, desperate to keep Judah's hands and lips on me, to keep this going, wanting anything he was prepared to offer. I'd never felt so owned, so controlled, and I fucking loved it. Whatever was happening in this moment, I knew I wanted it.

He drew a sharp stuttered breath and sat back on his heels to run his hands under my shirt, our dicks still nestled together through our trousers, all friendly-like.

"Fuck, look at you." He lifted a thumb to graze my lips.

I flicked out my tongue and caught it in passing, and he was back in my face in an instant, plunging his tongue into my mouth while I gave as good as I got. It was ridiculously hot. Fucking incendiary. And I'd never been kissed like it.

A shiver broke over my skin and I groaned, so close to blowing my load it wasn't funny, and I was still fucking dressed.

He pulled off and we locked eyes, barely centimetres between us. From there I couldn't miss the slight sway of his shoulders.

Shit. I cupped his cheek and felt his weight press into it. "What the hell are we doing? You're still woozy. Get your arse back on that bed now," I ordered softly.

And just like that, he rolled off and collapsed beside me, and I didn't know what was hotter. The fact he drove me like he owned me in the kiss? Or the fact he gave himself over to me when he needed to be cared for? Fucking addictive.

I scrambled off the bed and adjusted myself while he watched.

"Dicks and kisses and every unmentionable thing I want to do to you and have done by you can wait, understand?" I told him. "But right now, I'm gonna chuck that bucket and then get us some food."

"You don't have—"

My look silenced him.

"Fine." He rolled his eyes. "But I'm only a little shaky, nothing major. You're too fucking tempting." He aimed for a smirk and missed by a country mile.

"Yeah, well, blame me if you want, but you're too dangerous for your own good. You had me almost forgetting you've spent the last few hours residing in the land of spinning tops."

"Dangerous, huh? I like the sound of that. And while we're on it, you have no idea the length of the list in *my* head of all the things I want to do to you. I've been thinking on this for a while now, at least a week, which is a long time for us *younger* folks. I've even allowed for some intermission time in the event planned out in my head just so . . . you know, you can . . . recover."

Motherfucker. I sealed my lips over his before he said another word and he melted against them, soft and pliant, his arms circling my neck, keeping me close, no hurry, no pressure, just a teachable moment as we opened the books between us. And when I finally pulled away, Judah hummed softly, boneless, relaxed, and . . . quiet.

Huh. Well, look at that. I kissed his nose and got to my feet. "Stay here while I get those omelettes going. I cook, you eat. Once my dick relaxes enough to not be in danger of burning itself on the gas, that is."

Judah licked his lips. "You know I could help with that."

I snorted. "Behave."

"But I think you like it when I don't." He waggled his eyebrows, arched his back, and stretched.

His shirt slid north and those fucking pink jeans south, and . . . damn. I did like it, way too much. "Well, you're gonna have to wait to find out," I said failing to keep the roughness out of my voice.

"Don't need to." He closed his eyes, leaving only an enigmatic grin on his pale face. "I already know."

And I wanted to crawl right up that hard-muscled body and lick that sucker into next week. I turned away before I did just that, grabbed the bucket, and heard him chuckle as I left.

With the bucket disposed of, the familiarity of a kitchen and a freshly stocked fridge brought a smile to my face. This was my happy place.

I'd just begun cracking the eggs into a bowl when Judah called out.

"By the way"—

I'd learned quickly when it came to Judah, that nothing good ever came after that particular phrase.

—"does your family know you like to fuck boys, Morgan Wipene?"

The egg exploded in my fist and splattered down the front of my shirt. *Jesus, this man.* "Yes, Judah, my family knows."

He grunted, which I took for approval.

"Good. I can't be dealing with a closet case on top of everything else I've got going on," he said.

I went back to cracking the eggs.

"Though for you, I might've made an exception."

It was said so quietly, I almost missed it.

CHAPTER EIGHT

Judah

WHY IN GOD'S NAME HAD I SAID THAT? BUT THE FACT I MEANT every word was the true stunner that swept the air from my lungs. Meanwhile, Morgan was whisking the ever-loving life out of those damn eggs. I'd shocked him. Hell, I'd shocked myself. Closet cases scared the shit out of me. After years of fighting for the courage to live my life the way I wanted, I'd never considered ever giving it up for a man.

I was hardly your background-scenery type of guy—more your shine-that-damn-spotlight-this-way type. Just standing downwind of me was likely to get a man side-eyed, if not bagged and tagged. None of which made me good boyfriend material for someone in the closet.

Not to mention I had a particularly bad poker face when it came to men. The bossy side of my nature meant subtlety generally took a back seat. If I was interested in a guy, they knew it soon enough, hell most everyone did. I was no pushover. But Morgan was one out of the box.

Who'd have guessed I'd find a damned gentleman who walked

my side of the street in arsehole Painted Bay? I didn't know whether to laugh or shake my fist at the gay gods of destiny. Whichever one of them gazed in their crystal ball and thought this was a good idea needed to lay off the margaritas. Like I needed another complication in my life, particularly a man, a *nice* man, a nice man who seemed to like me for who I was. Fucking unicorns.

Should I fuck the gorgeous fisheries officer? Hell yeah. Who wouldn't want a piece of that? But that wasn't what was going on here and I couldn't pretend otherwise. For Chrissakes, the guy fell asleep on the floor beside my bed to keep an eye on me. Who the hell does that? I still had the lump in my throat from waking up and finding his body origamied into what had to be the most uncomfortable position just so he could be close if I needed him. So fucking beautiful.

Most of the people I knew in Boston—colleagues, lovers, ex-lovers—had taken the long way around my life once they'd found out I was done for as a dancer. No performer wanted a reminder of how the randomness of life could fuck up your career paraded in front of you every day. I got it.

But my so-called friends? We'd clearly had different understandings of the word. Mine erroneously included the idea that six years of sharing an eye-wateringly expensive three-bedded apartment in the centre of Boston might forge relationships worth more than a few awkward hospital visits, a month of actively avoiding me, followed by a dwindling number of texts, to a resounding zero level of contact once I left for New Zealand. Theirs? Not so much.

Diana was the last one standing who kept in contact. Though why she wanted anything to do with me remained a mystery. The fractured wrist and broken ulnar and radius sustained when I'd dropped her during my first attack had put her in rehab for six months.

Which brought me back to Morgan.

While he'd slept, I'd run my fingertips over that precisely clipped beard and wondered about the rest of the body hair he'd made damn sure I knew about. A few tufts peeking from the neck of his button-down, along with a tantalising glimpse of ink, was all I had to work with, and it was fucking killing me.

I'd never found the whole hair thing remotely sexy, just the opposite, in fact. And yet now I couldn't get the damned image out of my brain, or the thousand questions that went with it. How thick? How soft? What colour? Was his arse smooth, sprinkled, or needing a part. And what the fuck was that tattoo about? He didn't strike me as a tattoo kind of guy. And the not knowing was making me lose my mind.

Not to mention that kiss. Holy shit. He'd let me right in, handed over the reins, and opened up the doors. A big guy like that. It was heady stuff. And what's more, he'd enjoyed it, loved it even, at least if his enthusiasm was anything to go by. It cranked my shit big time, and by the end, I was close to coming on the brush of his cock alone.

But none of it solved the problem of where to go from here? That we wanted each other was hardly news. But there was a lot more to consider.

I slid my legs over the side of the bed and pushed myself to a sit. Not too bad. The tinnitus had drifted to the background and my head was okay-ish. My thighs ached and my battered Achilles twinged in protest. I hadn't stood at a barre or properly warmed up in months and it showed. Still, I was in no way ready for that particular come-to-Jesus moment.

Or I hadn't been. Hannah sprang to mind, but that was a bag of snakes I didn't have the energy for right now.

The ping of the toaster finally got me to my feet, and I could see Morgan above the half-wall, moving around my kitchen like he owned it, cooking for me. I watched for a few seconds, caught up in the odd domesticity of it, and the even odder sense of rightness about it. It wasn't something I'd normally find sexy. But then again, everything about Morgan was sexy, including having the man cooking in my kitchen. And the bald-faced truth of that was fucking with my head.

I tested my legs, and other than a slight shudder at the knees, they felt good. Go me.

Morgan glanced up, smiled, and indicated the table. "Take a seat."

I did.

"What's up between you and Kane?" he asked, dishing our food onto some plates. "You wanted him out of there pretty fast today."

I was so not up to answering that. "Let's just say he was one of my school-age terrors."

Morgan looked over. "Really? He's always seemed friendly enough. Not much to say for himself."

I couldn't contain the eye roll. "Pfft. In high school he had an awful lot to say for himself, at least to me. He hung around with Leroy, and yeah . . . he caused me a few problems. But I really don't want to go there right now."

"Fair enough. Anyway, I can see you've been shopping." He slid a plate under my nose and sat next to me.

"Yeah, well, someone might have made a recent comment on the state of my fridge."

Morgan's mouth quirked up at the corners. "Pffft. How rude."

"That's what I thought." I moved the damn snow globe I'd left sitting smack bang in the middle of the table.

"You liked it, then?" He took a bite of his eggs, then pointed his fork at the globe.

"Don't fish. I said so, didn't I?" I shovelled a huge mound of omelette into my mouth like the ravenous bitch that I was.

He watched me chew through the giant mouthful with a smile. "Impressive."

"Yeah, well," I answered once the eggs were down. "Short attacks leave me starving, but long ones can screw with my stomach for days. I'm taking advantage."

"You call a few hours short?" He added some salt to his food.

I shrugged. "I've had longer. They can be as short as a few minutes, but those are rare with me. Mostly it's a couple of hours, unless it's a drop attack. Those particular fuckers come without warning but only last seconds, minutes at the most. With the others I get something like an aura, I guess you'd call it."

"Like with migraines or epilepsy?"

"Similar. My ears get full and my tinnitus goes off the charts. Sometimes I get a bit spacey or woozy as well. It usually gives me enough time to get safe or find a chair or whatever. I'm trying to get better at picking it up earlier but . . ."

"But not today?"

I broke off a piece of toast and loaded it with egg. "Well, not exactly. Today, in my infinite wisdom, I ignored all the warning signs that I knew were there and just hoped I was wrong. I should've come back here as soon as I twigged, which was about fifteen minutes before it happened, but . . ."

"But?"

I looked him in the eye. I wanted him to know. "But I didn't want to break our coffee . . . *thingy.*"

Morgan stared at me, the disbelief plain as day on his face. "As happy as it makes me that you wanted to keep our coffee *date* so badly—"

"I can see that head of yours exploding."

"Next time listen to your body and I'll come to you."

"Yes, Dad."

"Can it. I'm not worth it. You're more important than a fucking coffee." He fired me a pissy look and went back to his eggs.

I watched him for a minute before answering. He was only trying to help, but it still rankled. "I do understand that and I don't need the lecture. I'm still learning my boundaries with this thing. Everything changed so fast when it happened, and some days I still just want to pretend that I don't have it, that I don't have to second guess myself all the time. I'm getting there, but it's not a perfect thing, you know. And for your information, you are very worth it."

Morgan froze, his fork halfway to his mouth. Then he looked up with the hint of a blush on his cheeks, and my heart skipped in my chest. He slowly put his fork on his plate and took my hand. "I'm sorry for being a paternalistic dick. I can't seem to stop putting my foot in my mouth when it comes to you, but I just don't want you putting me before your health, please."

I squeezed his hand lightly. "Thanks. And it's okay. But maybe we can think of something else to put in your mouth instead one day . . . just saying."

Morgan's blush deepened. "Yeah, I can work with that."

We locked eyes for a moment and shared a quiet smile, and if I didn't already know it, that one simple exchange confirmed just how totally screwed I was about this man. Morgan was a perfect fit for the hole in my life that I didn't even know I had. It was terrifying on every level, not least because that life was currently in total chaos and I barely knew where I fitted in it anymore, let alone him.

But that appeared to make not a scrap of difference to my heart which was busy bouncing around all over the place, like an excited toddler faced with a selection of their favourite ice creams and told they can have them all. I really needed to rein this thing in before I got myself in a lot of trouble. A few kisses were all we'd shared. Up until recently I was lucky if I bothered with getting someone's name for that kind of chicken feed. But Morgan? Man, who was I kidding?

I chanced another sneaky look to find Morgan smiling at me.

Goddammit. "Finish your dinner." I pointed at his plate with my fork. "You're giving me indigestion."

He laughed, seeing straight through me, and after a second, I shook my head and joined in. "We're ridiculous, you do realise that?"

"Absolutely." He flashed those dimples and I might've swooned, just a tiny bit.

We finished our meals in comfortable silence, or at least Morgan did. I kind of lost my appetite halfway. Every now and then we'd catch each other's eye like ridiculous teenagers. It was too fucking cute for words and made my damn teeth ache.

When we were done, Morgan slid down in his chair and laced his fingers together. "So, you wanna tell me more about this Meniere's disease?"

I sighed and pushed my plate away, figuring Morgan deserved at least that much. "CliffsNotes?"

He nodded. "Fair enough."

I took a deep breath. "Okay, well our inner ears are full of fluid contained within this membrane balloon. It bathes the balance and hearing systems so they function properly. People with Meniere's disease produce too much of that fluid for some reason, and the balloon builds pressure. This leads to an intermittent fullness in the ears, tinnitus, and vertigo attacks, like the one you saw. I'd had the first two on and off for a quite a while before the first vertigo attack actually happened, but I put it down to exhaustion and diet and a whole lot of other stuff. If the membrane actually ruptures, which it can do regularly, the fluid irritates other ear structures it's not meant to touch, which affects hearing and balance, long-term."

Morgan shook his head. "I've never heard of anyone with it."

"About two in a thousand people. My Boston doc told me there's about seven hundred thousand in the US. So it's not common, but it's not super rare either."

"Is there any cure?"

I let out a bitter laugh. "They don't even understand the exact cause. Some genetic, some environmental, the usual suspects. The aim is to manage it, not cure it. Low-salt diets and diuretics can help keep the fluid levels down. There are some drug and surgical options, but I'm too early for that and they have their own problems. Mostly it only happens in one ear, although it can occur in both. In some cases, the body resets the fluid production levels on its own and the condition improves, can even disappear. For others, it's a lifetime thing, and the docs can't really tell you where you'll fit in that spectrum."

Morgan stared at me. "Shit."

I blew out a sigh. "Pretty much."

He pushed my uneaten food back toward me. "Eat up. You must need it. So, I'm guessing copious alcohol would be a no-no?"

I rolled my eyes and pushed the plate away . . . again. "Correct."

Morgan pushed it back and stabbed a piece of toast with his fork. "Open up."

My brows hit my hairline. "Really?"

He nodded. "I cook, you eat. That was the deal. And I promise no more questions about Meniere's."

I stared at him for a moment, then opened my mouth. He slid the fork in and watched as my lips pulled the toast free. He brushed his thumb over my lips to catch a crumb and I nabbed it and licked it clean, adding a languid suck to finish before popping off.

It was all in super-slow motion and was sexy as fuck.

Morgan cleared his throat and shifted on his seat. "Jesus Christ, I think I need a cigarette."

I laughed and reached for his hand, threading our fingers together. "What the hell is going on here, Morgan?"

He sat back and studied me with a curious look on his face. "I have no fucking idea. I just . . . like you, Judah. And I can't seem to get past that. I had a nice time the other night before I fucked it all up. Then when I saw you go down today, I can't even explain what that felt like. I like being with you, and when I'm not with you, I think about being with you. Jesus Christ, I barely even know you. Fucking embarrassing if I'm honest."

A whirlwind of emotions ran riot in my chest, but I put a lid on every one of them. This had hurt written all over it, and I wasn't sure I was strong enough to deal with it right now. "You ever get interested in a man this quickly?"

A crease formed between his brows. "I pretty much *never* get interested in *anyone* in this way. Hook-ups? Sure, a few. But there haven't been a lot of those with men in . . . well, let's just say I'd need to brush the cobwebs off my dick with a broom."

My mouth quirked up in a brief smile, but that whirlwind of panic continued to knot in my chest. Some bi men had a preference, some didn't, and with others there was an ebb and flow, and where did that leave me? A short-term crush? I had no interest in that.

He squeezed my hand. "I can hear you thinking from here. I don't avoid men, Judah. I like men. Don't forget, I was married for five years and I haven't been interested in anyone much since Sally died. Plus, I've just never met a guy who piqued my interest quite so strongly . . . until now." He held my gaze. "Until you."

Oh.

"And Painted Bay is hardly overrun with available men, is it?"

He had a point. "What about women?"

"Nothing serious."

I shouldn't have been as relieved as I was. "Tell me about your wife. Was she pretty?"

He watched me for a minute. "Yes, Sally was pretty. Very pretty, very smart, and with the attitude of a T-Rex if you gave her any shit."

I couldn't stop the laugh from bubbling out. "She sounds awesome. And you loved her a lot, I can tell."

His brows dipped together. "I did. More than I thought possible."

I watched him, wondering what fond memories he was caught in. It felt almost intrusive and my gaze slid to the table. "That's good. I'm glad you found someone like that. Not everyone's so lucky."

He tipped my chin up with his fingers. "She'd like you."

Something stuttered in my chest. "You think?"

He nodded, then lifted his hand to lightly brush my cheek before setting it back in his lap. "We met in university and first sight was pretty much it for me. She majored in political science."

I rolled my eyes and he laughed. "Yeah, I know, right? And yes, she was a talker. But she was also full of life. She had this way of sucking all the air from the room. You couldn't miss she was there. In that way, you actually remind me of her."

"Me? Pfft." I swallowed hard. "You guys didn't have kids?"

His expression clouded and he didn't answer for a few seconds. "No. We were thinking about it when she got sick, and that put an end to it. The cancer was fast. She was gone in a year. Then, not long after the funeral, I came up here. But I was pretty much written off for a couple of years."

I squeezed his hand. "It must have been hard. Where are you now do you think?" You didn't forget a love like that. Everyone that came after would have a hard act to follow, and I wondered what Morgan saw when he looked at me and thought of Sally. Not that I had much to offer. A warm body, perhaps, something that had generally been enough for me, until now. With Morgan, I suspected it would never be enough.

He took his time answering. "I'd say I'm . . . okay."

Hardly the decisive response I'd hoped for.

He sent me an apologetic look but shuffled his chair closer. "I'm trying to be honest. *Okay* is actually a good thing. Maybe it doesn't sound so positive to you, but it feels pretty damn good to be able to say it and mean it. She was bright and feisty and left a mark wherever she went.

"I still miss her and I always will in some ways, but the pain isn't bone-deep anymore. It's more a background melancholy when I think about it too hard. Like finding myself, on occasion, still looking for her when I get home, or thinking I've heard her laugh, or reaching for her in the bed next to me at night. Almost like muscle memory.

"It's not holding me back, it's not raw and stinging. It's settling into my history, a part of who I am, but not all I am. Plus, her voice still rattles on in my brain, telling me what she thinks about what I'm doing with my life, so there's that. She always was an opinionated woman."

She sounded . . . wonderful. Everything I wasn't, except for the opinionated bit. Maybe she and I could've laughed over a glass of wine on that point. "Does she have anything to say . . . about me?"

Morgan blinked slowly. "She thinks you'll rattle my cage."

I snorted. "Smart woman."

"And she thinks that's a good thing, and I need it."

"Maybe not so smart."

"I think she's right."

Heat flooded my cheeks. "Says the man who buys manta ray snow globes. Your rational faculties are already under scrutiny."

Morgan's eyebrow twitched. "Don't think I missed the change in subject there. But yeah, it just looked like something you might enjoy."

I wrapped my hand around our joined ones. "It's perfect."

The air between us thickened into a big load of trouble.

"So, ah, did you date much before Sally? Any other relationships or was she it?" I clearly had a masochistic streak a mile wide.

Morgan shrugged. "Would you like signed affidavits?"

Fuck. "Sorry."

He flashed me an amused look. "Just kidding. Only a couple of women, and by relationship, we're talking six months or so."

Fuck. "No men?"

He held my gaze. "As I already said, none caught my eye. Not in the *relationship* way."

"At the risk of being a prick, can I ask if you've *ever been* with a guy?"

He cocked his head and bit back a smile. "You mean sex?"

"Ugh. You make it sound so dirty."

He chuckled. "Yes. So you can relax. But we're not talking double digits."

Which of course got me thinking. I leaned back in my chair and folded my arms. "So, virgin? Semi-virgin? Rocket or pocket, both, or neither?"

He laughed. "*Semi*-virgin? I don't even want to know. But definitely *not* virgin. And if you mean do I top or bottom, both, or none? I've mostly topped, more because of the hook-up aspect than preference, I think. It feels safer somehow. But the couple of times I *have* bottomed, have been . . . fine. I think guys just look at me and assume—"

"Top." I let my gaze roam freely over his hard body. The man was delicious. "Yes. Six foot something and all that hair and rumbling testosterone. It's the obvious conclusion. But it's only fair you should know that I *don't* think that. In fact, what I felt from you with my tongue down your throat was kind of . . . promising, for me.

And I really, really hope bottoming isn't a hard limit for you because—"

"You've got bossy fucking top written all over you." He quirked a brow.

I opened my mouth but nothing came out, so I closed it again because he was right. When other men saw the same thing, they didn't always respect it, but Morgan did, and that was worth rolling over on my tongue for a bit, just to appreciate the taste.

"I actually enjoy both," I finally said. "But I do think I have a flair for wrecking arses, so to speak. In the best possible way."

Morgan swallowed hard and I leaned across the table to whisper in his ear. "And I promise you right now that if you're ever interested, bottoming for me will be so, so much more than just *fine*, Mr Wipene. In fact, if that word ever crosses your lips after I've owned your arse, I'll personally hang up my dildos, ropes, handcuffs and whips, and take vows of celibacy." I sat back and watched his eyes bulge. Jesus, he was adorable. "Just kidding, of course . . . about the whip thing."

He fell back in his chair, looking like he wanted to eat me alive and I was so, so down with that. "I'm not sure I'm gonna survive you, Judah."

"The feeling's entirely mutual, Morgan," I said, deadly serious because I saw a ton of heartache heading my way like a fucking runaway train.

"Right." He sat back like he was waiting for popcorn and my stomach rolled over. "Your turn. Relationships?"

"I should get these dishes." I got halfway to my feet before a meaty hand landed on my shoulder.

"Come on." He steered me to the couch and pushed me down. Then he sat at the opposite end and hauled my feet onto his lap to massage them.

I could only watch with my mouth open. "Are you sure you want to touch those? Braver men than you have fled screaming."

He shrugged. "They're a part of you, so yes, I want to touch them, just like all the other parts of you." His smile turned wicked. "Now talk. Relationships, boyfriends, hook-ups? I'm all ears. It can't be that bad."

I threw him a horrified look. "Are you kidding me? I'm a gay ballet dancer, for Pete's sake. We're all about the body."

"I'm well aware." A flare of heat lit his eyes, and not for the first time, I was struck by how we seemed to have completely missed the introductory, warm-sparks-between-us of initial attraction and moved straight on to the burn-your-fucking-clothes-off incendiary fires of hell. Not that I was complaining.

I blew out a sigh and slumped back against the cushions, enjoying the feel of Morgan's warm hands on me. "And if you think kneading a piece of heaven into my feet is going to somehow make me eviscerate myself emotionally in front of you, you've got another thing coming."

"Aha." He lifted a shoulder but kept on working his thumbs into my foot, melting me into a pile of goo.

I squiggled my bum further down the couch with a satisfied groan. "All joking aside, as much as I'd like to blind you with an itemised list of my best hundred fucks in order of personal preference, I'm sad to say my love life is a lot less interesting than you might think." *Fuck.* So I might've underestimated his evil mind fuckery. Apparently, my emotional secrets could be had for the price of a foot massage.

I held up a finger. "One. Ballet is the best cock-blocking tool ever invented. You're either too tired, too hurt, too swamped with rehearsals and performances, or all of the above at the same time." I added a second finger. "Two. Because of all those things, ballet is mostly a closed world. Outsiders don't understand the hours involved and most relationships are doomed for that reason. And three. You spend a lot of time with each other, and I mean A. Lot."

"So you end up dating other dancers?" Morgan cottoned on.

"Yes, and almost singularly unsuccessfully. We're a fairly emotional lot, go figure. Not to mention, if you're in the same company, it can lead to all sorts of problems on and off the stage if the relationship blows apart.

"So, there's a ton of very good reasons to avoid dating altogether. Add to that the improbability of finding any genuine twenty-something dating material lurking in the downtown Boston gay clubs, and you have a conundrum. All of which leads me to the devastating realisation that my love life doesn't look too dissimilar from yours."

Morgan choked a little. "I'll try not to take offence at that."

I sent him a shining look. "Then you'll be pleased to know you've outdone me in the second category. I've only had one *relationship*, as such. Although I suspect there's a lot more cards in my hook-up files than yours." I eyed him pointedly. "A *lot* more." I made no apologies for loving sex and men, preferably together, and as often as I could get them. Or at least I had.

"Was that with another dancer?" Morgan cast me a speculative look.

And there it was. The fork in the road. Did I own up to what a total fucking dipshit I'd been? That I'd ignored the signs. That I'd been hurt in places I didn't want to look at too closely. That I couldn't think about the man with any objectivity until recently, until Morgan walked into my life. And wasn't that an eyeopener?

I sucked in a breath and blew it out slowly. "No. He was the artistic director of the ballet company I danced for. And he was a lot . . . older. A lot."

Morgan arched a brow but said nothing.

"And no, we shouldn't have been together. I should've had more sense. There was no hard-and-fast rule, but sleeping with the people who decide the roles isn't exactly viewed favourably by the other dancers.

"But Grant was a perfectionist—he never assigned a role based on the fact he was fucking you. If anything, he rode me harder than the others, pun intended." I flashed Morgan a wry smile, which he duly ignored.

"But he believed in me, or in my talent at least, and I was flattered and smitten, I guess. Can you work your thumbs in that spot? Mmm. Oh my god. Perfect." I quite possibly drooled.

Morgan nudged me. "Go on."

"When I look back now, I think he simply gets turned on by any talent and has to have them in his bed. Grant's a passionate man, in and out of the sheets. Driven. But there were days he wanted out of that seat, and so we clicked in that way."

Morgan cut me a sideways look, and his hands slowed like he maybe wasn't as comfortable with the conversation as he'd thought. I felt the urge to reassure him that he and Grant were different, but I didn't.

"I don't think he ever cheated on me when we were together, but to be honest, I don't know."

Morgan grunted dismissively and pushed the legs of my jeans up so he could reach above my ankle. It shouldn't have been as damn erotic as it was, but I was starving for more than just the man's hands, and two inches closer to my cock was always going to be a winner.

"But?" His expression was unreadable.

"*But*, as soon as it became clear that I wasn't going to be able to offer him another chance at perfection, he dumped my arse faster than you can say pirouette. Of course, it would've been nice if he'd actually told me to my face and not leave it to one of my rival dancers to plaster their two kissy faces all over Instagram in an epic Fuck You, but there you go. Lesson learned."

"Asshole," Morgan spat.

I glanced up and caught the flash of anger in his eyes. "I won't disagree."

Morgan dropped the foot he'd been working on back in his lap and started on the other. I tried not to think of the construction of the soft cushion currently under my heel and failed.

"Is it hard . . ."

Increasingly. My gaze shot to his but he was focussed on my foot.

—"when you dance, remembering how it was for you?"

Oops. "I um, don't. Dance, that is. Haven't since it happened. So I guess that answers your question, right?"

Deep lines cut across his forehead. "But, it was your life—"

"Exactly. Was. Not anymore. Besides, I hardly have the room in this place to stretch let alone dance."

Morgan drew in a long breath and studied me, his fingers still working my foot. "I obviously know nothing about your profession, and maybe ballet isn't in your life anymore in that way, but you've danced your whole life, Judah. I'm gonna go out on a limb here and assume that wasn't all about making money?"

My stink eye made him laugh. "You know damn well that's true, so don't try and be clever. I know what you're saying. That I should carry on with what I can because I love it. And I agree. I just haven't quite got there yet."

Morgan grimaced. "I didn't mean to put you on the spot. I know it must be difficult—and oh god, listen to me." He facepalmed. "I sound like all those people I left Auckland to escape after Sally died."

I stabbed a finger at him. "Aha! So you *were* escaping."

He narrowed his eyes. "Don't twist my words. I only meant that in lots of ways you're grieving, just like me. And there's no timeline for that. It is what it is till it isn't anymore."

"I think I got that part."

Morgan pulled my jeans back down and patted my feet. "Okay, so I'm only going to say one more thing." He smiled at my eye roll.

"Go on." I curled my legs under me. "I'm riveted."

"Thought you would be. But remember, this is only *my* experience. Sometimes grief becomes habit. You get used to not wanting or being too scared to try. It's safer, and you don't recognise when you need or are ready to move on."

I bit back a smile and flicked a finger back and forth between us. "Are we having a Yoda moment here? 'Cause if we are, I really need to be Obi-Wan, not Luke. That kid had some serious issues. Come to think of it, maybe that's where my liking for old hairy guys has its roots."

Morgan threw up his hands. "Oh. My. God. Just forget—"

"I'm sorry." I scrambled to the end of the couch and wrapped him in a hug. "I wasn't making fun. Well, not much. Except for the

Obi-Wan bit. I always found him oddly . . . hot. That growly voice and—"

Morgan stared at me like I'd lost my freaking mind.

"Come here." He grabbed me by my T-shirt and tugged me onto his lap. Then he cradled my face and pulled me in for a kiss.

I opened to the first touch of his lips, his tongue strolling around my mouth for a long, slow taste. By default, I tried to notch things up and take control, but a growl rumbled deep in Morgan's throat and I went still, my body deflating against his chest cell by cell until I was soft as a noodle, content to be held in place by his arms, our cocks snuggled nicely together, flirting a little but not insistent, and it felt good, so fucking good.

After God knows how long, he sighed, nipped my lips, and gently pushed me away. "Sit."

I did.

He studied me a moment and gave a satisfied grunt.

My gaze narrowed. "What? You're looking very pleased with yourself about something."

"I am." He waggled his eyebrows. "I just reset you. Before that, it was like looking at that screen of garbage you get when your computer's fucking up. And now look at you." He waved a hand my way. "All . . . mellow."

Huh. "I have a reset button? You mean the kiss? That's ridic— I do not . . . How did I not know this?"

He shrugged. "It's a gift."

I punched him on the arm. "That's nonsense. And I am not mellow."

"You are. Don't fight it."

"I'm not—"

He sealed his mouth over mine a second time and any remaining tension in my body oozed out my big toe and puddled on the floor. So okay, maybe a little bit mellow.

He pulled away with a self-satisfied smirk. "I rest my case."

My chin jutted. "I concede nothing. But for the sake of science,

I'm willing to further the experiment. You may kiss me on a regular basis whenever it seems necessary and we'll take copious notes."

"Of course we will. Now, back to the not dancing thing."

"Fuck. Is it enough to say that I *am* thinking about it. Hannah asked if I would dance for her, so yeah, I'm thinking about it."

"A good incentive."

"I know. I just . . ." I looked up at him. "It's hard. And being the dramatic tart that I am, I couldn't have my first vertigo attack somewhere sensible, could I? No. I had to launch this whole new juncture in my life, mid-performance, centre stage in the Boston Opera House, right in the middle of a catch and lift. My best friend Diana was my opposing lead, the catch to my lift. She broke her wrist and ulna when I collapsed and dropped her. After that—well, as you can imagine, there's not much call for a male ballet dancer with vertigo and a history of dropping the primas. Cue a whimpering return to Painted Bay to lick my wounds and grow a pair, as my brother would say."

"Stop it." Morgan's expression was caught between pissed off and stricken. "What's with the bad-taste jokes. Jesus Christ, Judah, you gave up everything for dance. I look at that photo in your room and I can't even begin to imagine what you've lost. How can you joke about it?"

To survive. I threw him a cool stare. "Do you think I don't know that? Do you think it doesn't feel like someone's cut off my fucking legs and thrown them on the garbage heap along with my heart and all my fucking dreams?" I pushed up from the couch.

He reached for me but I evaded his hand and crossed back to the dining table and sat. Two seconds later, he followed.

I could barely look at him. "I hate everything about this, Morgan, *everything*. But I am also so fucking sick of wallowing in it, of trying to drink my way out of the grief, or pretend it isn't happening. You've known about this for five minutes, and I appreciate your anger on my behalf, but I've lived with it for eight months now, and I'm only just starting to breathe again. And the *only* way I can keep my shit together sometimes *is* to joke, to minimise it, to try and dismiss it in whatever cringe-worthy way I can." I wiped at my eyes. Goddammit, I did not want to cry.

Morgan immediately slid from his chair to kneel at my feet, cupping my cheeks and forcing me to look at him. His thumbs brushed at my tears. I tried to wriggle free but he held tight.

"I'm sorry," he said, pressing his lips to mine. Then he kissed each damp cheek in turn, and just like that, the anger bled away.

And holy shit. I really did have a reset button.

I trailed my fingers down his beard and dropped my forehead to his. "I'm scared, Morgan. Scared this self-pity is going to eat away at me till there's nothing left and I spend the rest of my life hiding out in this fucking boat house becoming everything I hate. Because regardless of all that indulgent shit I just spewed, I *want* to live again. I want a life. I want to find a way through this.

"But right now, I'm fucked up. You don't understand me like you think you do, because I barely understand myself. And to be honest, you'd do better to walk away."

Morgan pulled back till our eyes met and then smiled, a big fucking smile with dimples for miles. "You are so full of crap."

I jolted upright in my seat. "You did not just say that."

He pulled me back down. "I did, and you know why? I don't pretend to understand you, Judah. But you also clearly know zip about me if you think that little set-me-free speech is gonna makes a cat's piss of difference in scaring me off. I thought we'd been through this. That boat sailed with the whole pink-jean thing, and I've got my eye on a ballet-tights rerun in my near future that I'm not about to give up."

Laughter bubbled out of me. "Oh, I see. You only want me for my potentially uncut dick."

Morgan's eyes popped comically, then his gaze drew heavy and he leaned in close. "I want you for a damn sight more than that, Judah Madden. But it's as good a place as any to start."

I turned and pressed my lips to his ear. "But what if you're wrong, Morgan Wipene? What if I'm, horror of horrors, cut, after all?"

I shivered as he sucked my earlobe into his mouth and nibbled on it. "I'm an equal opportunity lover, Judah." His breath blew hot in my ear. "As long as it's yours, I couldn't give a rat's arse if it's cut, uncut, or fucking tied up in a pink bow."

I pulled back with a saucy smile. "Now *that* I can arrange."

His lips slid over mine and I was lost in the salt and pepper taste of his mouth. My arms wormed their way around his neck, my body lighting up as his tongue swept through my mouth and—

"Judah?" An all too familiar voice called as my door rattled in its frame.

"Shit. My mother." I pushed Morgan away and squeezed my dick into submission in my still—fuck—unbuttoned jeans. I turned in my chair so my knees were under the table.

Morgan clambered back onto his own chair and smoothed his shirt. "Jesus, I feel like I'm fifteen and caught with my hands down my pants," he hissed.

"Ooooh, teacher-student role-play. I like it." I winked.

A key slid into the lock and my mother blew into the boathouse with an armful of containers.

"Oh, Judah, there you are. Why didn't you answer the door? Terry let me know about—oh." She caught sight of Morgan and froze mid-sentence. "Hello, Morgan. What are you still doing here?" Her gaze flicked between the two of us with obvious interest. "Terry mentioned you drove Judah home, but I had no idea you stayed. How . . . lovely of you."

Her eyes landed on the empty plates. "Oh, and you cooked?" A wicked gleam entered her eyes, and her tone moved from surprised to suspiciously gleeful.

"Mum, please." I tried to head the matchmaking off at the pass. "Leave the poor man alone. Morgan was just worried and wouldn't listen to me when I told him to go."

Morgan raised a questioning brow, but I fired him a warning

glance. The last thing I needed was to deal with Mum's interfering ways before I had to.

"Mmm, how perfectly gentlemanly of you." She eyeballed Morgan with a knowing smile that threatened to pin my mortified balls to my chair. "I'll just put these away." Her gaze swept the room and she faltered. "Judah? You've cleaned! Oh. My. God." She put a hand to my forehead and I brushed it away.

"You make it sound like I lived in a hovel."

Morgan cleared his throat, which earned him a glare, and he threw up his hands.

My mother merely raised her eyebrows.

For fuck's sake. "I think that's enough from the peanut gallery. It was time, that's all."

My mother bit back a smile. "Well, I for one am delighted." She shuffled her eyes once again between Morgan and me. "What do you think, Morgan?"

Oh. My. God. She was relentless.

"Ah, yeah, much better."

"So you've been here before then?" My mother looked positively victorious and I could see the moment Morgan realised he fallen into the trap by his horrified expression.

He looked my way, but all I could offer was a shrug. The man was on his own.

"Um, y-yes, once," he faltered. "Look, I should really be on my way."

I shook my head madly that I didn't want him to leave, but his gaze was fixed on my cock-blocking mother. "But first, let me put those in the kitchen for you, Mrs Madden."

"Mrs?" I mouthed, bug-eyed. No one had called my mother Mrs since I was a teenager.

"Pfft. Cora, please," my mother practically purred, the witch. "You've never called me Mrs Madden before, Morgan. I don't see any need to start now, regardless of what you two are trying to pretend you aren't doing."

I was pretty sure Morgan almost choked on his tongue as he blushed prettily—which surprised the hell out of me—then swept the containers out of my mother's arms and headed for my tiny kitchen at close to a gallop. It would've been cute if I hadn't been mortified for the poor man.

"Mum!" I hissed once he'd gone. "Stop it." But even as I tried to abort my mother's award-winning jump to conclusions, I couldn't drag my eyes from Morgan's fine arse as he unpacked the food into my fridge. My mother noticed. Of course she did. My tongue stuck to the floor in a pool of drool was likely ample indication.

She took Morgan's empty seat and leaned across the table. "The man has a lot of admirable . . . attributes, wouldn't you say?"

I ignored her.

"And he, um, seems to know his way around your kitchen quite well, sweetheart."

I turned to find her grinning like a Cheshire cat and hoped my threatening glare said all that was needed.

She shrugged. "Just an observation. How are you feeling, by the way?"

I feasted one last look at Morgan's rear end as he finished. "Better."

She took my hand and squeezed it. "I'm sorry it happened in town, but I guess it was bound to at some point."

"It's fine. Like you say, it was inevitable." *Please, just go.*

"Terry mentioned you'd bought a bike. Are you sure—"

"Mum please, can we do this later? You know I hate being fussed over." It came out sharper than I intended and I saw the sting in her eyes. It was also patently untrue as I was, apparently, more than happy to have Morgan fuss over me like an old mother hen—something I chose not to dwell on. "I'm sorry. That was cruel. It's just been a long day."

She nodded but it was clear I'd hurt her.

"Can we talk tomorrow?" I offered.

Her gaze softened. "That would be nice."

She got to her feet just as Morgan approached.

"Well I, ah, might call in tomorrow? Maybe see how you are, if you'd like?" Morgan glanced from me to my mother and back again. "But if it doesn't suit . . . ?"

I opened my mouth to tell him I'd call him later when—

"Pfft. Rubbish, young man," my mother interrupted, looping her arm through Morgan's and steering them both towards the front door.

His gaze shot back to me, more than a little rattled.

I followed them, hastily buttoning my jeans. I hadn't intended to let Morgan out of my sight without another taste of that sinful mouth, which meant my mother needed to leave first, a long way first. "Hey, Mum?"

She ignored me. "You can walk me to the car, Morgan. Martha gave me a lift."

"I can?" Morgan sent me another panicked glance, and I kept following.

She looked up, her head barely at the level of his chest.

"I mean, of course I can," he said, only slightly stumbling over the words.

She patted his arm. "Good. That way I can tell you what wine I'd like you to pick up for Sunday lunch tomorrow."

"Sunday lunch?" Morgan's voice held a terrified note that I would've found amusing if I hadn't been gobsmackingly horrified at my mother's suggestion.

"Well, of course," she sounded confused, but I wasn't buying it. The little minx. She was scheming. Innocence and my mother were two words that never belonged in the same sentence. "It's past time you paid us a visit. And since you've been so kind to my son, I'd like to repay that with a bit of hospitality. Terry and Hannah will be there too. And Martha's son, Fox. He's up from Stewart Island."

They will? He is? This was all news to me.

"And who knows," she continued with a lilting laugh that I thought I might shove down her throat till it choked her. "You might like it enough to come every week."

Morgan spun to face me and I could see fear in the whites of his eyes.

"Ah, Mum, can we talk a minute?" I put a hand on her shoulder.

She shrugged it off. "Nonsense, Judah." Those blue eyes that only I could see steeled and grew cool as she delivered her final offensive lunge. "You said we'd talk tomorrow, and that's exactly what we'll do. *Tomorrow*." Her expression brooked no argument and I knew when I was beat.

Mother, one. Son, zip. The woman had some serious skills. I bowed to her perfectly executed checkmate and delivered Morgan an apologetic shrug. "You can pick me up on the way."

His eyes popped, then rolled in surrender. "White or red?"

My mother looked up in approval. "I knew you were a smart man." She prodded Morgan toward the car where Martha waited in the driver's seat. I sent our office manager a wave, which she returned a little hesitantly, and I made a mental note to check in with her. She'd been riding my arse less than usual lately and it was starting to worry me.

Morgan threw one last panicked look over his shoulder as he was led away, and I wiggled my fingers at him.

I gave it seven minutes before he blew up my phone.

He took five.

CHAPTER NINE

Judah

8:00 AM.

Four hours until the Madden circus, otherwise known as Sunday lunch, kicked off. After leaving the boathouse with Morgan on her arm, my mother had turned off her phone to avoid any backlash. Smart woman. But if she thought it was going to save her arse, she was sadly mistaken. I wasn't about to put Morgan through the wringer of a family meal when we didn't even know what this thing was between us yet.

I had a plan, but I needed an accomplice, someone other than myself to tell my mother Morgan was held up and unfortunately couldn't come. Hearing it from me, the excuse would not only be instantly dismissed as the lie that it was but would likely earn me the protracted cold shoulder treatment along with an inundation of "olive branch" casseroles down the track, once she started speaking to me again. The cold shoulder I could handle, the casseroles, not so much.

I stood at my ranch sliders and applied yet another layer of watermelon lip balm while I contemplated the ripples of the outgoing tide and considered my options. Morgan had laughed and outright refused to pass off the lie himself, honest fucker that he was, so there went my first plan. I'd already called Terry, but he wasn't having a bar of it either. And when I instantly struck him off my friendship list and told him that, he just laughed and pointed out that as he was the only one on it, he wasn't unduly worried. I hung up on his sorry arse because he was right.

And because he was right, I had a problem. Accomplices, by their very nature, implied some kind of existing relationship, and I was admittedly running a little short of those in Painted Bay. My gaze wandered to the car park and landed on Martha's jeep. *Mmm.* She didn't usually work on Sundays, but that didn't stop my hamster-wheel brain flying into motion. With the right inducement, the idea had potential. I could offer to do the office books for a month. Martha hated that job and I had nothing to lose.

I grabbed my jacket against the unseasonably chilly southerly barrelling onto the wharf outside and headed to the office. The door was closed so I gave a quick knock and walked in.

"Martha, Martha, have I ever told you that you're my favourite person in all of Painted B—" My tongue lodged in my throat and blocked every scrap of air from entering my lungs. *Christ on a fucking cracker.* "I, um . . . shit, sorry . . . fuck . . . I'll, um . . . just wait outside. Fuck."

I leapt back through the door and slammed it shut, in the hope that might somehow protect me from what was inevitably coming, or at least give me enough time to change my underwear.

Shit. Shit. Shit.

There was not, nor would there *ever* be, enough bleach in the entire world to cleanse the image now burned into my brain of my mother in a passionate lip-lock with our office manager, her hand up under Martha's shirt—nope, fuck, I couldn't even think the damn words.

Christ, I was going to need therapy for fucking decades.

I was still trying to muster some vocabulary that didn't solely contain expletives when the door suddenly pulled open at my back and I all but fell into the office.

I stumbled to keep my feet while my mother calmly, *calmly* ran her hands down the front of her jeans, hands that had just been— nope, still not going there. She wore an amused smile and I wondered what weird and wonderful rabbit hole I'd fallen down this time.

Martha leaned on the opposite wall next to the old loading door that opened directly above the water. With her arms across her chest, she looked distinctly embarrassed by the unexpected outing, and my heart momentarily squeezed for her. I didn't want that for them, but . . . holy shit, I was still in recovery myself, because . . . *Mum*, and, and . . . well, to be honest, that was more than enough.

"Take a seat," my mother said, not a mortified wrinkle to be seen.

My mouth hung open, as it had been since I'd first seen them kissing and—nope, nope, nope. "What the fuck, Mum?" Only one expletive. Pretty damn good.

"Sit."

I sat.

"I imagine you have some questions," she said with a worried glance at Martha who was altogether too quiet.

I snorted, then had to wipe my nose because obviously, that was how I was rolling. "Questions? Who me? Can't think of a single one. Now if you'll excuse me, I have some things to—"

"Sit."

I sat looking anywhere but at my mother.

"Martha, would you come here, please."

And I had to look because . . . well, because I hadn't heard that soft tone in my mother's voice since . . . Dad.

My mother had her hand extended, and after casting a quick look my direction, Martha walked across and took it.

And I could do nothing but stare, stare as all the hugs I'd watched them share, all the times they'd arrived or left in the same car, the careful way Martha watched over my mother's feelings, the hours they'd spent in the office together, the way my mother's eyes softened every time Martha walked into the room, and the way all of it now made simple, clear, complete, and utter sense.

I stared until the pink roses on my mother's shirt blurred at the edges, their joined hands clouded, and the damp on my cheeks had me closing my eyes. The next thing I knew, Mum's arms were around me and I caved against her soft belly like a child.

"Shh." She held me close. "We were going to tell you, all of you, tonight while Fox is here. I didn't mean for you to find out like this. I'm so sorry if we upset you. But that's all I'm sorry for, understand?"

I pushed her gently back and got to my feet, lost in those gentle blue eyes that had watched over me my entire childhood. "I'm not upset, Mum." And I wasn't. "I'm surprised, shocked, and to be honest, feeling a little foolish that I didn't see this. It was right in front of my eyes the whole time. I always knew you guys were close."

My mother stepped back into Martha's waiting arms, which immediately folded around her. Watching them stand together like that, something inside me stilled. Then Martha dropped her arms and took a step back, but my mother grabbed her hand to keep her close. "This relationship is serious, isn't it?" I asked, though I didn't need to. It was clear in my mother's eyes.

"It is. But I need you to understand that we only embarked on something between us a little under a year ago. Nothing ever happened while Damien was alive. I loved your father. I was devastated when he died and it took me a long while to recover. But now, amazingly, I find myself in love again. I don't know what I did to deserve two loves in my life, but I'll take it. I love Martha, and I hope you'll be okay with that." She turned to Martha's shining eyes.

Holy shit. I didn't even know where to start, except for one certain thing.

"If you two are happy, then I'm happy for you. I don't need time to think about that. Hell, you've stood by me my whole life, Mum. You never batted an eyelid when I came out, so I'd be a bloody hypocrite if I was anything but supportive of you both. It's just . . .

well, a surprise, given how I'd thought you were straight my entire life. That part might take a bit of adjustment."

She snorted. "Yeah? Well, imagine my surprise, then. For over fifty-two years, I thought I was straight too. Martha's always known she swung either way, and it was something I knew about her. But I was clearly a slow starter."

She didn't know? Rats were eating my brain, it was the only explanation. "So, then, ah, how did you two . . . work it out?"

Mum looked to Martha who smiled fondly. "Your mother kissed me," Martha said.

I nearly fell off my chair. "You made the first move?" My eyes bugged at my mother.

She laughed. "I might be slow on the uptake, son, but when I know what I want, I've never been shy about going for it. Your father would've told you that."

I threw up a hand. "Stop. TMI. Please? We're gonna need a discussion about boundaries." I turned to Martha. "So, um, did you know how she felt?"

She shook her head. "Never saw it coming. But let's just say once she kissed me, I didn't need much persuasion after that. I've loved your mother from afar for a long time."

I had nothing left to say, or rather, I had a million questions but none of them needed answering now, or at all if I was honest. This was my mother's life, and if they loved each other, it was all good with me. Except—

Fuck. "Leroy."

My mother's smile slipped. "Ah, yes. Leroy. That's the sixty-four-million-dollar question. I'll talk to him after lunch today as I'd intended, but how he'll react . . ." She shrugged.

And I had one or two ideas about that as well, none of them good. "I've got your back," I said. "I can come with you if you want?"

She patted my cheek. "Thank you, dear, but I'm going to do this on my own. Martha will do the same with Fox, and then we'll see if they want to talk with both of us. Although Martha thinks Fox is already suspicious. He's been asking questions and doesn't seem unduly upset at Martha's vague answers, but we'll see. Anyway, that's kind of why we wanted a nice big family lunch today. The calm before the storm, so to speak."

Goddammit. There was no way I was screwing with that. Morgan was definitely coming to lunch.

Morgan

How in the hell had I managed to get myself invited to lunch at the Madden house? I lathered my neck and grabbed my razor from the soap tray, letting the scalding water sizzle down my back.

Although to be fair, *invited* wasn't entirely accurate. Strong-armed ran closer to the truth, and I wouldn't baulk at the term coerced or even intimidated. All of which applied to Cora Madden. The woman was devious and wielded guilt like the grip was custom made to fit her hand.

And as for Judah—all that feisty attitude had been thrown under the bus alongside me, and we were gonna have words, lots and lots of words. Still, I wasn't about to lie my way out of it as he'd cheekily suggested in a text. I had to live in this town, and if Judah and I lasted, I'd be seeing a lot more of Cora and I preferred that she didn't want to flay me alive.

One to the mothers of the world.

Still, it could be worse. At least I'd see Judah in his broader family environment, something I expected might be worth the invite alone. Cora, Judah, and Leroy in the same room would make for an interesting couple of hours. And I liked Terry and Hannah, so that was a win as well. And presumably, since I'd been instructed to pick Judah up, I might just get to take him home as well, and the potential in that scenario had me tingling in all the right places.

My soapy hand slid around my bobbing cock and . . . mmm. I

shouldn't have been as aroused as I was at the thought of being topped by Judah, especially since I hadn't lied about only bottoming a couple of times. But the fire in those eyes when he'd promised me so much more than just *fine* nearly melted my socks right off my feet. And with that single thought, I spilled long and hard against the shower tiles.

I was in way, way over my head with this man, and all I'd done so far was kiss him. I hadn't considered anything beyond a casual fuck with anyone since Sally died, and I was struggling to understand why things had changed so suddenly. Was it just time? Or was it Judah? And therein lay the problem. There was zero doubt I wanted Judah in my bed, but was I ready for more than that?

One thing I did know, I didn't want to hurt him. He was in the middle of a gigantic life clusterfuck. I'd never even heard of Meniere's until Judah. Was I a complication he didn't need? Because one thing I was sure of, Judah getting his life back on track was bound to include drama, with a capital D, something I avoided like the plague. Even without the Meniere's, I was pretty sure any relationship with Judah would entail all the excitement of a rollercoaster where the ride official had failed to check the safety bar was in place. Part of me thrilled at the idea, but mostly it simply terrified me.

I slammed off the water and reached for a towel.

"Feel free to jump in here any time, darling." I rested my hands on the vanity and stared in the mirror.

Nothing.

Typical.

"You know, I'd hoped having an interested party on the other side might come with a few more perks. But you're turning out to be a major disappointment."

Get over yourself. You like him, he likes you. The sex should be hot. Can't wait to see that go down.

Bitch. God, I missed her. We'd sent more than a few pairs of sheets up in flames in our time. Then I thought of Judah and a sizzle burned low in my belly. *Well, damn.* It appeared I was making room.

I grabbed a quick breakfast and headed outside to wait for Jon. He'd come up with a Whangarei address for the Laird brothers from the boat, and we were going to do a low-key drive-by of the house in Connie's Honda Accord to see what we could see.

An hour later we were sweltering in the car under a burst of late summer heat, with eyes on an attractive green-and-cream weatherboard villa about fifty metres away on the other side of the street. On our initial drive past, the bow of the white-striped boat was clearly visible in the rear of the section behind the house. So far, so good.

"So, you and the young Madden boy, huh?" Jon kept his gaze fixed down the road but it was impossible to miss the amusement in his tone.

"I think the word you're looking for is man, not boy." I took the bait. "Judah is twenty-five. And how the hell did you know?"

He chuckled. "The jungle drums beat loud last night. Plus Connie might've run into Cora at the store. Twenty-five you say. Well, that makes all the difference, then. You're what? Thirty-five?"

I barely contained the eye roll. "Do you have a point, or should I just open the door to let your drool roll out into the gutter, old man."

Jon choked on his Diet Sprite, sending a spray of it over his dashboard.

"Shit." He grabbed his jacket and mopped at it. "Damn steering wheel's gonna be all sticky."

I laughed. "Serves you right, you nosy bastard. But you don't seem surprised . . . about me and another man."

Jon pursed his lips. "Why would I be surprised? You'd already told me you were bi."

"Knowing it and seeing it can be two different things."

He shrugged. "Yeah well, none of my business really. Pass me a water bottle, will you?"

I reached into the back and handed one over.

He continued as he opened it. "But maybe in some ways it makes sense. After Sally, I imagine it would need to take someone quite special to catch your eye. And Judah is . . . special." He smiled and took a long drink.

I laughed. "That he is. And right now, we're just talking. I like him. He's different. Challenging."

Jon chuckled.

"You sound like you know him?"

He lifted a shoulder. "Mostly hearsay, though Cora's told me some. I know he had a hard time in school. I know he was swept off to Boston as a major ballet talent, and I know that his brother holds a bit of a grudge that's more about Leroy's choices than Judah's. Those boys need to sort that out, by the way. Cora doesn't need them at each other's throats. And I know he got sick, though I didn't know the name of it till yesterday. I might've done a bit of googling."

"Join the club. It's a shit of a thing."

Jon took a guzzle of water. "It is. And he's a bit lost by the sound of it." Jon eyeballed me. "I reckon he could do a lot worse than have the ear of someone who's seen a fair bit of shit in their time as well and who could do with a dose of flair in their own life, something I imagine Judah has in spades."

The surprise must've shown on my face.

Jon barked out a laugh. "What? You think I don't notice stuff? We've known each other five years, Morgan, and I've watched you mourn Sally through every one of them. The first three were hell on earth. I know that because I was there, lucky to call you a friend. I saw the pain and the lies in your eyes when you told everyone you were fine. The last two years have been better, much better, and I for one am pleased you might be willing to stick your toe in the water again. You and Judah were supposed to have coffee together, I heard, before . . . you know."

I shrunk in my seat. "God, this bloody town."

"Cares about you." Jon patted my arm.

"Yeah, but we hadn't intended everyone to know our business before we'd even been on a single damn date."

Jon arched an eyebrow. "When Judah went down in the main

street, you were at his side in seconds, pale as a ghost and with a face like thunder, at least to hear Henry tell it. It doesn't take a rocket scientist to put two and two together."

"Goddamn gossip. Not everyone knows I'm bi, you know? It's not an issue, it's just . . ."

"I know, and there's gonna be a few raised eyebrows for sure. You worried?"

Was I? I didn't have to think long. "Not worried as such, at least not about what other people might say. But I've never had a relationship with a guy. Hooked up? Sure. But nothing more. This is all pretty damn new to me, and I didn't want eyes on us so soon, or on Judah. He's got enough going on without people gossiping about his love life as well. Bad enough his mum walked in on us chatting last night and summoned me to family lunch today."

"Lunch?" Jon choked back a laugh. "Holy hell. You better make sure to eat something before you go, just in case."

I flipped him off. "Very funny. How bad can it be?"

Jon shook his head. "My lips are sealed."

I wound the window down to let a bit of air in and pulled my T-shirt up to wipe my brow. "You know I love this town, but it's like living under a damn microscope. I'd kind of hoped to keep everything quiet until I knew I wasn't going to screw things up."

Jon laughed. "You know damn well you've got two chances of keeping anything quiet in our town: zero and none at all. Besides I can't imagine you screwing things up. You've a hell of a lot more relationship experience under your belt than Judah has. If I was worried about anyone, it would be him. There's a lot of reasons that man might want the friendship of someone like you while his world's crashing."

I gave a derisive snort. "And that just shows how much you *don't* know about him. Until yesterday, I'd only met Judah twice, and both times had my balls handed to me for being an idiot."

Jon's eyebrows hit his hairline. "Really?"

"Really. Judah has more intuitive smarts than you think," I pointed out. "And he's none too shy about using them."

A twinkle lit up Jon's grey eyes. "Then I'm gonna have to re-evaluate my opinion of him, the fact of which makes me very, very happy. You need an equal, Morgan—someone to challenge your tendency to settle for less than spectacular in your life. It was something Sally was particularly good at from what you've told me."

It was, and my heart squeezed at the memory.

Jon's expression grew serious. "And if Judah has some of that in him, that's a damn good thing. So I hope you're not feeling guilty about giving things a go between you. There's no right time to try again. It is what it is. Five months or five years, only you can know. Plus, you're allowed to make a mistake, or to just want a good time, or some company. Do you think Sally would approve?"

"Of a gorgeous guy ten years my junior, kicking my arse and throwing my world into chaos? Hell yeah, she'd approve. In fact, I'm damn sure she's had a hand in the whole thing."

He nodded. "Then what are you worried about?"

Nothing. Everything. Judah turning out to not be what I hoped for. Judah turning out to be everything I hoped for. "I just don't want to make things more difficult for him. We're very different people and he's not in a great space."

Jon tut-tutted. "He's a man, as you so observantly pointed out. So, how about you let him make those decisions for himself."

I punched him lightly on the arm. "Look at you, all grown-up and shit. I guess that's what happens when you get to forty. That and your nuts shrivel up under your ribcage—" I ducked as his empty water bottle sailed past my head into the back seat and then threw up my arm. "Shit, stop, stop. There they are."

Jon spun back around to the windscreen to watch the brothers amble down the villa's driveway to meet a dark blue BMW X7.

"Nice car. Let's see if we know the driver." Jon reached for his binoculars and took a look while I got a couple of photos of the vehicle, its licence plate, and the brothers. The driver slid out of the front seat and proceeded to lean against the car as they talked. He was dressed in expensive-looking clothes with a pair of sunglasses pushed up on his head, relaxed, friendly.

"He looks familiar." Jon handed me the binoculars and grabbed his phone.

"Well it's not the third man from the boat, I can tell you that much," I said.

"I know I've seen him, dammit." Jon ground his teeth. "Call out that plate."

He punched it into his police laptop and waited while it ran. Meanwhile, the conversation looked to be wrapping up.

"He's leaving," I warned Jon. "What do you want to do?"

"Got him! Let's follow for a bit." He shoved the laptop into my hands and pulled out after the BMW, keeping a good distance. "His name is Leo Haversham. His photo and file came through as a person of interest a while back, that's why I recognised him."

The penny dropped. "Jesus, I know that name."

Jon passed a slow car to keep within visual of the BMW but still three cars back. "That makes sense. He's thirty-nine and owns several tourist operations in Northland, including running chartered fishing trips. No record as such, but there's a flag on him regarding possible gang connections and also organised poaching. Nothing concrete."

I threw my head back and groaned. "Shit. I must be getting old. The name's somewhere on my watch list, but he looks like he's too far up the chain for me to run into him directly." My brain buzzed. "What's he doing slumming it with these guys?. Can't see them as best mates."

"Me neither. Let's see where he goes."

The BMW pottered along in no hurry, stopping at a liquor outlet for a dozen beers before skirting the harbour, all the way around to Mangarei point where he pulled into a gated beachfront property with a long cypress-lined driveway.

Jon gave a low whistle. "Nice car, nice house. And it's his, according to the file."

I took a few more photos as we passed, then Jon turned us around and headed back.

"So what now?" I asked.

"Let's do a bit more digging with our bosses, and we'll both keep an eye out for that boat again. But right now"—he had a grin from ear to ear—"I'm gonna make sure you get back in time for your lunch date."

"Gee, thanks." I wanted to slap him.

CHAPTER TEN

Morgan

I'd been to the Madden home a few times collecting Leroy for rugby or on fisheries business, but I'd never had the grand tour. The 1860s house was gorgeous. Not flashy, just warm and inviting in that graceful but world-worn way, and bubbling with history.

With generous hallways and a maze of interconnecting rooms, it had wide honey-coloured planked flooring worn smooth with age, matching creaking doors—each the weight of a small country—towering twelve-foot ceilings, and broad sash windows some of which were tall enough to walk through onto a broad veranda that took in all the splendour of pocket-sized Painted Bay. Judah's boathouse sat to one side, it's windows and deck hidden from view.

Previous renovations added new bathrooms, a bright modern kitchen in pale cream and moss, and much-needed insulation and gas heating, leaving the open fires for ambience alone. Furnishing were nineties country comfort, a little dated but in keeping with the feel. And the walls of the open-style country kitchen were littered with dozens of family photos, including a lot of Judah on stage. The whole place smelled of floor wax, Cora's ever-present Jasmine perfume, a little sadness, and a whole lot of love . . . and lunch, whatever that was.

A huge plate of some kind of meat sat in the centre of the massive farmhouse table directly in front of me, alongside a casserole of what looked like pumpkin, a pale puffy soufflé thingy that eluded definition, a mix of peas and beans and broccoli that I could at least identify and which looked pretty safe, and a final dish that had me completely stumped.

I took a deep breath. It probably wasn't going to kill me, right?

Family and friends had survived years of this, so that had to mean something. Then again, maybe they'd developed a herd immunity. While Cora collected the last of the condiments and conversation sparked around the table, I swallowed hard and focussed on the meat. Not much you could do wrong with a roast, right? But staring at it wasn't going to get me any closer to establishing exactly what meat we were talking about, though I was placing odds on chicken, judging by the colour. But I wasn't about to put money on it.

A set of toes nudged my shin and I glanced up to find Judah smirking from across the table, eyes afire with mischief. We'd arrived fifteen minutes late as it was, ten of those consumed by a sizzling make-out session in his boathouse. An armful of sexy, writhing, and horny ballet dancer wasn't something to turn your nose up at, and I didn't. But getting out of there on time quickly became a lost cause. Call me a martyr.

Judah had been in a strange mood though—thoughtful, maybe even anxious, but also happy at the same time, and unwilling to talk about any of it. Maybe it was simply a little unsureness about this new thing between us, but I'd also noticed a wealth of shared looks pass between him and his mother, so who knew?

"Guests first." Judah handed me the serving tongs and slouched down in his seat with a smirk on his face. *Cheeky shit.* Then, as I put some food on my plate, that same foot tracked up the inside of my leg to brush against my cock, and I had an entirely different set of prob-lems to deal with.

Setting the tongs on the serving platter, I took my napkin from under my plate and calmly spread it across my lap while discreetly giving his big toe a solid wrench to the right. He shot up in his seat with a grunt of pain and I flashed him a steely glare. He responded by taking his lower lip between his teeth, looking for all the world like he was a whisper away from throwing me over the table and eating me for lunch instead. In any other circumstances I'd have been pretty much down with the idea, but popping a boner in front of his whole family and friends was definitely *not* on my to-do list for the day.

Terry choked back a laugh. *Damn.* Then I clocked Leroy watching from the far end of the table with a distinctly pinched and disapproving look on his face, and I realised if Jon was privy to the town gossip hotline, then Leroy had to have heard as well. And that wasn't even taking Judah's mother into account.

Fuck.

Not that it was any of Leroy's business, but Judah was likely to catch the brunt of it if Leroy didn't approve, and judging by the bile in his expression, he didn't. Not to mention Leroy was a friend and teammate of mine. Regardless of that, I narrowed my gaze to let him know he was out of line and ignored the way his jaw twitched, hopeful the full table would keep him in check and the conversation light.

Besides Leroy, Cora, Judah, and myself, there was Martha, Patrick, Terry, Hannah, and Martha's son, Fox—all gathered around the huge table.

No one seemed to have met Martha's son before, other than Cora, and all I'd gleaned so far was that he was a fisherman living on Stewart Island, as far south as you could get in New Zealand before hitting Antarctica. A tall man with dark, intense eyes, handsome features, and a brooding presence, he'd been working his boat in the depths of the Southern Ocean for ten years, was in the middle of a break-up, and was visiting to decide if he wanted to move his business north.

All of that had come from Martha, as the man himself had said about three words since he'd arrived. But whatever those three words were, they seemed to have instantly got Leroy's back up, and he'd spent the last forty minutes shooting daggers at the visitor.

Patrick, on the other hand, seemed barely able to drag his eyes away from Fox, and not for the first time I wondered about Cora's employee. A small, wiry young man from somewhere up north of Kaitaia, he'd arrived in Painted Bay a couple of years back. Cora had taken him on and made him one of her special projects as she was wont to do with the local strays. It was one of the things I loved about her.

"Are you waiting for a gilded invitation?" Judah's grin turned wicked as he nodded at the remaining plates of food I'd yet to touch.

I narrowed my eyes. "Just contemplating which delicious dish to start with."

Martha choked on a mouthful of bread and Terry looked like he was going to wet himself.

"Dig in, dear," Cora said to me as she took her seat next to Martha and patted her friend on the back. "You okay, Matty?"

Matty? In five years, I'd never heard Martha called by that nickname, and I noticed Fox too seemed startled.

"I'm fine." Martha squeezed Cora's hand, then fired a warning glance Judah's way.

He immediately blushed and I took the opportunity to send him a shit-eating grin which earned me a deeply satisfying scowl.

Cora raised her glass of rosé. "I found a couple of new recipes so today's a bit of an experiment."

Judah booted me under the table and I jumped.

"I do hope you enjoy it. To friends old and new, and bon appétit." She winked directly at me, and I knew in that moment from the smile on her face that she knew exactly what everyone thought of her cooking. I had to admire her fuck-'em attitude and so I winked back.

Leroy continued to glower, sharing his bad temper equally between Fox and me. *Whatever*. Then I glanced across to find Judah sat back in his chair simply smiling at me. Something instantly lit up in my chest and I realised his opinion was the only one that mattered.

He tipped his glass my way and I did the same. Then I helped myself to the other platters, taking enough to be polite without leaving myself a problem if any of it proved challenging, and we were soon all eating and chatting as if there wasn't this odd unnamed elephant or two in the room taking up oxygen.

I started with the mysterious soufflé, and by the end of the meal, I'd gotten through most of my plate and even gone back for a couple of things. The meat had turned out to be snapper, go figure, with some creamy sauce that wasn't inedible as such, but if you scraped it completely to the side, the fish under it was actually pretty good.

The pumpkin turned out to be potato in an orange curry sauce and the less said about that the better. The green veges were . . . well, green veges and nothing unexpected, which was a good thing overall. Something which couldn't be said for the soufflé. Beginning with that particular dish had been a grave error in judgement, which almost saw me doomed before I started, the ingredients remaining a mystery.

"I don't know what went wrong." Cora prodded at her own portion, which made me feel somewhat better. "There must've been a mistake in the recipe."

Martha patted her hand. "I'm sure you're right. But the fish was lovely."

"Here, here." Terry raised his glass in another toast, which everyone joined.

"It was yummy," Hannah piped up. She'd squirmed on her chair all through lunch and I wondered if her knees were giving her problems.

Cora sent her a shining smile. "And that's why you're my favourite girl and get to have two slices of dessert."

Judah pouted. "I thought I was your favourite girl?"

Leroy groaned and rolled his eyes, and I wanted to slap him.

Hannah didn't miss a beat. "You're a boy, silly. Even if you do wear makeup."

Judah slid me a sly smile. He'd put a lot of effort into his makeup today and it had been the first thing I'd noticed. One look and I'd made it a mission to de-gloss those lips in world record time. Hence the whole running late thing.

"I *am* a boy, you're right. And I think maybe you like my make-up." It was said for Hannah, but Judah's bright hazel eyes were fixed firmly on me and every nerve in my body sizzled in response.

"I love it," Hannah said cheerfully.

Judah leaned past Terry to ruffle her hair. "Thank you, pumpkin."

"How's school?" Cora asked.

Hannah glanced up at her father before she answered. "I'm helping with the school talent show next month."

"Oh, that's wonderful." Cora clapped her hands. "Can I come and watch? What are you going to perform?"

Hannah pushed nervously at her plate. "I'm not actually entering. I'm just helping other people with stuff."

Cora's gaze flicked to Terry, who shrugged. "They encouraged her but she said no."

Cora's brows knit together. "Oh, honey. I'd love to see you on stage."

Hannah stared at the table in front of her. "I can't walk right and I'll probably have to wear a stupid brace by then, won't I, Dad?"

Terry took Hannah's hand and kissed the back of it. "We don't know that for sure, but yes, maybe. You could still do something though."

My heart squeezed and I saw Judah watching closely, knowing exactly what was running through his brain. As if he felt my gaze, he glanced over and we locked eyes for a moment.

"Everyone will just stare." Hannah fiddled with her dessert spoon.

"I kind of think that's the idea of a talent show," Judah said quietly.

"They'll look because you're beautiful." Patrick eyed Hannah with a fierce look. "And I'd sit right up front, clapping."

"Me too, honey bee," Martha piped up. "We all would."

"Maybe you should ask Judah to help you," Leroy butted in from the end of the table. "He knows all about performing. Be good to see what we got for all that investment."

Motherfucker.

Everyone froze, including Judah, whose face paled. I held my breath. Oh yeah, Leroy and I were going to have a talk.

"Leroy!" Cora censured her son, her face white as a sheet. Martha grabbed her hand and shot Leroy a furious look. He had the decency to drop his eyes and appear a bit shamefaced, but not nearly enough to get him off my shit list.

"Would you help me?" Hannah's eyes went wide on Judah, completely missing the undercurrent in the room.

"Hannah." Terry put an arm around his daughter. "We talked about this—"

Her bottom lip trembled and I could have killed Leroy then and there, as could Terry and most of the rest of the table, if the angry looks being fired Leroy's way were anything to go by. What the fuck was wrong with him?

"Remember Judah hasn't been well," Terry explained to Hannah.

Hannah's eyes brimmed. "I know. I just . . ." She sighed and looked past her father. "I'm sorry, Judah."

Judah almost caved in on himself and I couldn't help but reach across the table for his hand. Six pairs of eyes followed, but I had less than a fuck to give. Someone needed to acknowledge what had just happened. Leroy had his head way up his own arse, and although Cora was trying, Judah was keeping his mother at arm's length. Well, that shit wouldn't fly with me. Judah was going to have to get used to support if he wanted us to have a genuine shot at something together.

He let me thread our fingers together—a surprise all around, seemingly also to his mother, whose eyes nearly popped out of her head.

"How about you let me think about it, okay, munchkin?" he said

Her expression brightened. "Would you?"

Judah nodded and squeezed my hand. It was a huge moment and I was so fucking proud of him.

Terry sent him an apologetic but grateful smile. "Thanks, mate."

"No problem." Judah turned and fired a decidedly stony look Leroy's way, which left no one in any doubt that trouble was brewing, big sibling trouble.

Martha broke the awkward silence that followed. "Right, I need a volunteer to clear the plates and then I'll get the dessert that *I* made with two helpings for Hannah, I believe."

Cora turned that shining smile of hers onto Martha, and I caught Judah watching the two of them with an enigmatic smile. Something was definitely going on.

"I'll clear." Judah shot to his feet, then pulled up short, grabbing the edge of the table for balance.

"Judah?"

Our gazes locked and he gave a brief shake of his head. "I'm fine." He stacked some plates and headed for the kitchen, but even I could see he was a bit wobbly.

Leroy gave his brother the once over, sighed, and got to his feet. "Sit down. I'll do it."

"Get out of my way, Leroy." Judah stepped around his brother, keeping his back to me.

Leroy moved to block him. "Why do you have to be such an arsehole? I'm only trying to help. Isn't that what I'm *supposed* to do?"

"Leroy, stop it." Martha sprang to her feet, her hand on Cora's shoulder to keep her sitting.

I didn't have to see Judah's face to know how supremely pissed off he was. It was clear by the stiff set of his shoulders and the way he almost vibrated with fury. I was about to intervene when Fox pushed his chair back and stormed across, a thunderous look on his face.

"Step aside, both of you. I'll do it. It's *my* mother's dessert, after all."

"I'll help." Patrick appeared at Fox's side and took the plates from Judah's hands.

Leroy looked from one to the other, his eyes lingering on Fox. He appeared about to argue, then gave a grunt and headed back to the table, his shoulder deliberately catching Judah's as he passed.

It took all I had not to get up and shove the insensitive prick outside for a quiet word. It was a side of Leroy I'd never seen and I didn't much like it. But when he sat and glanced my way, I swore I caught a brief flash of dismay in his eyes. I shook my head and looked away.

Cora stared at her eldest son, her lips a thin line, but Leroy was avoiding her eyes like the plague. Martha leaned in and said something to Cora, too soft for the rest of us to hear, and Cora breathed out a sigh.

Holy shit. Gotta love families. Not quite the lunch I'd expected.

Thankfully things settled after that and dessert was finished on almost friendly terms, mostly because Leroy didn't say another word. Terry, Hannah, and Patrick headed off the moment the dishes were done. Soon after, Cora steered Leroy outside—no surprise there—at which point Judah bustled us out of there with haste verging on rudeness, leaving Fox and his mother to hold the fort.

As soon as we were hidden from direct view of the house, I found myself flattened against the driver's door of the Hilux while Judah groped me shamelessly.

"Your place, now." He breathed the words against my lips in between fucking my mouth with his tongue and unbuttoning my jeans with lightning speed to wrap a hand around my surprised but eager cock. The man had moves.

"Jesus, Judah." My knees trembled as he gave me a couple of firm strokes, bringing his thumb up and over the head to dip into the slit.

"Look at you." He nibbled down my neck to bite my shoulder through my shirt. "You're already leaking like a fucking sieve for me."

Then he plunged that tongue right back where it belonged and I was glad for the door at my back to hold me up.

I deserved a fucking gold medal for having the presence of mind to remember his earlier wobble and pull back enough to look him in the eye. "Hang on. You sure you're okay?"

"No," he deadpanned, that beauty spot on his right cheek twitching. "I thought I'd just get us both worked up for nothing. Here, you wanna check?" And without blinking an eye, he unzipped his jeans and let his cock spring free, commando, commando and very—*damn* —uncut. Christ on a bicycle. I shouldn't have been as excited as I was, but I'd never been with an uncut guy, and Lord, Judah was beautiful. Saliva pooled in my mouth and I itched to touch him, suck him, anything that got me closer.

My fingers were already on the hunt when I suddenly remembered where we were and jolted back. "We can't. Your mum . . . the others—"

"Relax." He pressed a kiss to my cheek and whispered, "No one can see us here. Besides we're just fooling around. Your virtue's safe with me."

My gaze dropped to his cock jutting from his unzipped jeans. "I highly doubt that."

He dipped a finger under my chin and raised it till our eyes met. "So, now that you have the answer to your burning question on the state of my foreskin, how about a personal introduction?" He slid his thumb over the head of his cock and slipped it into my mouth.

I closed my lips and sucked it dry, nearly coming in my fucking jeans as his pupils blew wide.

"Yeah, now we're talking." He cradled my face and looked me in the eye. "I need this, Morgan. I need to feel more than Leroy's pity. More than an awkward problem. I need to feel strong, desired. And I want to feel that with you. If you want the same thing, that is?"

He stepped in and covered my mouth with his own, our exposed dicks shaking hands and making friends in the process, as he circled my waist with his arms and pulled me close, groaning into my mouth like I was everything he'd ever dreamed of. I could only hope because, Jesus, the man was sexy, and for a second, I panicked. I might've been ten years older but I had limited experience with men, and I didn't want to disappoint him.

Don't be an idiot. I tried not to think of that as Sally's voice because that was too damn creepy.

But Judah must've sensed my hesitation because he pulled off and rested his forehead against mine. "Hey, if you're not into it right now, I'll under—"

Shit. "I am. I'm just being ridiculous."

Judah's hips continued to move against mine, rubbing our dicks together in a delicious tease.

"I'm gonna come if you don't stop that," I warned.

"And that's a problem because . . . ?" He pressed his cheek against mine and hummed contentedly, still rocking those hips and pushing me closer and closer to the edge. "You feel so good."

A few seconds more and—

The front door slammed on the other side of the Hilux and jolted me back to reality. A swift check confirmed my fears. Leroy, his face a study in fury.

"Fuck." I pushed Judah away, and when he didn't immediately leap into action, I did it for him, desperately shoving his dick back in his pants, but yeah, big arse peg into small hole—never gonna happen without surgery. So, I pulled his shirt over top as Plan B and jammed the empty wine bag into his hand to cover his still gloriously bouncing hard-on while I tried to deal with my own conundrum.

Judah watched it all with an amused grin on his face that needed wiping off with my hand, or maybe my lips, possibly even my dick, it was a close call.

He laughed. "I take it we're in a hurry?"

"Arsehole. It's your fucking brother."

He turned to look over his shoulder as Leroy came into view. "Fuck him." But his expression was less dismissive. He glanced back at the house, again at his brother heading to his car, and then back to me. "I think I know what that's about and it isn't us. But I'm not inclined to pander to his sensibilities regardless. He was a dick today."

"Do you need to check on your mother?" I'd finally managed to jam my dick somewhat inside my jeans and get the zip up halfway.

Judah hesitated. "Nah, I'll do it later. Martha and Fox are there. I'll give her some time. Leroy can go to hell."

I blew out a sigh. "Unfortunately, I have to play rugby with the man, and I'd rather not have him catch our dicks playing peekaboo if I can avoid it. So get in the damn car, Judah. I want you naked and in my fucking bed, the sooner the better."

His eyes widened in surprise. "Well, why didn't you say so?" He sauntered ever so fucking leisurely around the back of the car, flipped off his brother who was shooting daggers our way, and got in the passenger seat. All slow as fucking treacle.

My list of conversational bullet points with the sultry man were growing by the minute.

CHAPTER ELEVEN

Judah

"Can you give me just an inch of wiggle room to get my damn key in the lock? Or we'll be out here all day," Morgan grumbled as I crowded him against his back door from behind, my hands running up his thighs and around to the bulge in his jeans, eliciting another sexy rumble from the back of his throat. With only a few inches between us height-wise, we were a good fit, the hard ridge of my cock snuggled nicely up against his crease as I gave another nudge.

"Fuck." The keys hit the deck for the second time. "You did that deliberately."

The delicious push back on my groin when he bent to pick them up and the shudder that ran through him when I slipped a hand between his thighs and palmed his dick through his jeans had me desperate to get him naked.

"Now why on earth would I do that?" I whispered against the back of his neck. That I'd managed to keep my hands off him until we got to the car was a fucking miracle as it was. Halfway through dessert, watching him tease me with Martha's chocolate pie smeared all over his damn lips, I'd given serious thought to breaking my rule about fucking in my mother's bathroom. It would've been the first time since I'd been sixteen, and seventeen-year-old Daniel Frobisher had thought for a half-second that he might be gay and asked me to blow him while his mother visited mine two rooms away while I was home for the holidays.

In my defence, I'd had only one dick down my throat at that point, and with a limited number of local opportunities, I leapt at the chance to double the count. Daniel got off in a disappointing minute or so, decided he wasn't gay after all, and left me hanging. He did, however, stop with the crappy name-calling whenever he saw me that summer, which counted as a not insignificant win on my part. That and I got my first genuine full swallow of the goods without a gag in sight. All up, not a bad payoff.

As for sexy Mr Wipene? I'd been getting increasingly antsy sat across from the man who was acting all buttoned-up and well-mannered in front of my family and friends, as if butter wouldn't melt in his hot little mouth. From the minute he'd picked me up at the boathouse, I'd been itching to take him apart one very proper button at a time and lay eyes on all that promising hair peeking out from those dreary clothes.

Good God, the man needed to be taken in hand and then to a store other than CamouflageRUs. So, if he thought I was going to be happy to simply stand back while he took his own good time riling me up, he had another think coming.

With the keys back in his hand, Morgan spun to face me, clamping his hands on my shoulders and pushing me back to arms distance.

I leaned against his hold, licking my lips. "I want you and I won't be kept waiting. You've been a fucking tease all day."

His pupils flared as he stuttered out a sigh. "Jesus, Judah. I'm gonna embarrass myself on my own back-door step in about thirty seconds if you don't give me some room. And I don't want that, not with you, not this first time. Quick and dirty with men is all I've known. I want this, us, to be different. And I want . . . you inside me when I come." His gaze travelled all over before landing on mine. "Please."

The words stopped me in my tracks. *I want this, us, to be different. Us.* And it hit me like a ton of bricks. The idea of *us* meant something to Morgan. I wasn't a quick fuck. Not simply a warm, young body in a bed. How long had it been since I'd felt like I was something special? Regardless of what I'd felt for Grant, I'd always known he didn't feel the same. Morgan and I barely knew each other, and he'd lost a woman he truly loved, but in this moment, there was nothing in his eyes other than his desire for me, all of me, battered and messy, he didn't seem to care.

My heart swelled and threatened to jump out of my throat.

I cupped his cheek gently. "I want that too. More than you know." I kept my gaze steady on his. "But if you don't get that door open in the next ten seconds, I won't be held responsible." I stepped back. "The clock's on."

He spun, jammed the key in the lock, threw the door open, grabbed my hand, and hauled me into the kitchen. "See, teamwork." He kissed me hard, then waved a hand toward the lounge. "Down the hall and to the left. Make yourself at home. Give me a few minutes to um . . . sort some stuff." He blushed furiously.

My brows bumped. "We don't have to go that—"

"Yes. Yes, we do." Morgan's eyes twinkled. "As long as you still want to. I haven't forgotten your promise."

I stepped into his space. "And I intend to keep it." My hands slid under his shirt and over the heat of that long, long back. His skin pebbled under my touch and a shudder ran through him as his lips found my neck, nuzzling a path along my jaw to my mouth before sinking his tongue over mine.

We made out lazily—tasting, nipping, licking—finding the hot points, the give and take of control, the smooth run of my mouth over the bristle of his beard; his lips on my eyelids, my cheeks, my ears;

teeth at my jaw, my throat. Amping up, pressing the limits. *Fuck.* It was so damn sexy.

Good God, I needed him naked, and I needed inside him like yesterday. I yearned for the taste of his spill, of his hidden places. The rough of all that hair under my hands. The wrap of his arse around my cock. The squeeze. The sounds he'd make when he came, when he couldn't bear it any longer. And I wanted the feel of his hands on me, his lips, his mouth on my cock, his fingers up my arse—*son of a bitch*—

"Stop." I stepped back, breathing hard as I palmed my cock and squeezed hard.

Fuck. Fuck. Fuck.

Morgan's turn to smile and waggle his eyebrows. "I'll, um, go do my thing then, shall I? Supplies are in the bedside drawer."

I narrowed my gaze. "Yeah, you do that. Tout suite, mister. I'll find my way. And don't be too long. I'll enjoy you any way I have you."

Morgan's brown eyes gleamed in the afternoon sunlight that split the small kitchen in two. "No clippers required then?"

I studied him for a long minute, then undid the buttons of his shirt and peeked inside before spreading the opening and shoving my whole damn face against all that beautiful dark hair. I rubbed my cheeks back and forth, inhaling deeply as I drank in the feel of him, delicious, but not nearly enough. Full, soft, and so fucking sexy. I trailed my tongue from his sternum to a nipple and drew it into my mouth.

Fingers threaded through my hair and he rumbled somewhere deep in his chest, the hum of it going straight to my dick. I popped off and took a shaky step back.

"No, definitely no clippers. Now skit." I waved a hand in dismissal. "I want my dick to tickle your tonsils from the bottom up."

He laughed and slapped my butt as he walked by. "Counting on it."

I watched him leave, every bunch and stretch of that scrumptious rear end, until it disappeared from view. Then I pulled out my phone and shot off a quick text to my mother to see how things had gone with Leroy. A few seconds later I got a reply.

Could've been better. Could've been worse. Fox is fine. Talk tomorrow.

Damn. Not like it wasn't expected, but I felt for her. Coming out was a bitch no matter how you looked at it. The fact we had to do it at all was a disappointing mindfuck, and I wanted to kill my brother for making it that much more difficult for our mother. I'd have a hug ready when I saw her, but right now I had other irons in the fire.

I took a minute to scope out Morgan's kitchen, not surprised to find it well stocked with an overflowing spice rack, a seriously equipped knife block, a pot rack suspended from the ceiling, and a butcher block chopping board that likely cost a week's wages. And through the window in the back yard—a vegetable garden the size of Manhattan. The man could obviously cook more than an omelette.

The sound of running water had me wandering into the lounge, determined to get a feel for the guy who was making such a serious and unexpected dent in my heart. But the reality brought me to a complete stop.

Instead of the functional, masculine retreat of a rugby playing, fisheries law enforcement officer, complete with obligatory large screen TV, brown furniture, and well-stocked bar that I'd expected, I found warm pastels, overstuffed sofas, colourful throws, and not a TV in sight. Instead, a massive bookcase filled one entire wall and a guitar sat on a stand in the corner.

I shouldn't have been as surprised as I was. Morgan Wipene was adept at the unexpected.

My hand trailed over the books as I passed—murder mysteries, paranormal, adventure, thrillers, anything and everything, not to mention an impressive array of gardening books. I smiled to myself. Another surprise.

I let my nose lead me down the hall, passing a selection of photos featuring Morgan and what looked like his parents, and maybe his brother and sister. I went back to switch on the light so I could better study them. They seemed a happy family, his dad looking the larger-than-life character Morgan had painted him as. I kept moving down the hall till I got to what looked like Morgan's bedroom and came to an abrupt halt in front of a half dozen photos of Morgan with a very beautiful young woman. This had to be the famous Sally.

My heart squeezed and something very like fear curdled in my belly. In every photo, Morgan stared at his wife like she hung the moon, thoroughly and unapologetically in love. I ran a finger over her image in one of the two of them standing on some tropical beach. Her head was thrown back laughing at something he'd said, and Morgan looked like he wanted to drink her up. I was damn sure no one had *ever* looked at me that way, and for the first time, I felt very . . . young, and very much *not* together. What the hell did Morgan see in me when he'd had someone like her?

An arm slid around my waist from behind and Morgan nuzzled my neck.

"She was beautiful," I said. "You must miss her. I can't imagine what that feels like."

He looked over my shoulder at the photo and blew out a long sigh. "She was. And I do." He turned me in his arms, backed me against the wall, and looked hard into my eyes.

I wasn't sure I liked the idea of what he'd find, but then again, as I'd just realised, he was naked—gloriously and deliciously naked, and I wasn't going anywhere. Clearly Morgan wasn't shy of his body, so I let him look all he wanted while I arched against him, the solid, thick heat of his erection lying flush against my hip. He pressed back and took my mouth in a hard kiss, then went back to studying me. In the end, I couldn't hold his gaze.

"Look at me, Judah."

And so I did.

"Sally was beautiful, yes. But she's also gone, five years now. I miss her and a part of me always will. But right now I'm with *you*, and I *want* to be with you. I'm not standing here thinking of Sally.

I'm not wracked with guilt or second-guessing myself. That might come, but I don't think so. Right now I'm thinking of *you*—about how beautiful *you* are, about what I want to do to *you*, and Lord help me, about what I want you to do to *me*. There's not going to be anyone in that bed except you and me. Understand?"

I nodded, trying to believe he meant it.

Then he laughed. "Although to be honest, I think Sally would give up her damn angel wings for a grandstand seat. She was always more . . . uninhibited that way than me."

My mouth fell open. "Wait. Did you guys . . . I mean, did she . . . ?"

He chuckled. "Never. I don't share, Judah, just so we're clear about that. And when I was with Sally, I never wanted anyone else. Though we watched a lot of gay porn together."

I wasn't sure why my cheeks lit on fire, but they did. "Oh, um, yeah. I guess I get that. Women, huh? You never know what's going on in their heads."

"Mmm." Morgan dipped his head to trail his lips from under my chin to the hollow in the base of my neck. "Now, can we stop talking about my wife please?" His breath ran hot over my skin as his tongue licked beneath the neckline of my T-shirt and his fingers found my nipple.

And, oh god. My head hit the wall as he rolled and lightly pinched it, my cock throbbing in my half-undone jeans.

"I'm kind of keen to move this along." He kissed back up my neck. "To the part where you fuck me to the back of my tonsils." He pulled back and sent me a challenging look. "I believe that's what you said."

A filthy groan fell out of my mouth as he tweaked my nipple, and yeah, that was new.

"And can we please do something about these fucking clothes?" He stepped back and pulled at my shirt.

And with the light on the front of his body for the first time, I finally saw it. *Holy shit.* My breath caught in my throat and I batted his hand aside. "Get in that room."

I shoved his naked arse into the bedroom directly under the light and then knelt on the bed for a closer look at his shoulder. "Come here, mister."

He did, wearing a sly smirk.

"And you can wipe that smile off your face. You never once mentioned *this.*" I ran my hands over the massive and intricate tattoo of a black octopus draped over Morgan's right shoulder. "Turn around."

The tentacles ran halfway down his back and over his bicep, while one licked down the front to his pecs. It explained the hint of ink I'd seen that one day, but I'd never imagined this. The work was detailed, beautiful, and so damn remarkable. Even more so because it appeared to be the only ink Morgan had.

"'I *like* octopus,' the man said," I muttered as I ran my hand over the exquisite design. "Kind of an understatement, wasn't it?"

He shrugged. "Does that mean you like it?"

I licked a swathe up the length of the beautiful creature, feeling the brush of all that soft hair over my tongue, all the way to Morgan's lips till we were nose to nose. "Oh, yeah, I definitely like. Now take my clothes off before I incinerate where I stand." I grabbed his hand and put it on my aching cock.

He had me out of my jeans and T-shirt in a blink of an eye, while I couldn't take my eyes off that damn tattoo. Between that, the fact I hadn't been laid in close to forever, and the ripple of muscle on his body as he worked, I had some serious control issues going on. He was fit, not ripped or tough, but firm, with just a soft edge of age around his waist that only made me want to sink against him and wrap myself in his arms. In. All. That. Hair. But when I went to pull him onto the bed to do just that, he shoved my hands away.

I raised an impatient eyebrow. "What now?"

"You can do what you want to me . . . soon." His serious expression was kind of adorable. "But since I suspect once you get your hands on me, I won't want you to stop; I've been waiting too long to not get a taste of you first."

Before I could answer, he took a hold of my cock and stroked it firmly, watching with fascination as the foreskin travelled up and over the engorged, red head with each pass.

"You are so beautiful." He leaned in and pressed a kiss to the dripping slit, keeping his head angled so I could watch. And I did, laser focussed, entranced as his tongue swiped at the beading moisture and then rested in place on the slit as he jacked the foreskin up and over, the tip of his tongue disappearing beneath. I'd never seen anything so fucking hot.

Holy smokes. I sank my hands into his hair to keep his head where I could watch, feeling my balls tighten with each pass. Then he pulled free of my grasp and swallowed me down to the root. My knees damn near buckled as he went to town.

For a man who hadn't had many male lovers, Morgan gave head like a champ. If it wasn't for the core strength I'd built over all those years dancing, he'd have sucked me right off the bed.

"Jesus Christ." I pushed him off. "On your knees." He sank like a stone and waited as I jumped from the bed to stand in front of him. *Damn.* It was like the best present ever. "So fucking gorgeous." I ran my thumb around his mouth and dipped inside. He suckled on it, eyes locked on mine. I lifted it to my mouth and sucked it dry. He groaned and reached for his cock. A deep brown, it sat long and thick, nestled in a rich tangle of dark hair at its root, a pair of heavy balls hanging low beneath.

I was sorely tempted to switch things around so I could feel the width of it stretch my arse, but that was for another night. Tonight I wanted to give Morgan what he asked for. I wanted him to have that. He was a freaking wet dream, *my* wet dream, and he deserved to be looked after.

"Open up."

He did and fuck, what a sight. Kneeling in front of me, waiting to take my dick, wanting that, wanting me, wanting all of it.

I grabbed my cock and tapped it against his lips, smearing the pre-come from one side to the other. Then I bent down and licked every scrap of it off, jerking myself while he watched, a strangled groan falling from his lips.

I stepped in and fed it to him in one smooth slide. I wasn't as long or as wide as he was, but that was in my favour. He took every centimetre with barely a flinch. And then he waited.

My fingers forked through his hair. "You want me to fuck your mouth, baby?"

He nodded.

Goddamn. I wrapped both hands around his head and thrust gently, testing his limits. But when his hands dug into the back of my thighs and jerked me forward, it was all on, and my hips snapped in rhythm. I loved it long and slow rather than hard and fast, and Morgan cottoned on quick, clamping down on the suction when I withdrew, prolonging the agony of restraint, and frying every nerve in my body along the way.

Then he slid a finger into his mouth alongside my shaft, and the next thing I knew, it was in my arse.

"Fuuuuuck!" I snapped hard into his mouth and his finger slipped higher and crooked to— "Jesus Christ." I jumped back and slid free of his finger and his mouth before I lost my load down the back of his throat.

He wiped his dripping mouth with the back off his hand and got to his feet.

"Come here." I pulled him into a hard kiss, sweeping the taste of me from his mouth onto my tongue. Then I pushed him to the bed and climbed on top to straddle his hips.

"Where the fuck did you learn to suck dick like that?" I rutted up against his stomach. "If that's what you're like after only a few hook-ups, I'll be done for in a month, a wizened husk of the man you see today, my entire brain sucked out through my dick."

He laughed as he reached for the bedside drawer. "I'm obviously a quick learner. Or maybe it's natural talent." He threw lube and condoms next to the pillow, then closed the drawer, but not before I spied a smallish dildo, a cock ring, and a butt plug tucked inside. *Huh.*

I waggled my eyebrows at him.

His neck flushed bright red. Fucking adorable.

I leaned over to nibble at his lip, putting my arse high in the air. "I'd like to give the contents of that drawer a test run at some stage in the future, if you're game for some play?"

He took a sharp breath and gave a single nod, his hands finding the run of my back. I shivered at the lightness of his touch, his nails just catching my skin, painting long lines from my shoulders to my hips.

"So fucking game." He breathed the words against my lips.

I laughed and shook my head in disbelief. Who was this guy and what had happened to my nice but somewhat buttoned-up and over-bearing fisheries officer? "You, ah, use them often?"

He ran his hands over the curve of my arse and dipped his fingers into my crease. "Now and then."

"Good to know." He might not need quite the prep I'd thought.

He caught my eye at the exact time he pressed his finger inside my arse and my whole body lit up like Las Vegas. "I like just an edge of pain," he muttered, as if reading my mind while he buried his finger further.

"Argh . . . also good to know." I threw my head back in a long groan, arching my back as I fisted the sheets. He lifted his head to snag my nipple, and for a few seconds, I rocked in place, the dual sensations of him finger fucking my arse while he sucked at my nipple almost sending me over. On the cusp of no return, I arched up like a cat and slipped free of both.

I slapped his hip. "Get on your knees, sweetheart. It's my turn to play."

He'd flipped before I'd even finished the sentence, and I knee walked between his spread legs to nestle our dicks together through his open thighs. Then I draped myself over his back and wrapped my arms around his waist, letting the scorching heat of his skin soak into my chest. I was falling and I knew it. It was fucked up and wasn't going to help my hot mess of a life, but Morgan undid me in places I didn't even know I had knots—quiet, needy places that only he seemed to know existed.

"Do you have any idea how hot you are?" I kissed my way all around that stunning black octopus and followed the tentacle that ran down his back to his waist as he trembled beneath me.

"Hair and all?" He chuckled.

I tweaked a couple of tufts in my fingers to make a point. "*Especially* the hair. I love every soft, curly bit of it." I reached the top of his crease with my mouth and slipped my tongue down between his cheeks to rest on his clenched hole, pressing ever so gently.

"Holy shit!" He dropped his head to the bed, putting his arse on perfect display. "No one's ever . . . fuck . . . damn."

No one? The rush of being the first to share this particular delight with Morgan spun my head, and he groaned as my tongue lifted from his hole.

"Patience," I told him, running both hands over the full curves of his arse to get a handful of each, while my eyes drank in every inch of that bare skin spread out before me, mine for the taking, anyway I liked.

I might not be the first inside him, but I was going to make damn sure to be the best he'd had. He deserved that. He deserved to know what a gorgeous man he was on every level, and we were going to start with this.

The thought tripped me up. That I felt so strongly. That what I wanted for Morgan was more important than my own urge to get off, and yep, those alarm bells rang louder. I ignored them, rubbing my thumbs down Morgan's crease instead, pulling those cheeks wide apart so I could delve right in with my tongue.

He grunted and white-knuckled the sheets. And damn, the noises he made. Filthy, sexy curses. Demands, threats, and promises that would've made me laugh if I wasn't so busy getting my tongue as deep as I could to set off another string of them.

I loved this. Loved rimming. Loved reducing a guy to a mess of trembling flesh. But doing this with Morgan? Getting him so hot and bothered that he dropped that ever-so-reasonable, mature, sweet mask he wore, and having him needy and demanding and totally begging for it? *Shit.* That was a power trip like no other.

I pulled off and slipped in a finger, then a second, watching as Morgan rocked back and forth on them, nonsense spilling from his mouth.

With my free hand, I reached between his legs, gave his weeping cock a tug, and he leapt halfway up the bed leaving my fingers in mid-air. "Shit—too close—fuck." He grabbed his dick at the base and squeezed.

I sidled up behind and ran my hands over his shoulders as I whispered in his ear. "I'd like you on your back, if you're game. I want to see you when you come. I'll make sure it's good."

"I'm in your hands." He flipped over while I suited up. Then I slicked both of us, taking time to feel the heft of his shaft in my hand once again while I contemplated the trust he'd so readily placed in me.

He quickly slapped my hand away. "You better get that beautiful dick of yours inside me or so help me God, I'm gonna hold you down and skewer you myself."

I choked on a laugh and the cheeky fucker winked. "As tempting as that is"—I elbowed his knees apart and shoved a pillow under his hips—"and believe me, it's really fucking tempting"—his eyeballs popped a little at that, but I was up for a dicking by this man any day of the week—"I'm gonna take a hell no on that right now, but a rain check later would be just dandy."

I lifted both his legs onto my shoulders and nudged my cock into position.

He white-knuckled a wad of sheet in each hand and grinned up at me. "Bring it on, ballet boy."

Pressed tight against his hole, I nudged a little against the resistance and eyeballed him. "Oh no. You did *not* just say that." One more nudge and I was in, just, and Morgan's eyes closed and his head fell back against the pillow with a groan. I paused just in case, but he was lubed up enough for a damn slip and slide and quickly tapped my thigh.

"More."

I pressed forward slowly, watching his expression for any indication I should stop but none came. His arse was a damn furnace, gripping my cock like a vice while I barely held on by my fingernails till finally I was fully seated.

"Jesus fuck, you feel huge," he huffed, breathing through the discomfort as I waited for him to adjust.

"Yeah, well anytime soon would be great. Just saying." I forced the words out between clenched teeth. A puff of air in the wrong direction would be all it took to tip me over. "But you take your time and all."

"Just a sec." Morgan lifted his head so our eyes met. "Yeah, okay, I think we're good." He cupped my cheek and blew me a kiss. "Don't hold back. I want the full Judah Madden experience."

My lips curved up in a smile and I started a gentle stroke in and out of that tight heat, watching as the slow build of pleasure drove those beautiful brown eyes black.

He wriggled his hips to get the pressure just where he wanted it, and I picked up the pace. I didn't give a flying fuck whether I got off or not, but Morgan was going to damn well fall apart with pleasure if it was the last thing I did. I kept him on and off the boil, slowing as he dug his nails in begging for more, speeding up when he relaxed and wriggled under me, changing the angle of my thrust till I hit that spot time and time again.

He groaned and swore and lifted his legs higher, opening himself right up so I could sink that extra centimetre, his dick squeezed tight between us as we rode it together.

"Close," he grunted.

Thank God. "Fine with me."

His hand wriggled between us and pumped at his dick. Once, twice was all it took before his body arched up and his eyes rolled back in his head, sweat running off his brow as he shuddered with every wave of pleasure pulsing through him. It was fucking glorious and I was spellbound for about five seconds, stroking him through it, until my own hit. I slammed deep inside once more, and that sizzle of pleasure surfaced and exploded as I spilled and spilled.

His arms wrapped around me, holding me close as I slowly came down, jerking with each residual pulse.

"Holy shit." I melted against the slicked-down hair on his chest, covered in sweat and quivering with pleasure. "Jesus, Morgan. I think my dick's lost somewhere north of your appendix. I hope you've got a locator beacon in that bedside drawer of yours, it has just about everything else—and we are soooo having a conversation about that, by the way, once I recover my faculties."

He snorted and brushed the wet hair from my eyes. "You looked so damn beautiful getting off like that."

I lifted my head to find a contented smile on his face and a question in his eyes that likely matched my own. *What the fuck just happened?*

"Can I have an adjective please?" I teased.

He studied me for a second, his eyes dancing in amusement. "How about abso-fucking-lutely mind-blowing. You just exploded *fine* right out of the water."

"And my work here is done." I laughed, rolled to the side, and my still-purring dick slid out from all that magnificent heat. Too overwhelmed to move, I just lay there, my tinnitus far in the distance for once, my heart up front and centre.

Morgan removed my condom and threw it aside, then tucked his body next to mine with an arm over my chest as if to make sure I couldn't leave. I hadn't the slightest intention. I could barely get any words to leave my mouth let alone my feet to leave the bed. I needed everything I could get of all things Morgan, to see me through in case reality hit and he realised the mistake he'd made.

A little help here, Sally, if you have a minute? How to keep Morgan 101? The crazy thought spiralled through my head.

Talking to the dead wife of the man I'd just fucked into oblivion pretty much summed things up.

A laugh sounded somewhere in my head.

CHAPTER TWELVE

Morgan

JUDAH SNORED LIKE A RABBIT. I'D BEEN UP ON ONE ELBOW watching him sleep for about fifteen minutes, marvelling at the coordination required to twitch your nose, wrinkle your upper lip, and snuffle cutely without waking yourself.

It was charming as hell, but waking up with Judah in my arms had thrown me for a complete loop. A what-in-the-fuck-is-happening-to-my-life loop. A very similar loop to the one I'd found myself in after the epic fuck he'd given me the afternoon before, and the one following the sizzling blow jobs we'd exchanged in the shower after dinner, and even the loop after a round of lazy hand jobs we'd exchanged before falling asleep exhausted around midnight.

I hadn't slept through the night since Sally died; that wakeful grief pattern had stuck like glue. But not last night. Not after Judah. I wasn't sure I'd ever had sex like it in my life. Sally had been uninhibited and adventurous in bed, and we'd had an amazing sex life, bar rimming, which I was pretty sure she'd have regretted not trying had she realised what we were missing. But she also tired of the natural leader role she carried in everyday life and preferred me to take over in the bedroom.

Judah was an entirely different animal in bed.

His tongue in, on, or anywhere near my hole had pretty much shot to the top of my all-time favourite things to do short of having his cock in my arse. I shouldn't have been surprised. Judah even breathed sex with a capital S, and I was pretty sure I could come from his slow sexy smile alone given the right circumstances.

He had this way of sliding inside my brain with just a look, and from there it was a hop skip and a jump to my dick. I'd always felt desired with Sally, but bottoming for Judah was something entirely new. It felt like he . . . craved me, like he needed to be inside me more than he needed to breathe. Add in a working sexual appendage that knew how to bring me to my knees and I was a total convert.

To hell with topping. No denying that shit was good, but compared to the stretch and burn of being filled, a dick dragging across my prostate, and an orgasm that blew me up from the inside and then swept like a mushroom cloud from the roots of my hair to the tips of my toes, and . . . well, just call me Nelly and be done with it. How had I not known this about myself?

I pulled a lock of hair free from the corner of his mouth and lightly brushed the backs of my fingers over his cheek. He snuffled and settled, the weak morning light through the crack in the curtains striping across his bare hips and all those layers of hard, lean muscle. I ached for the audiences that would never know his body moving in those fluid ways again.

I'd woken early and left him sleeping while I searched YouTube on my phone—video after video of him dancing. Even a nobody like me could recognise his talent. Then I searched for anyone who danced professionally at that level with Meniere's—not a one. Tragedy didn't even begin to cover it.

But I did find *something*. Several articles about how the brains of ballet dancers were helping medicine understand dizziness, offering hope to people learning how to deal with vertigo. About how, after years of training, ballet dancers somehow suppressed the natural signals from their balance organs in the ears in order to be able to do those endless spins. Their bodies simply ignored the warnings, and I wondered if Judah had read about it, if it might give him an edge in dealing with the vertigo, something he could work with? Did I dare even raise it?

His eyes blinked awake and he smiled up at me.

"Can I say it's kind of creepy waking up to you staring down at me?"

"You snore like a rabbit." I covered his mouth with my own and dipped in for an early morning taste. I wasn't going to miss the chance to kiss Judah at any time of day.

"Mmm." He pulled back and kissed my nose. "You're a brave man, Morgan Wipene. My morning breath has been known to slay a dragon at fifty paces. And I do not snore."

"Now that sounds like a challenge. And you do too snore. Cute as a button little bunny sniffles. Now come back here so I can test that dragon theory." He tried to wriggle away, but I took him in another kiss, this one deep and lingering. I made sure to dip into every musty corner I could reach, and then I pulled back. "Nope, I'm still here. Must be immune. Though I feel I'd need a lot more kisses for any conclusion to be statistically relevant."

"Hah! Good luck with that, bunny boy." His eyes sparkled. "And. I. Don't. Fucking. Snore."

"Of course you don't." I wiggled my nose and he tweaked it. "Ow."

"Serves you right." His expression grew thoughtful. "How are you feeling this morning?"

Was he serious? "Is that a trick question?" I rested my chin on his chest and he tunnelled his fingers through my hair, his touch waking up all sorts of other places as well.

"Not really. I guess I just wanted to check in about the whole bottoming thing, and the Sally thing, and the me-staying-overnight thing—any of which on their own could have easily rattled your cage and I wouldn't have blamed you."

I laughed and jiggled up onto my elbows. "Okay, so in order. One, the bottoming thing—hell fucking yeah, sore as shit and loving every minute of the reminder. You are a master."

He beamed.

"And you still snore."

He scowled.

"Two, the Sally thing—there is no Sally thing. I told you last night, I loved her, I always will, and she'll always have a place in my heart and my life, but not in my bed. I don't feel guilty. She would want this for me. It's more the whole change in itself that I'm adjusting to. Recognising that I'm coming out of a long period of grief. That things are changing. Finding my feet again. It's all very new. Having a *man* in my bed is also very new. I can't tell you more than that, but so far, I'm okay. I think maybe you're less okay than I am about it."

He shrugged.

"Number three, the you-staying-overnight thing—I loved it. I've been watching you sleep for ages. I like your body in my bed, I like *you* in my bed. And we are *definitely* doing this again."

His cheeks brightened and I traced them with my finger. "Are you blushing, Judah Madden?"

He slapped my hand away. "Don't be ridiculous. But I think you need to say it again just in case I missed something vital." He studied me through half-lowered lashes so I kissed each lid in turn, which sent another flush of pink to his cheeks.

I felt sure the crack of my heart was loud enough to wake the neighbours, but Judah never blinked an eye. I was in trouble, big, big Judah-shaped trouble.

"Again, huh? Okay then, are you listening?" I tucked a curl of hair behind his ear.

He took a hesitant breath and nodded.

I locked eyes with him. "I had the best time with you last night,

Judah Madden. Making love with you, bottoming for you, sleeping with you in my arms, waking up to you this morning. I wouldn't change a single thing."

The crease between his eyes grew deep. "Making love?"

The words were so soft I had to reach for them and my heart squeezed. In some ways, Judah could be so young, and then it hit me that, in fact, his heart *was*. My heart had been sorely tested on all sorts of levels. Judah's was still feeling its way, and I needed to be mindful of that.

"Yes, making love. Don't say it like the words are going to bite you." I pressed a kiss to his cheek. "Because you know as well as I do, what we did last night wasn't just fucking. I don't care how you spin it in your head or what any of it means for where we're going. It's sure as shit not something I planned on, and it's probably the last thing you need right now, but I'm not running. Are you?"

He stared open-mouthed as if I'd just thrown a hand grenade into the bed between us, but it was too late—I couldn't and wouldn't take it back. One thing I'd learned about life, there were no guarantees, and you let chances pass you by at your own peril. I didn't rush to fill the silence, just waited until his shoulders slowly unknotted and he rolled into my arms.

"Personally, I think you're nuts," he said. "I'm hardly a safe bet in anyone's books, but no, Morgan, I'm not running either. Having said that"—

My heart dropped.

—"my life is a shit show right now, no matter which way you look at it, and I didn't see things between us happening so fast."

I raised a brow because *us* in bed was *always* going to happen in my mind, sooner rather than later.

He grinned and fingered my brow back into place, then patted my cheek. "I meant *feeling* things, Morgan. Lift your mind from the gutter, babe." His eyes popped wide and his cheeks spiked pink. "Fuck, I'm sorry about that."

We burst out laughing at the same time.

"See, fucking feelings." He hid his face. "That's what they do. Take control of your mouth and before you know it, you're spouting cringe-worthy, sappy endearments all over the damn place."

I cradled his face and kissed him firmly on the lips. "I'll have you know I'm kind of partial to the odd cringe-worthy, sappy endearment."

"Really?" He eyed me dubiously.

I nodded. "Really."

He side-eyed me. "Okay, but you have to promise me one thing."

"What?"

"If I use one that Sally used, you have to promise to tell me. Because that would be just too fucking creepy for words."

"I promise. And I agree on the creepy angle, though she wasn't big on pet names, so you're pretty safe." I slid my lips over his and licked my way into his mouth. He groaned and pressed the length of his lean body against me, and fuck, it was tempting to just pull up the covers and stay there all day.

Judah was a puzzle, a confusing blend of cocky determination, hesitant insecurity, anguish about the upheaval in his life, and sweet innocence—all wrapped up in a hot as hell body. It was as addictive as shit, and I pulled back from his mouth reluctantly.

"So, you were saying about things happening fast?" I asked, not sure I really wanted an explanation.

He licked his lips and blinked slowly. "Right. I just meant there are things I need to work on, to change, if I'm gonna build a new life for myself, but also if we want to give things between us a real chance. I have to pick up the reins of my life again . . . *myself*. It has to be a priority."

"Agreed." I could work with that. "So what do you need from me?"

He took my hand, brought the palm to his lips, and pressed a kiss there. "Talk to me. Bring me coffee. Text me. Take me on . . . dates." He waggled his eyebrows. "Be there, but let me work things out for myself. And like you, I'm in unfamiliar territory here. I don't know where this new life I want will lead me, whether I'll still be in Painted Bay in a few months, or not."

My stomach dropped but Judah was right. He had to get some kind of life back, wherever that led.

He threw me a nervous look. "I have a specialist appointment coming up in Auckland. I can't imagine I'm gonna learn anything new from it, but I need to start doing something for myself, and I can't let this thing between the two of us stop me from doing what I need to. Knowing that I can't make any promises, I understand if you can't—"

"Of course I bloody can. I can't make any promises either, Judah. Would you let me take you to this appointment? I need to visit my brother and his family anyway. Maybe we can grab lunch with them while we're there?"

Judah studied me with wide eyes. "With your *family*, you mean?"

I nodded. "Just my brother and his wife. Why not? I've had lunch with yours. And it might keep them off my back for a bit. I'd, um, like to introduce you, but no pressure. If you don't want to, then we'll just go somewhere on our own."

Judah took a moment to think. "I'm not sure that fits in with the 'let's take it slow' option, but yeah, okay. I'll be tied up all morning. The appointment's at 11:45 am but there's a mass of tests they want to run beforehand."

"No problem. Text me the details and I'll clear it with work and give Cody a call. As for the other, we might be taking it slow, Judah, but you're already so far under my skin."

"Like hives, right?" He gave me a lopsided grin.

I laughed. "On some days, yeah. But I'm a patient man. I'm not wanting to rush whatever this is either."

His eyes sparkled. "So, does that mean we're like . . . boyfriends and everything?"

I almost swallowed my tongue and the little shit knew it, a smirk as wide as Cook Strait on his face. *But holy shit.* My first boyfriend. I felt about fifteen. *Jesus, Sally, what've you gotten me into?*

"Yeah," I choked the word out. "I'm more than okay with boyfriends. You?" It sounded a lot simpler out in the open than in my head.

He frowned and tapped his finger to his lips. "Well now, I don't know. Are you gonna pop for sodas? Do I get to wear your jacket? Your class ring?"

I found his dick and squeezed it, hard.

"Argh." He arched up against me. "Yeah, yeah, okay, I'm good with the boyfriend thing. But if you *were* keen for my ring, mister, it's a little further back and you are more than welcome to wear it." He waggled his eyebrows.

And so I did.

Which meant we were both late for work. I rolled up to the wharf ten minutes after Judah was supposed to meet Leroy, and based on how things had been left between them the day before, it was no surprise to find Leroy's face like a thundercloud.

Judah ignored his brother and scooted to the boathouse to change while I wandered across to face the music between us.

"So you're fucking my brother now?" Leroy grumbled, a deep scowl crossing his brow.

"None of your business, Leroy."

"It is if it interferes with him doing his job."

I kept walking till I was almost up in his space. "Still not your business, though I apologise for getting him back late—my fault."

Leroy snorted. "I doubt that."

I narrowed my eyes in warning. "Be careful, Leroy. I don't care what stick you have riding so damn high in your butt about him, but Judah is pretty damn important to me now, so you better get used to it."

Leroy's gaze slid off me to the boathouse and he grunted noncommittally. It wasn't nearly enough.

"Hey." I walked back into his line of sight. "You and I are friends, or I thought we were. I sure hope you respect that enough to understand what I'm saying here so we can keep that friendship. But fair warning, Leroy, the next time you start in on Judah like you did yesterday, with his friends and workmates watching, you better believe I won't be letting it go."

Leroy lifted his shoulder in a half shrug. "That was a family thing."

My fists balled at my sides. "No. It was a slap-in-the-face thing, and I won't just let it happen again. I don't get you, Leroy. He's your fucking brother and life's just dealt him a shitty hand. Judah says you've never even raised it with him? What the hell is that about?"

Leroy took a step back. "If he pulls his weight a bit more, I'll have no complaint. He's unreliable."

"Like hell he is."

"What the fuck do you know? You've been in his life two seconds. He doesn't even try to look after himself. He drinks too much."

"Not anymore."

Leroy's lip curled. "Says you."

"Talk to him."

"I don't need to—"

"Talk to him." I walked off just as Judah reappeared from the boathouse.

He looked between the two of us, frowned, and jogged my way. "What happened?"

I shrugged. "Nothing. Your brother's being an arse."

Judah's gaze jerked sideways to Leroy. "Nothing new there. Did he give you shit about us?"

"As I said, just being an arse. You be careful on the boat today."

Judah smiled and lifted on his toes to give me a quick kiss. Likely as much for Leroy's benefit as mine, but I'd take it. I was quickly learning I'd take Judah anyway I could get him.

"I will," he said. "But you don't need to fight my battles for me. To be honest, I'd rather you didn't."

"I know, but he's my friend as well as your brother, and that puts some of my own skin in the game. Plus, you're important to me, and I just needed to lay that out there between us. I won't apologise for caring." I cradled his face. "Boyfriend 1 0 1, right?"

He eyed me suspiciously. "Mmm. Sneaky. Go on then, scoot. Before I'm tempted to give my brother an eyeful he won't forget in a hurry."

"Promises. Promises. I'm still waiting for the whole bendy ballet boy thing. I hear you guys can really lift your legs."

He ran a hand down my chest and grabbed my dick through my jeans. "You have no idea. See you later . . . babe." He winked and I watched his arse swing all the way back to Leroy, trying and failing to ignore how much I fucking liked him calling me that.

When I got back to the Hilux, my phone buzzed with a text from Jon.

You wanna go flying?

I called him back. "What's this all about?"

"Got a message from Auckland's joint task force on poaching, after our report. They want an up-to-date scope on Laird's property via chopper. There's some buzz on the ground about a big Southeast Asian pāua shipment going out soon. I cleared it with your boss. You in?"

I hated choppers, which Jon knew only too well from the last time when I'd thrown up on the floor of the damn thing, mid-flight. "You better be buying lunch," I told him. "After."

He chuckled. "Thought you'd have leftovers from Cora's lunch?"

"Fuck you. As if I didn't feel nauseated enough. You did this deliberately, didn't you?"

"Riiiight. Like I want you spewing on my shoes again."

"Hey, it could've been worse."

"Yeah, well, bring a bag this time. Meet you there."

It was the last thing I needed. But at least it got me out of my car for the day. I watched Judah and Leroy loading up the boat and a smile broke my lips. What a difference a weekend could make.

Before I headed to the airstrip, I sent four words to my brother.

I have a boyfriend.

Three, two, one, bang . . . my phone blew up with the first of a dozen texts, all of which I happily ignored.

Judah

I watched Morgan drive away and then spun to Leroy. "What did you say to him?"

"Nothing." Leroy turned his back and headed back for the boat, which was heaving in the thickening swell coming in from the east. It was gonna be crap out there today.

I threw my hands up in disgust. "Don't walk off on me."

Leroy turned around. "Why not? You've spent a whole lifetime walking out on us."

My jaw dropped open. Even for Leroy that was low. In fact, this whole thing was well past a joke, but I could tell by the look on his face he was itching for a fight, and I wasn't about to put myself on the sacrificial altar. I wasn't sure our relationship would survive it.

Besides, there was no way this wasn't really about Martha and our mother.

"I'm gonna pretend you didn't say that," I warned him, "and put this down to you having fucked up big time with Mum yesterday. I take it the idea of her and Martha offended your sensibilities, pretty much like I do, right?"

"It's not the same."

Like hell. "Why not? And keep your voice down."

"They're not here. And it's not the same because she's not gay . . . or lesbian, or whatever the hell you want to call it. She was married to Dad for twenty-five years for fuck's sake."

Jesus, he could be a self-righteous prick at times. "Oh, and you'd be the expert on her sexuality, of course, right? There's such a thing as bi or pan, you dipshit. And not everyone knows who they are from an early age. Besides, I thought you didn't have a problem with people's sexuality? But that's not true, is it? Because you said you were fine with Morgan, and then you suddenly go off at him because he's with me." I paused as it hit me. "Or maybe it's just *me* you have a problem with? Yeah, that's more like it. Well, at least I'm used to it from you. Mum deserves more." *Shut up.*

A wave of crimson tracked up his throat. "I don't need to be an expert. And I don't have a problem with anyone's sexuality, yours included. Doesn't mean I like having it being rubbed in my face."

What the hell? "When have I ever rubbed . . . no, you know what? I don't want to know. I don't give a fuck what you think about me. But Mum—"

"Just you being *you* rubs it my face. Look at you! You're wearing makeup now? For fuck's sake!"

Don't react, don't react, don't react. "So what if I am?"

"So . . . why? Why do you always have to go the extra fucking mile? No one gives a shit that you're gay. But you make it so hard on yourself. Just like in school. Being gay wasn't enough for you, you had to scream it to the world with your clothes, your ballet, your ridiculous flirty snark, and now, Jesus Christ, makeup? You have to be different. You can't stand not being the centre of attention. Shit." He hung his head as if suddenly realising what he'd said.

But it was too late. Shocked didn't even begin to cover what I felt. Offended, hurt, insulted, and degraded were a few others to add to the mix that had my heart reeling. I sucked in a breath and tried to keep my anger under control, telling myself over and over that this was about Mum, not me. I could handle whatever shit Leroy threw at me, but if he'd said anything like that to Mum, I was going to smack him into next week.

Martha's car pulled into the car park and I knew we needed to wind this up quick.

"We're not done here," I warned him. "But I won't have Mum hurt any more than she already is."

He at least had the grace to look somewhat ashamed.

"But you better not have said anything like what you did just now to Mum."

Leroy swallowed hard and wouldn't meet my eyes. "Of course I didn't."

"But you didn't make it easy on her, either, did you?"

He jerked his gaze my way. "Why should I?"

"Because she's our mother, arsehole, and she's in love. We should want her to be happy, regardless of who it's with. She's been there for us our entire fucking lives."

His gaze shot over my shoulder to where I guessed Martha was heading for the office, and for a second, he looked . . . devastated.

What the . . . ?

Then his jaw set. "She loved Dad. She loves this place. She loves us. She's lonely, I get it. If she wants something with Martha? Fine. Believe it or not, I don't care. I just don't get why she needs to tell everyone like it's this huge fucking announcement. And I don't want that arsehole son of Martha's anywhere near this place or the mussel farm."

What the hell did Fox have to do with it? I shook my head, needing to stay on topic. "Maybe she wanted to come out to us, to her *sons*, because we're important to her, because she loves us."

Leroy winced.

I continued, "Because that's what she did, you realise that, don't you? She *came out* to you. And even your pea brain has to know how hard that is for *anyone* to do and how important it is for your family have your back." I left that hanging for a second. "And maybe she wanted to come out because she *loves* Martha as well. Loves, as in, 'doesn't want to hide it, wants the world to know, might even get married someday' kind of love. Would you deny her that after losing Dad?"

Leroy's face turned ashen. "Married?"

Martha hesitated at the office door, her eyes on us. I waved. She lifted a hand and returned the wave with a wary smile. Leroy simply turned his back, and I saw the sting of disappointment on her face.

"Don't you fucking dare," I hissed at him. "Martha's been good to us, more than good, and Dad would be so fucking disappointed in you."

He glanced at me, almost stricken, then turned and gave Martha a brief nod of acknowledgement.

"Jesus, Leroy, you better get your head out of your arse before you do or say something you can't take back. I'm not sure that you haven't done that already, because you'll never get the chance to redo your reaction to her coming out to you ever again. Now you have to live with it, and so does she." I headed for the boat and left him standing.

CHAPTER THIRTEEN

Judah

With my feet spread for better balance, I gripped the helm chair and counted to ten. I'd been spinning on and off for about an hour, and my anxiety had spiked into the red zone. The last thing I needed was an attack now, on the boat, in front of Leroy.

We'd barely talked for four days, since Monday's argument about Mum and Martha and Leroy's standoff with Morgan, which he wouldn't say anything about other than to bitch that I was screwing with his friendships on top of everything else.

Whatever. I was done caring. Leroy could go fuck himself. Mum was keeping tight-lipped about what had gone down between them, which was fair enough, it wasn't my business, but I could tell she was hurting. I'd done my best to reassure her Leroy just needed time, but I wasn't so sure about the truth of that myself. I thought I'd made some kind of point with him in our *discussion*, but Mum said he hadn't spent any time at home or even eaten there since they'd talked on Sunday.

I was rapidly losing patience with my dickhead of a brother.

Poor Martha looked nothing short of exhausted. I'd stopped by the office for a couple of long hugs as I came and went from the boathouse, and it was clear she was grateful. Fox hadn't been as surprised as he maybe should've been. According to Martha, he'd handled the news well, happy for them both. And with his previous relationship going up in flames, he was thinking of moving to this end of the country, which pleased Martha to no end. I hadn't had a chance to talk to Fox myself, mostly because we'd been spending long days harvesting, and now he'd flown back south.

Leroy was lucky I hadn't decked him a half dozen times over the last few days with the mean-arse attitude he'd been leaking everywhere. I was pretty much done with it and just waiting for an excuse. I also hadn't seen Morgan for three days, three days too fucking long, which wasn't helping things. He'd been busy with some poaching ring they'd gotten wind of, and he and Jon had been busy tracking them down.

In addition to the detective work, he'd been out as an observer on a commercial fishing boat, monitoring and recording and not returning till late. Between both our jobs, we simply hadn't actually managed an actual face to face. We'd texted, sure. Hell, we'd written bloody novels to each other. And since Mum had given me permission to tell Morgan about her and Martha, that had taken up a fair amount of call time as well. He'd been surprised but also thrilled she'd found someone who made her happy, and he wanted her to know he was happy to talk anytime, one bi, or whatever, to another.

I nearly cried.

I had hopes he would call by the boathouse after he was done today. My fingers itched to touch him, and I was wearing out my favourite emojis, which had taken to hiding at the very end of my user list in protest. The man's company was addictive. Things happened in my body whenever he was within touching distance. And I wasn't just talking about lust. There was also this weird calm, like someone dumping Valium on my hyper-frazzled fringes.

The only time I'd felt anything similar was on stage, where my inner world stilled to this fine point of light as I *got in the zone*. Like a batter at the plate or a rugby winger with his eye on an incoming ball just before the try line, only you and that narrow margin of focus, the rest of the world dropping away. Morgan did that to me.

As a dancer, I lived for those moments, craved them, breathed them in like a drug, and I knew I had to be careful about letting Morgan step into that vacuum. I couldn't let him fill that hole, because if he left I'd have to start again. How I changed my life had to be for me, not for Morgan. And I had a plan, one I'd been working on since Monday.

"Throw me some rope ties," Leroy called from the bow. "They're in the bag by the floats."

I made my way to the back of the boat, grabbed the bag of ties, and was heading forward when I was suddenly thrown sideways. *Goddammit.* My shoulder hit the helm, spinning me around only seconds before I faceplanted on the deck. *Shit.*

"Judah! What the fuck? Judah!" Leroy's feet crashed over the deck to where I lay stuffed under the helm.

I wanted to tell him to fuck off, but you know, complete body-brain disconnection and all that. I was pretty sure my face was white as a sheet although that copper tang on my tongue was a sheer give-away that I'd split something on the way down. Bad enough to have a regular garden variety vertigo in front of Leroy, but a drop attack? Fuck. Just the excuse he needed to cut me out altogether. If I could've crawled under the canvas tarp covering our gear, I would've.

"What happened?" Patrick called from the other boat where he'd been seeding some ropes. "Judah, are you okay?"

"Judah!" Leroy knelt at my side and rolled me over.

And it was then I saw it—the bone-deep fear in his eyes that maybe I was really hurt, or worse, and the raw depth of it stunned me. But when my muscles began to fire again and I started fighting to sit up, the fear was quickly replaced by anger, as if he was embarrassed to be caught caring.

Fuck him.

"I'm fine," I called over to Patrick as I struggled to a sit.

"You can head back to the wharf," Leroy told him, shuffling out of my way. "We're done for the day."

"Okay." Patrick was clearly hesitant. "Are you sure?"

Leroy raised a brow at me and I nodded.

"We're sure," he said, then turned back to me. "So, what the hell was that?" he demanded as if I'd somehow engineered the fall deliberately.

I rolled my eyes. "*That,* dear brother, was a Tumarkin's Otolithic Crisis, otherwise known as a drop attack. It's like being pushed and having all your strings cut at the same time. Now if you'd get out of my way, I need the first aid kit."

He suddenly registered the blood running down my cheek. "Fuck, you're bleeding."

"I'll get it," I snapped as he reached into the cabinet under the helm.

He pushed me back. "Don't be an idiot."

"Oh nice. Push the dizzy guy who's bleeding."

"Shit, sorry." He even managed to look a bit sheepish as he set about cleaning the cut on my brow and lip while I gritted my teeth and let him. "Does that happen a lot?"

I pulled back and stared up at him. "Why the fuck do you care? You've shown not the slightest bit of interest before now."

He sighed and dabbed at the wounds. "I know, all right. So I might've been a bit of a prick."

I arched my uninjured brow.

"All right, I've definitely been a prick. But *that,* just before. Man, that was weird. It was like someone shoved you sideways, like a fucking ghost."

I shrugged. "Feels like it too."

"I thought you got that aura thing before you got dizzy? Mum never said anything about any drop attack."

Got 'dizzy'? Understatement of the fucking year. "I asked her not to."

"Why?"

"Because you've been a total arsehole about the whole fucking thing, Leroy, that's why. Case in point. *Got dizzy?* You have no idea, do you?"

He went quiet and finished putting a dressing on the neat slice I'd put in my eyebrow.

"Your lip should be okay, and all right, fair point. I don't really know much about it. But I'm asking now." He sat on a pile of floats opposite me.

"Why?" I shot back, reaching for a tarp to put between the wet deck and my soaking butt. "So you can decide whether I'm a danger to you out here? 'Cause that would just be bonus points for you, right? Then you could refuse to let me help and have even more reasons to throw insults at me for how useless I am."

His eyes bored into mine. "Yes, partly. I need to know you're safe out here, for everyone's sake. But I don't think you're useless. What the hell, Judah?"

"Could've fooled me. You tell me often enough, always on my case about stuff I can't control? I didn't ask for this, you know. Do you think I *want* to be stuck here? Do you think I enjoy dragging myself out here on days when my head's spinning so fucking bad I can hardly tell which way is up? Do you think I wouldn't rather be back in Boston, dancing?"

His expression cooled. "No, believe me, we *all* know where you'd rather be, where you've always rather been, and that would be *anywhere* but here."

I gritted my teeth. "That's bloody unfair. Dancing was my life and my *job,* Leroy. Not some fucking whim. I worked my arse off for that opportunity, and I know you don't care, but I was good. I was really fucking good."

His eyes slid off mine to the water behind me, the reflection dancing in his dark eyes. "I know. Mum showed me the reviews."

What the . . . ? You could've knocked me over with a feather. "You saw the reviews?" I threw my hands in the air. "Well gee, thanks for not saying anything. At least when I thought you hadn't seen them, I could give you the benefit of the doubt."

"And exactly *when* did you ever say anything to me about what *I* was doing?" Leroy's eyes fired bright with anger.

"I—fuck." I tried to think and came up with nothing.

He gave a disdainful snort, the veins in his neck pulsing with fury. "Yeah, not once. Not when I made the first fifteen rugby team in school, and then the regional rep team."

"Why the fuck would I? You watched me get bullied by half of those guys for years and said zip. They were your fucking friends, Leroy. And you sat back and did nothing. I was just a kid."

He kept talking as if I hadn't said a word. "You said nothing when I was accepted to vet school, which was really fucking hard to get into, I'll have you know. And again nothing when I gave all that up to come home to look after the farm and help *our* mother get her life back together after Dad died. Not once have you said anything to me in the last five years about me saving this damn place from the bank while you were somewhere thousands of miles away forgetting you even had a fucking family."

"I never forgot." My heart pounded in my chest, guilt flushing through my body. "I called Mum. She understood. My life wasn't as easy as you seem to think, and I didn't get paid enough to come home."

His lip curled up. "You called every month or so. Big fucking deal. I hope that didn't put too much of a dent in your savings."

It stung, more so because it shaved too close to the truth, and I didn't dare risk responding in case I blurted out that very fact. Then it occurred to me what he'd just said. "What did you mean when you said you'd *saved* the place from the bank? Dad always said the business did fine."

Leroy pulled a face. "He didn't want us to worry. It was tanking, Judah, big time. If I hadn't come home when he died, Mum would've had to sell. She couldn't afford the workers. She was always taking on more people than she could afford, you know her."

A wave of cold crept through me. "You never said anything. You never told me."

He threw up his hands. "She wouldn't let me. Your ballet was always this precious untouchable thing, and she didn't want to risk you giving it up, not after everything they sacrificed to get you there. Everything we *all* sacrificed."

"What the fuck does that mean?" But something in me sensed what was coming, something I'd never wanted to ask or even consider, and a heaviness settled in my chest.

Leroy's lips flattened and his expression turned stony. "They sank a ton of money they couldn't really afford into your fancy training and boarding school in Wellington. Which meant I had to take out a fucking student loan to even get to university, not to mention pay my halls of residence. You wonder why I gave up vet school? It wasn't just because I needed to run the farm. The fees were crippling me, Judah. I had to make a decision. I didn't have the luxury of any backup."

I didn't want to believe it, but deep in my heart, I knew Leroy was speaking the truth. It was clear in his eyes. But I didn't want to feel sorry for him, I wanted to fucking run.

"No one asked you to," I grunted, an epically unfair statement. "Maybe Mum would've been happy to let the place go." It came out sharper than I'd intended, but I was still reeling from the loan bomb. I couldn't fathom why Mum and Dad would do that to Leroy when they'd helped me so much. I'd always assumed he'd gotten the same treatment. I'd screwed up.

He deflated in front of me. "No, you're right. No one asked me to do this. And maybe I wasn't loving vet school as much as I should've, so that played a part too, but at the time it felt like I didn't have a choice. And Jesus, Judah, you could've at least checked in with me about how things were going."

Yes, I absolutely should've. But the truth was, I hadn't wanted to know. I'd buried any questions I might have had under my determination never to come back to Painted Bay.

But Leroy wasn't done. "And you got to do your shit over there, live your dream free of worry *because* I was here looking after Mum. I was the ticket so you could focus. But did it ever occur to you that it wasn't always a good thing for me either, coming home? That it might've been nice to have some brotherly support?"

It hadn't. Not once. I'd just assumed, god, there I went again, I'd assumed Leroy wanted to be in Painted Bay—that he was only pissed with me because I didn't. I should've thought about the gift he was giving me in making my life a little easier, but I'd been barely twenty, young and so full of my own self-importance that I'd never even considered it.

"No, I didn't," I admitted. "And I'm really sorry about that." I was. "And I didn't know about the fees, either. What the hell were Mum and Dad thinking?"

Leroy sunk back against the helm. "I did ask Mum, and to be fair, she said they'd always intended to reimburse me when they retired and sold the farm, unless I wanted to work it myself. But then Dad died and there was too much debt. And Mum still needed an income, so . . ."

What a mess. "I'm sorry I never asked, but Leroy, why the hell didn't you tell me or say something, anything?"

Leroy looked at me in disbelief, and yeah, I got it. I wouldn't have been exactly receptive.

"Okay, I might not have welcomed your call, because you're right, I pretty much walked away from here at sixteen. But I should've been told things were bad with the farm. I deserved to know that much at least, don't you think? And in my defence, you were a total arsehole to me in school. I don't take that back. This thing between us wasn't all a one-way street, Leroy."

His cheeks pinked and his gaze slid off me to the choppy sea beyond. "And you're right, I should've said something in school. I could've stopped some of the crap that was said."

Tears pricked at my eyes even after all that time, and Leroy saw them. "I'm sorry, Judah. It was a shitty thing to do, but it just seemed you were the golden child in so many fucking ways and—"

"You thought I had it coming?" I fired back, my voice breaking as I desperately tried not to dissolve into a complete wreck in front of him. "You're right. It *was* a shitty thing to do. And you wonder why I didn't want to come back here. And it wasn't just words, Leroy. Did you know it was your mate Kane who put a tear in my fucking kidney?"

Leroy's face drained of colour. "Fuck. No . . . shit, I . . . fuck. I thought it was just some name-calling, maybe a bit of elbowing—"

"Oh, and that made it okay?" I pushed to my feet and stormed to the other side of the boat. I was two seconds away from punching Leroy in the face. A seagull landed on the top of one of our surface buoys. A shift in the wind was kicking up a few white horses, but the mussel farm mediated the swell and I was surprisingly steady on my feet.

I felt rather than heard Leroy approach.

"I said I'm sorry and I am, more than you know. I *was* an arsehole to you. And I didn't know about the heavy stuff. You have to believe me when I say I wouldn't have let that go without saying *something*."

I turned and flashed him a withering look.

He flinched. "I guess I deserved that. And I'd take it all back if I could, but we were four years apart, Judah, and we had nothing in common. We weren't close. I was a stupid teenager, and I was so fucking angry with you—with all the time Mum and Dad spent making sure you got what you needed.

"And you were this strange kid who loved to dance, wore bright clothes and fucking lip gloss, and who knew he was gay since he could walk and wasn't backing down for anyone. My friends gave me such shit about you and I just wanted to fit in, so I acted like I agreed with them. Yes, I was a real jerk, and although I would never have said anything at the time, I was actually pretty proud of you. You were so brave, man."

My breath caught in my throat. "You thought that I was brave?"

He shrugged. "Much good it did you. Would've helped if I'd said something, right?"

I snorted, trying once again to keep the tears from my eyes, but this time for an entirely different reason. "Yeah. It would've been a start. I thought you hated me like your friends. Hated the fact I was gay. And to be honest, it still kind of sounded like that the other day."

He swallowed hard and looked away, rubbing a hand over the back of his neck. "What I said on the wharf was way out of line. I, ah, wasn't dealing with Mum's news very well. What I didn't tell you was that she's thinking of selling the farm."

I gaped. "What?"

He shrugged. "Yeah, that was the part I was really pissed about. After all the work I've put in, and she wants to sell it. Said that she and Martha are thinking of buying a house in town, together. She offered the farm to me but I doubt I could swing the money and she needs the cash to buy."

Shit. That explained a whole lot. "I'm sure she wouldn't rush something like that."

He didn't look convinced. "We'll see."

"Did you tell her how you feel about the farm?"

He turned his head away. "Not really. I, ah, kind of lost it. I was too shocked, by everything."

I put a hand on his arm and he let me, which was something. "Then will you at least talk to her, again? Please? She thinks you're mostly upset about Martha and that's not fair. It's punishing her for things she can't control. Tell her what you want for the farm. Put a plan together."

He breathed out a long sigh and faced me again. "I was going to, tonight. It was never really about Martha, or not most of it, anyway."

I snorted. "Doesn't mean you weren't a total dickwad, though."

His shoulders slumped. "Yeah, I guess. But can you please tell me now about these damn drop attacks. I promise I won't ban you from the boat. I just need to know. And you've got to stop coming out on the boat if you feel like crap. I can manage with Patrick or on my own. I did it for years, you know?"

I arched a brow. "You won't get on my case about it? Believe it or not, I won't shirk. I'd rather come out with you than sit home all day."

He squinted at me. "Will you promise to look after yourself better?"

I nodded. "Already trying. Will you promise not to be such an arsehole?"

He nodded. "Already trying."

"Pinky swear?" I extended my hand.

"Fuck off." He pushed me toward the helm. "For that, you can take us back in while I put my feet up."

His gaze softened and warmth flooded my chest.

Maybe everything wasn't lost between us, after all.

We made it back to the wharf at just after six, and although I wouldn't say things were rosy between Leroy and myself, not by a long shot, they were at least a bit less . . . openly hostile. But there'd been a lot of hurt and pain on both sides, and it was going to take time for that to heal.

I wasn't sure mine ever would, at least not about the bullying thing. I understood Leroy's reasoning—that we were both kids and that he didn't realise the full extent of it—but I couldn't forgive him turning a blind eye, not yet. That twelve-year-old boy who didn't fit in, and just wanted to be left alone to dance, still hurt right down to his gay little toes. Maybe I always would. But at least I saw my part in things now, and Mum and Dad's. There was plenty of blame to share around.

Martha and Mum were waiting at the pier and picked up on the changed mood between Leroy and me straight away. Their curious gazes flitting between us and two pairs of eyebrows peaked when

Leroy actually said hello. Then Mum spied the dressing on my fore-head and the cut on my lip and gasped.

"What happened?" she asked, grabbing me by the chin to hold me still for inspection like I was ten years old. "Did he hit you?" She spun Leroy's way, clearly ready to let fly.

"No, Mum." I grabbed her arm. "It wasn't Leroy. I had another drop attack, but it's all good. I caught my head on the helm is all."

"You had a—" She glanced again at Leroy and lowered her voice. "Was it okay? Did he say anything?"

"I can still hear you," Leroy said drolly.

"It was fine." I looked across at my brother. "We, ah, talked."

"Oh, good. That's . . . good." My mother nodded at Leroy.

I could tell she was dying to know what had been said, but Leroy's concerns weren't mine to share.

"Maybe it's time you both talked, again. About *everything*."

"What do you mean everything?" She studied my face closely.

I nodded. "Everything. Dad, Martha, the farm, your plans, his plans, you know . . . everything."

"Oh." She looked over to Leroy who said nothing, just gathered a long coil of seed rope and headed for the storage shed. "Yeah, maybe that's a good idea."

We unloaded the rest of the gear in silence and thankfully Mum left well enough alone, although Martha gave me the hairy eyeball as I headed for the boathouse. I mouthed the words *all good* at her as I passed. She let out a big breath and her mouth curved up in a genuine smile for the first time in days. Then she tipped her head to the boathouse and winked. "You've got mail."

I approached my front door, wondering what that was all about. The bike I'd bought from Terry was still chained up outside mocking me, waiting for me to get the courage to ride it. This weekend. It was one of the things on my plan.

But it wasn't the bike that had my attention. It was the extremely large package that sat alongside it. Or two packages, to be precise. The first, about two metres long and half a metre wide, and the second, about one and a half metres square. I hadn't ordered anything, so what the hell? I dumped my stuff and hauled them inside to open.

Five minutes later I collapsed on the floor next to their contents, my heart thumping. Polished wood slid seductively under my fingers as I ran them along the two portable ballet barres, igniting a thrum of excitement low in my belly.

Eight words stared up at me from the delivery note, but no name.

Use it or not, it's up to you.

It had to be Morgan. There was no other answer, and I didn't know whether I wanted to curse and yell at him for interfering and forcing me to face something I didn't know if I was ready to or kiss him senseless for caring enough to offer me a choice I wasn't yet brave enough to risk for myself.

It only took a minute of staring at the object of my dreams and nightmares before I grabbed the instructions and a muesli bar and set about putting the framework together. It was made to hold two barres at different heights, each fully adjustable, and the whole thing was absolutely perfect.

Forty minutes later I was done.

Ten minutes after that, I'd changed into practice tights, stretch canvas flats, and a T-shirt.

Another five minutes of pushing some furniture out of the way to make room before I fell into my first plié.

From there, time evaporated as I stretched and worked all those neglected muscles, waking them up and reminding them what they could do. I didn't stop till the barre was wet with sweat and my tights clung to me like I'd just finished a performance. I was so unfit it wasn't funny, but I floated on a high the likes of which I hadn't felt since Boston.

It hadn't all gone smoothly, though. Dizzy spells meant I had to pause and change down the exercise—adapt. My transitions and processes were clumsy, heavy and unrefined. The tinnitus irked and disrupted my thinking. But I made it through a decent first session, and my body sang.

Endorphins and joy bubbled through my veins like soda. Not because I'd achieved some amazing feat. Not because I thought I had a chance of returning to professional dance—if anything, I was clearer about the fact that wouldn't ever be happening. I'd lost too much of the intuitive pinpoint balance that marked any professional ballet career, and it wasn't likely I'd ever regain it. In that respect, nothing had changed.

But the joy of dance was still there, and it hit me how terrified I'd been that I'd lost that too. My life had revolved around excellence in performance almost my whole life. I didn't know if my heart could find a home in the simple art of dance for dance's sake ever again, and I'd been too frightened to try.

I fired a text off to Terry, asking him to tell Hannah I said yes to helping her with her talent show entry. And then I slumped to the floor, dropped my head, and let the tears fall.

CHAPTER FOURTEEN

Morgan

I GRABBED A QUICK SHOWER AFTER GETTING HOME AND THEN headed to Judah's. I didn't text, I was too damn terrified for that. The ballet barre had been delivered, I knew that much from the courier's text. And I'd seen Leroy's boat tied up at the wharf on my way home, so that meant Judah must've opened it. But I'd heard nothing from him, and I was shitting myself.

The idea about the barre had come to me after that conversation at Cora's lunch with Hannah asking Judah to help her. He said he'd think about it, and I could see how badly he wanted to be there for her, but he looked so trapped. I don't know why I did it and I probably shouldn't have. No, I definitely shouldn't have. I'd been second-guessing my decision all week, but it was too late to change my mind. All I could do was deal with the fallout.

Had I gone too far? Yep, the answer to that one seemed clear. Would it be too confronting? Probably, but I was about to find out. Would it push him away? Maybe, but I didn't think so and that's what spurred my hope. I simply wanted him to have the choice. If it was too painful, he could get rid of it or store it somewhere until he was ready. But he wouldn't know if he didn't have the option. And if nothing else, he'd benefit from the physical stretching and some balance exercises which I'd read was important, not that I'd admit to googling more shit about it. I valued my balls way too much for that.

My hand shook as I knocked on his front door. Music filtered from somewhere inside, and when he didn't answer, I tried again. His voice rose in song and I smiled. Guessing he couldn't hear me above Taylor Swift, I made my way to the deck on the far side and knocked on the open slider.

Judah's head poked around the corner of the kitchen, and a broad smile broke over his face. The air whooshed out of my lungs. It didn't appear he was going to kill me right away, at least.

"Did I lock the front door?" He sauntered toward me and my tongue hit the roof of my mouth.

He was shirtless, wearing nothing but a pair of those damn ballet tights moulded to that exquisite, sculpted body. And it was pretty clear he had zip on underneath as my gaze zeroed in on the swell of that ample cock and balls trapped inside.

He noticed, of course he did—my eyelashes were practically tickling his damn foreskin, but I tried for at least a modicum of decorum and cleared my throat. "Ah. I didn't want to assume anything, and I could, ah . . . hear you singing so I, um . . . came around back."

He pulled his lower lip between his teeth and I followed every little tug and nibble, my cock plumping to strain against the zip of my jeans. Jesus Christ, the man was sexy.

As though he could read my mind, Judah's mouth curved up in a slow, sexy smile and he leaned on the door frame, his gaze raking over me from head to foot. "Cat stolen your tongue, babe?"

Along with every other workable part of me. "Possibly. But I'm thinking it might also have run off with the rest of your clothes because, damn, Judah, I'm not sure my heart was quite ready for this. You look fucking delicious." I scrubbed my hand over my mouth and drank him in.

He opened his arms a little. "Would you like a bite?"

"Is that a trick question?"

He yanked me inside, slammed the slider shut, and pressed my back hard against the wall, rubbing his body against me until I swore I sparked like kindling, two twitches away from igniting in fucking flames.

Then I noticed the steri-strip and pushed him back. "You're hurt." I fingered his brow. "What happened?"

"A drop attack . . . on the boat." He pulled my fingers down and proceeded to suck on them, which pleased my dick to no end, but—

"Shit, quit that," I freed my fingers and breathed myself down. "Did Leroy see it? What did he say?"

Judah dropped my hand and latched onto my neck instead, nuzzling his way up to my jaw. Every neuron in my body got to its feet and screamed hallelujah.

He lifted his head, kissed me on the nose, and planted a string across both cheeks. "We talked." *Kiss.* "About stuff." *Kiss, kiss.* "It's good, well, it's better between us." *Kiss, kiss, kiss.* "But let's talk about that later." He pulled back to look me in the eye, and I nearly incinerated on the spot.

He looked a half-second away from devouring me, and I was so, so down with that.

He leaned in until his mouth was alongside my ear. "There's something more important we need to discuss first, *Mr* Wipene. And I think you know exactly what that is."

A flurry of nerves seeded in my belly and made their way north. This was it.

"You bought me a barre," he whispered, then latched onto my neck hard enough to leave a mark. I groaned and fell back against the wall while my brain figured we were likely gonna be good about the whole barre thing.

"I did, um . . ." *Oh god, I wasn't going to survive this.* Somehow, Judah had my shirt off and was already working on my jeans and I was leaking from my cock like a damn faucet. "Was the barre . . . oh shit." My knees buckled as his hand grazed my cock. "Was it, ah, okay?"

He kissed a line from the dip in my throat to my stomach. "More than okay. Now lift your feet."

"What?" I looked down to find my jeans and briefs puddled around my ankles and I was standing there naked. "Oh, right." I stepped out of them, and Judah sent them flying with a kick.

Then he stood back and stared at me, hazel eyes glinting in the late sun, his heavy cock thick with arousal.

My mouth watered like I hadn't been fed in weeks.

"You really should've asked," he said, his expression unreadable.

Shit. "Yeah, I know. I'm sorry. I didn't mean—"

"I love it." His eyes danced like stars in a night sky and he smiled. "It's fucking perfect." He grabbed my hand and pulled me into the dining area. "So, I've been trying to think of an *appropriate* way to say thank you, and—" He pushed me face-first on the table before covering my body with his and kicking my legs apart. "I wondered if this might work?" His rigid cock rammed hard against the back of my balls. "What do you think?"

He thrust again and I saw fucking stars. "Oh, shit. Yeah, ah . . . good choice . . . fuck, right there."

He thrust again, while at the same time finding the back of my neck with his mouth and sinking his teeth, and—*God and angels and hell and damnation, all tied up with a Christmas bow*—I wasn't going to last a fucking minute.

He nibbled his way around to my ear, and a wet finger slipped inside my crease to press on my hole. One, two, three taps and he was inside and—*son of a bitch*—I arched beneath him, pushing back till his finger slid over my prostate, and *damn.*

"You are so fucking sexy." He breathed the words hot into my ear as he continued to fuck me with his fingers, first one, then two. "I don't even know what I want to do to you first."

I wanted to tell him that was a moot point because if he even whispered the word *come*, I was gonna spill in an instant, but my tongue had packed its bags and left the building.

"But . . ." He continued lapping at my ear while that wicked finger ploughed in and out of my arse, shattering any residual control I might've had. "I believe there's one particular fantasy you've had running around in that filthy mind of yours."

Was there? And he was gone from my back just like that, leaving me spluttering in protest. I didn't give a brass razoo about any fantasy, I just wanted those fingers of his back on my skin and preferably inside me Right. Fucking. Now.

At least that was until I pushed myself up, still grumbling, to find him standing facing the barre, one leg stretched horizontally along the wood and everything, *everything* on display, and within reach . . . all barely concealed by those damn white tights.

My mouth dried to dust and I was on him in an instant. Starting at his toes and kissing my way up his leg and under his thigh until I could mouth his balls from below, through the thin membrane of material. He groaned, went up on tippy-toe, and then ground down on my face, palming his cock till I slapped his hand away.

"Mine."

"Goddammit, Morgan. Get me out of these things. They're strangling my dick."

Nope. No way in hell. "*My* fantasy, *my* way," I muttered. I'd been dreaming of these fucking ballet tights since the first day I'd seen him in them. I'd jerked off to them in my shower, in my bed, on my couch, and once even in my kitchen, and I knew exactly what I wanted. I needed him free to handle but not much more.

With that in mind, I grabbed each side of the seam and ripped them open front to back leaving the waist intact, so his arse was flying free in the breeze.

"Yes," he cried out. "Thank fuck. Yes."

Grabbing them again at the crotch, I flayed the seam open between his legs till his balls dropped out and his cock popped free.

"Lube and condom, right side bedside table," he huffed. "Hurry." He grabbed my wrist as I passed. "I want you to fuck me, got it."

I nodded and smiled to myself. As if I'd ever thought for a moment *I* was in control. I was back at the barre in seconds, supplies in hand, and so fucking hard my cock was on a hair-trigger. If I even brushed against Judah too hard, it might all be over.

"Are you okay like that for a bit?" I asked, not sure how the hell he kept his leg up for so long, but I really, really hoped his answer was yes.

"I'm fine."

"Excellent."

He flashed me a wicked smile.

I suited up, because I wasn't sure I'd have the wherewithal to do it later, and then lubed my cock and drizzled some more down his crack.

He hissed with the cold but I soon warmed him up, sliding both hands over the cheeks of his arse, moving one through his legs to stroke his leaking dick while the fingers of the other played with his balls, and my thumb slipped into his hole.

"Jesus fuck," he groaned, as I worked on all three hotspots at once.

Then I went to my knees and added my tongue to the mix.

"What the hell . . . shit, shit . . . I'm gonna come. Morgan, stop!" Judah pushed my head away and dropped his leg, then bent over and grabbed behind his legs, his head almost on his knees, doubled in two. "Gotta stretch out. Hang on."

Like hell. The man was bendy as shit and I almost came at the sight of his arse in the air and that beautiful slick hole right there for the taking . . . for *my* taking. "Don't move."

He looked up at me from his upside-down position and smirked. "Oh, it's gonna be like that, is it? Like what you see, huh?"

"Nope. I hate it. Gonna slap a FedEx label and get it outta here fast." I smacked his arse. "You have no freaking idea how much I like what I see. But will you be okay . . . you know, like that?"

"Not quite." He reached a hand out for the chair to lean on and brace himself and uncurled just a little. "This is easier."

I still marvelled at his position. "How the hell do you do that?"

"Years of dedication, now fuck me before my head says it's had enough."

"Oh shit, yeah. Sorry." I walked between his legs and ran my hands over the powerful globes of his arse, feeling him shudder at my touch. He was so stretched I didn't even need to look, I just lined up against that open hole and slid inside all that tight, moist heat, counting sheep and camels and fucking aardvarks to stop from coming on the spot.

"More." He pushed back, taking me deeper.

My hand trailed the length of his back and then I folded over him, thrusting in and out as he groaned and swore with every pass.

"Harder."

Like I needed to be told twice. I slammed into him, my arms wrapped around his waist, and we rode like that for a dozen more thrusts until I couldn't stand it any longer.

"Dammit. I want to see you." I pulled out and he stood and turned. I cupped his face and slid my lips over his, and we crushed together, our slick cocks tangling as we rutted.

"I want to ride you," Judah huffed in my ear. "Right here, on the floor."

Holy shit. I dropped in an instant and held my dick stable.

He straddled my hips and then used all those concrete core muscles of his to squat until he could reach my cock and guide it in. His head fell back with a grunt as I lodged deep in his arse, and he took a couple of long breaths while I did my best to hold on and not embarrass myself.

Then those bright hazel eyes flew open and he started fucking himself, his gaze locked on mine. He didn't go to his knees, just squatted up and down, thighs of steel. It meant everything was on display and it was hot as shit.

"You feel so damn good, Morgan. Look." Judah tipped his head to the mirror by the front door.

I followed his gaze and saw my dark dick sliding in and out of his pale hole, and that was it. I was one errant thought away from exploding, so I reached for his cock to get him there as well. It only took a few strokes and he grunted, arched up, and spilled all over my chest.

I slowed as he shuddered through it, and when he was done, I nudged him onto his back on the floor, whipped the condom off, and knelt by his shoulder.

He licked his lips and grinned. "Fucking do it."

Three more strokes were all it took to finish all over his face, waves of pleasure crashing through me. His tongue darted out to grab what it could and my heart stuttered in my chest. *Don't think about it.*

I swiped some of his spill off my chest, licked my fingers clean, and then I fell on his mouth and fed it to him off my tongue. He groaned for every last drop. I licked his face clean and we shared that as well.

After a minute or so, I suggested a shower, shuffled to my knees, and promptly banged my head on the barre. We collapsed in each other's arms once again and laughed ourselves into a sweaty, sticky puddle on the dining room floor.

When we calmed, he looked down and pulled at his ripped tights. "Really, Morgan? This is gonna be a fucking expensive fetish."

I nuzzled into his neck. "We'll buy them in bulk."

Judah chuckled. "Fuck you."

I grinned against his shoulder. "Yes, please. Just give me ten."

CHAPTER FIFTEEN

Morgan

"Are you going to eat the rest of that pizza or do I get another slice?" I watched as Judah raised his fingers to his mouth and cleaned them slowly, one by one, while my jeans got a little tighter. "And you can stop with those pitiful attempts at sexy distraction; I'm immune to your Jedi mind tricks. I want my pizza."

He snorted and handed over the box with its two remaining slices. "I only promised to tag along while you did your private-eye thing on these bozos *because* you promised me pizza, Morgan. I could be sitting on my couch watching the Russian Ballet in the comfort of my own home."

"At the risk of sounding petty, I feel the need to point out that you've already finished your pizza. That one's mine, sweetheart. You said you hated pepperoni, remember?"

"Hate's a strong word."

"And you're supposed to be on a low-salt diet."

"I'm having a day off."

"Oh, for fuck's sake." I gave him the last piece and he flashed me a shit-eating grin.

"I'm really only saving you from yourself," he said, reaching over to pat my stomach. "It's a selfless act on behalf of your adoring public."

I slapped his hand away. "That wasn't what you said last night when I was down on my knees for you. Then, you were praising every square inch of my, and I quote, 'perfect fucking body.'"

His cheeks turned a lovely shade of pink. "Pass me some water."

I raised an irritated brow.

He smiled sweetly. "Please."

I handed him a bottle and went back to staring at the green-and-cream villa while Judah finished his—my pizza. I'd spent the last three Saturday mornings parked in the Laird brother's street in the hope of nailing some of their contacts, fishing or otherwise, and today Judah had offered to keep me company. The poaching task force had a man on the inside of the ring and he seemed pretty certain the brothers were involved in some capacity, but at this point, they were more interested in who they met up with than nabbing them for any small-time illegalities.

Follow and photos only were my instructions. No confrontation, no risks, all low-key and off the books. And so here I was in Leroy's old green Corolla that he'd lent me to keep things on the down-low, sharing a pizza with Judah, and staring at the villa where it seemed everyone inside was doing what we should've been—having a beer and watching the Super Rugby game on TV.

We'd been taking turns planning dates over the last three weeks of our adventure into boyfriend land. Some of the highlights had been a *Die Hard* movie night with three flavours of ice cream; a Judah-cooked meal complete with slow dancing to a variety of Frank Sinatra numbers, colour me shocked on both counts; a picnic down at the wharf complete with submerged light and fish display, which had earned me an epic blowjob in front of five hundred million baitfish;

and fish and chips and skinny dipping in the shallows at a secluded nearby beach.

That one had been Judah's idea. I was pretty leery about him being in any depth of water in case of drop attacks, so I'd kept us no more than waist deep and remained glued to his side like a fricken leech the entire time. He'd called me cute and gone down on me in the lapping shallows under a half-moon. I'd called him reckless and nailed his arse over a log, under a giant pohutakawa hidden from the car park. We'd both called it fucking perfect.

So yeah, all up, this dating thing had been pretty successful so far. And in between, I'd attended two more Sunday lunches and survived both in one piece, more or less. Cora's potato bake recipe had been a surprising success; the lamb stew, less so. But the mood around the table had been much improved, Leroy even participating in a toast Judah made to Martha and Cora's relationship. He still avoided commenting in any conversation about them, but at least he wasn't openly hostile, a win all around.

There was only one problem with the last three weeks and that was me. I was falling hopelessly further and further under Judah's spell with every minute I spent in his company. He wasn't just sexy and unpredictable, he was smart, funny, thoughtful, and surprisingly open with his feelings once he let you in, more than me as it turned out.

It wasn't that I was holding back, but yeah, I was holding back. Half of me wanted to wrap my heart and trust around Judah Madden and hold on for the ride. But the other half knew that ride was going to be hell in places with no guarantees of a future. And the tender places inside me that had only just healed from losing Sally, simply weren't sure they'd survive losing Judah Madden as well, if he decided he wanted out. For all that grief and guilt and Sally *weren't* holding me back, fear was. I was still raw in those heart spaces, tender, like a broken bone newly knitted, and I could feel myself protecting it, trying and failing to keep some distance.

I was falling in love and there wasn't a damn thing I could do about it other than try and hide it so I didn't scare him away or make his decisions even harder. Judah was ten years younger. He had a new life to craft, one that had to hold the weight of his loss and his health issues. He was getting on better with Leroy, but mussel farming in Painted Bay was never going to be Judah's thing, and I wouldn't have him settle for second best just to accommodate this new relationship. As a couple, we wouldn't survive the fallout of a decision like that, long-term. And so I did the only thing I could. I hoped and prayed and kept the depth of my growing feelings to myself.

"Just so you know, this doesn't count as a date," Judah said, wiping his hands on a paper napkin.

"I beg to differ," I told him. "You and me together, food, drink, and conversation aplenty with the added interest of a stakeout—ergo, a date."

"You're working."

"Not officially."

He reached a hand to my groin and squeezed my dick. "So, that must mean we can fool around, yeah?"

I was about to agree when the front door of the villa suddenly opened and the two brothers spilled out and into Paul Laird's Everest parked in the drive.

My heart ticked up. "Here we go. Buckle up."

Judah dropped his hand and his bottom lip. "Like I said. Soooo not a date."

I leaned over and kissed him quickly on the lips. "I'll make it up to you."

"Promises, promises." He pulled on his seatbelt as I threw Leroy's old Corolla into gear and followed the brothers at a distance.

They appeared to be in no hurry, making their way into town to a coffee shop on the main street where they offloaded to a window seat inside. I got a park close by so I could watch through the glass. The whole thing was beginning to look like a lost cause. If they ate and went home, I was calling it a day, and I said as much to Judah.

He unbuckled and turned sideways in his seat to face me. "So."

His wary tone had me suddenly nervous, and I kept focussed on the café as he continued.

"I've, ah, been applying for a few jobs. I don't want to be working on the mussel farm forever. I need to find something I actually enjoy doing."

"Of course." I tried to keep my voice even. Judah hadn't mentioned anything about looking for work. "How's it going?"

I felt his eyes on me while I kept mine rigidly focussed on the brothers and off the fact of my heart skipping out of my chest. There were no points for guessing where this was going.

"Not great, as it happens. Not having transport is a big problem, as I expected. There's nothing in Painted Bay unless I want to wash hair for May in the salon. I even thought about that for three seconds, which only shows how desperate I am."

"She's a great hairdresser."

"She is." He ran his fingers through the back of the trendy new cut she'd given him. It was a take on his Boston cut but left a little longer around the ears, and it looked good on him.

"That means I'd have to catch a bus or find a ride to a job somewhere else," he said, then added, "if I want to stay in Painted Bay, that is."

I still couldn't look at him, too scared of what my expression might reveal. "Right."

"And then there's the Meniere's. I can't do anything that requires heavy lifting or driving machinery, and I don't exactly have a bunch of skills to offer. Not a lot of call for ex-ballet professionals who can do a mean tour en l'air in Northland New Zealand."

I finally glanced his way. "I'd hire you."

He smiled and brushed the backs of his fingers down my cheek. "I think there's room for only one uniform in this relationship, and it looks a lot better on you."

"They're getting food." I watched the server set plates on the Laird table and slid down in my seat. "We could be here a while."

"Are you deliberately avoiding talking about this?" he asked bluntly.

Yes. I turned in my seat. "What about university? Or some online courses. What are you interested in?"

"Dance."

I sighed. "What else?"

"Ballet." He stared at me. "I mean it, Morgan. I've looked at a ton of stuff like that, but it boils down to the fact dance is what I'm good at, and not just good, excellent. Nothing else feels the same, and I was never good at school. I barely made it to graduation. If I try and study something that doesn't grab me, that I don't love, especially online, I'll fail. And I can't afford to waste money."

"I can help—"

"No," he leapt in, then sighed apologetically. "Thank you, but no."

"Can the farm business extend you—"

"The farm's barely keeping its head above water." He looked away.

Shit. A heavy silence filled the cramped car and I suddenly felt too tight in my own skin. I reached over and threaded our fingers together. "I don't want you to leave."

He squeezed my hand back. "I don't want to go. But it doesn't matter which way I look at it, I don't see a future for me here. I'm a prisoner in this town with no car, no public transport worth a damn, no shops, and nothing with my interests to build a life around."

Except me, but don't go there.

"In a bigger city, I'd have buses and Uber and education options. I could do barista training or any number of things that at least gave me some independence while I decide what I really want."

It made sense. Absolute and terrible sense. Except for the part where he fucking left. *Shit.* "You've talked about teaching dance? Teaching ballet?" Talked, but of course I'd ignored it like I ignored anything to do with him leaving. I needed to start being supportive.

His gaze slid off me and back to the café. "It's still a good option, and I've emailed my old ballet school in Wellington to see what would be involved in the training."

Fuck.

"But it's another thing there's not a lot of call for in Painted Bay, is there?"

Shocker. "You need to go where you'll do best, Judah. You've got a life to build. It's important."

He glanced at me but said nothing, an odd look on his face. But Judah would die the death of a thousand cuts teaching backwater dance to half-interested kids.

He looked away again. "I haven't decided anything. I'm just feeling my way through the options. I can work on the farm as long as I need while I make up my mind; Mum's been clear on that. And even Leroy's been surprisingly understanding, though he's still an arsehole at times."

"Are the two of them doing okay?"

Judah shrugged. "Better. They've talked and agreed to shelve any decision about selling for a year, see where the business and Mum and Martha's relationship stand then. In the meantime, Mum's going to move into Martha's house."

"Wow. Things are getting serious then. I'm glad they sorted things out."

"They're good together. It still feels a bit strange but I'm happy for them both. Hey, look. Your guys have company." Judah pointed to the café.

My head swivelled back to where two men had joined the brothers at their table. I grabbed my phone and zoomed in for a couple of shots. They weren't too clear through the reflections in the window, but there were a lot of gesticulations happening.

"I wish I had a microphone," I lamented watching the energetic conversation.

"Well, they know you but they don't know me." Judah opened his door. "I feel the sudden urge for a coffee. Pick me up down the block when they leave."

I reached for him. "Don't—"

"I'll be fine," he brushed me off, and then he was gone.

Goddammit. The man would be the death of me, and I cursed him seven ways from Sunday as I watched his sexy butt saunter across the street and into the café, bold as brass. I could just make him out at the register putting his order in, after which he took out his phone, apparently engrossed in whatever it was he was pretending to do on it, while hovering not too far away from the table where the four men sat. I had to give it to him, he was a pretty good actor. I wouldn't have looked twice and neither did the four men.

Five minutes later and his order was ready. He came out, completely ignored me parked across the street, and headed up the road to the park on the corner where he sat on a bench and pulled out his phone.

My screen lit up and I answered immediately, still watching the table in the café. "What the hell were you doing?"

Silence, then, "Are we going to have to have this conversation again, Morgan?"

More silence.

"Okay, whatever." I wasn't going to start an argument for being a protective arsehole.

"They make good coffee by the way."

"Judah," I warned, picturing that damn smirk of his.

"Does that mean you don't want the photos I took?"

The cheeky fucker was lucky he was out of reach. "I want them."

"Coming your way now. You can thank me later." He positively purred.

"Don't hold your breath." I put the call on speakerphone while I took a look at the images. "Okay, so I know this younger guy. Harry Brewer, I think it is. We had a heads up about him last year. He was one of a number of arrests in Christchurch for supplying large quantities of pāua and undersized crayfish, but they had to let the whole lot go over a technicality. So I guess that puts the brothers in the right arena of interest, at least. But I've no idea who the other guy is. What were they arguing about?"

Judah sighed. "I can't be much help there but it had something to do with dates and needing a different boat, and that was all I could make out."

"Okay, well, it's good stuff to take to Jon and my boss. So, um, thank you." I felt Judah's smile as if he was next to me.

"You're welcome," he said. "Just give me a second to pull all the daggers out of my back."

I couldn't help but laugh. "Yeah, don't think this gets you out of trouble. You and I are still gonna have a talk."

Judah snorted into the phone. "I like it when you get grumpy. And I think a stern talking to is definitely in order, maybe even sending me to my bedroom for, oh, I don't know, hours and hours should do it. But under strict supervision, of course, just in case I don't take it seriously enough and need further *instruction*. I could be so, so down with that, Morgan. What would you have me do? Get down on my knees? Hands on the shower wall, legs apart? Or maybe a pair of those new tights that arrived this week with my leg above my head against the wall?"

My breath lodged in my throat as a rerun of the last time he'd done that exact same thing ran through my brain. I couldn't believe a guy could stand and lift his leg that high and I'd fucked him till I couldn't see straight.

"Would that make everything better, Morgan? Would you like that?" His voice slid like silk down the phone and my body responded like Pavlov's fucking dog. Judah Madden had my dick on speed dial and there wasn't a thing I could do about it.

"Ah . . ." I cleared my throat. "I . . . yeah, I ah, think that would do nicely."

"Mmm. Good to know. Maybe I could—"

"Wait . . ." The four men at the table were heading for the front door of the cafe. "They're leaving," I told him. The men hit the sidewalk and headed off in two different directions, the Laird brothers for their car. I made the decision to let them go and focus on the others. "The new guys are coming your way. See if you can spot their vehicle."

"Oh, but wouldn't that be too dangerous for someone like moi?" Judah mocked in a falsetto voice.

"Don't even go there," I answered coolly. "And don't take any chances either. Oh, and don't get seen."

"Yes, sir. That's a lot of don'ts in there."

I watched as Judah stood and ambled into the park like he was simply enjoying the sunshine and finishing his coffee. The two men paid him no mind and crossed the road toward him before heading out of sight. Judah followed at a distance, keeping inside the park till I lost sight of him too.

Meanwhile, the Laird brothers got into their car and took off back the way they'd come. I figured I'd learned about as much as I was going to for an unpaid Saturday's work. A minute later Judah texted me the vehicle's plate, and to come pick him up. And when he jumped in the passenger seat, he looked so fucking smug I wanted to throw him in the backseat and have my wicked way, public indecency be damned.

"Jesus, Morgan. If you keep looking at me like that, my dick's gonna burn to a fucking crisp. You need to take me home." He fisted my shirt and pulled me into a fierce kiss, then let me go just enough to stare into my eyes. "I've been a bad, bad boy, and I need to be *punished*."

Holy smokes. I kissed him once again and pushed him back into his seat. "Buckle up now. And start thinking about those goddamn tights. I'm in the mood for white, and I think we'll get through more than one pair."

He laughed but got that belt on faster than you could say pirouette.

Two hours and three orgasms later, I left a boiling hot, naked, and snoozing Judah in his bed, hobbled my aching arse into his shower for a quick clean-up, and then headed to Jon's house for a catch-up on our guys. He opened the door in his boardies and nothing else and I held my hand up to my eyes.

"Holy crap, there's enough sun reflecting off that lily-white skin of yours to cause a fire halfway down the block. Warn a guy next time. I think you just fried my retinas."

"Fuck you." He swatted my hands aside and laughed. "And come inside before you let all the heat in. Connie's relented and switched on the air con. We're sitting in front of it counting the dollars floating through the air with every minute. Still, at least I'm not fucking melting through the floorboards. It's gotta be a million degrees out there today and pissing humidity. This is supposed to be the end of summer."

"I know." I kicked off my shoes and followed him into the lounge. "Man this cool air feels good. Hey, Connie."

"Hey, Morgan," Connie appeared from the kitchen. A whip-smart lawyer, she spent four days a week working out of her Auckland practice and staying in a small apartment they rented there. The commuting wasn't a lifestyle I envied—an image of Judah sprang to mind—but it seemed to work for them just fine. They'd had no luck trying for children, and after a range of failed fertility treatments, they'd decided to just get on with life.

"Sorry to interrupt your Saturday." I grabbed a seat on the couch and Connie shoved a beer into my hand. I took a long swallow and feasted my eyes on the spectacular view through the wall of glass facing the sea.

Jon and Connie leased the ultra-modern clifftop house with its panoramic view over the Pacific Ocean, a far cry from the humble police house that came free with Jon's job, just down the road. The perks of being married to a successful lawyer, and I didn't begrudge them a single minute of it. Being separated four days a week had to suck, but sinking money into a permanent house in Painted Bay would've been foolhardy when Jon could find himself moved somewhere else in the future.

"Not a problem." Connie bent to kiss her husband on the cheek. "I have some prep to do for a trial next week, so you've saved me getting *the look* for disappearing into my office on a weekend."

"As if." Jon slapped his wife's arse as she turned to leave. "I'll get dinner. I'll call you when it's ready." He watched his wife go, then turned to me. "So, how'd the information gathering go?"

I told him, including Judah's eavesdropping and photos. Jon's eyebrows hit his hairline but he didn't say anything, for which I was grateful. Instead, he studied the photos with a decided frown. I told him my take on the younger well-dressed newcomer to the table.

"And I know the other dude." He tapped the older man in the photo. "Stephen Pryor or Peyton or something. I'll have to look it up. He's a mid-level gang affiliate. Does some of their dirty work, and he's been inside for robbery and drug possession. Nasty piece of work. Your guy is new to me though. I wonder, what's he doing in our neck of the woods? I'll run it by the team. Something's going on. Another?" Jon held up his empty bottle.

I nodded. "Go on. I left the Hilux at Judah's and walked. I'll roll back down the hill if I have to."

Jon laughed and got us another couple of IPAs. "So, how is the young ballet star? The grapevine has been surprisingly quiet on the two of you lately."

I snorted and raised my beer in a toast, which Jon returned. "Too busy with the scandal of Martha and Cora, no doubt."

"Very likely." Jon threw his legs up on the footstool, looking like he was settling in for the night. "The volume's still cranked high on that particular morsel of gossip. Mind you, I wouldn't have picked it in a million years either. Not because of the bisexual thing," he was quick to point out. "But because it was Martha. That woman scares the shit out of me most days."

I almost choked on my beer and had to wipe my chin. "I know what you mean. But I've watched them at the last two Sunday lunches now they're out in the open, and Martha's very different around Cora. Very protective, but if anything, she seems to almost step back and let Cora lead the way. Not at all what you'd expect. It's all very interesting."

Jon took a long swallow of his beer. "Well, I wish them luck. Not enough love in the world as it is. How's Leroy about it now?"

"Better. But I think there's a lot more going on in his pot than just his mum and Martha."

"Mmm. So, back to Judah. No more vertigo attacks in the main street, I take it, or I would've heard."

"No. He's had a couple, one at home and one on the boat, over the last three weeks, but that's a big improvement. He's got himself a health strategy—no drinking and a low-salt diet that's supposed to reduce the fluid build-up in his ears. He hates it but is willing to give it a decent try before making his mind up. The fact he's having fewer attacks is a good sign it might be working. I'm driving him to Auckland for his specialist appointment this week. There's a whole lot of tests involved, so he might learn more."

"Sounds like he's getting a plan in place. I can't imagine suddenly finding myself having to deal with something like that. I wouldn't be able to do this job, for a start."

"Same here. Gets you thinking, doesn't it? How you'd handle it? I wouldn't do well, I don't think."

We finished our beers in silence, my gaze, as always, drawn out the window to the view. Thick slate-coloured clouds rumbled on the horizon. "There's a storm coming."

Jon followed my gaze. "Explains the humidity."

I leaned forward with my elbows on my thighs, dangling my beer between my knees. "He's been looking at jobs."

Jon turned from the glass with a carefully neutral expression. "I take it from that, you don't mean local."

I dropped my gaze to the polished concrete floor. "There's not much for someone like him around here. And transport's a big problem."

"I can imagine. So are you guys good together? Does this thing between you have potential?"

I looked up. "He needs to get a life going for himself first. I can't come before that."

Jon continued with a flat stare. "That's not what I asked."

"Maybe not, but I can't influence him. He's ten years younger and his life's in a mess. I can't ask him to stay in Painted Bay because of me. This thing between us is too new. And I love it here, you know that. I don't want to move, and he'll probably have to, would even choose to. He has no idea what he wants to do with his life."

"Again, that's not what I asked."

I slumped back in the chair, scooting down against the cushions until I was nearly horizontal. Then I peered at him through the bottle. "I know what you're asking, and yes, I like him, I really like him. And yes, we have potential. And yes, I'm pretty sure he feels the same way. But, and this is a big but, I still can't be a priority for him, not right now. Once he gets his life together and we see where he ends up, then maybe we can do something. But right now I can't be sure if the only reason we're working is because he needs me and likes my company. Maybe, when he gets his life back on track again, he won't feel that way."

"Well, he certainly won't if you don't tell him what you feel and what you want and that maybe you want to be a part of what he decides."

"I *don't know* what I want. It's too soon."

"Don't you? How long did you know Sally before you knew she was it for you?"

I closed my eyes and let my head drop back. "It's not the same thing."

"How long?" he insisted.

"A couple of weeks." I lifted my head and met his gaze. "But that was entirely different. She knew what she wanted, she had a plan, and we both had lives on the go."

Jon stared at me hard. "That's pretty condescending, don't you think? Assuming Judah doesn't know what he wants when it comes to you, even if he's not sure about the rest of his life? Especially since he's not working with all the information he needs."

I didn't answer. I didn't need to. He was right. Not that it changed anything.

"You're scared." He eyeballed me. "You came here when Sally died and the world got too much for you. I'm not saying you don't love it here, because I know you do. But how many people get a second chance at love thrown their way?"

"I don't love Judah."

"I'm not saying you do. I'm saying you have a chance to find out if it could become that, and I'd be very careful about letting Judah slide out of your reach just because you feel comfortable with your life here. Maybe you two will work, maybe you won't, but you would've said that about Sally as well—shit. That's what this is all about, isn't it? You're scared of going all in and losing someone, again."

I rolled my eyes at him and tried to check the tears. It was the last thing I needed.

"Fuck. I'm sorry. I'm such an arse."

"I think it's time for me to go."

"Morgan, I'm sorry. Stay. I'll shut my mouth, I promise."

I put a reassuring hand on his shoulder. "Don't worry. It's not you. I'm just not ready for this conversation. Text me what the team says about our guys and we'll talk later, I promise."

I left with him following me out the front door still apologising.

Out of sight of the house, I took a seat on one of the town's clifftop benches overlooking the sea and caught my breath. I wasn't angry with Jon. That's not why I left. I'd left because he'd been far too close to the truth for me to continue without dissolving into an embarrassing mess on the floor.

I was scared. Of course I was, terrified, if I was truthful. But Jon would never really understand the why of it without experiencing it like I had. I'd packed a lifetime of love and expectation into what Sally and I had built together, and we had everything on our side. We had every reason to think we'd make it, and yet I still lost her. I'd lost her and almost didn't make it back from that.

Whereas this thing with Judah had tons more risk attached to it, way more opportunities for things to go wrong. I didn't trust the universe any longer. It hadn't delivered when I'd ticked all the boxes, so why the hell would I trust it to deliver when we had so much working against us?

No matter how I looked at it, I couldn't see Judah settling down in Painted Bay, and I couldn't imagine leaving. Judah was like a fucking rose in barren soil here, whereas Painted Bay had fed my heart and healed me. How were we supposed to make that work?

No. Judah needed to decide what was best for him first, and then I'd see if I could risk committing all of my newly healed heart once again.

CHAPTER SIXTEEN

Judah

"Stretch, sweetheart. Use your crutches." I held Hannah's leg at the knee as she lifted it as far as she comfortably could behind her, using her crutches for balance at the front. "That's it." I dropped my hands a little and she held the position for a five-count before I supported her again. Her foot wasn't more than a foot off the ground, but a week ago she hadn't managed even half of that.

I squatted down and gave her a big hug. "Well done. I'm so proud of you." I switched the music off from my phone and pulled over a chair for her to sit.

Hannah's eyes lit up at the praise. "I've been using our towel rail and the shelves at the store, and Dad's been helping."

"Well, you tell your Dad, you're doing awesome and we'll be ready for him to take a look by the end of the week."

"Really?"

I nodded. "Really."

We'd been meeting in the side room of the community centre for three weeks and the improvement in Hannah's flexibility was already showing. Of all the things I'd thought Hannah might want to do for the talent show, dance hadn't been among them.

"Danielle said I'm walking better too."

Hannah's physio had called to tell me the exact same thing. Terry had given permission for us to consult so I would know exactly what Hannah could and couldn't do, and anything I had to be aware of.

The unexpected degree of improvement wasn't necessarily going to stop Hannah needing a leg brace in the near future—the arthritis in her right knee was simply punching too hard. But it would maybe push the need back until after the show. I had my fingers crossed, but I'd also made sure her routine was flexible enough in case we needed to accommodate a brace.

"I think I could do the longer dance option if you wanted?" Hannah studied me closely.

"I'm sure you could," I countered, keeping my expression neutral. "But I think we should stick with what we're doing now. We know you can manage this, and I don't want to push things too hard for a first performance."

"Okay." She was disappointed but there was relief in there too, and I knew I'd made the right decision. She brightened. "But you're still going to do the beginning dance with me like you said? A duet, right?"

And Lord help me, I was. The little minx punched well above her weight in the manipulation stakes having agreed to enter the show only if we did the first part of the dance together, and I'd been freaking out ever since.

But watching Hannah work so hard to learn her steps had shamed my fears. What's the worst that could happen? I have a vertigo attack in front of the East Bay Primary School parent and teacher population? Hell, centre stage of the Boston Metropolitan Opera House beat that by a few lifetimes at least.

"Yes, munchkin, I'll be right there beside you, although I have to warn you I might let you down if I have one of my *moments*. Are you ready to go on without me if I do?"

I'd kept Hannah's solo routine very simple, trying to incorporate her crutches like extensions to her arms so they became a part of her body rather than something to hide or minimise. But the part we danced together had a little more meat to it since I was there to help with her balance and provide an element of strength she couldn't summon herself.

Lifts were obviously out, as was anything where I took her full weight, just in case I had a drop attack. I hadn't had one in three weeks, but I didn't trust my body to risk Hannah like that. But I could take her feet on mine and do a few more fancy moves, plus help with some of her turns and slow twirls and other moves where she stayed still and I did all the work circling her instead.

"Of course, silly." She nodded enthusiastically. "And if it happens while we're practising, I call Dad and sit next to you and hold your hand, right?"

Fuck me. "Yes, perfect, munchkin. That's exactly right." We'd talked about my Meniere's when we first started working together, and just as well. I'd had a bad attack in our third rehearsal and Hannah had done exactly what I'd told her and used my phone. Terry came straight away and got me back to the boathouse. Then they both ignored my protests and stayed with me until Morgan got there.

Hannah hadn't batted an eye—one person living with a chronic condition to another. She'd simply kissed me on the cheek and said she hoped this one didn't last too long. It was a sobering reminder of how much the little girl knew of pain and poor health already at such a young age, and it gave me yet another kick in my arse.

It had been Morgan's idea to use the community centre for rehearsals since we were going to need some space, and also because the school had booked it for the talent show itself. But I'd asked Hannah to keep the fact that *I* was dancing with her a secret. Partly as a surprise, but also so I could chicken out if I needed to or if the Meniere's threw a fit at the idea.

I couldn't believe twenty seconds of simple ballet, no big leaps and nothing tricky, had me terrified—as nervous as the first time I'd ever walked on stage. But it did. My solo part gave Hannah a chance to rest and catch her breath. She would turn slowly in place, centre stage, while I did a short solo dance around her. I'd added a few spins and a small jump, because why the hell not? I wasn't going to kill myself if I fell during them and I was sick of playing it safe. If I was going to do this, I was fucking going to do it.

We chatted away as Hannah let me remove the support shoes Terry had bought her especially for dancing and packed them into her dance bag before her dad arrived to pick her up.

"You guys done?" Terry barrelled into the room and clapped his hands. "Chop-chop, honey bunch. We've got a birthday party to get to."

"Bye, Judah." Hannah reached up on her tiptoes and I bent down to receive the kiss on my cheek. "See you tomorrow."

"Saturday," I corrected. "I've got my doctor's appointment tomorrow, remember? But there's only one week left till the concert, so keep practising."

"I will. Bye."

Terry took Hannah's bag and sent her ahead to the car. "Things go okay?" he asked.

"Great. She's amazing."

He grinned with pleasure. "Did she tell you she practises in the store? She won't let me see the whole thing, just snippets, but a month ago she wouldn't have been caught dead doing any of that on her crutches, not where people might see her. You've worked miracles, Judah. I can't thank you enough. She's even talking about the braces like they might not be the worst things ever."

"That's good news. But it's not a one-way street. She's teaching me too. You've got an incredible kid there."

Terry flushed with pride. "I know, right? Her damn mother doesn't know what she's missing."

"She's not coming to the show?"

Terry snorted. "Too busy. I offered to pay for her flight from

Dunedin, but she still won't come. Fuck her, right?" His smile missed his eyes by a million miles.

"Right. But Hannah will have a huge cheering section if Cora and Martha have anything to do with it."

Terry brightened. "And my parents will be there, so yeah, she'll do fine. I'd just hoped for Hannah's sake that maybe . . ."

I touched his arm. "I know. It sucks."

"It does. But I have a party to get her to, so I'll see you Saturday. Good luck with the appointment. You're heading to Auckland with Morgan tonight, right?"

"Once the evening rush settles." I followed Terry out the door to where Hannah sat waiting in their car with the window rolled down. "See ya, munchkin. Be good. Don't eat too much cake."

She pouted. "Pfft. Parties are meant for stuffing yourself with cake."

I laughed. "An excellent point." I waved them off and was heading back inside when someone cleared their throat behind me. I turned to see who it was.

"Judah?"

I had to blink a couple of times to be sure. "Kane? What the hell do you want? I haven't got the time or energy for any of your shit."

Kane's face drained of almost all colour as he stood with his hands in his cargo shorts' pockets, shuffling from foot to foot. If I hadn't known what an A-grade arsehole he was, I might've even said he looked nervous. But Kane Martin, terror of my teenage years and all-around dickhead, had never done nervous, not with me.

His deep blue eyes skittered over my face and I tried to ignore the fact that the lanky, awkward teenager I'd hated with a passion had somehow grown into a strikingly attractive man. *Son of a bitch.* Sometimes life sucked and karma didn't do its job.

"You have every right to hate me," he said.

I cocked a brow and said nothing.

"I *was* a total shithead to you in school."

I snorted. "That's hardly news to me, Kane. And total shithead doesn't even begin to cover it. You made my life a nightmare."

The flush crept up his neck and over his face, and I had to mentally shake myself before I started to feel sorry for the guy.

He swallowed hard. "I know I did. And I don't have any excuse, just that there was a lot going on . . . at home, but I shouldn't have taken it out on you. I'm sorry."

I bristled. Kane Martin had been the primary reason I couldn't get out of Painted Bay fast enough. "No, you fucking shouldn't have. I was a kid, Kane. A kid who had no choice about fitting in. I never did, and I was never going to, no matter how hard I tried. And you were a complete arsehole to me."

I clenched my teeth and tried to quell the burning anger in my gut. "I don't know what this is about. Terry said you'd changed, and maybe you have. But if you think a little enlightenment and a quick apology is going to make up for everything you did to me, you've lost your fucking mind. I'm not going to absolve your guilt on the basis of a few words of remorse. I appreciate the balls it took for you to say something; it's just a shame you didn't have more of that all those years ago when I could've done with a fucking friend rather than a tormentor."

He scrubbed a hand down his face and I noticed it was trembling. *Goddammit, do not feel sorry for him. Do. Not.*

He sucked in a shaky breath. "I know, and as I said, I have no excuse. I don't expect forgiveness. I just wanted to say I was sorry."

My gaze slid over his shoulder to the inky-grey sea beyond, the stiff off-shore wind cutting up white horses and sending them galloping into Painted Bay. "Well, you've said it. Now, how about you leave me alone so I can get on with my day?" I glanced back in time to see his eyes widen.

"I, ah . . . sure. I'll leave you to it. Thanks . . . for listening." He hesitated as if he might say something more, then his shoulders dropped and he headed for the corner of main street.

I waited till he'd nearly reached it, then called out. "And Kane . . ."

He turned, a little too eagerly. "Yeah?"

"Next time you see me and you're tempted to say hello . . . don't." I turned my back on him and disappeared into the community centre.

Two metres inside the door, I crashed against the wall and slid to the floor clutching at my chest. *Holy crap.* Kane Martin had just apologised to me. And I'd told him where to go. Nowhere on my bucket list had that exchange ever been conceivable.

I was shocked and totally pumped at the same time. I'd had Kane pegged for a redneck, dyed in the wool, irredeemable, homophobic dickwad. And I'd been right . . . ten years ago. Now? I didn't know what to think. *You could've heard him out,* a voice that sounded suspiciously like my mother's carped in my ear.

Yeah, I could've.

But it had felt so fucking good, just for a second, to see the sting in his eyes. A tiny reflection of all the times he'd cornered me at school and hurt me with his vicious words. All the times I'd held on just long enough to get to the bathroom before I broke down at the hateful shit. Payback. I'd earned it. Hadn't I?

Maybe.

But as I sat on the floor with the adrenaline finally crashing, all I felt was a numb disappointment in myself and a lot of uncomfortable questions.

Fuck it. I didn't have time or space in my head for anything more right then. I slid my track pants from my leggings underneath and headed back into the rehearsal room where I changed the music to my favourite ballet. Kane Martin wasn't going to take anything more from me.

This had been a good day. A day where I felt solid and well balanced for a change, and where I'd just handed my childhood bully his arse on a platter. I felt an urge to beat my wings a little, test my body while I felt good. I stretched through my warm-up and then let my body take me where it wanted. And what it wanted was to fly. I sailed around the room, adding a few complicated foot changes and spins to my regular routine. And it felt good. More than good. It felt . . . redeeming.

And as the minutes passed, all those thoughts screwing with my head dissolved into the rhythmic pattern of the dance that filled my soul. In the three weeks since Morgan had given me the barre, I'd grown in confidence, my muscles increasingly familiar, stronger, more supple. My fitness was returning, and the ballet, along with finding the courage to use my bike around town, had me feeling more human and independent than I had in a long time.

Not that the vertigo had miraculously disappeared, it hadn't, but it was definitely improved. Whether it was the exercise, the diet, the no alcohol, Morgan, the medication, or whatever, it was enough to have me feeling a lot more positive that I'd find a way through this to something more.

Cinderella filled the room, carrying my feet over the wide oak floorboards, rushing through my blood, firing my heart, and quickening my step. I tried to think of the last time I'd danced it. New York? Dallas? I couldn't remember. I landed a restrained jeté, my heart pumping, only to come to an abrupt halt a few metres from Morgan who was leaning against the door, watching me with the sexiest damn smile that went straight to my balls.

"Afternoon, babe," he drawled, and I might've flushed just a little.

I never got sick of hearing that word fall from Morgan's lips. In three weeks, I'd turned into a total sap.

He pushed off the door and crowded me up against the wall, one hand cupping my firming cock through my leggings. The man had a fetish, there was no doubt about it. But it was one I was more than happy to indulge. Some of our best sex happened after he watched me dance. Ballet and performance had always been a point of arousal for me, and it seemed Morgan was also a fan, of the attire if nothing else.

I pushed hard into his hand and his grip firmed while his mouth found its way to my neck. I angled my head to give him more room to work those sneaky lips. "These are brand new tights, Mr Fisheries Officer," I scolded, groaning as he nipped and kissed his way down my throat. "Don't you dare ruin them."

"I can't be held responsible for my actions," he answered, then sucked the skin of my bare shoulder into what was sure to be an impressive hickey. "You look so fucking delicious, and the way you move, I just . . . I can't even find the words."

I slipped sideways and spun him so we traded places, sliding my hands up under his shirt into all that glorious hair. My mouth found his and I dipped inside for that familiar taste of coffee, salt, and today —a bitter-sweetness. I pulled back, licking my lips. "Chocolate?"

Morgan waggled his eyebrows. "Jam's brownie. I was filling in some time at his shop till you were done."

"Hmm. That man has his sights set on you." I knew Morgan wasn't remotely interested in the shop owner, but I loved giving him a hard time about Jam's flirting. "Better not be fudge brownie is all I'm gonna say."

Morgan exploded in a fit of coughing and I laughed. "And my work here is done." I kissed his cheek and set about packing up my gear.

———

We got to our fancy Auckland hotel just before nine. I'd left the booking to Morgan because he'd threatened me with intense bodily harm if I didn't. The salary of a professional dancer had left me an unrepentant cheapskate when it came to accommodation, a side Morgan wasn't about to indulge. He liked his home comforts.

Going along with that, he ordered room service rather than pizza, and we exchanged blow jobs in the obscenely large shower while we waited for the food to arrive, and not for the first time I thought I could perhaps get used to being spoiled, though I'd prefer to have a better income so I could return the favour.

That was, however, a touchy subject, and one I was trying not to dwell on. I'd had zero luck nailing down a local job that paid even half-decent wages or that would employ me at all, to be honest. And since our brief chat in the car the previous weekend, it was clear Morgan wasn't keen to raise the subject between us again, either.

I was pretty damned confused. Staying in Painted Bay had never been a consideration before Morgan, and I wasn't sure that should change just because he and I were a *thing*. There was nothing here for me. My family? Yes. But Leroy had the mussel farm, Mum had Martha, and I didn't fit into the town any better than I had as a kid. And if I was ever going to consider teaching dance as a sideways career move, I was hardly going to find the numbers I needed in Painted Bay or it's rural surrounds.

And yet the idea of simply leaving and chucking what Morgan and I had started tore at my heart for reasons I wasn't prepared to look at too closely, not while I didn't know how deeply he felt about us.

I'd never fallen for a man like this. Never hung on anyone's calls or texts or ached for the sight of them, the touch of them, the smell of them. It was new and intoxicating and so damn scary. And I felt very, very alone in it all.

Morgan liked me, I knew that much. But more than that? I had no idea. He was trying not to influence me, I understood that, but the mere fact he could remain so calm and hands-off had me almost convinced he was still very unsure about us at all. And I couldn't make such an important decision on such a shaky foundation.

His brother had offered to put us up at his house rather than us get a hotel, but I was too nervous about all the tests and the appointment to handle a long round of excruciating small talk with Morgan's family. And to be honest, he hadn't needed much convincing.

We shared a bed most nights, but the luxury of a night together with no work demands, a super king bed, a room-for-two shower, and room service? Hell, what's not to love about that? I'd packed enough condoms and lube to cover a pride parade and a bottle of ibuprofen to smooth the edges of what I hoped would be a delicious afterburn for both of us. I might've had an unapologetic preference for topping most of my life, but I was definitely developing a taste for Morgan's dick in my arse and the feel of all that soft hair tickling my southern geography.

"You worried about tomorrow?" Morgan pushed his empty plate to the side and wiped his mouth on the napkin.

I nodded and downed my utensils, having only managed half the food on my own plate. "I don't expect to hear anything new, necessarily." I spun my empty apple juice carton on the table between us. "But I'm a bit nervous about what the tests might show six months down the track from the last ones. Would, ah, would you mind coming with me? Not to the tests, but the appointment after?"

Morgan's mouth opened, then closed, then opened again, and a brief smile played over his mouth. "Of course, if you're sure you want me there?"

"I do. It'll be good to have someone else's ears there in case I forget something after. But if you'd rather not—"

"I'll come." He reached over and squeezed my arm. "No problem."

A rush of air left my lungs and I felt myself relaxing. "Thanks for that."

He took the squished carton from my hand and threaded our fingers together. "You're welcome. I know it sucks, but you can't change what tomorrow's gonna bring. It is what it is. At least you'll have some facts to work with and a better idea of what to expect and plan for, right? You said some people find things settle after a few years and they can almost return to a normal life? Maybe you'll get lucky."

I wrinkled my nose. "Some, yes. But most of those don't get drop attacks in the early stages, either, or get this as young as me. And so far, I haven't exactly been a poster boy for positive outcomes."

"But you don't know that, not yet."

My gaze slid to the table. "No, not yet. But a lot of my planning hinges on what I hear tomorrow." I sent Morgan a pointed look. "A lot."

He ran his free hand over his face. "Judah, I—"

"It's fine, Morgan. I understand." *Maybe too well.*

He watched me for a few seconds, then shifted back on his chair and stretched his legs out, keeping hold of my hand. "Did you hear back about the ballet teacher training?"

And not for the first time I wished I could see inside his brain. But I wasn't going to put him on the spot and ask what he was thinking about us. If Morgan wanted to keep us together, I needed to hear it from him freely.

I sighed and pulled my hand free. "My dance degree from Boston works fine as a base, but for credibility and to be able to run my own studio and teach students for their examinations, I'd need further training, which would also mean some extended periods working with dance students under supervision in someone else's studio. There are some choices in how I'd do that from Diplomas in Dance Teaching right through to a bachelor's programme, but none of them are cheap and I wouldn't be earning much to start."

"Where would you go for this?" Morgan began stacking our plates back on the tray.

I watched his awkward unease and swallowed a sigh. "Auckland or Wellington, most likely. Australia has some good training programmes too."

He hesitated in his stacking. "Oh, okay."

Okay, good? Okay, bad? Okay, no, please, I don't want you to go? Bloody hell. For a straight-talking guy, Morgan was suddenly all kinds of vague when it came to my future plans, and I wanted to slap him.

He shoved the tray outside the door of our room and took a seat on the massive bed a good three metres away. If I could've rolled my eyes any further, they'd have fallen out the back of my head. I wasn't sure who was the grown-up here anymore.

"Which would be better for you?" he asked with a blank expression.

I eyed him in disbelief. "Which would be better for *you*, Morgan?" I returned, equally deadpan.

He frowned in confusion. "What do you mean? I wouldn't know anything about it. Which is the better school?"

I crossed the distance between us, shoved him on his back, and straddled his hips. The guy could be as dense as a log. I lifted his hands above his head and held them there as I leaned forward, my face hovering just above his. "And *I* meant, would you rather I be as far away as possible because you don't want to do the distance thing at all? Or within driving distance because you want to try?" I swallowed the mounting fear in my throat, but for fuck's sake, one of us had to ask the damn question.

I waited, watching as he formed an answer, his eyes locked on mine, which was something, at least.

"And if we try, what happens after the training?" he asked softly. "I can't imagine you teaching ballet in Painted Bay?"

Shit. "Do we need to have the answer to that now? Can't we just give things a go and see how we do first? It would only be for a year or so."

He blinked slowly. "Says the man ten years younger than me."

I released his hands, flopped down on the bed beside him, and stared up at the ceiling. "Age has nothing to do with this and you know it."

He turned on his side to face me and reached for a lock of my hair, which he then twirled in his fingers. "Maybe not age, but I've lost a life partner already, Judah, and I've done a lot of reflection in the last five years—the kind of stuff you're doing now, to be honest. And I know how that can change a person. I'm ready for another relationship, I know that now, but I'm not sure I could survive losing another someone special to me quite so soon. I guess what I'm saying is that I need to have some clarity around your plans before I can say I'm all in. I need you to have some of your own answers, first."

My heart jolted in my chest and I rolled to face him, his breath hot on my lips. "Are you saying I could become someone that special?"

His expression softened and he let go of my hair to run his fingers the length of my jaw. "I'm saying you already are, Judah. I care deeply for you, too fast, and way more than is good for me. But that doesn't necessarily solve our problems."

I wasn't sure how right he was about that, but I took the crumb he'd thrown my way and revelled in the fact Morgan Wipene cared deeply for me. We were dancing around each other's words, hinting at more, but it was enough, for now.

I brushed my lips over his and cradled his face. "You're pretty special to me too, and I need you to promise you'll keep talking to me. I know you don't want to influence my decisions, but you do, simply by being you, and I need to know what you're thinking."

He studied me for a long moment, then nodded. "All right. I promise. As long as you promise to make the decisions that are best for you."

How the hell was I going to do that? "I promise." I fired him a wicked grin. "Now can we skip to the part where we move temporarily into denial and use that obscene amount of lube I packed? My dick has an appointment with your prostate that I'd hate to miss."

Morgan laughed and rolled me on top of him, pinning me in place with his legs locked around my waist. "Wanna toss a coin for the first round?"

"Pfft," I scoffed and tweaked his nose. "It's like you don't even know me. You've got one minute to get naked and be on your hands and knees with your arse in the air."

He made it in thirty seconds.

CHAPTER SEVENTEEN

Morgan

THE DOCTOR'S OFFICE HAD THAT FAMILIAR AIR OF TRYING-TOO-hard neutral-toned serenity, that only made you more nervous because you knew exactly what they were trying to do. I sat on my hands and did my best to look like the décor was working as we waited for Judah's doctor to collate the morning's results.

Anything *but* calm described Judah, sitting alongside me, fidgeting his body into the next century.

"Sit still," I whispered. "You're wearing out the chair."

He fired me a glare and the doctor glanced up with a smile.

"I won't be long," he said, flicking through the papers.

Judah went back to fidgeting and I clamped a hand on his thigh. He covered it with his own and started jiggling his leg. *Lord, help me.*

Not that I could blame him. After getting way too little sleep, Judah had spent three hours weaving his way through a number of waiting rooms, from one set of tests to another until we'd finally met back at his specialist's rooms to hear the results. He was strung so far out I doubted the space station could see him.

Judah's doctor, Peter, was somewhere in his fifties and with the kind of easy approach and crinkled-eyed smile that spoke of years of laughter and a positive can-do attitude towards life's troubles. I could imagine his patients loved him, but as I watched him scanning the results, I had the uneasy feeling he wasn't liking everything he saw, and I had no doubt Judah had picked up on that as well.

After a few moments, Peter sighed, shuffled the papers back into some sort of order, and sank back in his chair.

Judah and I let out a simultaneous sigh and waited.

"There's good news and bad news," Peter began.

Judah said nothing but the clamp he had on my fingers ramped up to tourniquet level.

"The good news first," Peter continued. "Your blood results are good, Judah, and I think the lifestyle changes you've made in diet, drinking, and exercise seem to be making a difference. The drop in the frequency of your attacks says a lot about that. It should also give you some reassurance that you're on the right track.

"The addition of the steroids by your GP on a temporary basis while you made those changes was the right decision, but we'll probably look at tapering those off soon. I'm gonna give them another week and then get you to follow the pharmacist's instructions for weaning off them. I'm also going to change your vestibular suppressant—the one you take when an attack happens since yours are consistently lasting several hours. It can't hurt, and if we can shorten the length of an attack, that's a good thing long-term."

I wrote notes on my phone for Judah to read later. The doctor had been less keen on recording the session and I understood his concerns.

He studied Judah carefully and I could sense he was holding back. "In seventy per cent of patients, diet and medication control the attacks to a manageable level. We'd obviously prefer to get rid of them, but as I'm sure you're aware, that doesn't happen as often as we'd like."

Judah let out another long sigh. "What about the drop attacks?"

Peter's brow wrinkled. "Ah, yes. It's rare for someone your age to have to deal with those, but you said you were mostly free of them until you came home, am I right?"

Judah nodded.

"And you've only had one in the last three weeks since you've been taking better care of yourself?"

Another nod.

Peter seemed happy with that. "Then I think we can assume that number will continue to decrease if you keep up the good work. They were likely brought on by stress, diet, and . . . alcohol." He peered over the top of his glasses and Judah's cheeks pinked up. "Enough said, I hope."

"I got the message," Judah answered quietly.

"Many people can return to a drink now and then; others can't. When things stabilise, you can try. And if the drop attacks don't improve on their own, then we'll consider other options like steroid injections into the middle ear, but it's too soon for that now. All the more invasive procedures have their own set of problems, including permanent damage to your hearing and balance."

God almighty, this disease was a fucking nightmare.

Peter continued, "But I *am* going to refer you to our support group because everyone needs help to cope, *everyone.*" He paused for effect. "And I'm also sending a referral to my vestibular rehab therapy nurse. She'll arm you with a whole range of exercises to try and retrain your balance system. You can talk with her via Skype if you need to, and your ballet training will be surprisingly helpful with that side of things, as I think you're already aware—learning how to balance with all those spins."

Judah nodded and I wished I had raised what I'd found on Google and not been so worried about his reaction.

"What about alternative treatments?" Judah asked. "Acupuncture and stuff like gingko biloba that my mum found out about."

Peter nodded. "As long as you run them by me and your pharmacist so we can make sure they won't cause any complications, I have no problem with you trying anything that might help. This is a shit of a disease, Judah, and we're open to anything that helps, just talk to us first."

"Good to know."

"How's the brain fog?"

Judah wrinkled his nose. "Depends on the day. If I haven't had an attack for a while, it's okay. Other days my concentration is for shit and I can't make a decision to save myself let alone think straight, pardon the pun."

Peter laughed, those eyes crinkling up in delight. "And that's where the support group may be of the most help—not the gay part." He chuckled again. "But with the brain fog. There's lots of techniques you can use, and I'm sure the group as a whole will have tried them all."

"Dance helps a lot, as long as I'm not shaky at the time."

That had been the best development in the last month. Judah couldn't always do everything he wanted to, but he always felt better, more solid on his feet after a dance session.

Peter's face lit up. "That's excellent news. Creativity is one of the best-known ways to improve the fog. It's like a step class for your brain." Then he sat back and the smile dropped. "Now for the not-so-positive results."

Judah's shoulders tensed and I scooted closer, looping my arm around the back of his chair. He leaned ever so slightly against me and I tugged him in.

"Your audiometry results have me a little concerned. There are early signs of damage in your right ear, not surprising in itself, but the level is more than we would've expected in someone as young as yourself."

You could've cut the air with a knife.

"What does that mean?" Judah pulled away when I put a hand on his back.

"It's too early to say for sure, and it's maybe that you've had a bad

few months since you've been home, but let's just say it's not encouraging. It may mean that even if we get on top of things over the next couple
of years, you might be left with a degree of hearing loss, regardless."

Judah froze. "How much loss?"

Peter shrugged. "It's impossible to say. But there's also early
evidence of left ear involvement, as well."

"My *left* ear? But—"

Goddammit.

"Do you ever get tinnitus in that ear?"

I saw the answer in Judah's devastated expression, and he almost
collapsed in on himself. "I . . . just, I thought it was only . . . shit." He
put his face in his hands for a moment, then looked up again. "It's not
as bad as the right and not all the time. I didn't want to . . . I mean, it
doesn't usually happen in both ears, right?"

"Not usually, but in fifteen to twenty per cent of cases, yes,
though not always at the same time and not always to the same
degree."

Silence filled the room, and to his credit, Peter didn't try to fill it,
giving Judah time to absorb the news. I risked another hand to
Judah's back and this time he let me.

Eventually he cleared his throat and looked up. "So what does
this mean for me now?"

Peter steepled his fingers. "Nothing different to what I've already
said. But it's one of the reasons we won't rush into more serious treatments. We keep doing what we're doing, but I want to see you back
for more audiometry testing sooner rather than later. We'll send you
an appointment."

"But if it continues in the left ear as well as the right, I could
potentially lose hearing in both. That's possible, isn't it?" Judah
pushed.

Peter hesitated, then answered, "Yes, it's possible. Every time you
have an attack, it does damage, and the damage becomes cumulative
and irreversible. Even if your Meniere's improves in a few years, there

will still likely be damage. But the degree of loss can't be predicted. It could be minor."

"Or it could be a lot more."

Peter nodded. "It could. We simply don't know. And I don't want to scare you with another layer of what-ifs and concerns, but the risk is real, especially for people with both ears affected. And for that reason, I'd be remiss if I didn't suggest that you consider learning whatever you can now that might help with that hearing loss down the track. I tell this to all my patients, not just you. Hearing aids can help, but it's complicated with Meniere's, and you have a long life ahead of you. Some hearing loss is almost inevitable and it makes sense to be prepared."

Fucking hell.

Judah's brow furrowed in thought and I saw when it hit him. "You're talking things like sign language, right?"

Peter nodded. "Just something to think about, with both ears involved. You might never need it, Judah, but it's a worthwhile skill to have, regardless."

"Holy shit. I can't believe this." Judah slumped back in his chair.

Sign language. If I was reeling, I could imagine what Judah was feeling, and one look at his face told me everything I needed to know.

Devastation didn't even begin to cover it.

"We don't have to go," I told Judah for the millionth time. "My brother will understand. You've had a huge shock." But I may as well have been talking to a brick wall for all that Judah was listening, sitting like a slab of glacial ice in the passenger seat.

"Pfft." He stared out the front windscreen, refusing to meet my eyes. "Just another bend in the Judah Madden Road to fuck town, right? I mean, it's not like I need to hear music to dance, is it? No balance and now no music—walk in the fucking park. How am I supposed to teach dance if I can't hear the music?"

"You're getting way ahead of yourself. You heard Peter, there's all levels and degrees of loss, and years till any of it might happen. He was just preparing you. Judah please, let's head back to Painted Bay."

"I'm fine," he snapped. "I want to meet your brother. And you need to see them. We're going, Morgan. Just drive, already."

But Judah wasn't fine. He was as far from fucking fine as it was possible to get. He hadn't said a word after we'd left the doctor's office until we got to the car. And then all he'd said was, "I hope your brother has some beer."

Wonderful. Could this day get any worse? Of course it could.

We drove to my brother's in silence. Every time I tried to get Judah to talk, he just ignored me and stared out the window. I wanted to shake him. I wanted to fold him in my arms and block out the world. I wanted to cry with him and rage at the unfairness, but all I could do, all I was permitted to do was drive.

When I pulled into Cody's driveway, Judah wiped at his eyes and repaired his face, pinning on that false smile from the first night I'd met him, the smile I fucking hated from the minute I saw it. Then he got out without a word. The lunch had disaster written all over it, but in a mood like this, Judah was impossible to reason with. It was like the last month and a half between us had never happened.

He must've caught my mood because he fired me a pointed look. "Don't do this. I don't need your pity on top of everything else." He pasted that godawful smile back in place and headed up the path toward my brother who was on his way to meet us.

Motherfucker.

Once inside I had to keep pinching myself to remember what had gone down in the doctor's office just an hour earlier, because you wouldn't have known it, watching Judah charm his way around my brother, his wife, and Logan, their three-year-old. He said all the right things, complimenting the house and the décor and getting on the floor with Logan to set up a farmyard complete with animal noises. Cody and Tess sent approving smiles my way, and I could see them already imagining Judah and me providing nephews and nieces for them in the future.

Considering the state of Judah's life and our relationship, that would've been laughable had it not been for the fact that I couldn't drag my eyes from him either, my heart squeezing at how easy he appeared around kids, and that they seemed to love him. Logan was a quiet kid, an introvert more likely to bring you a book than anything else. He'd rarely be so comfortable with a stranger, squealing with laughter, and scolding Judah for braying like a donkey when Logan was holding up a pig.

"You've got a good one there." Tess touched my arm as she passed on her way to the kitchen.

Didn't I know it. But *good* wasn't a guarantee of anything with Judah. The news that his hearing was already affected and what the future might have in store for him hadn't just been a shock for Judah. I'd left the office with flashbacks to when Sally had gotten her bad news. Meniere's wasn't terminal like Sally's cancer, but it was going to have profound long-term effects, greater than I'd first thought, greater than even Judah had bargained on. Today had shredded that pretence and brought the challenges he might face front and centre for us both.

Judah caught my eye with a genuine smile, and all my worries faded for a few seconds, lost in that sassy attitude and the soft vulnerability that lay just beneath it. That openness was a big difference between Judah and Sally. The word vulnerable and Sally rarely mixed in the same sentence, and I'd seldom felt the need to protect her emotionally, even in those last months. But Judah brought those instincts raging to the fore, and I was shocked by the urgency I felt at times to stand between him and the world.

I'd fallen hard, there was no use pretending otherwise. I was well on my way to being in love with this beautiful, challenging man. But holy crap, did we have some shit to negotiate, which only ramped up my determination that Judah do what was best for himself, and I would deal with the fallout. I'd keep talking as I'd promised, but watching him play with Logan, I wasn't so sure I was the problem in that regard any longer. Since leaving the appointment, Judah had shut like a clamshell.

For all of that, lunch went well. Cody and Judah got on like a house on fire, Judah hiding his fears with barely a crack in his façade. He drank two beers in quick succession, but when he caught me watching, that jaw of his steeled in defiance and I knew not to say a word. Whether it was me or his own common sense, he didn't have a third. I should've been pleased, but instead, I was slowly fuming, the unanswered questions from the morning eating away at my mood.

When Logan pulled Judah outside for a look at his sandpit, Cody and Tess took the opportunity to drag me into the lounge for the designated grilling.

"He's great," Cody said, his gaze drifting to the ranch slider where Judah and Logan were visible on their hands and knees playing dumpster trucks.

"He is," I answered, finding a grin as Judah fell on his side and Logan climbed on top.

"We watched him dance on those links you sent. He's really good." Tess smiled warmly. "And he's got an amazing body." She sent me a sly wink.

"Oh god, no!" Cody covered his ears. "I do not need to hear that about my brother and his boyfriend." His eyes flew wide. "Shit, my brother has a *boyfriend*."

I laughed and punched Cody playfully on the arm.

"And you obviously like him," Tess added.

"I do." I stared through the slider again. Judah caught me and stuck out his tongue.

"I sense a *but*." She studied me. "You've been quiet since you got here, Morgan. Did something happen this morning?"

I blew out a sigh. "Judah is great, better than great, and to be honest, I think I'm falling for him."

Tess and Cody exchanged not-so-subtle delighted smiles.

"Slow down," I warned them. "He also has a health condition.

Meniere's disease, though I think it's more of a syndrome than a disease."

Their eyebrows popped in unison, and this time the looks they exchanged were concerned.

I raised both hands. "It's not cancer."

"All right, we're listening," Cody said.

And so I told them what I could, using the condensed version Judah and I had talked about for times like this while leaving out the news from the doctor that morning. When I was finished, they both sat like stunned mullets.

Cody finally blew a low whistle. "Jesus, Morgan. You sure know how to pick 'em."

I flipped him off and slouched down in my chair.

He winced. "I'm sorry, that was rude. But . . . just, wow."

Wow, exactly. "Yeah, I know, right?"

"It's just a lot. For him and for you. Are you sure you're ready for this? I know we said it's been five years and you should maybe consider dating again, but that last year with Sally was pretty intense, medically speaking, and this guy—"

"You're a great guy, Morgan," Tess chimed in. "Losing Sally was so tough on you, we felt like we'd lost you as well. And Judah must be feeling a bit lost himself. Do you think it's the best thing, for either of you?"

I bristled. "What is this? Do you think none of that's crossed my mind? And if you think Judah's leaning on me, you don't know him. He's fiercely independent—"

"We don't mean that." Cody sent Tess a warning look. "I think it's just that it would be nice if maybe you didn't have to deal with anything heavy again, medically speaking, just yet."

"We're not trying to tell you what to do," Tess backtracked.

I raised my brows. "Pretty much sounds like you are."

Her cheeks pinked up. "Sorry. It's just that, well, are you sure you're ready for this? He's gonna need a lot of support."

"Yes, Morgan, are you sure you're ready for this?" Judah breezed into the room, Logan in tow.

Goddammit. Just my luck.

"Judah, we didn't mean anything by it." Cody came to my rescue. "We're just concerned. It's no reflection on you or what you guys have. You're clearly great together. Morgan only told us the basics."

"Stop." Judah held up his hands and sat next to me on the couch, threading his fingers through mine. The relief that went through me almost stole my breath. I squeezed his hand and got one in return. "I know Morgan wouldn't say anything we hadn't agreed to. But I'm here now. So, feel free to ask what you want."

Tess and Cody looked at each other, then nodded. And the next few minutes were spent answering their questions right down to the specialist appointment and Judah's potential hearing loss. Judah answered honestly but his demeanour was tense and he never faced me once. I tried to read what I could into the conflicting messages he was sending my way but eventually gave up.

Tess and Cody listened politely, but the way their eyes kept flicking to me, it was clear they were worried, and I was beginning to think letting Judah talk me into going forward with the lunch had been a bad, bad idea.

Cody and Tess became increasingly quiet as the discussion continued, and I was tempted to kick Judah in the shins. He was being blunter than he needed to about a lot of it, as if he was painting it in the worst possible light. My heart sank when I figured out what he was up to. I'd had enough.

"None of this is certain," I finally interrupted. "Everyone with this condition is different, and the hearing loss could be anything from mild to severe. No one can predict it, not even Judah." I eyed him pointedly. "Correct?"

He gave a petulant nod. "But—"

"No buts. There's no point catastrophising when we don't know anything for sure. Plan, yes, but stay positive. I always found that was the best way to deal with this kind of uncertainty. God knows Sally and I lived with enough of it. You just have to let it go and move on."

"I'm not Sally, Morgan." Judah said in a clipped voice, eyeballing me. "And it's *me* dealing with this, not you. We're not the same, *it's* not the same. I don't want this situation compared with what you and Sally went through, and I don't need a caretaker."

The air whooshed out of my lungs and you could've heard a pin drop. A quick glance at Tess and Cody revealed their faces pale and shocked, though I couldn't tell if it was directed at my thoughtless words or Judah's.

"I-I . . ." I stammered. "I'm so sorry. I didn't . . . we didn't, it was . . ."

"Shit." Judah pulled me in for a hug. "I know you're only trying to be there for me. I didn't mean it that way, I just . . ."

I lifted my head and pressed my lips to his. "I know you didn't. And I didn't mean to compare you, I just . . . " I realised Tess had left the room with Logan, and Cody was watching me, worry etched on his face. "Let's talk later, huh?" I said to Judah, then turned to my brother. "I think we'll go. It's been a long day."

"Of course." Cody got to his feet and Tess appeared with some leftovers for Judah to take.

"I'll meet you at the car, if that's okay?" I said to Judah.

He studied me for a second, then nodded and thanked Tess and Cody and headed out the front door.

I turned to my brother and his wife. "I like Judah. I like him a lot. And I know you mean well, but you need to stay out of this. Sally is dead"—they both winced—"but I'm not. And Judah makes me happy. She would want that for me. We don't get to choose who we fall for, and the fact Judah has a health issue is really none of your business, other than to support us both if we need it. Would I have married Sally if I'd known she was going to get sick and die? Yes, I would have. Would you have walked away from each other if one of you were in the same position? I guess only you can answer that. So thanks for lunch and for talking with Judah, but please don't think you know what's best for me."

"Morgan, it wasn't about—" Cody's face fell. "Shit. I'm sorry, okay? And I hope Judah's all right. Please give him our apologies and tell him he's welcome again any time. We didn't mean to upset either of you or cause any problems."

"I know you didn't, but it still happened."

To their credit, they said nothing more other than to repeat their apologies. Everybody hugged, but the goodbyes were awkward and excruciatingly polite, and I drove off with a pit the size of Lake Taupo in my stomach.

CHAPTER EIGHTEEN

Judah

I STRETCHED MY ARM ACROSS THE BED AND TOUCHED . . . nothing—the first time I'd woken up alone in ten days. My heart ached. These days it seemed Morgan was always in my bed and I'd grown to love it. It's just how it happened, like we'd been doing it forever. He'd stayed one night after I'd cooked him dinner and simply never went home. I'd always been happy to go to his, but Morgan loved the boathouse, loved sitting on the deck, morning and night, with his coffee, the two of us reading or chatting as the tide came and went and the seagulls hung around, ever hopeful.

I barely recognised myself. Even when I'd been with Grant, we'd only overnighted a couple of times. Grant was always keen on his own space. Looking back, I should've recognised that for the message it was. And we'd certainly never chatted over breakfast or held hands during a movie. I could almost feel my fillings pop from the syrupy domesticity of it all.

If I dug deep enough, the sharp edges of the Judah who'd arrived back here, brittle, angry, self-absorbed, and at odds with the world, were still there, primed and ready to shred any offer of help. But that Judah rarely made his presence known with Morgan any longer. Morgan had mellowed those defences, exposing the fragility I kept well and truly hidden.

What the hell had I been thinking yesterday? I knew Morgan hadn't meant what he'd said, at least not in the way I took it. But I was hurt. From the doctor's warnings, from overhearing Cody's and Tess's take on Morgan and me, and from the reminder of Sally all over the walls of their lovely house, and the way they still spoke of her, almost reverently.

Morgan wasn't comparing Sally and me because there was no comparison. Sally had it much worse, wasting to nothing and then leaving with a quiet grace that Morgan spoke of in awe. Well, he sure wasn't in awe of me, a petulant child striking out in anger to hurt the one man who cared for me. I'd seen the photos of the two of them on Cody and Tess's wall, as if I needed the reminder of how wonderful, funny, and strong Sally had been, and how I wasn't any of those things.

Morgan had tried numerous times to get me to talk on the two-hour journey back to Painted Bay, but after apologising for my thoughtless words, I had nothing more to say. Not because I was being a prick, but because there was a hole where my feelings should've been. An emptiness that needed consideration before I made any more promises.

Arriving back at the boathouse, I'd told Morgan I needed time to digest everything. I'd challenged him to keep talking to me and yet I was avoiding just that with him. The irony wasn't lost on me. He kissed me, concern filling those beautiful brown eyes, and then did what I asked. The minute I'd stepped inside, however, I'd taken one look at the oppressive emptiness of the small space and almost texted him to come back.

But it was time to be a grown-up. I didn't think I was leaning on Morgan like Tess had suggested, but the words still stung, and I needed to be sure.

I dragged myself into the shower and started getting dressed. Hannah and I had a rehearsal later in the morning and I wasn't about to disappoint someone else. After that, Leroy needed help on the boat, so I had a full day. Three previously unread messages sat on my phone from Morgan, the final saying he'd bring dinner at six, but I wasn't at all sure I was up to that either.

And I was avoiding my mother and Martha like the plague. They wanted to know about the appointment and had left a note on the boathouse door saying to call them when I got back. Yeah. Nah. Neither had I returned any of their texts. I didn't want or need any sympathetic looks or patronising concern.

"Anyone home?" Terry popped his head through my open front door.

"Come in." I answered over the half-wall of my bedroom, still putting my shoes on.

"How'd it go?" Terry took a seat at the dining table.

I told him all about the doctor's appointment as I finished getting ready, including a little about lunch, barring my screw up, and he listened in silence. It was one of the things I appreciated most about Terry.

When I was done, he gave a low whistle and shook his head. "Fun trip then, by the sounds of it."

I snorted and threw a pair of socks at him from the clean washing.

"So, exactly how much wallowing do I need to allow you before I kick your butt into action again? Just a rough guide will do. Are we talking a day's sulk, two days, three? Although personally, I think you'd be pushing it at three."

I flipped him off and joined him at the table. "Your bedside manner leaves a lot to be desired." I kicked him lightly on the shin.

"Ow. I'll have you know I can be very sensitive."

"Yeah, right. I'll believe that when I see it. Where's Hannah?"

"Keeping Jam company and dusting his shelves for some pocket money. Thought I'd come and give you a lift to the community centre. I imagine Morgan was a nice distraction for you in your hour of need."

"What do you mean?"

He rolled his eyes. "Come on, the man's car has been parked down here that often, I'm surprised he hasn't got his own labelled space."

Jesus, this town. "No. As a matter of fact, I sent him home. We both have stuff to think about."

"Oh. My. God." Terry's mouth set in a thin line. "You're such a dipshit."

I bristled. "What's that supposed to mean?"

"Did you even talk to him about it?"

"Yes . . . kind of."

Terry grunted.

"He keeps telling me I need to do what's best for me, and then we'll see where *we* fit into that. So, I'm just doing what he says."

Terry picked up the snow globe, gave it a shake, and my heart shook with it. "How very convenient for you."

I snatched the snow globe from his hands and put it out of reach.

He bit back a smile.

"Not a word," I warned him, then slid down in my seat and sighed. "I possibly didn't tell you everything."

Terry rolled his eyes. "Colour me shocked."

"His brother and wife are really great, and their kid's a blast. But the whole time I was there, I couldn't shake the feeling that I was an intruder, you know?"

"Because of Sally?"

"Partly. They had lots of photos of the two of them, but that didn't bother me too much. And it was fine when they didn't know about the Meniere's, but when they found out, it was clear they were concerned. They were nice about it, but I could tell they were worried about Morgan getting involved with someone else who had health issues."

"But yours are nothing like Sally's."

"No, they're not. But they're not minor either, and I agree with what they said. He deserves an easier time, you know?"

"They told you that?"

"I, ah, might've overheard."

"Oh, for fuck's sake." Terry fell back against his chair.

I waved his concern aside. "It wasn't anything against me as such. Just that Morgan's already been through a lot. And what if I do lose my hearing? That's huge, Terry. That's more than just an inconvenience."

"I'm not disputing that. I have a daughter with a chronic condition, remember? You're preaching to the choir here. But why don't you let Morgan decide if he's up for it or not? He might surprise you."

"But he loves it here. This is his home. And I can't see myself staying, especially now. I'm gonna need education of some sort for a new career, not to mention the hearing services I can access in a bigger city. I have to give myself the best chance."

Terry looked like he wanted to say more, but thankfully he seemed to think better of it. "Okay. But promise me you'll at least talk to him."

"I will."

"Good. Now come on, there's a girl waiting to dance with you. And that's not a sentence you'd hear very often, I imagine."

I grinned and slapped him on the shoulder. "You'd be surprised. The fact I'm not interested doesn't always stop them coming to my yard, man. My body is a magnet, what can I say?"

Terry slapped me up the back of the head. "Would somebody please switch the man off?"

———

"Hang on, Jude, we're almost there." Leroy propped me against the door while he got the key in the lock and I tried not to throw up on his shoes . . . again.

"Judah," I croaked.

"Sorry. *Judah*." He grabbed me around the waist and hauled me through the front door where my body gave up the fight and I hurled all over the entrance floor.

"Fuck. Did you have to?" He stared down at the mess I'd made of his trousers.

"No, I just thought it'd be fun, arsehole. Get me into bed."

"I suppose you want me to clean that up before I go?" he grumbled.

"If it's not too much bother." I tripped over my feet as the walls spun another three-sixty and the bed appeared to move of its own accord. Leroy manhandled me under the sheets and got my shoes off before drawing the duvet over top.

"How'd you manage to miss yourself and get it all over me?"

"Good aim." I shimmied down and tracked the weirdly moving walls till my gaze landed on the dance photo, bringing a swell of relief. "Can you get me a bucket, a bottle of water, and my pills, please. And close the curtains. I'll be good to go after that. And don't forget the floor." Even sick as a dog, that was worth it for the grunt of disgust Leroy gave in reply.

"Yeah, fine. Whatever. You sure you'll be okay?"

"I'll be good. Can I ask why the hell you won't call me Judah?"

He smirked. "Because it pisses you off, baby brother."

"Fucker."

"Bastard."

He left the room and I started my routine of deep breathing and fixing on my still point to get my mind calmed. Water ran in a bucket, then the clatter of a mop was quickly followed by dry retching and string of curses. A smile crossed my lips.

"Okay, I'm off." Leroy strolled back into the room and propped some mail against my bedside lamp. "Found these in your box. You want me to call Morgan?"

"No." It came out sharper than I'd intended, but I'd yet to do more than exchange a few texts with Morgan in the days since we'd got back from Auckland. He'd been busy with some secret poacher mission takedown thing he and Jon were involved with. He hadn't come to Sunday lunch either, and I was . . . well, I was avoiding him, plain and simple.

"Okaaaaay. I'd ask but I really don't want to know about you and your boyfriend's little spats."

"It's not—"

"I'll let Mum know."

"Tell her not to come down. Give me a couple of hours at least."

"I'll try, but you know her. And take tomorrow off."

"I'll be fine."

"Take it off," Leroy ordered. "Patrick's available. He's been asking for extra hours."

Thank Christ. "Why are you being so nice to me?"

"A question I ask myself daily. Get some rest."

He got to the front door before I called out, "Hey, Leroy?"

"What?"

"Thanks, for bringing me back early. And I'm sorry we didn't get the seed ropes finished."

"No problem. It'll all still be waiting tomorrow."

The front door closed and I breathed a sigh of relief that lasted all of a minute until Morgan Wipene strolled into my head, as he always did, and sent what was left of my equilibrium spiralling south.

I needed to talk to him. I wanted to. I just didn't know what I wanted to say. My brain had settled around the hearing issue to a point of almost fatalistic acceptance. I couldn't change it, I couldn't predict it, so I just needed to look after myself the best I could to minimise the number of attacks. That would help minimise the damage. It sounded a lot like what Morgan had suggested at his brother's house. Plan for it, but don't catastrophise. Go figure. Another apology owed.

But the planning for it was something I had to take seriously. And that, plus trying to cobble together ideas for a new career, were taking up enough space in my head without adding my conflicts about a relationship to the mix. But I wanted to. I really, really, wanted to.

Enough. I reached for my phone and sent Morgan a text. *I miss you. Come for dinner tomorrow.*

However many hours later, in the fog of my recovery from the vertigo, my phone buzzed with a reply.

I miss you too. You had an attack?

Bloody Leroy. *It's finished. Just gonna sleep.*

Good. See you tomorrow. I'll bring dinner

I smiled and texted, *Pack a bag.*

He answered with a string of emojis that made me laugh. I might not be able to keep Morgan Wipene in my life long-term, but I was going to damn well enjoy as much of him as I could before the inevitable happened. I threw the phone on the bedside table and my eyes landed on the mail Leroy left there. The name of my old Wellington dance school stood out from the pile.

My heart lurched as I picked it up.

CHAPTER NINETEEN

Morgan

"THAT WAS DELICIOUS." JUDAH PUSHED HIS PLATE ASIDE, leaving a couple of mouthfuls of steak uneaten.

I reached across and snagged them. "Not bad, even if I say so myself." I'd brought rib eye steak to grill on Judah's barbecue, and all the salad fixings and veges came straight from my own garden. Not a word had yet passed between us about the last few days, but it was coming. It stretched like a thin glass bridge between us, and I wondered who'd be brave enough to take the first step. I looked up to find him eyeing me like I'd just eyed the last pieces of steak on his plate. Then he leaned in.

"You know, ever since I first went to your place, I've had a fantasy of fucking you in that vegetable garden of yours, with you wearing nothing but your gumboots."

I nearly choked on the last piece of steak in my mouth, and he laughed.

"As intriguing as that sounds," I said primly, "there's only a low fence between me and the neighbours, and I do have a professional and community reputation to consider."

He waggled his eyebrows. "You could always keep your uniform on. I can unpick the back seam of your trousers. I'm good with my fingers . . . or so I've heard."

Goddamn. I couldn't keep the images forming in my filthy brain. I cleared my throat, unsuccessfully, and had to clear it again. "Well, um, I'm not sure that would work . . . in terms of selling the whole we're-not-having-sex thing. You'd have to be very close to my, you know, and then there's the *thrusting,* and all those *sounds* you make . . ."

I reached over to wipe a smear of dressing from the corner of his mouth with my thumb and then licked it clean, slowly.

His hazel eyes darkened and fixed on my mouth. "Well," he said, licking his lips. "I'm quite partial to being close to your, you know. And we could always slow the thrusting down, take it real slow, spin it out, keep you gagging on that knife-edge you seem to love so much."

And I was pretty sure that was a squeak that slipped through my lips.

"And as for the sounds, we could try that oh-so-very-professional tie of yours across your mouth, what do you think?"

I couldn't think. I couldn't do more than palm my cock and glare at him. That and marvel at how the hell he managed to do this to me every time I came within ten metres.

Because he's perfect for you.

Oh great, now you decide to show up. I booted Sally out of my brain and stared Judah down. "I know exactly what you're doing."

He batted those long lashes at me.

"But it won't work. We need to talk. You know it as well as I do."

He deflated on the spot. "Killjoy."

I reached to cover his hand with mine. "But just in case you've forgotten, I've missed you."

His expression softened and he turned his hand palm up to

thread our fingers together. "I've missed you too. I just needed a bit of time to process."

I raised a brow and he winced. "Okay, that was a lie. Mostly I was just shit scared."

I sagged against the chair, happy he was at least being honest. "Me too. But now we talk, right?"

He held my gaze. "Now we talk."

I drew in a long breath. "Cody and Tess—"

"Care about you. I understand." He sighed dejectedly.

I frowned and looked around the room. "Excuse me, but did I miss something? This was supposed to be a conversation, right? As in, I talk and then you talk, got it?"

He pouted and slid down in his seat. "Smart alec."

I squeezed his hand and rubbed circles on the back with my thumb. "You're right. They do care about me. But they don't know me as well as they think they do. I understand their concern, but they were out of line and I told them that."

"So was I and I'm sorry."

"I was too, and I'm sorry as well. You're *not* Sally in so many, many ways, all of which I like about you." I winked and he smiled. "You have a health condition, sure, but it doesn't scare me off."

"It should."

I put a finger to his lips. "Shhh. And it doesn't. What happened with Cody and Tess was mostly my own fault. I haven't kept in touch with them as well as I should have, so they don't really know where I am now or how much things have changed. Plus, you're the first guy they've ever seen with me. Knowing I'm bi in theory isn't necessarily the same as seeing me with someone. They both thought it was a lot of change in a very short time, and maybe it is. But I realised I'm okay with that. And they also asked me to pass on their apologies and hope it hasn't put you off visiting again."

"Really?" Judah was obviously surprised.

"Really. And I was there for everything the doctor said as well, remember? I know it's going to be hard, I'm not pretending otherwise.

But, and I'll say it again, it doesn't scare me off." I lifted his hand to my lips and kissed the back. "Now it's your turn."

He squirmed a little in his seat. "Well, I'm not sure if this is the best follow up to all that, but—" He reached for an envelope on the far side of the table and handed it to me. "—this came yesterday."

I glanced at the sender's address and raised a brow. "Your old dance school?"

He nodded. "Read it."

I did, and my heart and hopes sank with every fucking line. By the end of the short letter, I could barely think. I kept staring at the last few words to avoid the conversation I knew was coming like a fucking freight train.

"Wow. This is . . . amazing." I lifted my eyes to find Judah studying me intently, his fingers worrying his beauty spot. "I mean, you'd be crazy not to be interested. It's a great offer." I held the letter out for him to take.

He did and slumped down in his chair. "It is. I'm still shocked."

"But this is good news, right?" I struggled to keep my voice even and my expression positive. "They have to think a lot of you to propose something like this. Are you excited?"

"I guess." He studied the letter, looking anything but excited. "It's a long way away." He looked up at me and we both knew what he meant, but I couldn't let any worry about what might happen to us ruin an opportunity that could potentially provide the answer to so many of Judah's problems.

"How about you look at it before coming up with all the negatives?" I hated every positive thing that came out of my damn mouth. "They said to call and discuss it further. Have you?"

He nodded. "This morning."

Fuck. He really was interested. "So, what did they say? When would they want you?"

He sighed and the first glimmer of a smile tugged at his beautiful mouth, those bright eyes sparking to life. Yeah, he was excited. I'd been right to hold back my fear.

"After I'd contacted them about what I would need to do to get my teaching qualification, they got to thinking how they could use me themselves. They've been following my career and they're looking for a new dance teacher. But they also want someone who could mentor some of their up-and-coming dancers about the realities of a professional ballet life."

"Judah, sweetheart, it sounds right up your alley." It so fucking did, and I hated it.

"They'd take me as soon as I could get there."

Of course they would.

"It would only be part-time at first, while I was working on my qualifications, but they said they'd subsidise the costs of those as well. I'd need a medical clearance. Not to dance, just for their peace of mind. And there's great hearing services in Wellington, too. They're gonna fly me down for an interview." He'd clearly done some research and the excitement in his voice and gleam in his eyes revealed just how tempting Judah found the offer.

I blinked a truckload of sand from my eyes before they brimmed, because the job was, in a word, perfect. "This is a career they're talking about, not just some fill-in. It's exactly what you were looking for."

He took my hand in both of his. "Except for one thing. It's in Wellington and you're . . . here."

"Hey." I pulled him onto my lap and he wrapped those lean legs around my waist, his arms around my neck. "One step at a time, remember? You're going to take up their offer to fly down and talk first, right?"

He nestled his face into the side of my neck. "Thursday. I'll fly there and back on the same day from Whangarei."

"I'll take you and pick you up." *God, help me.*

He pulled back and stared at me. "Really?"

"Really. Judah, all I want is the best for you, and dammit to hell, this sounds like a great opportunity. And I'll want to hear all about it the minute you get ba—"

He cut me off before I finished, covering my mouth with his and shoving his tongue down my throat to show just how happy he was. And pretty soon, with an armful of wriggling and excited Judah, it was hard to remember why I had this gnawing hole in my chest that felt suspiciously like my heart had been ripped through my rib cage and a sharp pain in my butt that would've fitted Sally's size eight boot.

But I ignored it all and carried Judah through to his bed while he continued to kiss like a fiend. Once there, he pushed me off and wriggled out of his clothes in seconds like a long-limbed slinky cat, then starfished across the sheets, wearing a wicked twinkle in his eye and nothing else, while I gaped like an idiot

"Take everything off, slowly," he said, fisting his hard cock and stroking slowly.

I blushed like a damn school girl but did my best to give him a sexy striptease. Judah's breath hitched and those hazel eyes bled black, so I figured I must've done a reasonable job.

"Damn, look at you," he said huskily as I threw my briefs to the floor and crawled up his body. "Who knew the heart of a sultry performer beat under all that uniform starch? And I'm the lucky guy who gets to unbutton all that sexy potential." He cradled my face and looked right into my eyes. "You undo me, Morgan, in so many, many ways. You're absolutely fucking perfect for me."

I had to kiss him. Kiss him before I listened to my heart and ran as fast as I could to escape the pain headed my way. Because I knew this ballet school would love him, knew he'd take this job, knew he couldn't turn it down because it was too fucking perfect for him, just as he was too perfect for me.

I kissed my way down his hard-muscled body and swallowed his cock down the back of my throat so my tears would be overlooked. I loved the taste of him, loved taking him in my mouth. And he was so damn responsive. I never had to guess at his hot points; those little groans and soft grunts gave me everything I needed. The way he tilted his hips to encourage my fingers to his arse, one of his favourite things, and mine. The way his hands caught in my hair and trailed down my cheek while he watched me work his cock, dropping his fingers to my lips so he could feel the stretch and slide where he disappeared inside me.

Above everything else, I loved the keening sound he made when he came undone, the wide-eyed pleasure on his face as he watched me swallow his spill, the sharp tang of it on the back of my throat, the heat and clench around my finger on his prostate as he arched up when the wave hit.

I catalogued every one until Judah was done, blissed out and boneless on the sheets. As if by remembering them in detail, I might be saved the anguish of their loss when the time came. Then I crawled up beside him and he rolled to his side and claimed me in a soft, unhurried kiss. Then his hand wrapped around my solid shaft, full and aching for him, and he sighed with pleasure.

"I love that you're so hard for me, baby. Tell me what you want. Anything for you."

Except one thing.

"I want you to fuck me, bare," I answered without even needing to think.

His eyes sprang wide. "But—"

"Your test was negative, right? You said Peter did that with the other bloodwork."

He nodded, still hesitant.

"I am too. So, please. I want to feel you, Judah, all of you with nothing between us. I want to feel you run out of me, marking me. I can't believe I'm even saying those ridiculous words, but I want that, with you."

He gave a soft smile and kissed me on the lips, his cock thickening between us, even at the thought.

"If you're sure."

Never surer. "I am."

His mouth curved up in a shining smile. "Then hell yeah. I want that with you, too. But I want to see your face, understand? I've never done this with anyone else, and I want to remember every second of it."

Not nearly as much as I do. After Judah, I wouldn't be looking for another man in a long, long time.

He rolled on top and we made out for a bit, slow and gentle, grinding softly till his dick fully caught up to speed. He kissed his way up the tentacle of my tattoo and over my shoulder, then reached for the lube and slicked us both up, taking his time, making sure I was open and needy and desperate for more than his fingers.

"Please . . ." I reached for his swollen cock and tugged it gently. "You feel so fucking good like this, nothing but skin and heat and so fucking hard. I can't wait."

"Slowly, sweetheart." Judah rocked forward on his knees and pressed a kiss to both my eyelids. "You're so beautiful. We're gonna take our time. Just let me love you."

My eyes flew open, but it was like he hadn't heard himself say the words, trailing his mouth down my body. He blew long breaths and hummed in pleasure through all the hair he seemed to love so much, teasing first one nipple with his teeth and then the other, before finally lifting my legs onto his shoulders and shuffling forward till his cock pressed at my hole.

Just a couple of nudges and he was in. So huge, so hot, so slick and tight, and so not like anything before.

"Oh god," Judah groaned as he sank in further. "Holy shit, Morgan, you feel fucking amazing. This is . . . son of a bitch, you're like a damn furnace . . . I hope you've got your running shoes on because I'm not gonna last."

He wasn't going to last? Hell, I was barely hanging by a thread, partly from the sheer delight on Judah's face, that being inside me was so hot for him. And partly because he felt so damn good, skin on skin, heat on heat, no drag of rubber, just slick skin. Knowing he was going to spill right up inside me and that part of him would stay there when he pulled out, safe and warm, something to try and hold onto, if only in memory.

I held my breath as Judah bottomed out and held still, head thrown back, blowing out his breaths as if he was too scared to move. Then his head tipped forward and his mouth tugged up at the corners. He opened his eyes and my breath caught in my throat. He might not have heard himself say the words, and maybe he didn't mean them the way I hoped, but the depth of his feelings for me were written in metre-high letters in those bright eyes, and my heart clenched. What the fuck were we doing?

"Hot, damn Morgan. I'm putting dibs on this parking space, because Jesus, you feel good."

I shoved the wrenching misery aside and returned his smile. "Valet service all the way, babe. Now, do you think you can move so I can at least say I lasted more than a couple of strokes before embarrassing myself?"

He snorted. "You and me both, babe. You and me both. Hang on."

He drew back, then slid home, again and again, building force, angling to hit my prostate just right, until I was fisting the sheets to stop my skull from slamming into the headboard. He lifted up so he could watch himself, and I was so close, the look on his face alone almost pushed me over the edge.

"Let go, babe." His gaze lifted and drilled into mine.

And that was all it took. I arched beneath him, breath held, head slammed back in the pillow as I spilled and spilled between us, shuddering with pleasure.

Judah followed a few strokes later, slamming into me with a series of soft grunts as he came apart. Then bending low to press gentle kisses on my chest as he came down, licking the come from high on my belly, before collapsing on top, completely shattered, safe in my arms.

It was a promise that wasn't going to happen, but I wanted him there as long as I could.

Eventually he softened and went to move but I held tight. "Stay inside. Please."

He looked at me with enquiring eyes but didn't ask, settling back in my arms for as long as he could. But when I finally couldn't hold him inside me any longer, he slid to the side and I let him go.

"Can I?" He glanced to where my arse was currently regretting its life choices.

"Sure, but I want to see too."

He scuttled out to the front door, returned with the big mirror, and got me into position so I could see.

"Damn. That probably shouldn't be as hot as it is," he said as we both watched his come trickle out my arse. "Why is that not gross?"

I nudged him with my toes. "Because it's you and me, as close as two people can get. And that's not all there is. When I get up tomorrow, some of you will still be inside me and I'll feel you, see where you've been, remember how you felt, remember what you said."

Judah caught my eye and held it, and a thousand what-ifs and maybes passed between us. He suddenly looked very young and very unsure. I scooted onto my side and patted the bed. He collapsed, and I tucked him into my side and enveloped him in my arms. Then, pressing my lips to his hair, I pulled him close and rocked us together.

After a minute or so, he lifted his chin slightly onto my chest, eyes hidden behind a swathe of dark hair, and spoke in a voice almost too soft to hear. "I think I love you, Morgan."

I froze, my head wanting to run, my heart wanting to take a shovel and dig a hole so big under the two of us that he could never leave me. I nuzzled into his hair and cradled him closer. "I love you too, Judah."

Not that it changed a thing.

Not that it didn't change the world.

CHAPTER TWENTY

Judah

THE SOUND HIT ME FIRST. THEN THE SMELL. THE MUSIC, THE laughter, the soft thud of canvas on boards, the beat count and shouts of the choreographer. Closely followed by the scent of Tiger Balm, Deep Heat, perfume, and sweat. The slightly musty odour of costumes, the particular scent of the steamer used to remove creases as I passed the dressing room, and the waft of hairspray. It brought a wave of nostalgia that had me reaching to steady myself on the door jamb before my knees buckled.

Nothing to do with vertigo. Everything to do with loss.

"Take a look." Colin pushed open the door to the studio for me to walk through, completely oblivious to the chill in my heart and the nauseous pit growing in my stomach.

"Thanks." I slipped inside and stood against the wall, stepping back almost ten years to the first time I'd done this as a raw sixteen-year-old wannabe ballet star, newly arrived in Wellington with dreams too big even for this city. I'd been so freaking elated to be out of Painted Bay, I spent the first month wandering the halls of the ballet school with my mouth hanging open and my eyes bugged.

Now, as I watched the class of late teens being put through their routine, I felt this strange and newly minted tug back to my home town, or more specifically, a certain man who lived there. In unspoken agreement, Morgan and I left our confessions of love between the sheets of my bed when we'd got up on Tuesday morning and had said nothing more since. It was all too new, too unsure, too risky to speak of further. He'd been right. I needed to consider this offer seriously. I couldn't simply dismiss it because we thought we loved each other. If I decided to stay just for him, I might not only regret it, but I might grow to resent him as well.

Rock and a hard place had nothing on this, and when I'd left Morgan in the car at the airport that morning, things had been quiet between us. He'd wished me luck, of course, but the smile never reached his eyes.

A fresh-faced, beautiful young boy caught my eye on the far side of the dance studio. Long and lean, he stretched at the barre and returned my stare as if trying to place me. Then suddenly his eyes widened, and his gaze shifted to the front of the class where a line of photos graced the wall—those who had left this studio to begin successful careers. Mine was one of them. The boy grabbed the arm of his companion and excitedly pointed my way.

The choreographer, Damien, who had also taught me, noticed the boy's excitement and turned to see who'd interrupted his class, no doubt ready to deliver one of the scathing blasts he was known for. But when he saw me, he gave a broad smile instead and ushered me across. I met him in the middle of the room and was immediately enveloped by his broad arms. He'd put on a little weight since I'd seen him last but still had that larger than life presence I'd always adored.

"Delighted to see you, my boy." He stood back to take a good look. "Not bad." He patted my stomach with the back of his hand. "Still fit, I see. Good. You'll need that." His smile dropped. "I was devastated, utterly devastated when I heard you'd had to retire. Incomprehensible. I'm so sorry. You had the world at your feet. One of the best we've ever had."

Had, had, had. Past tense. I needed to get used to that.

Back in Painted Bay, few people had followed my career or even gave a shit about ballet, full stop. In many ways I'd been sheltered from the pity and sympathy of those who'd lived in my professional world. Today that had been stripped away, and never had I felt my loss so keenly than amongst all these excited young faces.

In this world, they knew me, knew the life, knew the cost. Here I wouldn't be able to escape what I'd lost. I was up on the freaking wall for fuck's sake. It would take some getting used to having to face it every day, but if it meant I could stay in this special world, part of a team as passionate about ballet as I was, and help to train new stars, then my skills wouldn't go to waste. I still had something to offer.

The young dancers crowded around as Damien introduced me and talked about what I'd achieved, including my brief stint as a principal dancer in Boston. There were suitable oohs and ahs and lots of questions, and it was heady to have that recognition. I found myself relaxing under the onslaught, smiling and answering their questions with genuine enthusiasm.

Damien left me with the group while he went to chat with Colin, and the two watched from a distance, no doubt discussing me and the role I might play in the company.

The young dancers eventually got around to asking about why I'd left Boston, and I answered them honestly. The change was immediate. Things became quiet and there were uneasy glances and murmurs of sympathy, the same type of tension I'd felt with my fellow dancers in Boston before I left. No one who had eyes on the pinnacle of a physical profession like dance or sport wanted to be confronted with the random ways that particular dream can be crushed.

I got it. I did. They were young. They wanted to hear all about the dance, the stages, the talent, the travel, all of that. But they didn't want to hear about my failure to achieve their dream, and I realised if I accepted this role, I'd need to carefully edit that part of my career so as not to affect their self-belief. They wanted to learn and they wanted advice, but they didn't want or need to know about my personal downfall. Still, it seemed a small price to pay to stay in the world that had become my home.

I danced a little with them as Damien and Colin watched on—no leaps, no big spins. I took no chances but enjoyed the camaraderie, relishing the joy of being part of something special. I even taught the boys a couple of tricks I'd learned to improve the height on their jumps, which sent them scurrying to a corner to madly practise. Hannah's face sprang to mind, and I couldn't help but think she'd love to sit in on one of these classes. Maybe Terry could bring her down for a visit.

The meeting with the senior company managers and artistic director was quick and positive. It had more to do with me explaining about the Meniere's, and in what ways it might potentially impact any work I did for them, than about my skills themselves, which they seemed more than happy with. They seemed to have no doubt about my teaching potential, unlike me. They just needed to be clear whether Meniere's would be a problem.

Didn't we all?

By the end of the interview, they seemed satisfied that any issues would be limited to the occasional cancelled class and necessary rescheduling, which they felt they could work with, but wanted to put me on a six-month contract to start, just in case.

The short contract did present a slight hiccup. If I was going to make such a big change, I'd have preferred longer, but I understood. Their confidence in me as a dancer, albeit in the past and what I might have to offer, more than made up for the rest, and it felt good to be appreciated again.

I boarded the plane back to Whangarei on a high that lasted until

I saw Morgan's face as he waited to pick me up. His gaze searched the crowd as the passengers came through in a confused jumble from baggage claim, and just for a second, I was struck by how damn excited he looked. For me. It seemed ridiculous, but my heart still kicked up. Then I registered my own excitement and smiled. We were such dorks.

To hell with decorum, I ran across and jumped into his arms, wrapping my legs around his waist. Fuck what anyone thought. He gave a grunt and grabbed me under the butt before I fell, his lips finding mine in a long, slow kiss that melted our audience away.

"I missed you," he said, letting me slide to the floor while keeping hold of my hands and ignoring all the looks we were getting.

"Of course you did." I patted his uniform collar back down. "It's been eight hours, after all." I kissed him again, just because I could, and because he looked delicious in his prim and proper fisheries guise, and because he smelled of the sea and everything Morgan. "I missed you too. And I bought—" I unzipped my bag to expose a carry box."—ta-da . . . donuts." I waggled my eyebrows, knowing how much he loved the heart attack balls of deliciousness.

His lips curved up in a slow sexy smile. "And that's why I love you." He grabbed my backpack and hauled me out the main door before I even registered what he'd said.

Fuck, fuck, fuck. Clearly the moratorium on the *I love you* words was over.

I pulled him to a stop. "Whoa there, mister."

"What?" He turned, looking genuinely confused. Then he smiled shyly and it was enough to make my knees wobble. "Oh, you caught that, huh?"

I folded my arms across my chest and stared him down. "Yes, I did. I thought we'd agreed we weren't doing any of that since I might not be staying and all."

He shrugged. "Well, technically we never actually talked about it. Therefore, technically we *couldn't* have agreed. And then I got to thinking, in the excruciatingly long eight hours you were away, that *maybe* we should do as much of that as we can, precisely *because* you might not be staying . . . and all."

I took it for the challenge it was—to step up and own this thing between us, because there was no doubt my heart thrilled at the words.

"Mmm. Very tricky of you." I kept my eyes locked on his. "But let's say *technically,* I might consent to said change in our agreement. I need to maintain the right to change those terms if shit becomes too hard."

He studied me for a moment, then nodded. "Agreed. Now hurry up, I want to hear all about your trip . . . after a donut."

He tugged at my hand, but I didn't budge.

"What now?" He spun back around with a sigh.

I stepped into his space and slid my arms around his waist so we were face to face and I kissed him. "I love you too." Then I grabbed my backpack from his shoulder, laughed, and ran toward his Hilux. "The cronut is mine," I yelled over my shoulder, knowing it was his favourite.

He set off after me. "Why you little . . ." He didn't catch me till I'd made it to his vehicle, where he pinned me against the passenger door, both of us breathless.

"How badly do you want it?" I puffed, snagging my lower lip between my teeth because I knew it drove him nuts.

"Toss you for it." He gave a sly grin that failed to hide the two spots of pink on his cheeks. "And not the kind of toss you're thinking about."

I leaned forward until I could lick his lips. "Oh, I think it's exactly the kind of toss I'm thinking about. You know a spot we can go, close by?"

He thought a minute. "I do."

"Good." I kissed my way to his ear. "Last to come, wins."

Those brown eyes turned black. "You're on."

Morgan

With Hannah standing on the top of his feet, Judah circled them both around the stage, while Terry and I watched from the back of the community centre. With only three days left until the talent show on Friday, their rehearsals had moved from a side room to the stage itself, and from what I could tell, they seemed more than ready.

And I wasn't just talking about Hannah. Judah's increasingly pissy mood over the week reflected just how important this was for him as well. He'd never danced for his home town, not even in school. Drama, yes. Dancing, no. It had been his line in the sand, he'd explained. He didn't care what people said about his acting, but if the bullies started in on his dance, he wasn't sure he'd have survived. I was so damn proud of him.

"Who's the other girl?" I nodded to a young girl about Hannah's age, sitting off to one side of the stage watching Hannah and Judah rehearse.

"Natalie. They met at a swimming class Hannah's physio runs for kids that need a bit of extra help. She lives with cystic fibrosis, and she's had a pretty crap time of it lately, missed a ton of school. Her mum was wondering if Judah would do some sessions with her, later on in the year, to help her confidence. She watches all the dance shows on TV, by the sound of it."

I blew out a sigh. "How'd that go down? You saw how reluctant he was to do this, even with Hannah, and you're his best friend."

Terry shrugged. "He was good about it. He didn't fob her off, just said he might not be here for much longer and left it at that."

Like I needed the reminder.

"He's surprisingly good with kids," Terry commented, watching his daughter squeal with delight as she managed to get her leg a bit higher on the finish. "He'll make a great dance teacher. Hannah's barely mentioned the brace in two weeks, except to say it might make it a bit harder to dance with, and she might have to change how she balances." He turned to me. "Can you imagine? A month ago she burst into tears at the thought of wearing it, and now she's talking about dancing with the damn thing. I honestly can't thank him enough. I don't know what's going to happen if he leaves."

"Does Hannah know?" I watched Judah press a kiss to Hannah's hair and an unsolicited image suddenly popped into my brain of him teaching our child to dance. *Our child. Holy shit.* Another bag of snakes. Just what I fucking needed.

"I told her that there's a chance he might leave, but she didn't want to talk about it."

That made two of us.

"What about you?" Terry turned those preceptive eyes on me. "You guys seem pretty close."

I avoided his gaze and studied the floor. "I'm channelling my inner Hannah and refusing to talk about it."

He snorted. "Good luck with that."

I drew the toe of my shoe through the dust on the floor, creating a line that was anything but straight. Story of my damn life.

"I won't hold him back." I looked up to where Judah was helping Hannah to stand a little taller for her finishing bow. "He needs this job, Terry. It's perfect for him. He's already making enquiries about flats and bus routes. What's he supposed to do? Stay here in Painted Bay and wash hair for May for the rest of his life, slowly growing to hate me for the chance he gave up."

Terry rubbed a hand down his jaw and over his mouth. "I know. It sucks. But what about what you want? Are you happy to just let him go?"

Was I? "What do you think?" I bit a little too harshly. "Sorry. And no, I'm not happy. And to answer your next question, yes, I'm thinking about it."

"Moving with him?" Terry sounded genuinely surprised.

Well, join the club. The thought fucking terrified me. "I haven't said anything to Judah, and I don't know why I'm even telling you now, but yes, I'm thinking about it. Or rather, I'm thinking about what it would mean to think about it."

Terry put his shoulder to the wall and faced me. "Not to be a wet blanket or anything, but you guys are still pretty new."

Hammer meet nail. "I know. And if it was Auckland, I'd be happy to just rack up the miles for a few months and see where things went. But Wellington? That's a long way, Terry. And neither of us truly see commuting that distance as an option. My job has crazy hours and he won't have the money or time."

With the rehearsal done, Hannah headed for Natalie and the two girls hugged. Then Hannah helped Natalie wheel her way over.

"Did you see me, Dad?" Hannah asked excitedly. "Judah says I'm the best student he's ever had, and I think he's the best dance teacher in the world."

Terry grinned and took over pushing Natalie's chair. "I did see you. And that's wonderful, pumpkin."

I raised an amused brow at Judah who shrugged. "It's all true."

"Come on, girls, it's ice cream time. See you guys later." Terry nodded our way as he manoeuvred Natalie's chair towards the door.

I steered Judah into my arms and began kneading the muscles down his back. "Can I interest you in a lemonade at the pub, Mr Best Dance Teacher in the World?"

Judah groaned with the pressure of my fingertips and rested his head on my shoulder. "Your pick-up lines need some work, but yes, just give me a few minutes to change. Then I'm cooking lamb chops for dinner. I'm starving."

"Sounds good."

He headed to the change room in those damn ballet leggings, every sizzling muscle on display, every impertinent swish of those sexy hips sinking another nail into that tiny coffin of hope I had that I'd get over him any time soon.

I'd practically moved into his place since his trip to Wellington, wanting as much time with him as I could get, hearing the clock ticking in my head. His mother had been delighted about the job, of course, though she'd been warier with me and hadn't raised the subject, for which I was grateful.

Leroy had merely grunted and talked about being able to lease the boathouse to earn some money for a change, and for a stupid second, I'd considered putting up my hand for it. Couldn't get much closer to Judah than that. Then I thought about him coming home to visit and being so close and unable to touch him, and I was thankful I'd kept my mouth shut.

He hadn't given the ballet school a final answer yet, saying he wanted to take the full two weeks they'd given him to think about it and talk to his specialist and so on. But I was pretty sure he just wanted to put off the inevitable decision screwing up what we had, for as long as possible. And for that I was grateful. I could do an impersonation of an ostrich as well as the next man.

My phone buzzed in my pocket with a call from my boss.

"Keep Saturday free," he started with.

My interest immediately peaked. "Why? Something going down with our friends?"

"Could be. There's word of a big pāua shipment going out, and the task force's undercover guy reckons they're gonna try and get the stock centralised in Auckland this Saturday night. They want you and Jon to sit on the Laird brothers from lunchtime on. The police will watch Haversham and get a tracker on his boat. Jon's in the loop."

"Great. I'll get in touch and see how he wants to do it. Keep us up to date."

"Will do."

There went the weekend. How many more I'd have left with Judah wasn't something I could think about.

I watched the change room door and thought of Terry's words. *Could* I follow Judah down there? Could I give up the life I'd built for myself after Sally and take that risk? There'd be no coming back, not for a while. Fisheries jobs were hard to come by in Northland, the climate and lifestyle were big draws.

Wellington had more regular openings, but it was a big city with more harbour work, more travel, more officialdom and oversight, and a lot less independence. The thought gutted me on so many levels, but compared to losing Judah . . .

Make some calls. Sally's voice rang in my ear.

I'd make some calls.

CHAPTER TWENTY-ONE

Judah

THE DAY OF THE TALENT SHOW BROKE WARM AND SUNNY AND I stretched next to Morgan who still lay sound asleep sprawled half on my side of the bed. Huh. *My* side of the bed. Since when had this become *our* bed with designated sides? Since the first time Morgan stayed the night, that's when.

Waking up to the gorgeous man was the highlight of my day. It didn't matter the temperature outside the bed. Inside it Morgan pumped out heat like a freaking radiator, and it was one of my all-time delights to stretch and snuggle against all that warm hair tickling my back and arse, his morning wood nestled in my crease, right where it belonged. With a bit of luck, he'd fling a hairy arm around my chest and all would be right with the world. And—

Oomph.

—there it was.

He tugged me back against him. "You're purring." He breathed the words in my ear as his hand drifted south to cup my wide-awake cock.

"I'm kind of hoping you'll work me up to a roar." I thrust into his fist to make my point, and he rubbed his thumb over the head.

"You're leaking. Should I call a plumber?"

"Would he move faster than you?"

Morgan rolled on top of me, pinning me to the bed. A hot, hairy, possessive, and growly Morgan, covering me head to toe? It didn't get much better than that. He got up on his knees and rubbed against me, every sizzling, furry centimetre of him, and a trail of sparks caught my skin alight, or close enough.

"Argh . . . don't you have a sting, or whatever you call it, to plan with Jon for tomorrow?" I arched up to add a little more pressure to the fire he was kindling between our dicks. "And I, ah . . . fuck, right there . . ." He tweaked the angle just a fraction to catch the underside of my balls, a particular hot spot of mine. "And I promised to help set up the community centre for tonight." I grabbed his arse in both hands to keep him right where I wanted him.

"How very civic-minded of you." Morgan nipped at my jaw, then buried his head in the curve of my neck while we rutted like teenagers.

It didn't take long. A few spine-tingling thrusts, a succession of grunts and suitable profanity, a single threat to end his life if he adjusted position one more time, and I was there, my legs wrapped around his waist to ride out a spectacular orgasm as the sun striped the bed and caught the sun-kissed gold at the ends of Morgan's dark hair. He crested seconds later, sinking his teeth into my neck with a lengthy contented moan.

I held him in place for a few moments until I lost all feeling in my legs and had to roll him to the side.

"Damn, that was almost better than coffee." He snuggled close and pressed his lips to my throat.

"Almost? Best dick you've had in your life, sunshine." I pulled back and raised a brow, daring him to disagree.

He dropped a hand under the sheet to wrap around my softening cock. "Damn right." He squeezed and I jumped.

"Quit that." I picked up the damp sheet between my thumb and forefinger and screwed up my nose. "Shit. These were clean. I'm gonna have to change the damn things again before Hannah comes to stay tonight. One minute we were talking about me taking her out for ice cream as congratulations for all her hard work, and the next thing I'm hosting a movie and sleepover night. And guess who's sleeping on the couch? You could've swapped Terry's eyebrows for McDonald's arches when I told him. I can't believe he trusts me to keep her alive."

Morgan's mouth curved up. "Stop fussing. You're gonna love it."

I sniffed dismissively, because I would.

"And she'd be perfectly happy on the couch," he pointed out.

"Maybe. But her hips aren't great at the moment."

Morgan kissed my cheek. "You're a soft touch, Judah Madden."

I flung a hand over his mouth. "For fuck's sake, keep your voice down. I have a reputation to maintain."

He licked my palm and I jerked it away.

"Soft as butter," he repeated, running his fingers up my belly until they popped into view covered in our combined come. He licked them clean, then leaned in to take my mouth in a hard kiss, his tongue sweeping over mine. "I love you, Judah Madden."

My heart stuttered in my chest. Hearing those words from Morgan never failed to undo me in ways I couldn't understand. How was I ever going to walk away from him? I shoved the question back where it belonged in my ballooning mental file labelled *denial and survival*, right next to the one labelled *abject terror about performing again*.

I kissed him instead. "I love you too." Then I pulled a face and fingered the burgeoning hickey on my neck. "You do realise I'm going to need makeup to cover this tonight."

"Sorry, not sorry. What's the time?"

"I turned and gave my phone a tap. "Eight."

"Damn, I have to get moving." He flung off the sheet and scrambled for the bathroom, dick flapping in the breeze. "Jon's picking me up in thirty minutes and we're heading to Whangarei to chat with the rest of the team. What time do you have to be at the centre?"

I snuggled down to appreciate the view of Morgan standing starkers in front of the bathroom mirror. "Not till midday, but Leroy's given me the day off. I'm going nowhere for a bit."

"Bastard. Here, take your pills." He threw two bottles my way.

"Yes, Mum."

A spray of freezing water landed on my chest and I squeaked.

"We agreed no mention of mothers in the bedroom."

"Understood. Now keep shaving." I waved him around mostly because ogling his furry arse had become one of my all-time favourite things.

He jiggled his bare butt right at me because he knew all of my fetishes.

I leapt out of bed to grab a handful.

"I think that's the last of them, Judah." Jocelyn Street, the forty-something principal of Hannah's school plonked her butt in a chair next to me and slipped low. "Cripes, I'm unfit."

Behind her, Jam was busy testing the sound from his booth at the back of the room. "Is that going to be loud enough?"

Jocelyn raised her hand in a thumbs up without even turning. "If we get more than two hundred tonight, we're screwed," she said. "How long till lift off?"

I checked my phone. "Two hours. Have you got the order of appearance?"

She handed me a folded paper from the bag propped next to her. "I've left you off it. You can pencil the two of you in where you think best. If Hannah gets too nervous, her balance and walking always suffer."

I snorted. "That makes two of us."

She patted my hand in understanding but said nothing. I'd liked her immediately. On the ball but no fuss.

"I think we'll go second." I wrote our names in. "Let the first kid set the scene and then we'll get ours over with before either of us can talk ourselves out of it."

Jocelyn studied me for a few seconds and I felt ten years old all over again. "It's a good thing you're doing here, Judah. We've all noticed a change in Hannah. She smiles a lot more, for a start, and she's stopped trying to hide her crutches or *accidentally* leave them in the classroom at break time. She's more confident, and that's all down to you."

And there I went. Hot cheeks and definitely ten again.

"Hey, I had the time, and it was . . . fun, actually. I really enjoyed it." Which I had, more than I'd thought possible. "Thanks for letting her take me on stage as her partner. I know it rules her out of a prize—"

"It was never about the prize for Hannah." Jocelyn nudged me with her elbow. "And I know it wasn't as easy as you make it sound. Getting a kid who lacks confidence in her body, like Hannah, to trust you? That takes a lot of energy and a special connection."

Jocelyn ran her fingers through her hair and her eyes flicked to where May was busy setting up her makeup and hair station. The kids were getting the full-enchilada experience, and I loved that the school was going all in. May had even found Hannah a great rainbow almost-tutu costume and pimped her crutches with coloured tape.

Jocelyn eyeballed me. "Word has it from the older teachers that confidence or, rather, courage was never something *you* lacked. Though I suspect you had your challenges."

I returned her steady gaze. "One or two."

She nodded. "Have you thought about working with kids? Teaching maybe?"

My mouth dropped open. "Me? A teacher?"

"Yes, you, a teacher. Why so horrified?"

Had she lost her mind? "I don't know where to start. One, I suck at school, always have, and I suspect there's a fair bit of that involved in learning to teach, right?"

She bit back a smile.

"But teaching dance, on the other hand? Yes, and that's definitely where I'm headed."

"It'll be a shame to lose you to the area. Good role models are hard to come by."

I barked out a laugh. "Now I know you've lost your mind. I'm not sure anyone has *ever* considered me a good role model, and not just because of the whole gay thing, or the sarcastic thing, or the drama thing either. And in case you haven't noticed, I am actually a little short on confidence lately, and a lot short on patience and reliability, though I'm working on it. I wouldn't say I've coped with my current health challenge in an admirable way at all."

"Well, *I* think you're an excellent role model." Jocelyn grabbed her bag and stood. "And it's exactly *because* of the gay thing, as you call it, *and* the bullying thing I heard about, *and* the confidence dip thing, *and even* the health thing."

She put a hand on my shoulder. "If you'd aced a major health challenge like that without screwing up, Hannah wouldn't be hanging off your every word. She's not interested in that glittering career you had; she's interested in you now and how you've handled things, the good and the bad of that—the courage you're showing. *That's* what she relates to. If she sees you can screw up and still get on with it, then she knows she can too."

"Well, that's something I actually did ace in school."

Jocelyn laughed, brushed the dust off her bright red trousers, and straightened her gingham shirt. "Anyway, I'm off to grab some dinner and try and not freak out at how many calls I'm going to get after Ruby Lowe sings her version of 'Like a Virgin' tonight."

I nearly choked on my tongue. "Yeah, good luck with that."

Her words continued to roll around in my head for a few minutes after she'd gone as I tried to get a handle on something she'd said, something important that had struck a chord in my foggy brain. But whatever it was, it refused to be fished into the daylight.

Two hours later, I peeked through the curtain at the side of the stage and searched the back of the packed audience for Morgan's face. He'd texted to say he was running late but was almost there. Meanwhile, ten-year-old Brendon White pounded out the middle verse of "The Gambler" on a guitar that almost dwarfed him. The kid's voice was actually pretty good, if only someone had tuned the damn guitar.

I spotted Morgan at last, racing in through the back doors. Two hundred people turned as one to shush him and he slid to a red-faced stop. Too adorable for words. He saw me, smiled, and held up a huge foam finger glove that I imagined he had every intention of waving after our performance, the dork. Did I mention adorable?

Hannah stood next to me, her hand super glued into my own, as it had been from the minute May had finished getting her ready. She was terrified and ready to pull out. I had to remind her I'd bought a new pair of glittery ballet tights especially for the occasion, and she'd looked them over, suitably impressed, and agreed it would be a shame not to show them off. But impressed *wasn't* the word I'd have used to describe the looks and muttered comments I'd gotten from a small number of the men in the audience as I strode by in full princely costume. Surprisingly, I hadn't found a single fuck to give. Some of the mothers, however, were definitely more . . . receptive to the outfit, and I'd received my fair share of appreciative whistles as well. Which of course annoyed those same men, not that I was petty enough to take any pleasure from that, of course.

Best of all, I was having a good day health wise—solidly balanced, tinnitus sticking to the background, wobbly knees remarkably absent. I might not have been able to leap or spin as in my heyday, but even at half speed, I knew I could put on a show. Those men were about to choke on their small-town, redneck assumptions, and I couldn't be happier.

While Brendon and Kenny Rogers were winding things up, Hannah and I finished our stretches and warm-ups, and I tried to keep her as relaxed as I could. Thank God for second spot. I might've been confident about my ability, but I was worried sick the stress might prompt a Meniere's attack. Hannah knew the drill if it happened. She'd keep dancing if I left the stage, and Terry or Morgan would come to help me. All I could do was hope.

I'd danced on some of the biggest international stages, and here I was freaking out at a primary school talent contest, in a nowhere town in coastal New Zealand. Go figure. Then it hit me. What I'd been trying to remember in my conversation with Jocelyn. It was about Hannah not being interested in my glittering career, but in who I was now, and what I could teach her about dealing with tough shit. Not to mention what she could teach me, I thought ruefully. It was about being prepared to put myself out there and still be me.

With that, the fear left me.

And when Brendon ran off the stage to rapturous applause, I kissed Hannah on the cheek and gave her a big smile. "Let's show them, sweetheart. Have fun."

She squeezed my hand and we made our way to centre stage.

I'd chosen the ball scene from Cinderella, my favourite piece of all time, and it fitted well with the part where Hannah danced on my feet. That introduction led into a solo from Hannah, using her crutches, and then I picked up a short routine that saw me dancing around her before we finished with the two of us again.

As Hannah placed her feet on top of mine and got her crutches into place, you could've heard a pin drop. Then Jam started the music, and I counted the beats with my eyebrows, a secret language we'd developed together. My wink was our cue, and when she returned it, we were off, waltzing around and around the stage in a large circle, her skirt billowing up behind her, her face a delighted mix of joy and earnest concentration.

My eyes fixed on her, while my instinctive understanding of where my body was on stage guided us and kept us safe. After a few circles at a change in the music, we parted for Hannah's solo. With a sweep of her arms, she got her crutches into place, and I sank to one knee so she could dance around me. I risked a quick glance at the audience to find every eye in the front row locked onto her. A few tissues found their way into hands, while behind Hannah, in the wings, Terry had clearly lost it completely, tears streaming down his face.

It was almost enough to break me, but I held it together until Hannah finished her piece, twirling her rainbow crutches before crossing them over my back as she bent to kiss my head.

That was *my* cue. I checked my balance as I took the first couple of steps, but I was solid. A rush of relief rode through me as I gave myself the green light for the extra spins and two leaps I'd planned for if I felt good enough. I didn't want to upstage Hannah, but she'd insisted on some "flashbang stuff" and I tried to oblige.

The short piece flew by, with surprised gasps and murmurs of appreciation from the audience. In the end I didn't risk the second leap, deciding it wasn't worth the risk, and this wasn't my show, it was Hannah's. I scooped her back onto my feet and we finished with another short waltz around the stage and finished with a bow.

The audience erupted, and Hannah's nervous glance sideways to see her dad's reaction turned into a huge beaming smile and then another bow as the audience got to their feet and demanded more. I stood back as Hannah made up her own little encore to the delight of everyone, and my struggle to hold back my tears finally failed.

Then from the corner of my eye, I caught sight of a huge foam finger waving madly in the air, and I couldn't hold back a snort of laughter. Morgan—jumping up and down like the idiot he was, with Cora, Martha, Patrick, and even Leroy, hooting and whistling alongside.

I grinned at them and gave a quick bow, then startled at the sight of Kane standing behind them. What the hell? He gave me an unexpected thumbs up and then turned to leave. Had he only come to see Hannah, or me? That made no sense, but I filed it away for another time.

Right then I had no time to do anything but bathe in Hannah's delight and blow a kiss to Natalie who was waving madly from her wheelchair with a look of such yearning, it almost stopped my heart.

A voice from the wings called time, and I looked to Hannah to make our exit. I held out my hand like a good prince should. Hannah gave me a regal nod, held her head high and, using her crutches, walked across to take it. We then left the stage as any prince and his princess should.

As soon as the curtain closed, Terry swept his daughter up into his arms and tried to mask an endearing ugly cry with zero success. Hannah patted his head, then snuggled into his neck, and I ushered them both out of the way so the horn and drum trio could set themselves up.

A woman I didn't know patted Hannah's back and said something in passing, then headed my way.

"Danielle," she said, holding out her hand. "Hannah's physio. We've talked but haven't met."

I shook her hand, then wiped at the damp sweat on my face with a towel someone had shoved into my hand. Back on stage, the trio had started up with loud but very mixed success. I pointed to the quiet corridor which led to the parking lot, and Danielle led the way. She looked to only be in her thirties, which came as a surprise since I'd pictured her as a much older woman from our phone interactions.

"That was absolutely brilliant, Judah." Her eyes shone.

"Thanks, but it was all Hannah."

"Don't be ridiculous," she spoke sternly. "I've been trying for over a year to get Hannah to take a chance on something. You should be proud of yourself."

Her words brought me up short and I realised I *was* proud. We'd achieved something together, Hannah and I, and not just for her. And even if it was only a small blip in the scheme of things, it was something that mattered. It was going to make a difference in her life and how she saw herself. But the biggest surprise was that I could already feel the difference it was making in mine.

"Lots of people can dance, Judah, maybe not as well as you, but few people can do what you just did with Hannah. You should think about that. There's a lot of kids like Hannah in the world. I know something about Meniere's and what you've lost. But the man I saw on that stage with that little girl, who thinks you've hung the moon, will always find a way to thrive. Take care, Judah. I hope to see you again."

Before I could absorb what she'd said, Leroy, Martha, and Mum blustered their way around the parent help backstage, and Danielle slipped quietly away. I went in for a peck on the cheek, but Mum reached up on tippy-toe and dragged me down into a crushing hug while Leroy and Martha looked on, clearly amused.

"I'm so proud of you, son." Mum wiped the tears from her eyes and promptly smeared her mascara.

I cleaned the smudge with my thumb, my heart brimming, and marvelled at my luck.

"I never thought I'd see you dance on our little stage," she continued. "Hannah was wonderful, of course, but you were . . . oh god, I'm going to embarrass myself . . ." She blinked furiously and drew in a stuttered breath. "I wish your father had been here to see what you did for Hannah, and to see you dance again."

My cheeks burned, tears pricking at my eyes. "I miss him too, Mum. But it really wasn't much—"

Leroy clapped me on the shoulder and there was genuine regret in his eyes. "I should've got that stick out of my arse and watched you dance sooner. It was pretty impressive, bro."

I held his gaze and nodded, accepting the apology for what it was, a step in the right direction between us. "Thanks."

"Well done, Judah." Martha pressed a kiss to my cheek. "You've made a little girl very happy, and a certain big girl as well." She slipped an arm around my mother's waist to make her point, and I saw a couple of locals do a double-take. Gossip was dying down, but the two women had received their fair share of comments, good and bad.

"You better go and watch the rest of the show." I ushered them back toward the door to the audience. "I'll see you Sunday for lunch."

"Morgan too?"

I shook my head. "He's working this weekend."

"Have you signed the contract yet?" Mum eyed me warily.

I pushed her through the door. "Bye, Mum."

With the door shut on my family, I finally took a breath. No sign of Morgan. I swallowed a slight sting of hurt, but I'd catch up with him later. Right now I needed some space to gather my thoughts about the evening. I headed down the hall and out the side door to the parking lot, leaned against the wall of the building, and stared up at the sky, wondering what the hell had just happened and why I felt like someone had simultaneously given me the best present in the world while gutting me like a fish.

CHAPTER TWENTY-TWO

Morgan

When Judah's family reappeared from backstage, I headed that way myself, not wanting to encroach on their time with him. Cora nodded as she passed, but her gaze was skittering and unsure. She wanted badly for Judah to sign on the Wellington offer, and I was sure she worried our relationship was muddying the waters for him. I'd have been more than happy to dump a whole paddock of soil into that mix, but hey, that was just me.

Leroy grunted what could have been a hello. Who knew? Things between the two of us were still a little cool and I really needed to do something about that, but my mind had enough to deal with worrying about Judah. Making up with Leroy could wait.

I pushed through the backstage door in time to see Judah disappear down the back corridor. I was so damn proud of him, not just for what he'd achieved with Hannah, but also his courage in reclaiming something for himself.

He'd looked amazing on that tiny stage—elegant, strong, beautiful, and with bags of undeniable talent. He'd left me hard, breathless, and so fucking full of emotion, it cut through every bullshit excuse I'd given myself over the last few weeks and left me raw with certainty.

If Judah agreed, I was following him to Wellington. It was a done deal in my head and left me wondering why the hell it had taken me so fucking long to see the light. Painted Bay might've given me solace and a safe place to heal my past, and yes, I loved the town, but Judah offered me a future, and I'd be worse than a fool to turn my back on that just because I was scared. It might take months to get the transfer, likely longer, but I wanted him in my life. Now all I had to do was convince him of that.

I pushed through the door to the parking lot and scoured the area for any sign of him.

"Looking for me?"

I spun to find Judah leaning against the wall behind me, tucked into the shadows next to the door. I stalked over and pressed my body against his. "If you mean am I looking for the sexiest man to ever dance on the community centre stage with a nine-year-old on his feet, then yes, I am most definitely looking for you. Come here." I cradled his face and brought our lips together, pouring everything I felt about him into that single kiss—every scrap of love, worry, fear, want, hope—everything.

He gave as good in return, spinning us around till my back hit the wall and shoving his thigh between mine so I could ride it while his fingers found the hem of my shirt and dipped under to slide around my back. We made out like teenagers till my dick ached and I could barely catch my breath, his tongue so far down my throat he needed a mining licence. Then he abruptly pulled away and pressed our foreheads together.

"I'm not sure about this," he panted, "but I suspect that molesting the local fisheries officer in the community centre car park, while wearing a royal crown, tights, and sporting an erection the size of Kilimanjaro, wouldn't be considered appropriate behaviour."

I palmed his swollen dick and squeezed. "Fucking tights. You know damn well I can't be held responsible when you wear these things. But you have a point. And just for the record, your crown is crooked."

"Damn." He straightened it. "Whatever will my loyal subjects think?" Then he stepped back and attempted to rearrange his dick as well, with less success.

"Here, take my jacket." I threw him my jacket and he held it over his arm to hide his . . . interest.

"Better?"

I shrugged. "Not for me, but I'm sure the parents will appreciate it."

"Very funny." Judah turned for the door but I grabbed both his hands.

"You were wonderful tonight." I held his gaze, pleased to see his eyes soften and his cheeks brighten. "Both of you, of course, but particularly you. I could watch you dance forever, and it's not just the tights. You are so damn talented."

He rested his forehead on mine and our breath mingled. "I'm pretty sure I wouldn't have gotten there without you. Such a dork. Buying me that bloody barre. You stole all my excuses away."

I kissed his cheek, tasting the salt. "I just gave you a little push. You're a special man, Judah." I had to pause and swallow. "Shit, I, ah . . ."

He stepped back to frown at me. "What's wrong?"

"Nothing's wrong." I took a deep breath and straightened my shoulders. Here goes. "I love you Judah, and I don't want you to leave—"

"Oh, shit, Morgan . . ." His eyes screwed shut.

"Without me."

His eyes shot open. "Without you? But . . . what do you mean?"

I reached across and stroked his cheek, and he leaned into the touch. Everything about this felt right. "I mean that I want to come with you if you'll have me. If you want to give us a shot, I'll get a job closer to Wellington."

Judah's eyes went wide, then narrowed almost immediately. "But you love it here, Morgan. I can't ask you—"

"You're not asking me. I want this. I want to try. It might take a while to set up a job down there, so if you're not sure . . ."

Judah fisted my shirt and pulled me close. "Shut up, you crazy, beautiful man. I love you, Morgan, you know I do. Of course I bloody want to try. The very idea of walking away from you has been killing me. It's the biggest reason I haven't signed the contract. I've been trying to find a way around it."

That took a second to sink in. "The *biggest* reason? There's something else?"

He closed his eyes and dropped his head for a second. "I don't know. It's crazy, right?" He searched my face. "It's such an amazing opportunity. But I feel like I'm missing something. And tonight . . . ah, forget it. I'll get it signed and posted back on Monday."

I circled his waist with my arms and he relaxed into me. "It is an amazing opportunity. But don't think they're doing you a favour. Watching you with Hannah these last weeks, I know you'll make an awesome dance teacher. They'll be lucky to get you. I really do love you, you know that, right?"

"I do."

He tipped his head back, holding his crown, and I licked my way into his mouth, sinking into the kiss. He smelled of spicy cologne, an edge of sweat, and a large dollop of . . . "Liniment?" I pulled back and screwed up my nose. "Good God, how did I miss that the first time around? You smell like a freaking locker room."

He grinned. "Dick distraction. And I guess I'm used to it. I pinged a calf muscle yesterday."

"Dick distraction, huh?" I pulled his hips against mine. "You wanna remind me how that goes again?"

He waggled a finger in my face. "Nope. In case you've forgotten —fisheries officer, royal crown, tights, and a public car park. And also, I've got Hannah tonight. Our celebration sleepover, remember? Terry even managed to get himself a hot date, though he won't spill the details."

I narrowed my gaze. "I hadn't forgotten. But in that case, I have a proposition for you. My car in two minutes. I'm parked at the far end under those trees. Quickest blow job known to mankind. Leave the tights on and bring a change."

His gaze flicked to where my car was parked and back to me. Then his face broke into a huge grin. "You're on."

I got back to my tiny house around eight after the talent show finished and prizes had been given out to every child for something—the overall winner going to a young boy who'd played a pretty good piano rendition of "Johnny B. Good." Hannah picked up a certificate for Outstanding Personal Achievement, which she accepted standing tall on her crutches and bursting with pride. Judah got a hastily scrawled certificate for the best set of legs, which had all the kids in hysterics and even tugged a smile out of some of the disapproving fathers.

And to top it all off, Judah and I must've come damn close to setting the record for the fastest blow job known to mankind, clocking in at an impressive one minute and ten seconds for Judah, and a more sedate two minutes thirty for me. Admittedly, I hadn't played fair, destroying his tights to get my finger in his arse, while my uniform trousers were a little more argumentative.

I stood in the lounge of my house and just looked around. When I'd first arrived in Painted Bay, it was a welcome retreat, a chance to start again in a fresh place, with none of the memories of the house Sally and I had shared. Now it just felt . . . empty, and I felt . . . strangely disconnected.

Because it's done its job. It's time to move on. My voice, not Sally's this time, though no doubt she agreed.

I grabbed a glass of water and headed for my bedroom. It would be one of the few nights I'd slept in my own bed since Judah and I had become a thing, and I needed a good night's sleep if I was going to be on my toes for the stakeout tomorrow. Jon was picking me up at nine, and from there we'd head to Whangarei and take over from the night shift who currently had eyes on the Laird's house. I was pumped to get these guys. I might only be a cog in the task force, but this coastline was my patch, my responsibility, and during my time in Painted Bay, no matter how hard we tried, the shellfish stocks continued to be plundered. If I was going to Wellington, I wanted to leave on a win.

But it wouldn't be easy. No black-market ring worth millions of dollars was going to hand anything over without a fight. Jon would be armed, and I'd be wearing all the protective gear I could while keeping my eyes open. Judah hadn't said anything when we'd parted, but the worry had been clear on his face, and I wasn't about to risk a future I was only just beginning to glimpse.

Which brought me back to the man himself. Judah.

I slowed as I passed the photos in the hall, pausing at the one of Sally and me at her brother's wedding. Never would I have believed I'd fall for someone again as deeply as I had for Sally. I reached out a finger and ran it over her image.

"Thanks, gorgeous, for everything. You taught me to believe in happy endings. The fact you died too early doesn't change that. And now I get a chance at another. Who would've imagined that was even possible?"

Silence.

I blew out a sigh. I didn't need an answer. Everything inside told me I was making the right decision. Was it a risk? Absolutely. Could it blow up in my face? Of course. Was I going to miss Painted Bay? The nauseous ache in my belly answered that. Would I regret it if I didn't try? Hell fucking yeah, I would. Losing Judah from my life was not an option any longer.

I'd fallen hard and far, deep under the spell of a pair of hazel eyes and a sassy mouth. I loved everything about Judah, even the parts that drove me up the wall. Like how he could step over washing for days like he didn't see it. Or how he never put the electric toothbrush back on its charger, or the coffee back in the cupboard. Everything, even that damned Meniere's, because without that, he wouldn't have come into my life, and I couldn't imagine being without him.

Come Monday, I'd make enquiries with my boss about Wellington, but there was something else I needed to do first. Cody and I hadn't really talked since the whole lunch fiasco, although to be fair, he'd tried.

I fired him a text asking if we could talk over the weekend, then threw my phone on the table, determined to get some sleep.

CHAPTER TWENTY-THREE

Judah

THE SOFT SNORT-SNUFFLE CLUED ME IN AND I DRAGGED MY EYES off Belle tripping the light fantastic with her Beast, who would've looked great in a leather harness—a missed opportunity there—and angled my head forward for a peek beneath those curls.

Hannah's eyes were closed, her warm body curled against my side, a bowl of popcorn perched precariously on her lap—sound asleep. I teased a piece of caramel corn from her hair and grabbed a pillow to slide between us so I could leverage myself out from under. My arm fired with pins and needles and my neck sported a crick the size of the rift valley, but I wouldn't have traded either for the world.

Three hours on the couch next to an excited nine-year-old wearing Daisy Duck pyjamas, braiding her hair and watching Disney movies? It didn't get much better than that. In addition, I'd fielded a couple of phone calls from parents of kids who had a few extra life challenges and who wanted to know if I could teach them some dance. All of which begged the question of who the fuck was this person I'd suddenly become. Not to mention, sending my hot as hell boyfriend home for the night so I could have a girl's night in with a nine-year-old? Don't even go there.

Had I lost my freaking mind? Almost definitely. I could've been stretched out in bed, still tingling after an epic fuck, but no. I was stretched out on the sofa, still tingling after my arm had fallen asleep because I was too scared to move in case I disturbed Hannah. So yeah, go figure.

At least the fastest blow in the west competition between Morgan and I had gone some way toward slaking my lust, but not by much. It was also likely to become a semi-annual event, if I had my way, possibly including a trophy. I had pretty good stamina as a rule, but damn, the man had moves. A set of official rules was definitely called for.

I stared down at Hannah and brushed the hair off her face. As the younger son—and with a life that consisted of twelve-hour days, between school and dance, from the age of forever—I'd never been around kids. Most dancers in ballet circles avoided kids until their careers were over, especially the women. Kids just weren't a part of my life.

But Hannah? I let her fall back on the pillow before draping the blanket over her shoulders. Hannah was special. And she'd opened a door to the possibility of kids in my own life that I hadn't even considered.

I threw some fresh sheets on the bed and a new duvet cover, then switched off the TV, carried Hannah over, and tucked her in. Could something like this become a part of my future, Morgan's and my future? My thought sent a warm glow right down to my toes. He would a make a great dad. The solid, practical, outdoorsy one, to my artsy, hyper, enthusiast, and irreverent one. It could work, if he didn't kill me first for playing hooky with our kid to go watch a ballet, instead of going to school. I smiled at the thought.

Which brought me back to the fact Morgan wanted to come with me. I'd been completely broadsided. Hell yeah, I wanted him to come, but since we'd parted, I'd started second-guessing the idea.

Would he cope back in a big city? Would he resent me for it down the track? He belonged in a place like Painted Bay, just like those jack mackerel belonged under the wharf. That was their sanctuary. Painted Bay was his.

And like the flash of those silver stripes under the water, Morgan's face caught the light of this bay and reflected it too. It was part of his joy. Would that change? I wasn't sure I'd survive the guilt if it did.

And under all of that ran this niggly sense I was still missing something important. The audience appreciation had shocked me, not that they were clapping for Hannah, that went without saying. But because they were also clapping for me, catching my eye with nods and thumbs up.

Even some of those big strapping knucklehead old-school farmers I'd known and hated from my teenage years. The ones whose sons made my life hell and who glared at me in the after-school pick-up area as if my mere presence would turn their precious young boys into lip-synching, cocktail-drinking, limp-wristed, nelly bottoms like me. Well, minus the nelly bottom part, although it appeared I was currently in training for that as well—go figure.

Things had changed in this town. I might not have wanted to admit it, but they had.

I dimmed the lights in the boathouse and poured myself a much deserved zero-alcohol beer. I could've thrown caution to the wind with a half glass of wine, but I had Hannah to consider, and I wasn't taking any chances inviting a vertigo attack now. Terry had his phone on standby just in case, but zero-alcohol beer and I had sparked, if not a friendly relationship, then at least a bearable one.

I stretched on the couch, pulled out my phone, and sure enough, there was a text from Morgan.

Goodnight my tiny dancer. See you Sunday.

A lump caught in my throat at his words. *Tiny dancer.* God, I was ridiculous. I fired back a text and then threw my phone across the couch so I could pretend I'd had nothing to do with it. **Nite, pooky bear.**

Please, somebody kill me now.

I managed half the beer before the day caught up with me and my eyelids hung like bags of cement. Thumping the couch cushion into submission, I stretched out and hauled the blanket over top. With only a half-wall between us, I'd hear Hannah if she needed me. A few deep breaths and I was gone. Hannah wasn't the only one exhausted.

I couldn't have been asleep long before the churning thrum of an outboard startled me awake and I shot upright on the couch.

What the hell?

I reached for my phone but my flailing hand came up empty.

Damn. Where was it? Something pinged in my memory but then disappeared just as quickly as the engine rumbled louder. I'd lived in the boathouse long enough to differentiate between a small fishing tinny belonging to the local boys, larger recreational launches, fishing boats, and other commercial traffic. This didn't fit any of them. Too much power for an average launch, but not quite right for a commercial boat either.

I peered at the clock on the oven. Nearly midnight. Morgan popped into mind but I was reluctant to wake him unnecessarily. I spent another fruitless minute searching for my phone, then pushed to my feet. Thankful I still had sweats and a T-shirt on, I made my way to the ranch sliders, stubbing my toes on the leg of the coffee table on the way.

"Goddammit." I hopped the final couple of steps and pried open the curtains just enough to see across the small bay.

And there it was. A big launch, bigger than most that used our wharf and with its running lights turned off. No moonlight pierced the thick wall of cloud cover, but I could see a figure on the bow of the boat with a handheld spot, guiding it in. Everything Morgan had told me about poaching boats flooded back. Was this part of the sting he was involved with? Maybe it was police or customs? But then, why no running lights?

I headed back to the couch and made another search for my damn phone.

Still nothing.

The soft glow of headlights caught my eye through the window by the front door and I quickly made my way over to take a look. A dark van and a small truck pulled right up on to the wharf and parked close to the pier. The van driver got out and the snap of shattering glass was quickly followed by a blanket of darkness as the car park light fizzled out. Definitely not police or customs.

I thought of all the gear we had stored in the sheds, the boats, all that investment. And what about the boathouse? What if they decided to check it out? I glanced to the bed but Hannah was still sound asleep. I needed to let someone know, to get some help. *Shit, shit, shit.* Where the hell was my phone? I threw the couch cushions off and checked underneath, but my search still came up empty.

The boat pulled alongside the pier, the engine cut, and the light from the bow winked out. Muffled voices floated in the light breeze along with the sound of something heavy being dragged across metal and wood, but I could barely see a thing in the pitch black, other than a small glow from the boat itself and the cab lights from the truck and van.

And then I remembered. The phone in the office. It would only take a few seconds to run across to the door and I'd be out of view for all but the first ten metres. I was still debating whether to risk it when a shadow passed in front of the storage shed next to the office, and the padlock on its door rattled. Then the office door opposite shook on its hinges.

Fuck.

I ducked back behind the curtains and counted to ten before chancing another look. The figure was now standing about five metres away, staring at the front door of the boathouse. I froze, thanking every god I knew that I hadn't left a light on, but then he didn't seem to have seen me.

My heart nearly jumped out of my chest when he took a few steps toward the front door. And then someone on the boat shouted and he stopped. But he didn't leave immediately, staring at the boathouse for what seemed like forever until finally he turned and headed back to the others, and the breath I'd been holding came out in a whoosh. Something had grabbed his attention, and I was terrified he'd come back to check it out.

But if I grabbed Hannah and left through the front door, we'd be seen as soon as we cleared the office, and then where would I go? I didn't have a car, and the homestead was a good half a kilometre up the hill, past the truck and van. And going out the deck way, up through the field, wasn't an option with the tide near on full and complete cloud cover. Hannah couldn't run. I'd have to carry her.

I glanced again at the bedroom. She was tucked up on her side, arm flung across the spare pillow, still sound asleep. I needed to get to that office phone. I pulled on my jacket, shoved my feet into a pair of sneakers by the front door, and grabbed a flashlight. Then I eased the front door open and slipped out into the night, pulling it shut behind me. Two minutes. That's all it would take.

My breath fogged in the cool night air and my skin pebbled, catching me by surprise. I crept up the path, then alongside the wall of the wharf office, the voices from the launch getting louder with each step. Hushed arguing and someone trying to calm things down. I peeked around the corner, still keeping in the shadows.

Four men stood talking on the pier above the boat, which wasn't a launch but a smaller commercial boat with a large flat deck out the back. Three more men were manhandling large plastic containers from the boat up onto the wharf while the others talked, or argued, more like.

It didn't take a rocket scientist to work out what was likely in those containers, nothing legal for sure. My gaze flicked to the van and the truck. The cabs were empty as far as I could tell, but from that angle I could just make out the plate of the van from the light inside the open back doors. I was trying to memorise it when one of the men spun and pointed to the boathouse, turned back, and continued talking. *Fuck.* I had to get to that phone.

I slid back along the office wall, keeping well out of sight. At the door, I had to go by feel and memory as far as the touchpad was concerned and had just finished entering the code and opened the door when—

"Judah, why are you out here?"

Hannah. *Fuck, fuck, fuck.* My gaze swept around to find Hannah in her Daisy Duck pyjamas, inching her way on her crutches from the front door of the boathouse, over to where I stood. If anyone looked, they'd see her for sure.

I ran and scooped her up in my arms, keeping my back to the pier.

"Hey, you!" a man's voice called from the direction of the boat.

I froze.

"Judah?" Hannah's voice filled with fear.

"Shh, sweetheart. Don't say a word. Hang on."

Her fingers dug into my back.

"Hey! I said stop," the man shouted and someone started running.

Fuck. We were closer to the office than the boathouse and I could only pray that in the dark, with my back to them, the men might not have seen Hannah, only me. And I needed a phone more than ever. What the fuck had I been thinking? If anything happened to Hannah—

I covered the few metres to the open office door in seconds and pushed my way in. I slammed it shut with my back, a surge of relief flooding my body at the electronic hum of the lock sliding into place. But as I went to drop Hannah onto her feet, the room swam and a roar kicked up in my ears.

Son of a bitch. Not now.

Bootsteps rang closer and the old wooden door thundered on its hinges as a body slammed into it, and a man grunted in pain.

A hundred years old, you fucker, and thick as a porn star's dick.

"I'm scared, Judah. Make them go away." Hannah's eyes brimmed.

"Open up!" The door crashed again.

"Shh." I cradled Hannah's face, feeling her tremble as fists continued hammering along with rough-voiced shouting. "I need you to get under the desk," I whispered. "Right back, behind the filing cabinet, up against the wall."

Hannah stared at me with terrified eyes. I felt her nod, my hands wet from the river of tears coursing down her cheeks. Then she slid off the chair and crawled under Martha's massive desk, dragging her crutches with her.

"Good. Now you have to keep quiet. Don't let them know you're here. I'm gonna call for help, okay?

I turned and reached for the landline but every local number I'd ever known by heart disappeared from my head in an instant. 111 would take time to redirect to Jon, and it would be faster to call him or Morgan direct, but fucking, fuck, fuck, my brain was a useless ball of cotton wool, my balance already shaky, my ears full, and my body starting to check out. I leaned against the wall for support with the phone in my hand and breathed down the nausea. I hit 111.

"He's got a fucking phone," a voice shouted through the window after a beam of light sliced through the dark causing a starburst of colour to shimmer at the edge of my vision.

"Open this fucking door."

I barely got my name to the operator before the window above the desk fractured with an almighty crack and glass exploded into the office along with a large float that landed on the desk and knocked the phone from my hand.

There was a sharp intake of breath from Hannah, but nothing more. Then a man's body pushed through the empty frame and I shot to the far side of the huge office hoping to draw his attention from where Hannah cowered under the huge desk, six metres away.

The guy scrambled to his feet, yanked the phone plug from the wall, and then flicked the lock on the door to let the second man in. With the flashlight beam trained in my face the whole time, I couldn't see a fucking thing, and the room swam like a damn merry-go-round, its walls heaving in and out in a nauseating roll.

"You're too late. I already got through," I shouted, struggling to keep my feet as I backed against the wall. I figured I had about a minute max till I hit the floor, and I fired up a prayer to anyone who was listening to keep Hannah safe and an apology to Morgan and Terry.

"That's unfortunate, for you." The men moved toward me.

I could barely lock onto their faces, let alone see if they had any weapons, not that I was in any position to put up a fight. And there was nowhere to go. I just needed to keep them focussed on me so they didn't start looking around the office. They had to believe I was their only witness, and if that meant taking a beating or worse, so be it.

Morgan's smile swam before me and my breath caught in my throat. I'd been such a fool.

"Time's up," one of the men said as they came within striking distance. "Nothing personal."

And then I felt it—the jag of cool metal where my hand pushed on the wall behind, trying to keep myself upright.

The bolt on the over-water loading door.

A sea of coloured lights pierced through the blackness, and some-where outside a boat engine roared into gear. A look shot between the two men, and an arm lunged to grab me. I yanked the bolt back against its home plate and the huge door instantly swung back on its massive hinges, and I let myself fall back with it. The frustrated shouts of the men as they tried to grab me sailed above my head.

In the few seconds before I hit the water, all I could do was pray Hannah kept herself quiet and hidden and that the men came looking for me instead. And then deep water smacked on my back like a hard flat of wood, and I was under.

A cold rush swallowed me up and I sank like a stone. Down, down—direction lost in the chaos in my head, my world teetering on oblivion as the vertigo bit hard and consumed me.

Bile hit the back of my throat and I tried to swallow it down, fighting the desperate urge to suck in some air. *Calm down. Let go. My body will know the way up. Find the still point in my head. Be the spin.* But my head was screaming. A surge of bubbles washed around my back and up my side on their way to the surface and I tried to let myself follow. But the cold water sucked my head into a mind-numbing spin and I threw up in my mouth as the inky depths pulled me down.

CHAPTER TWENTY-FOUR

Morgan

I THREW AN ARM OUT TO GRAB MY PHONE JUST BEFORE IT vibrated itself off the edge of my bedside table.

"Get down to the wharf, now." Jon sounded frantic.

I put him on speakerphone, flung myself out of bed, and started pulling on clothes. "What's happened? Is it Judah? Fuck. Is it Hannah?"

"Hannah? What's she doing there? Shit. Never mind. Two minutes ago I got a call from police emergency to say someone had called 111 from the wharf."

Fuck. I shoved sockless feet into my shoes, grabbed my jacket and the phone, and headed out the door.

"Then almost straight after I got a call from the task force to say the tracker on Haversham's boat showed him in Painted Bay and that a team was on its way. They got the jump on us and moved up the timetable. And when I told them about the emergency call, all hell broke loose. Just get yourself down there. I'm leaving now."

I threw the Hilux into gear and headed out for the two-minute drive to the wharf. My heart squeezed tight in my chest, every nerve firing in panic. *Judah. Hannah. Please, dear God, no. This couldn't be happening.*

I called Terry as I drove, waking him up. There was another voice in the background that I couldn't make out and had no time to think about. I told him all I knew and sent him to Cora's to wait for someone to call. No one was to come down until we knew what we were dealing with. The voice in the background said something about driving him there, and I thanked God for that. I was almost sure I recognised who it was, but that wouldn't have made any sense.

At the turnoff to the wharf, I briefly registered how dark it was, bar the red-and-blue flash of Jon's police lights and a spotlight on a light fishing vessel. Someone had killed the security lighting.

Jon's four-wheel drive was lodged close behind a small truck, so I wedged myself in on the other side, blocking it off completely. I got out, kept low, and tried to focus. A couple of dozen large storage containers were stacked on the pier beside the fishing boat, but my attention was immediately drawn by shouts coming from the direction of the wharf office. I spun to look and saw Jon wave me over to where he was pressed up against the side of the supply shed. The office door, across and just around the corner from his position, stood partially open, the window completely missing. What the hell had happened? A quick glance at the boathouse confirmed my worst fears, its gaping door cracking my heart wide open. *No.*

Halfway to Jon, an engine fired up from the direction of the pier and the boat hauled arse from where it had been berthed. I froze. Where was Judah? Hannah? Were they in the boat? Jon shouted at me to let it go and that was good enough for me. Seconds later I was at his side.

"The boat—"

"Has a tracker. I made six guys. Two were unloading at the pier when I arrived, so I'm guessing they decided not to hang around. Two more made it to a van before I could block them, but there's at least two more still in the office, judging by the voices, but there could be more."

Jesus Christ. "What about Judah and Hannah?"

He flicked me a worried glance. "I don't know."

"Well, I'm not fucking sitting here if they're inside that office."

"We don't know they're in there."

"Well, someone is."

"We need to wait—"

Shouts broke the night, followed by a loud splash.

Judah! I ran.

Sirens split the air and the entire hill road lit up in blue and red flashes as two figures burst from the office.

"You check inside," Jon shouted as he took off after the two men making their way to Leroy's boat. Three police vehicles hit the bottom of the hill and drove right up to the pier, offloading a sea of officers who immediately split up to cover the area, weapons drawn.

I charged into the office in time to see Hannah crawling out from under the desk.

"Hannah, are you okay?"

She nodded, but her eyes were frantic. "Judah's in the water. He was having an attack." She pointed to the open loading door.

"Stay there," I told her, racing to the opening, but I couldn't see anything except black water ten metres down. *Shit.* Fear ripped through my chest. A vertigo attack in the water was a sure-fire way to drown.

"I've got her." A police officer pushed through the door. "Go find your friend."

I kicked off my boots, shucked my jacket, and jumped. Then I prayed with everything I had and started swimming.

"Judah!"

If he was under the water, I'd never see him; it was black as ink.

"Judah!"

I kept swimming and calling his name. A light appeared through the loading door and lit up the water. A police officer dived in to help, and for ten minutes we swam back and forth calling Judah's name but getting no reply.

"We need more light," the officer called over. "I'll get them on it. Check the shore."

"Okay." I barely recognised my own voice, my teeth rattling in their sockets as I feared the worst. "Tell them to get Hannah's dad down here. He's up at the homestead." The officer promised and headed back to the wharf while I headed for shore, still calling Judah's name.

My feet hit sand and my gut clenched in fear. This couldn't be happening. I would *not* lose someone I loved again. Judah was alive. He had to be.

I collapsed on the sand, turned, and searched the dark skin of the bay for something, anything. But other than the soft lapping pressure waves from the action under the wharf, the water lay almost flat as a black sheet in the near windless night.

"Morgan."

The voice was so soft, I spun to my left and scoured the shore, not sure if I'd just imagined it. "Judah? Judah, is that you?"

Silence, then, "Morgan. Here."

I was on my feet in a second, sprinting along the packed sand, but it was so fucking dark. "Judah, where are you?"

"In the water. I can't stand. I'm spinning out."

A light swept over the water and I yelled toward it. "Over here."

The light tracked back and forth till it finally hit on Judah lying face up in the shallows, the water lapping at his chest.

I grabbed him under the arms and pulled him up on the beach, then collapsed on my knees beside him, tears running down my face.

"Oh, thank God. Thank God." I pushed the hair from his eyes and smothered his face with kisses, then cradled him against my chest, rocking back and forth as people ran toward us.

"Hannah?" he mumbled against my chest.

"She's fine, I think."

I pulled his shaking body close and buried my face in his wet hair. "Don't you ever, ever scare me like that again, do you hear me? If you can't be trusted to keep yourself safe, I'm going to fucking tie you to our bed."

He muttered something that sounded suspiciously like, "*Our* bed. I like the sound of that." Which earned him another load of kisses wherever I could reach. That was until he started to dry heave.

Then the team arrived and pushed me aside, just in time for Judah to unload his stomach all over their nice clean equipment. They threw a space blanket at me and I wrapped it around my body, sinking to the sand so I could watch them work.

"Morgan?" Judah's head turned, his flicking eyes searching for me. And when they finally landed, he smiled.

And I'd never seen anything so beautiful.

CHAPTER TWENTY-FIVE

Judah

I SQUINTED AT MY PHONE, WHICH MORGAN HAD FINALLY unearthed when we got back to the boathouse the previous night. It had been lodged way down the side of the couch cushions, and it took him several attempts to retrieve it.

A groan broke my lips. Ten hours. I'd been spinning for ten fucking hours. *Holy shit.* My worst one yet. Still, it hadn't exactly been business as usual the day before and I'd probably got off lucky with that. Drowning in the middle of a vertigo attack would definitely have been a less cheery alternative.

Sliding the phone back on the bedside cabinet, I studiously avoided waking Morgan who was plastered to my back like a wet T-shirt. Let him sleep.

I wasn't ready to face the world. Not ready for the questions. Not ready to talk. Not ready to relive the fear of that endless crawl to shore, of trusting myself to let go and float, of choking half a ton of seawater into my lungs. And absolutely not ready for the smack in the face realisation that I might not see Morgan or anyone again. That I might just die in that bay with only the jack mackerel as witness. Not ready to take inventory of my mistakes and the sad state of my body. Not ready to hear Morgan's stream of worry and relief.

Let him sleep.

I owed him that much.

And Hannah was safe. With that knowledge, I could breathe . . . and think. Last night had started a sea change somewhere inside my heart that was gaining momentum, and I wanted to turn it over in my foggy brain while it was all still fresh.

I'd fucked up. I'm not sure what I could've done differently at the time, but I'd put Hannah in danger, and I'd be lucky if Terry ever talked to me again. And I didn't even want to think about Morgan. As soon as I showed a glimmer of recovery, that man was gonna nail my arse to the wall, and I deserved every fucking, agonising moment of the dressing down that was coming my way.

But for all of that, a seed of something else had been sown last night, something good, and that nameless niggling sense of something I wasn't seeing finally had a name.

Belonging.

Here.

In Painted Bay.

I'd fought it. This fucking town had hurt me in so many ways, but fighting it did diddly squat to stop it burrowing its rude way under my skin like the boil on my life that it was. But then somehow along the way it had morphed into this damn beauty spot that I wasn't sure I wanted and still wasn't sure I trusted. But I was thinking about it.

Because, homophobes and rednecks aside—since there would always be those wherever I went—standing in front of that audience, I'd been welcomed for who I was by the vast majority, and that was new. And not just welcomed. Congratulated, admired, thanked for what I could offer and for who I was in this town, warts and all. Maybe *especially* the warts because, fuck me, if Meniere's hadn't been part of building that bridge. It had brought Morgan into my life.

And it had brought Hannah, and her tenacity had been exactly the kick in the pants I'd needed. And wasn't that a fucking miracle?

"I can hear the cogs of your brain whirring from here." Morgan's arm tightened around my waist. "How're you feeling?"

I took a second to think about it. "My body's not too bad, considering. My head's still a bit spacey, not quite grounded yet. When can we check on Hannah?"

"Terry said to give them the morning, then call. How about the rest of you? That was quite the night."

I wriggled around to face him but couldn't quite meet his eyes. "I wouldn't blame you for walking away."

He tipped my chin up. "Why in the hell would I do that?"

I ran my finger over the frown line between his eyes. "Oh, I don't know. Maybe because I brought everything down on myself and Hannah last night. I shouldn't have gone outside and I'm sorry."

His expression didn't give much away as he took a moment to answer. "You were trying to get help."

I managed a decent eye roll considering I was still a little off-balance. "She wouldn't have been in danger in the first place if I'd just stayed put."

Morgan shrugged. "You don't know that. The guy was standing right outside your door. What if he'd decided to come back?"

"If I hadn't lost my damn phone—"

"Things happen. You did everything you could."

"I'm not so sure. But I promise I would've called you first if I'd found my fucking phone."

He kissed the end of my nose and I hoped that boded well. "Did they catch them?"

Morgan rolled onto his back and rubbed at his eyes. It brought all that delicious hair into sharp focus and I couldn't resist drawing patterns through it with my finger, following the black octopus tentacle down from his shoulder to his pec. He lifted his head and watched in amusement.

"Jon texted about three while you were still out of it. They got your mates from the office, and Whangarei police picked up the boat from its tracker and arrested those ones. There was a mountain of illegal pāua on board, so that was a win. Haversham's been taken in for questioning, but his story is the men leased the boat and he had no idea what they intended to do with it. Whether any of them will finger him is yet to be seen, but if it's all gang-related, that's not likely. And the van was found abandoned just out of Whangarei, empty. So the two men in that are still in the wind."

He cupped the back of my neck and pulled me in for a kiss. My entire body responded, surging as my tongue swept into his mouth. I'd nearly lost this; nearly lost him; lost the chance of a life together. The sharp scruff of his clipped beard brought a smile to my lips and I tugged on it with my teeth before delving back into his mouth. He tasted of musty morning, hope, and home, and I couldn't get enough, wouldn't ever get enough.

And when he finally pulled away, I chased his lips for more. He indulged me with a warm chuckle that fired through my body, all the way to curl my toes. Then I settled my cheek on his shoulder and got my thinking ducks in a row.

"I'm not leaving."

"What?" His head jerked to face me.

"You heard me. I'm staying here, in Painted Bay, with you."

His jaw dropped open. "But . . . Wellington? The contract?" He pushed up on his elbow, dislodging my head from his shoulder, and stared down at me. I pulled the pillow under my cheek and traced a finger around his lips.

"I'm turning down the offer," I said firmly. God, he had a beautiful mouth.

He grabbed my hand and tucked it against his chest. "No. You can't do that. I'm fine going with you. You don't have to—"

"It's not for you."

He narrowed his eyes. "Then tell me why?"

I took a big breath. "A few reasons."

He cocked a brow and waited.

I couldn't hold his gaze so I focussed on that short pert beard instead, every perfectly placed hair in it, desperate to muss it with my fingers. "I know it sounds weird after everything, and I've always said I hated this place. It was never part of the plan for starting a new life, and then you came along and I fell in love. This place feeds you, Morgan. You belong here."

"I thought you said the decision wasn't about me." His frown deepened.

"Shh." I put a finger to his lips. "It's not, not entirely."

Morgan slid onto his side, so our faces were only centimetres apart. "Okay, I'm listening."

He had the deepest brown eyes, and I took a second to appreciate them before I explained. "I *did* hate this place, I wasn't kidding about that. But I realised yesterday that I'm not that scared, desperately out-of-place, gay teenage boy anymore. I've grown. I'm much stronger, and Meniere's is a part of that."

He raised the hand he still held and kissed the back of it.

"But equally, this town isn't the unwelcoming place I remember it as, either. There's some really good people here. Terry, Jam, you, my family, and lots of others. People who cheered for Hannah last night, even for me. I've been looking through old glasses, wanting to believe things hadn't changed, because that made my decisions so much easier, if that makes sense?"

Morgan nodded. "Perfect sense. I think I felt something similar when we visited Cody that day. I had to admit to myself that I'd escaped Auckland to get away from my family and then avoided going back because Sally and my family were so entwined. But then when I did go back, things had changed. Cody's house didn't feel so full of Sally any more, just of Cody, Tess, and Logan. And I realised I was missing out on making new memories rather than rehashing old ones. I needed to stop hiding and take back that part of my life."

The understanding in his eyes cloaked me in warmth. "Exactly. I think that's why I've been avoiding signing the contract. And then last night happened and . . . things became really clear, really fast. Thinking I was going to drown in that water, I knew three things. I wanted you. I wanted a life, and maybe a family." I sneaked a look and saw the surprise on his face. "And I wanted all of those things in Painted Bay, if I could."

"A family?" Those brown eyes crinkled up the corners and I saw cautious hope there. "You'd want that? With me?"

"No, I meant Patrick." I poked him in the ribs. "Of course I meant with you." I stole a quick unsatisfying kiss, mostly because Morgan's mouth was still hanging open.

"I, ah . . . I just never . . . I didn't want to presume—wow."

"Would you please just fucking kiss me, already." I grabbed his chin and pulled him forward.

And so he did. Long and slow until my toes curled. Then his beard crawled its way down my neck to my nipples, and everything south went *hello*.

"Wait," he pulled off a nipple.

I scowled. "You better have put a bookmark there."

"What about work? What will you do?"

"I have a few ideas. If you can handle me spending some time on and off in Auckland, then I think I might look at getting certified in dance therapy of some sort for kids. I kind of like them as it turns out, and I seem to be good with them. Unexpected, right?"

"Not to me." Morgan locked eyes and my heart went all squidgy.

Fighting the urge to get all up in Morgan's business and in particular his arse, I bit my cheek and focussed on answering his question. "I'm going to talk with Hannah's physio. She mentioned there's a lot of kids in Northland who could benefit from dance therapy but that there aren't many teachers. Enough interest that maybe I could keep most of my classes here in Painted Bay and they'd come to me. But there's a lot to think about."

Morgan's eyes shone bright. "There is, but I think it's a fucking brilliant idea. Are you sure you won't regret taking up the Wellington contract though? What about all those dance careers you'd be part of fashioning. What you're talking about would be very different."

He was right and there *were* things I would miss. "It would be totally different, I get that. And no, I wouldn't get the exposure to the dance world I've known all my life. But when I visited my old school, something became apparent really fast. Although I enjoyed the atmosphere and all the recognition, they wanted who I'd been *then*, the old Judah, my past achievements. And as far as the Meniere's went, they either didn't want to know about it or it was simply something to be dealt with and made allowances for.

"But after Hannah and I had done our thing on stage last night, I realised that she, the teachers, and everyone in that audience respected me for who I was *now*, Meniere's included. They weren't interested in my past, other than to appreciate what I'd achieved. They wanted my *future*, the person I was *because* of what I'd lost, not *in spite* of it. And that means fucking everything . . ." I couldn't finish, my eyes brimming as a tide of emotion rolled through me.

Morgan pulled me close and my body shook like a tree in a storm against his chest. We stayed that way for minutes, hours, who the fuck knew how long. I didn't care. Safe in Morgan's arms, in our tiny boatshed, the rest of the world could take a fucking number and wait.

I'd survived last night when I'd thought I was going to die. I'd managed to get myself to shore, me, on my own, Meniere's be damned. No one was going to take that strength away from me, not now that I knew I had it.

Morgan pulled back a little and cupped my face. "I hope there's still a place for me in that bright future of yours? Because I love you, Judah Madden. And I don't need anything more from you than that."

Oh god, this man. I leaned in for a soft kiss. "You don't need a *part* in that future, baby. You *are* that future, my future, our family's future." I rubbed my cheek against his beard. "But right now there's something important I think you've forgotten."

His brows crunched.

I licked a path across his lips. "Bookmarks, sweetheart. Bookmarks."

His mouth curved up in a wicked smile and he disappeared under the sheet.

EPILOGUE

Morgan

6 months later

"Corrine, do you need a break, sweetheart?" Judah called to the ten-year-old whose face was a study in concentrated effort and frustration.

The young girl had spent twenty minutes trying to master a speedier turn in her chair so she'd keep abreast of her partner for the second part of the choreography.

"No, I can do it," she muttered, her palms red from her determination to get it right.

Judah crossed to her side and went down on his knee, taking her hand. "We'll just slow it down. It's not a problem."

Corrine's dance partner, Joseph, an eleven-year-old with a cheeky grin and a mouth to match, rolled up and nudged her chair with his. "It'll be better slower, Rin. I almost canned out on that last one."

Not true and everyone knew it, but Jo had a soft heart, and for most of Judah's students, with all the various challenges they faced, it was the journey that counted not the destination. The way they supported each other still blew me away. It was a huge difference from the professional dance world Judah had known, and it was his greatest joy.

"Well, how about we call it a day for now. Practise at home and when you come back next week, we'll see if we need to change it or not."

Corinne smiled shyly and nodded.

Judah ruffled her hair, then stood and turned to the other four students watching. "That goes for all of you. Next week we'll finalise any changes we need to make, so come rehearsed and prepared. Halloween is only a couple of weeks away and May wants to sort out your costumes, and your parents know they can call me any time with questions, right?" Judah turned to the line-up of parents on the back wall of the barn and threw a huge smile when he saw me watching along with them.

The barn still needed a lot of work to convert it to the dance studio Judah had envisaged, but it was getting there. A new floor, plumbing and wiring, accessible bathroom and change room, and some much-needed insulation and heating had dealt with the worst of the problems, although the council had still been slow in their consent approval for use, especially with the range of challenges faced by his students, and this was only the second week Judah had been able to make use of it. Until then he'd continued using the community hall. But the barn was only fifty metres from the boatshed and a much larger space. It also meant if he had an attack, he was close to home.

Someone was always on call during his classes for just that reason. If not me, then Terry or Cora or Martha or Jam, or any number of other locals who'd offered their time with the renovation of the barn and anything else Judah might need. It had been a humbling experience to see who came out of the woodwork to help when they heard what Judah was doing.

I was so fucking proud of him.

Judah ushered the last of the kids and their parents out the door, then stalked over, took my mouth in a hard kiss, and as always, I became totally immersed in everything Judah Madden, the rest of the world be damned. In the eight months we'd been together, nothing had changed in that regard. He still owned me. He still lit those dark corners of my soul on fire with just a look. And he still captivated my heart in its entirety.

And he'd never once looked back on his decision. When he'd told his Wellington school he wouldn't be signing and why, they couldn't have been more supportive. They'd even brought a small dance troupe north to Painted Bay just last month. They spent a day with Judah's students, who were beyond excited in the way only a bunch of six- to thirteen-year-olds could be, and they'd also put on a small performance in the community centre, which had packed out for the event.

Judah danced with the Wellington troupe that night, and it had been a test in so many ways, but it hadn't changed his mind. He loved what he did. I had to admit I'd been worried, and seeing him so secure in his decision was a huge relief.

Cody and Tess had brought Logan up for the performance, but also to continue getting to know Judah. They'd witnessed one of his attacks and I saw some of that concern returning, but they didn't say a word and I loved them for it.

The vertigo attacks had stabilised, hitting only once every couple of weeks or so, and although Judah had hoped for better, it was still a win in my eyes, especially since he hadn't had a drop attack in months. He still couldn't drive, but Hannah had pimped out his bike, painting it rainbow colours. People could see him coming for miles. He grumbled non-stop about how sappy it was, and how it was ruining his rep, but I knew he adored it.

He'd also invested in a personal alarm wrist band which gave us both peace of mind. It was much easier to operate than his phone when he was spinning out, and it accessed his cell to send his location to a designated group of people in case he was caught alone, or away from home.

He'd told Hannah it was his leash saying, "If I fall, it tugs a few people I know to come get me."

She'd just smiled that sunshine smile of hers and said, "Cos you need help sometimes too, like me, right?"

Yeah, just like you, sweetheart.

Someone in Judah's support group had mentioned a service dog and that had him all kinds of excited. They could apparently sense attacks coming before they happened, but I think Judah just liked the idea of a dog, period, and so did I. It would also give him some reassurance if and when we started a family, and I was all over that idea like a rash.

"You wanna come back to my place, sailor?" Judah waggled his eyebrows as my hand slipped down to cup his arse over those fucking leggings I so loved. Nothing had changed there, either. And between Judah and my fetish, we were likely personally responsible for keeping the New Zealand dance legging industry solvent.

"You gonna make it worth my while?" I leaned forward to nibble on his ear and felt a shiver run through his body.

"Are you done for the day?" He cradled my face and rested our foreheads together, his eyelashes tangling with my own.

"I am. I finished early since you're heading back to Auckland tomorrow."

Judah pressed a line of kisses down my cheek. "It's only for a few days, then the online exam, a practical in December, and that's it till February. Then this time next year, I'll be fully certified."

"I'm so proud of you."

Judah's mouth curved up in a rare shy smile that took my breath away. "I'm kind of proud of myself, actually. And maybe I can get a dance class going over the summer break. Get some extra hours in and up my loan repayments."

My scowl reached to my boots. The *loan* was a constant irritation to me, and one I had plans to sort out permanently. It wasn't a damn loan at all. After three months of living together, with dream plans to double the size of the boathouse and renovate the old barn for his dance studio, Judah, Cora, and I had come to an agreement . . . after much stomping of feet and shouting on Judah's part, I might add. Not to mention a lot of indulgent smiles from Cora, who had just moved in with Martha, which left Leroy rattling around in the big house on his own.

With the money from the house Sally and I had previously owned in Auckland, I bought two acres of Cora's land, which included the boathouse, the barn, and some of the beachfront, and put it in both our names. Judah threw a hissy fit at the second part, which admittedly I hadn't told him about, and then insisted on paying me back. At the time, I'd let it ride, but when I could get a ring on the frustrating man's finger, we'd be having a serious come-to-Jesus moment about the whole thing. Until then, I simply shut my mouth and set his *loan* repayments money aside to offset his student debt, which he also wouldn't let me clear. None of which fooled Judah, but neither of us spoke about it, so there was that.

The sale of the land also gave Cora enough cash to put off any need to sell the mussel farm for a while longer, which put a smile on Leroy's face, at least on occasion. He and Judah were getting along a lot better since they'd stopped working together, and since we'd bought the boathouse, separating their two lives nicely.

"Maybe you could *not* get a summer dance class going and we could take a holiday instead?" I eyeballed him.

"Really?" His eyes went wide. "A holiday?"

"Why not, I have some owing and you're an unemployed student, after all."

He pulled a face. "Don't remind me. I should really get some work so I can—"

"No."

He cocked his head and that steely jaw set. "Excuse me?"

"You heard me. I said, no. You can wave that bossy dick of yours around in the bedroom as much as you like, but outside of it, you don't got nothing. And this time, you're listening to me. We are going to take a holiday, end of discussion."

He stared at me for a minute, his jaw working, the wheels turning in his brain. "So I don't have any say in this?"

I shook my head. "No. It's been a big year for both of us. I *need* a holiday and I want to share that with you, my partner, the man that I love. Is that too much to ask?"

He pulled that bottom lip between his teeth and worried the fuck out of it. "I don't have any money."

"Did I ask you to contribute?"

"I don't want you to—"

"What? Spoil you? Treat you? Crave your company enough to need you with me? Want to have our first holiday together? Love you so much I don't want to go without you? Which of those things don't you want, Judah?"

Those bright hazel eyes grew shifty. "The spoil and treat part. I'm a grown man . . ."

I kissed the rest of the words from his lips and he went soft as butter in my arms as always. "Well," I said coming up for air. "Thank Christ for that. Since a grown man would surely be secure enough in himself and his relationship to allow the man who loved the shit out of him to take him on holiday."

Judah's eyes narrowed. "Very tricky, Mr Wipene. And that was nothing to do with any off-button rubbish, by the way. I just felt in the mood to let you kiss me. But okay, I'll let you take me on holiday. On one condition. That you add my half of the cost *to the loan*." He lit up in a smug smile.

Jesus fucking George. It was all I could do not to throw him over my knee and paddle his damn backside. For fuck's sake. Stubborn had nothing on Judah.

It was time to pull out the big guns.

"Not happening. No man of mine is going to pay for their own *wedding present*. My wedding gift to you is our honeymoon."

Judah froze, bug-eyed, slack-jawed, and white to the very roots of his hair. "Wedding . . . ? You want . . . Honeymoon . . . ? Are you asking me . . . ? Holy shit." His hand flew to his mouth.

I dropped to my knees and took both his hands in mine. "Judah Madden. I love you with every breath in my body, inside and outside of those tights, and I would be honoured if you'd take me as your husband. I promise to always circle your light in whatever waters we find ourselves in. I give my heart and body to you, and I promise to hold yours safe in return. Will you marry me?"

He stared long enough to have a flicker of doubt tickle at my heart. Then his mouth curved up in a huge grin, and he dragged me to my feet and slammed me against the wall.

"Yes. Yes, yes, yes." He crowded close and sealed his answer with a hot, hard kiss. "Fucking A, I'll marry you. And I'll even let you pay for the damned honeymoon. But you *are* going to let me repay it . . . in kind."

I swallowed at the fierce look in his eye. "In kind? Ah, in what form might that take, may I ask?"

His look turned sultry and he licked his lips, slowly. "In every fucking possible form you can imagine, Mr Fisheries Officer, until you're dripping with come, bloated with pleasure, and don't recognise your arsehole without my dick in it."

Holy fuck. I wasn't sure the zip on my uniform trousers was gonna survive the walk back to the boatshed without giving at the seams. But Judah hadn't finished by a long shot.

"So, I'd pack lots and lots of ibuprofen in that honeymoon bag you're planning," he dropped his voice and cupped my aching dick. "And enough lube to keep a formula one team on the track for a week, because I take my debts and my marriage prospects very seriously. Am I making myself clear?" He gave a solid tug on my cock, then rubbed himself against me like a hard-muscled cat, and I saw fucking stars.

And then he kissed me, slow, sweet, and deliciously decadent. Taking his time, tasting every corner, humming against my lips, wrapping his arms around me like I was the most precious thing in the world.

You are. Sally's voice popped into my head for the first time in months, and I couldn't help the smile that crossed my lips.

"Well, what did he say?"

Judah's head jerked toward the voice and my lips met air. "Terry?" he sounded confused.

Shit.

"I take it from the heavy make-out session that you said yes?" Terry fell into the room, pushed from behind.

"He said yes, right?" Cora followed Terry inside, trailed by Leroy and Martha and a very excited Hannah.

Judah turned to stare at me with wide eyes. "They knew?"

I shrugged. "Well, you do love an audience."

"What if I'd said no?"

I straightened his sweatshirt, pulling it down over his rigid cock and patting it in place. "Let's not talk about that."

"Well?" they all said together, and I bit back a smile.

Judah shook his head and laughed. "Yes, I said yes. All right? Now, as lovely as it is to share this moment with you all, I have a man I need to have a serious and looooong conversation with. So if you don't mind . . ."

He bundled everyone outside, locked the door, and crooked his finger at me.

"I thought we were going back to the boathouse?" I walked into his arms.

"Why, when we have everything we need here. You." He kissed my neck. "Me." He pulled my shirt off and ran his fingertips over the octopus on my shoulder, following it with another kiss. "This fucking uniform." He pulled at the button on my trousers till he had it undone and the zip down. "A barre." He pushed me over to the brand new barre he'd had installed only last week. "My tights." He pulled off his sweatshirt and put my hands on his arse. "And this." He reached high above the barre to a small shelf from which he removed a large tube of lube and a familiar-looking butt plug.

I took the plug from his hand and twirled it in my fingers. "It appears you've been in my drawers, Mr Madden." I flashed him an accusatory look.

He stole back the plug and popped the lid on the lube. "Not nearly as much as I'm about to be, Mr Wipene. Now I do believe you're wearing too many clothes."

The End.

Thank you for taking the time to read

OFF BALANCE
Painted Bay 1

If you enjoyed Judah and Morgan's story please consider taking the time to do a review in Amazon or your favourite review spot.I didn't realise until I was an author just how important reviews are for helping our sales and spreading the word. Thank you in advance.

Don't miss the next book in the series:
ON BOARD
Coming 2021

Have you read my
SOUTHERN LIGHTS SERIES
set in the beautiful Southern Alps in New Zealand?

POWDER AND PAVLOVA
Southern Lights 1

ETHAN SHARPE is living every young Kiwi's dream—seeing the world for a couple of years while deciding what to do with his life. Then he gets a call.

Two days later he's back in New Zealand. Six months later his mother is dead, his fifteen-year-old brother is going off the rails and the café he's inherited is failing. His life is a hot mess and the last thing he needs is another complication—like the man who just walked into his café,

a much older...

sinfully hot...

EPIC complication.

TANNER CARPENTER's time in Queenstown has an expiration date. He has a new branch of his business to get up and running, exorcise a few personal demons while he's at it, and then head back to Auckland to get on with his life. He isn't looking for a relationship especially with someone fifteen years his junior, but Ethan is gorgeous, troubled and in need of a friend. Tanner could be that for Ethan, right? He could brighten Ethan's day for a while, help him out, maybe even offer some... stress relief, no strings attached.

It was a good plan, until it wasn't.

Reviews

"Powder & Pavlova is charming, sexy and poignant; funny at one moment, heart-breaking the next, and I loved every minute of it."

. . .

-All About Romance

A really, really sweet age gap story that'll make you love Jay Hogan more! A love story... that will make you swoon and just fall in love again!

-Love Bytes Reviews

MORE BY JAY HOGAN

AUCKLAND MED SERIES

First Impressions

Crossing the Touchline

Up Close and Personal

Against the Grain

You Are Cordially Invited (2021)

SOUTHERN LIGHTS SERIES

Powder and Pavlova

Tamarillo Tart

Flat Whites and Chocolate Fish

Pinot and Pineapple Lumps

PAINTED BAY SERIES

Off Balance

On Board (2021)

STANDALONE

Unguarded (May 2021)

(Written as part of Sarina Bowen's
True North— Vino & Veritas Series and published by Heart Eyes
Press)

Digging Deep
(2020 Lambda Literary Finalist)

ABOUT THE AUTHOR

JAY IS A 2020 LAMBDA LITERARY AWARD FINALIST

She is a New Zealand author writing in MM romance and romantic suspense primarily set in New Zealand. She loves writing character driven romances with lots of humour, a good dose of reality and a splash of angst. She's travelled extensively, lived in many countries, and in a past life she was a critical care nurse and counsellor. Jay is owned by a huge Maine Coon cat and a gorgeous Cocker Spaniel.

Join Jay's reader's group Hogan's Hangout for updates, promotions, her current writing projects and special releases.

Sign up to her newsletter HERE.

Or visit her website HERE.

CPSIA information can be obtained
at www.ICGtesting.com
Printed in the USA
LVHW011618160621
690393LV00008B/737